REPUBLIC OF DIRT

REPUBLIC OF
DIRT

A RETURN TO WOEFIELD FARM

SUSAN JUBY

HARPERAVENUE

Published by Harper Avenue, an imprint of HarperCollins Publishers Ltd

First edition

HarperCollins books may be purchased for educational, business,
or sales promotional use through our Special Markets Department.

HarperCollins Publishers Ltd
2 Bloor Street East, 20th Floor
Toronto, Ontario, Canada
M4W 1A8

www.harpercollins.ca

Library and Archives Canada Cataloguing in Publication
information is available upon request

ISBN 978-1-44342-395-3 (original trade paperback)
ISBN 978-1-44342-396-0 (library hardcover)

Printed and bound in the United States of America
RRD 9 8 7 6 5 4 3 2 1

For Eggy

REPUBLIC OF DIRT

SEPTEMBER

Prudence

September is the season for canning, drying and freezing. It's the time to save seeds and to review your successes and failures in order to plan next year. Pride has no place in this assessment. The only thing that matters is what worked. In the case of Woefield Farm, September is also the last chance to make a decent showing at the final farmers' market of the season.

Our table has always stood out at the Cedar Farmers' Market. At first because it was so bare, but as time went on, we stood out because everything we sold had a bit of a diseased and/or stunted look to it. But I'm proud to say that by late August, our raised beds were finally producing fine, standard-size things. Unfortunately, they were the same fine things everyone else sold: zucchini, tomatoes, radishes, peas, chard. The only thing we had that no one else did was a small crop of very hot peppers. The pepper plants were given to me by my friend Kimi when she came to visit. We'd been neighbors and friends in New York, and she and I loved to visit restaurants that specialized in extremely hot foods.

She brought me a 7-Pot pepper plant, a Bhut Jolokia and a Trinidad Scorpion.

"Now, Prudence," said Kimi, an artist. "Be safe with these. They can do damage."

We laughed and laughed. That was the whole point of hot peppers! To test oneself and get the old endorphins flowing. Kimi and I used to take dates on spicy food excursions. Anyone who showed a lack of spirit or fortitude was quickly dispatched. Only Kimi found someone who could match us: Cali passed the test. In fact, Cali went on to become a firefighter in the Bronx and she and Kimi ended up moving in together.

I planted my ferocious pepper plants in the most premium of our raised beds. I used copper mesh to keep vermin off, and Sara, the eleven-year-old who has been living with us since this summer, made a sign: "Caution: Dangerous Peppers Ahead."

The plants had arrived with small peppers already on them and they flourished in the heat of the late summer on Vancouver Island. Soon all three hung heavy with fruit.

A single 7-Pot pepper, as the name implies, is said to be good for seven pots of stew. Bhut Jolokia, also known as the ghost pepper, has long red fruits, each one about 125 times hotter than a jalapeño. The Trinidad Scorpion, or Butch T peppers, are squat, angry-looking things that measure 1,463,700 on the Scoville scale. For those not conversant in hot peppers, that's very hot.

When the peppers were ripe, I went to the Fred's Famous hot pepper website and printed off hot sauce recipes. The three resulting sauces were absolutely delicious.

"Help me name them," I said to Earl, Seth and Sara as we stared at the pots of bright sauce. A haze of heat shimmered over them and the smell of garlic and onion filled the kitchen.

Earl was suspicious. No surprise. Earl is always suspicious. He essentially came with the place when I inherited it from my uncle last April. Earl's in his early seventies and he lives in a cabin on the edge of the property and he recently bought a half ownership.

Not long after I moved to Woefield, I learned that Earl is a cult figure in the roots music world. His brother is Merle Clemente. They were the High Lonesome Boys, a foundational bluegrass band, until Earl decamped for reasons unknown.

Earl's creativity with the banjo does not translate into adventurousness when it comes to food or drink. He's learned to tolerate a diet heavy on organic greens and brown rice but still finds any coffee that doesn't look like lightly used dishwater too powerful. Naturally, he drew a hard line at my hot sauces.

"I ain't touching that. Just standing near them pots is making my eyes water," he said.

"Keep an open mind. Hot food has positive effects on the mood. Besides, capsaicin is odorless."

Earl made a face. His general appearance is that of someone who has spent a lifetime breaking rocks in a quarry for low pay. This in spite of the fact that he's spent most of the last thirty years in a recliner, watching TV. He has longish white hair on the sides of his head and is bald on top. He wears his work pants pulled up high, courtesy of a pair of wide suspenders. Earl's customary expression is that of a man who would automatically say no to any question you cared to ask, but his eyes, which are small but clear and brown, are, in unguarded moments, even a little twinkly, though I would never tell him that because he'd probably start wearing sunglasses.

"I just got over my heartburn from our trip to Ron's Pizza Parlor," he said.

"Serves you right. You and Seth knew I'd made Swiss chard and white bean casserole."

"Exactly," said Seth.

Seth is twenty-one and has been living with me since he was kicked out of his mother's house across the street from the farm. He came to the door looking for room and board in exchange for work. He was in terrible shape. Apparently there was some trauma at his school that rendered him alcoholic, agoraphobic and highly dependent on the Internet for all his social needs. I took him in, put him to work and set him on a new path. He's been sober for three months and I give farm life much of the credit. It's my belief that healthy food and hard work can cure just about any problem.

In contrast to Earl, Seth looks exactly like what he is: a heavy metal fan who spends too much time on his computer when he's not working outside. Over the summer, his pasty white skin had begun to show signs of healthy circulation, if not an actual tan. But his natural pallor returned with the change in the weather. He trimmed his long black hair so that it now just brushes his shoulders. Seth almost always wears either an Iron Maiden or a Judas Priest ball cap. The first time I saw him without either one, I was startled to realize that his hair is lovely and thick. The persistence of the cap made me think he was hiding early baldness. He's lost his junk food gut and his hunched posture has straightened somewhat. Seth is even a bit good-looking, in his way.

Seth may appear somewhat less scurvy-afflicted than he did when he arrived, but he's still devoted to processed foods. He and

Earl sneak off to Smitty's and Ron's and any other purveyors of junk food every chance they get. Worse, they bring Sara with them.

Sara is the final member of our household. We met when her parents asked if she could board her fancy show poultry with us. Soon after the chickens moved here, her parents' marriage disintegrated under the crushing weight of their mutual loathing and Sara joined her birds. She's a serious and competent child who spends her time reading educational books and drawing up plans for practical things and tending her flock. She gets up early and goes to bed at the same time every evening. She is young but she's a farmer through and through. Earl, Seth and I compete to entertain and engage her because we feel bad about the situation with her parents and we live in fear of the day that they come to their senses and ask for her back and because Sara's smile is the kind that changes a day. She doesn't suffer fools and deep down I think most grown-ups suspect we might be fools.

Sara stood with Earl and Seth, alert but quiet.

"Seth, just try the sauces," I told him, dipping the spoon into the pot and holding it out to him.

"I've got a bad stomach from my drinking days," he said.

"You've got a bad stomach because you consume two liters of Coke every day."

"It's not Coke. It's *cola*. The difference is about three bucks a bottle and the taste."

I sighed and held the spoon out to Sara. She took the spoon from me and tasted the sauce. It was the mildest one.

Her nose wrinkled and she considered for at least ten seconds.

"It's good," she said. "Spicy."

"Ready to try the next one?"

She nodded.

I handed her a glass of water and then dipped the second spoon in the second pot. Sara tasted and her eyes widened.

"Hot," she said. She puffed out her breath a few times. "My lips are burning. My nose is running. It's good though."

I paused the spoon over the third pot, the one featuring the Trinidad Scorpion.

"Oh, no you don't," said Seth, gently getting between Sara and the sauces.

"You're going to ruin her tongue!" said Earl, putting a hand out to stop me.

I sighed and dipped the spoon into the Scorpion sauce. I tasted it. Delicious. Hot and peppery. Sweat popped out on my brow and exhilaration bloomed in my chest.

"See?" I said. "Don't be scared."

"Stand back!" said Seth. He put his long hair into a ponytail, picked up a spoon and puffed out a few steadying breaths like a powerlifter getting ready to snatch up a particularly large weight.

Seth

In spite of the terrible pain I was in, I tried to help name the hot sauces. For the allegedly mild one, which tasted like nuclear fallout, I suggested Hot as Fuck. For the medium one, which tasted like seven lit cigarettes applied firmly to the tongue, I suggested You'd Have to Be an Idiot to Try This, and for the Scorpion sauce, which was so hot I think it gave me permanent nerve damage, I suggested Lawsuit Followed by Complete Financial Collapse.

She ignored all my suggestions and went with Woefield Hot Sauce 1, Woefield Hot Sauce 2 and Woefield Super Mega Hot 3. Prudence may be a hard worker and have an inhuman capacity to eat hot things, but she's no great shakes in the naming-shit department.

I told her those sauces were too hot for Joe Public but she went ahead and bottled up the Condiments of Destruction anyway, and off we went to the last farmers' market of the season. Probably should have had a police escort.

Earl called the scene that followed "goddamned mayhem." Only

Earl has a problem with word use and actually said "goddamned mayhew." Which is excellent and part of why I still live on this farm. It's just too bad that we made exactly the wrong impression on a few key people.

Earl

Some people take vegetables way too serious. Prudence is always giving me hell for not wanting to talk much about our "wares," which is what she calls our vegetables when we take them to market. Well, what's there to say? These are goddamned cucumbers and that's a head of lettuce. What more do you need to know?

The other thing that gets me is how them vegetable lovers get so pushy. They got their cloth bags and old baskets and seem to have about six elbows apiece when they sniff out a bargain or some rare kind of tomato.

I knew putting sauces too hot for human conscription for sale was a bad idea. Don't get me wrong. Prudence has made a hell of an improvement on this place from when she first started, especially if you consider that until she showed up all the farm produced was rocks and a few blades of grass that died of fright as soon as they poked their heads out of the ground. Our raised beds is neat as you please, and there's sure as hell a lot of them. Prudence works like three sled dogs, but that don't stop things from going wrong.

Me and Prudence and Seth and Sara was behind the table. Prudence and Sara had all the bags of greens on the sides of the tables and bunches of radishes and zucchinis and peas and what have you laid out like you'd see at a grocery store. Then Prudence brung out them damned killer sauces in their skinny glass bottles with the string at the top and the brown paper labels. She got Seth to put out little wooden spoons like you'd use to try ice creams, and some crackers she made herself that taste like they're made with sawdust and dehydrated chicken feathers, but she thinks they're just delicious. I figured people would give us a miss like they usually do. They would have, too, except for the rugby team that stopped by the market on their way back from a weekend tournament in Courtenay. Those guys were already in bad shape when they got into Prudence's hot sauce.

You want to see mayhew in action, I recommend a drunk rugby team and a table full of hot sauce. I just wish Sara's parents didn't see the whole thing.

Sara

My mom and dad cancel our weekend visits quite a lot. It's okay with me, but they feel bad when they do it and so they usually come to say hello at the Sunday farmers' market. They don't usually show up at the same time, though. They just come, one at a time, to our table, say hello to me and hello to Prudence. At least my mom does. My dad ignores everyone except me, usually, although sometimes he glares at Seth.

On the day we sold the hot sauce, my mom came over to tell me how sorry she was that she had to cancel our visit last week because she hadn't been feeling well. My mom is kind of depressed and it's hard for her to do things.

My dad overheard her when he walked up and he said, "Not this again. You have responsibilities, Sally." Which was ironic because my dad canceled our visit this weekend so he could take an extra shift driving his taxi.

My mom said, "Mind your own business, Dean. You're half the reason I don't feel well."

Prudence asked if they'd like to try some baby carrots.

They said they needed to talk in private, which meant that they were going to have an argument. I hoped they wouldn't yell. It's very embarrassing when they do that.

That's when we heard the rugby players. Their bus had just pulled over to the side of the road, and when they came out, they were swearing and hollering but they sounded happy. It was good timing because they made so much noise that even if my parents ended up in a loud fight about why they didn't spend time with me, no one would notice because they'd be looking at the rugby players.

When the team walked into the market, a few of them were drinking cans of beer. I don't think you're supposed to drink beer at a Sunday morning farmers' market, even if you play rugby.

They started buying stuff from every table they saw, even the craft tables that not many people visit. Then one of them saw us, or at least he saw Prudence. She's very pretty and smiles a lot and people always like her as soon as they see her, which they should because she's really nice.

"Shit," he said. "I already bought my spinach off some ugly dude in a straw hat." Then he threw the bag of spinach off to the side and it landed on the ground.

"That was a waste," said Prudence.

"I'll tell you what's a waste. You hiding your light behind a bunch of carrots." The rugby guy was probably thirty or maybe even older and his head was shaved. He had a black eye and a torn shirt, but he seemed to be in an excellent mood.

A few other guys from the rugby club came up to stand beside him. "A flower!" said one. "Bart has found a rare and beautiful flower."

Prudence smiled at them like she smiles at everyone. She's very good with people and doesn't seem embarrassed even when she's called a beautiful flower.

Earl grunted and stared at the rugby players. There were five or six of them, with more coming. Seth held up his cell phone and took pictures, saying something about maybe needing evidence later.

"My name is Bart," said the one called Bart. "And we're the Cowichan Try-Athletes Rugby Club. We played a tournament in Courtenay yesterday. Got our asses handed to us, but we don't mind because we'll do better next year. Just heading back to Duncan now." Bart put his arm around another man, who was wearing a pink tutu. "Right, Tony?"

Someone had shaved off one of Tony's eyebrows and drawn it back on with black felt pen so he looked very surprised on the one side. He said something but I couldn't understand what.

"You know what you all need?" said Prudence. "Hot sauce."

"Hot sauce!" said Bart. "I love hot sauce. Figures you'd sell my favorite thing."

Soon all the rugby players were lined up to try the hot sauce and other people saw the lineup and so they joined it and we were the most popular stand in the whole farmers' market, which had never happened before!

I noticed my parents had finished arguing and were watching the lineup. I felt proud that they were seeing how popular we were. Maybe they'd feel more comfortable about letting me stay at the farm. I know they feel guilty sometimes but it's really for the best.

The first rugby player tried the mild sauce and his face turned bright red but he said it was the best hot sauce he ever tasted. He bought two bottles.

"Let me try it!" said Tony. Two of his friends were holding him, so Prudence had to put the cracker directly into his mouth.

Seth told the guy that if he wanted to drink that was his business, but if he wanted to stop that was Seth's business. But no one paid attention to him, because I don't think they knew what he was talking about.

I saw my dad frown when he saw Prudence feeding hot sauce crackers to the drunk rugby players and he frowned even more when they started saying they wanted to lick the hot sauce out of her hand.

Luckily, she didn't let them do that.

I think Earl noticed my parents watching and he told me maybe I should sit in the truck until the rugby players were gone, but I didn't want to. It was really fun.

Prudence and Earl and Seth gave out lots of samples of Woefield Hot Sauce 1 and Woefield Hot Sauce 2 and most of the rugby players bought a bottle, even though it cost eleven dollars, which is a lot of money for sauce.

It seemed to take a long time for the players to realize how hot the sauce was because they had been drinking a lot of beer and weren't sober, but they eventually noticed when the burning got bad.

"Water!" shouted one.

"Beer!" shouted another.

"Holy crap, my lips are on fire!"

A few of them crowded into the coffee stall, where they chugged cup after cup of coffee.

My mom and dad were watching everything and my mom said something and my dad said something back and they didn't look very happy but that was normal since they never look very happy. Earl kept looking from the yelling rugby players to me and then at my parents.

Then a short, dark man in a blue tracksuit with stripes on the arms and legs reached the front of the line.

"I see you have three sauces. I'd like to try the hottest," he said.

Prudence looked at the rugby players staggering around in front of our table, pawing at their mouths and saying how much pain they were in.

"I think that one might be a bit hot for most people."

"I'm not most people," said the man, who was about the same height as Prudence. "I'm from India," he said. "Originally. We moved here when I was three. I don't think you need to worry about me and a little heat." He winked at her.

"Are you sure?" she said.

"If it's hot, I can handle it," he said. "Not like them." He looked at the rugby players like they were weak and he wasn't.

The whole area around our table was a mess. Tony had torn his pink tutu off to use it to wipe hot sauce out of his mouth and then trampled it into the ground. He had sweated so much, most of his drawn-on eyebrow came off, and he was sitting with his back against the Environmental Action table, right near where my parents were standing. He kept moaning. Bags of produce and pot holders were scattered all over the ground.

"I come from the land of warm weather and warmer food. And of beautiful women," said the little man, winking at Prudence again. He might have had a twitch or Tourette's syndrome like the kid in my class who shouts unusual things during tests and other stressful times. I think that kid is very creative, because you never know what he's going to say.

"Well," Prudence said to the twitchy man. "I have to admit that this one is certainly *my* favorite."

She poured some on one of her crackers and handed it to the little man.

If I was her I don't think I would have done that. Seth kept shaking his head and wincing, but none of us like to tell Prudence what to do, because she doesn't like it.

"Dude, are you crazy?" said Bart to the small man. "My eyes are on fire. My *balls* are on fire. There's hot sauce and then there's . . . I don't even know what to call this." He waved the bottle of sauce around like it might blow up.

The small man smiled at the rugby player. "It's no problem for me. I'm a spicy guy."

Then he put a whole cracker into his mouth.

"Good," he said. "Just like home. No problem." But then his face turned purple and sweat started pouring off him.

"Oh my," he said. "Yes. Good."

"Dude, you okay?" asked Bart the rugby player. He stared at Prudence. "You might be cute but you're kind of deadly."

The small man's teeth showed and his eyes rolled around in his head. He started panting so he sounded like a dog left in a hot car.

"Oh yes," he said. "Oooh yes."

Then he grabbed at the front of his own shirt and fell down.

Prudence

Some people have a tendency to look on the dark side. Not me. I'm sorry the hot sauce caused a medical furor, but at least it wasn't a serious one.

The paramedics both reassured me that Anoop Sandhu would be fine and that he'd just had another of his panic attacks. His mother calls 911 every time he gets one and so they know Anoop well. Still, I was sorry that Sara's parents had to see the uproar. The market should be a place of nutrition and community, not a place filled with drunken athletes and emergency personnel.

Her mother came over as the paramedics were loading Mr. Sandhu onto a stretcher, just in case.

"Is everything alright?" she asked.

Sara nodded and I did my best to convince Mrs. Spratt that everything was under control. "Oh, this is a lot more excitement than we're used to at the market! Usually it's so quiet," I said, faking a laugh. Lately, I've been feeling a bit out-of-body-ish, particularly during stressful moments. It's like parts of me are going to sleep with no warning at all.

"Sara?" said Mrs. Spratt. "What's going on here?"

"It was just the hot sauce," said Sara. "It was too hot."

"We're heading straight home," said Earl. "Too much nonsense around this place."

Sara's mother, who has a lot in common with a limp rag, looked slightly mollified. "Sara can come home with me if things are too . . . busy at the farm," she said, unforcefully.

"No!" said Seth, Earl and I at the same time. Sara looked at the ground.

"Sara's fine. As you know, we love having her. Until you and Mr. Spratt are settled."

"He had to go to pick up a fare," said Mrs. Spratt. That was a relief. I hoped he'd missed at least part of the mess with the hot sauce and the rugby players and the panic-attack man. Mr. Spratt is an angry individual.

"Okay. But Sara, please don't touch any of that sauce."

"No way," said Earl, quickly shoving the remaining bottles of Woefield Super Mega Hot 3 into a cardboard box. "Going to get rid of them."

He would do no such thing, but I didn't correct him in front of Mrs. Spratt. No need to show we were not united on the home front.

Mrs. Spratt summoned Sara for an awkward hug and then walked away.

"Close call," said Seth, before he wandered over to try and flirt with the girl at the organic coffee stand.

Earl shook his head as he loaded the last of our produce into the back of the truck.

He was right to be concerned. If we wanted to keep Sara, we had to show that we could give her a safe and loving home. Her parents have spent a little bit of time at the farm, most notably when they came to the bluegrass concert we put on this summer, but since then their feelings toward us have cooled. I think it's because they feel guilty for leaving Sara in our care.

I was relieved that Mrs. Spratt was not around to see Liam, the manager of the market, stop by to tell me Woefield would not be welcomed back next year. I was about to protest when we were joined by Werner Guurten, the most successful grower in the area.

"Prudence!" said Werner, nearly shoving the overly earnest Liam out of the way. At seventy, Werner is at least six feet two and 250 pounds. If you include his charisma, he's twice that size.

"I have a proposition for you," said Werner. "Remember when I ran into you mooning over the Kubotas at Big T's Tractor and Trailer Emporium?"

I nodded. We couldn't afford to buy a tractor, but it was fun to imagine one parked in the field.

"Well, I have something like that for you and I think you're going to be real excited."

"Excuse me, Werner. I was just telling Prudence that we're rethinking the vendor mix here at the market," said Liam, attempting to get back to the business at hand. "For next spring."

"Be quiet, Liam," said Werner.

"But Werner, the incident today with Woefield's hot sauce could have been—"

"Prudence here is one of our most promising young growers."

"What if that man had been seriously injured from her sauce?" asked Liam, plaintively. "We've got to think about the liability."

"Nonsense," said Werner. He turned to me. "Prudence, you'll be back next year. And I've got an offer that's going to make it easier for you to work that farm of yours."

"You have an old tractor for us?" I said, excitement banishing the tiredness creeping up on me. I cast a glance at Sara and Earl, who'd stopped packing up in order to listen intently.

"Better," said Werner. "I've got a mule for you."

My breath caught in my throat. A mule! If there was one thing I wanted more than a Kubota tractor, it was a mule! A farm is not a farm without animals. We'd made a good start by boarding Sara's show chickens and of course there was Bertie, my late uncle's depressed sheep, but a mule would take us to the next level, livestock-wise. According to everything I've read, a mule is one of the strongest and most useful creatures a farm can have. We could use a mule to plow the fields, pull stumps, keep the grass mowed. We could even ride it around!

"Now, we don't have much use for a mule. Our operation is pretty much automated, but I know you like the old-timey ways," said Werner.

"Nice try, Werner," said a deep voice. I felt big hands close around my waist and a soft kiss on the top of my head as Eustace, my boyfriend, joined us. I melted a little at his touch but, as was becoming our pattern, ignored his words.

"I am very much interested in having a mule," I said.

"Is it trained?" Eustace asked Werner. He is a veterinarian and thinks he knows everything about training and proper accommodation and fencing for animals. I think he loses sight of the fact that everyone has to start somewhere. Learning as you go is a legitimate approach to matters agricultural.

"Well, he's trained to eat his weight every day," chuckled Werner, a touch evasively.

"Is it safe for inexperienced handlers? What sort of temperament are we talking about?" asked Eustace.

I looked at him, feeling resentment grow. My boyfriend is basic-ally a Hallmark version of a vet. He's as tall as Werner and, with his disarray of brown curls and sculpted facial features, he's almost too handsome. On the other hand, he has a tendency to interfere and our politics do not align.

"We'll learn," I said.

"Werner, you know there's no barn on Woefield right now. What's wrong with this mule? Why are you trying to get rid of it?"

Werner took offense or at least pretended to. "Nothing, Eustace. Come on now. You're making it sound like I'm trying to put some-thing over on Prudence instead of doing a favor for a fellow farmer."

Liam looked from Werner to Eustace and silently admitted defeat. His shoulders slumped and he walked away.

Werner beamed at Eustace and then back at me.

"Prudence, this is the best-looking mule I ever saw. Could prob-ably get a fortune for him if I put him on the open market. But I'm willing to let you take him for a season. See how he works out for you. Then, if you like him, we can get a payment schedule going."

"How much did *you* pay for him?" Eustace asked Werner, taking off his ball cap and running a hand over his curly hair.

"That's not important," said Werner. "What's important is that Prudence should be given the support she needs to farm the way she's always wanted to."

Eustace looked at me. "I would strongly advise against doing this right now," he said.

I ignored him.

Seth

I was talking to the girl in the "I ♥ Pugs" T-shirt at the coffee stand (who turned out not to want my number, even though I told her I also love pugs, which I don't, because they look fucked up), so I wasn't around when the deal was struck. I was left thinking the big excitement of the week would be the fact that Prudence nearly killed some poor guy with her hot sauce and the poor impression we left on Sara's parents, but Prudence had another trick up her sleeve. Mule up her dress? I can't decide which cliché to use. Of all the livestock that could have been foisted on us, we ended up with an animal that isn't even a single species! Correct me if I'm wrong, but a mule is one of those degenerate concoctions: half horse, half donkey. It can't have sex or at least it can't have babies. I don't know what all it can't do, but I know it's a lot.

Prudence is open-minded to a fault. Seriously. There are things that shouldn't be: apples that are half pears, raspberries that are half blackberries, and mules.

About three days after the last farmers' market of the year, forever known as the Great Hot Sauce Debacle, Sara and I were weeding the front beds and I was posting sarcastic comments to accompany pictures of vegetables on Instagram when a clip-clopping noise on the road caught my attention. I looked over at the road and there came Prudence leading a giant red mule with an abundance of spots on its ass. They reached our driveway and the mule came to a dead stop. Prudence started hauling on its leash for all she was worth. The mule, obviously smarter than it looked, was having none of it. My guess is that it was using its superior animal instincts to detect the incompetence rising off this place like mist off a moor.

That was the moment the Morrisey kid chose to set a new speed record on his dirt bike. He isn't even supposed to take it on the road because he has no license. He had the thing revved so high it looked and sounded like the space shuttle *Challenger* seconds before detonation.

Well, that mule knew a prime excuse for a conniption fit when it saw one. It reared up. Looked fairly magnificent, actually, for a spotted red mule. When it came down, it yanked the leash out of Prudence's hands and galloped away like a cross between Secretariat and Usain Bolt. Fast. What I'm trying to say is the mule was much faster than you would imagine.

Thanks to dumb luck, it didn't head back the way they'd come. Instead it pirouetted and did the fifty-yard dash across the street into my mother's yard. The luck was mitigated by the fact that my mother's place is probably the single most hazardous half-acre in all of Cedar, thanks to her habit of using the property to store half-finished craft projects and everything we've ever owned that has either broken or gone out of fashion.

The mule jumped three pieces of decaying twig furniture, narrowly avoided crashing into my gone-and-nearly-forgotten old man's derelict Firebird, cleared by three feet an old sectional my mom uses to entertain outside when the three-piece *indoor* living room furniture gets too confining, darted around an old washer-dryer set, before crashing directly into and *through* the trampoline that my mom picked up years ago from a friend who works at the dump. The trampoline was part of my mother's plan to encourage me to become more athletic. I was fifteen. You show me the fifteen-year-old heavy metal fan who wants to take up trampoline sports and I'll show you a guy who has more problems than me.

Anyway, while the mule was rampaging around my childhood home, I screamed, Prudence screamed, Sara screamed. I'm pretty sure even the mule screamed before doing the smart thing and freezing in place, both front legs having ripped through the rotten fabric of the trampoline, back legs splayed out behind.

The only one who didn't scream was Earl, who'd been working behind me, clearing blockages out of the drip irrigation system to prepare it for winter.

When all the yelling stopped, he said, "Well, Jesus Christ, what's next? It never ends around this place."

And then we went over to see if we could help. I went slowly, because mules are not among my core competence categories and I never liked that trampoline from the day my mom brought it home. I was just glad Sara's parents weren't around to see the latest show of poor role-modeling and unsafe home environment on the part of Woefield Farm's management team. I'm starting to think Prudence should go see someone.

Earl

I used to know a gal who rode a mule. Her name was Ella Grace and she was a crackerjack little rider. Even invited me to go double on that mule of hers, but I was never much for riding. I guess that gave me an appreciation for mules, 'specially ones with nice markings. The one Prudence come dragging up the road was a handsome bastard, even when he found himself stuck in a goddamned trampoline across the road.

It's a good thing that mule is smart. This one waited still as a statue while Prudence got some wire snips to cut him out of that contraption kids is supposed to jump on but that usually end being leaf catchers out in the backyard. Mule didn't flinch at all, though he got a real sour look on his face and bared his great yellow teeth at her a few times like he was getting ready to take a bite.

She told us the mule's name is Lucky and I figure that's a piss-poor name for an animal that ends up living here.

When she got him loose, the whole bunch of us, Seth, Prudence, Sara and me, led that mule out of that mess of a backyard and up the road to our place. He come along just fine. Head high, swinging side to side, big ears swiveling around, looking around like nothing happened. He was probably embarrassed and I can't say as I blame him. It's hard to keep your pride in a place like this. Just ask me.

I wonder what ever happened to Ella Grace and her mule. I lost touch with her after the incident with her and my brother Merle. There wasn't a woman anywhere he could keep his hands off, not even the only one who ever offered me to ride double on a mule. When Prudence came to the farm, she got to digging into my private history and figured out my brother was Merle Clemente and that I was what some people called the Lost High Lonesome Brother. Stupid thing to call me. I was never lost. I was right here on Woefield Farm.

Prudence convinced Merle to come all the way here to play a reunion concert with me as a fund-raiser for the farm this summer. Every bluegrass fan came out of the woodwork for that one. We raised a few dollars to keep the bank off our backs and Merle give me my cut of the money he got from selling our family place and I bought myself a half ownership on this place, even though what I really wanted was to get myself a truck and camper and get on the road. Couldn't do it though. Didn't want to leave little Sara or Prudence, who is energetic but also a little haywire.

Me and Merle left it on good terms after the concert. He keeps calling to ask me to come on tour with him and I keep saying hell no, and he says okay. Then he calls a few weeks later to ask the same question all over again. My older brother didn't get to be the so-called godfather of bluegrass music by not getting his way. He's always got some command performance, awards ceremony, special appearance up his sleeve. I'm getting real fed up with his harassing on me. I told him the last time he called that if he wants to play together he can come here because I ain't leaving the farm.

I need to keep my mind on all the responsibilities I got here. Like I said, I'm a co-owner now, and I got concerns about how it's being run. It ain't professional. That's the long and short of it. Course, it never was, so there's that.

Our sheep, Bertie, is still sleeping on my porch, nights, and the mule has started waiting near the steps for her. I figure he must be from an Appaloosa horse, which is how he got all them spots on his hind end and shoulders. Showy as hell, them spots, but they say an Appaloosa is probably the most attitudinal horse there is. Tough and smart and no-bullshit. Add that to a donkey and you've got yourself quite a combination. Too much animal for this outfit, I figure.

I got Seth to string a tarp off the side of my cabin's roof so Bertie and the mule can get out of the rain, but that ain't good enough. We're into late September now and the nights is getting cold.

I'm glad Prudence said we're going to go ahead with the new barn. I don't want a sheep and a mule on my porch all winter. No sir, I do not.

Prudence

From Eustace's reaction you'd think Lucky and I had been hit by sniper fire on our way from the Guurtens' to Woefield. I may not have a lot of direct mule experience, but I'm fairly certain that the fact that I was able to walk Lucky nearly two miles on the side of the road with hardly any problems, except a small hiccup near the end of our incredible journey, is a very positive sign.

That said, the sudden arrival of a mule means we really need to get the barn built and it will have to be on a different scale than I'd first imagined.

"I can build it for you," said Eustace.

"You're working twelve hours a day already," I said.

"I just don't want you to get ripped off by some contractor."

"We won't get ripped off. And I'll be right here to supervise the work. So will Earl and Seth."

"How'd it go at the doctor?" he asked.

He's been after me to see someone about my lack of energy and increasingly poor memory.

"Haven't had a chance," I said. In fact, I forgot that I'd agreed to get a checkup. I even forgot to put it on my to-do list.

"Do you want to see my doctor?"

"I'll find my own," I said, trying not to sound as defiant as I felt. "I only see physicians who appreciate and understand alternative and complementary medicine."

"As long as they also have some understanding of actual medicine," he said, darkly. We were on the porch swing, watching the dusk settle over the farm. I felt cozy under his arm as well as slightly claustrophobic.

"You don't need to look after me and this farm," I said. "I am quite capable of handling things."

Even in the failing light I could sense him struggling not to argue. But to his credit, he just nodded and squeezed my shoulder.

"Can I at least recommend a few guys? For the barn?" he said.

"Hiring contractors is part of my job. I need to learn to trust my instincts. I can't allow myself to become dependent on you."

"Are you sure? Because I'd sort of like that."

"I know you would."

We were just about to kiss when Sara came onto the porch with the phone in her hand.

"It's Mr. Sandhu's mother," she said.

For a moment I couldn't place the name. Then I remembered. The man from the farmers' market. The one who had the panic attack after tasting our hot sauce.

"His mother?" said Eustace as I took the phone.

"Hello? This is Prudence."

"It's Mrs. Sandhu. Anoop's mother."

"Oh hello, Mrs. Sandhu."

31

"You are knowing that you nearly killed my son?"

"I'm sorry. He told me that he liked spicy food."

"He is not liking food so spicy it stops his heart!"

"The paramedics said it was a panic attack. They said he gets them all the time."

"A heart panic attack!" said Mrs. Sandhu. "He was maybe about to get engaged. To a very nice girl of forty. But now she hears about his heart and she's not sure anymore."

"I'm sorry to hear that."

"Are you married?" asked Mrs. Sandhu.

"Well, no."

"Are you maybe looking for someone who likes spicy food? But not too spicy?"

"No, thank you. I have a boyfriend."

"Anoop's cousin Gurbinder, he's pre-law. He's top of his class. Top half, anyway. He is going to Trent. You ever hear of Trent University?"

"No, I'm afraid not."

"It's good," she said. "Very good."

"Okay," I said, not wanting to inflame her and not understanding if she was bragging or threatening.

"I wanted you to know."

"Is there something I can help you with?"

"Do you know any single girls? Anoop plays video games. He says he will get a job after he gets married."

"Oh," I said, not following.

"He plays video games all day and all night. He has friends online. None of them work. It's time for him to get married."

"Ah," I said.

"You can call if you know of a girl," she said. "Or activities where he might meet a girl. I'll give you my number."

It occurred to me to wonder how she'd gotten my number but I was too tired to ask.

"We will come visit you sometime," said Mrs. Sandhu, before hanging up. "In case you think of anyone."

I clicked the receiver off and stared into the dark night. I woke up to find Eustace carrying me inside to bed.

Sara

The time I have spent living at Woefield with Prudence and Seth and Earl is my favorite time in my life, so far. When my mom asks when I want to move home, I never know what to say. Our old house in Shady Woods Estates is for sale, so I guess I would live with my dad in his basement apartment near the Tire Depot on Cedar Road, or at my aunt's in Duncan with my mom. My mom has asked about me moving home three times since she saw what happened at the farmers' market with the rugby players and the man who had to go away in an ambulance. Last time we talked, she said that she feels like people, such as my aunt, are looking down on her for not taking care of me herself.

It's sort of funny that she wants me to move home, since I don't think she enjoys our visits very much. We always do the same thing. We go to the A&W across from Southgate Mall and then we go to the big library in Nanaimo. Or we clean the house in Shady Woods, even though no one lives there and it's not dirty. In Jr. Poultry Fancier's Club, I learned that keeping things clean is part of good husbandry, but cleaning things that are already clean is not a good use of resources. Sometimes my mom cries when she cleans. She even cries at A&W. I think she's depressed. The only time she doesn't cry is when she writes in her journal, which is what she does when we go to the library. She also does it at night when she should be sleeping.

On my visits with my dad, we watch TV. He enjoys watching poker and other sports. He says he's sorry to be boring, but he's really tired. He doesn't mind if I read while he watches TV, so at least I'm getting something done. He's also asked about when I want to move home, but he always says, "We should think about you moving back with your mother soon."

My other news is that I've taken three mule books out of the library and am looking forward to reading them.

My teacher, Miss Singer, sent me home with a notice about parent-teacher interviews. She said she's aware of my "situation" and she said I should give the form to my custodian. Which is funny, because the custodian is the janitor at the school! I hope it doesn't sound mean when I say that I'd rather have the janitor go to my parent-teacher than try to figure out whether I'm supposed to give the form to my mom or my dad. If I tell them things they both need to know, such as that they have to go to a meeting or something, they call up the other one and have a fight on the phone. When they get done fighting, my mom cleans and cries or writes harder and my dad watches TV even more and then says he's sorry for being such a cliché. I just looked that word up and it means typical. I think he might be misunderstanding the definition. Most of the kids I know who have divorced parents get special fun treatment from at least one of their parents. It's okay though, because I have fun at Woefield. Everyone there is really nice.

Maybe I'll put my parent-teacher notice on the fridge at Woefield. Prudence will know what to do.

Seth

Lately I've begun contributing to *The Cure*, this online recovery magazine. My column is called Half Measures. I asked my editor if I could name it Fucking Half Measures, but she said Half Measures was inflammatory enough.

If you don't get the joke, then you are not a twelve-stepper. In the interests of killing the thing entirely by over-explaining it, there's this line in AA's Big Book that says, "Half measures availed us nothing."

Personally, half measures have availed me over three months of continuous sobriety, my own column, and a new life across the street from my mother and her boyfriend, Bobby. If I gave a full measure, I'd probably be running the country right now.

One thing about my new writing gig: I think I might be in love with my editor, Tamara. She gives good email. The fact is, since I sobered up I'm half in love with every woman I meet.

I shouldn't say too much about Tamara right now. My sponsor, Eustace, who is Prudence's devoted-like-a-dog boyfriend and studly vet about town, said it's normal for me to get the hots for numerous women while I'm in my early recovery, because my health is returning, but he thinks it's somewhat abnormal for me to get the hots for *every single* woman with whom I come in contact. That sounded dismissive to me and so I added him to the resentment list that I already wrote about in an article for my column.

We live in an age of repurposing content and I fully embrace that shit.

Unfortunately for the purposes of what Earl refers to as my ambition to "tomcat around," I'm trapped here on the farm due to not really receiving much in the way of a salary. At the moment, the farm generates approximately negative twenty thousand dollars a year. As a result of these sad circumstances, I don't meet many women. Sure, there are women at AA meetings, but Eustace said that I have to maintain a hands-off policy on them until I've been clean and sober for a year. That's probably good advice. For someone else. Yes, I realize that some of the newcomer girls have issues. That's very attractive to me. There's one girl who cries every time she shares. She says, "My name is Brittiana, and I'm an alcoholic." This declaration is followed by precisely five minutes of crying. She gets on some people's nerves, but I think it's considerate of her to never go into overtime with her crying.

Thoughtful as she clearly is, she's off limits. Eustace is uptight about rules in the program. The guy looks like a Greek god, and I seriously doubt he stayed out of the relationships in his first year, but he said he'd fire me if I got into a relationship, especially with a girl in the program. I figure he doesn't need to know about my relationships with girls who are *not* in the program, if I should meet one. I'm not being sneaky and dishonest. I'm being discreet.

It might sound like I'm paranoid and grandiose, thinking people are talking or thinking about me. Well, they are. The entire twelve-step community is always ass-deep, if you'll forgive the expression, in each other's business and I can't face the thought of getting a new sponsor right now. If necessary, Eustace can fire me next summer. By then I'll probably be ready for a more high-profile sponsor such as Eminem or Robert Downey Jr.

In addition to desiring all women over twenty, I'm also concerned about Sara. Since she moved in with us she hasn't brought home any little friends. I think she might be unpopular. That would just about fucking break my heart.

Then there's the parent-teacher notice on the fridge. I have no idea what the protocol is when you're looking after a minor whose parents are total nonstarters. I presume *they're* supposed to go to the interview. But will they know to ask the teacher if she has any friends? I saw the way they were eyeballing us at that farmers' market. It's like they don't trust our judgment, which would be the biggest example of the pot calling the kettle scorched in kettle history. But they're the parents and they can pull the plug on this child care arrangement at any time.

In other last page news, the mule is kind of cool to look at, but I fail to see his purpose. I mean, if you want a creature to wreak destruction on your sporting and playground equipment, Lucky's your man. If you want a beast of burden to pull your plow, then you might want to look elsewhere. At this point, Lucky is a thousand-pound tapeworm who hangs around looking like he could give a shit what anybody thinks.

Oh no. Here comes Prudence. I just know she wants to talk about farm matters. Raised beds, mules, barns, what to do with all the remaining bottles of killer hot sauce.

Prudence

After interviewing contractors for two days, I was beginning to doubt I'd find the right person. Sure, they all had that calm, competent air that people who build things cultivate. They were all broad-shouldered and square-jawed, even the lone woman I spoke with. I would have chosen her, too, because I think there should be more women in the trades, but her quote was too high. All the quotes were too high.

"You want steak on a bologna budget," said Seth. "I understand because I want bologna on no budget."

"Just let me handle it," I said, as I prepared a delicious dinner of baked butternut squash, assorted dark greens and quinoa. I am normally energized by the dish, but I felt full and exhausted by the time I'd finished half my bowl. I've been gaining weight recently, so that was just as well.

"I liked that woman you talked to," he said. "She had a really nice truck."

"Her quote suggested that she has big payments on it."

"Why don't you ask Eustace? He could do it himself. On a Saturday afternoon. With one arm in a sling and a blindfold on."

I paid no attention to Seth, who is uninterested in the power of independence. "Have you ever tried squash hummus?" I asked.

"No, thank Christ."

I hoped that I'd distracted him enough that he wouldn't remember to tell Eustace that the quotes came in higher than we could afford. Until I learned basic construction skills myself, I should at least be able to hire someone to help out. Self-reliance is a core value of mine. Well, that and teamwork.

At risk of revealing myself to be psychologically predictable, I'm the product of parents who (a) sent me away to boarding school when I was eight so they could focus on their golf games, and (b) died when I was twelve. From them I learned that people in general and women in particular need to take responsibility for themselves. Becoming an orphan at an early age taught me that organization and productive activity bring pleasure, as do list-making and crossing items off lists.

I have never allowed my boyfriends to do things for me that I can do for myself. Just because I'm running a small but labor-intensive farm doesn't mean I'm going to change. I dated a junior hedge fund manager before I left New York. Leo wanted to get access to my (extremely modest) trust fund in order to make it grow. Not three months after I declined, the market imploded and Leo was one of the few Wall Street guys to lose his job. See? Self-reliance is the byword.

That said, I was beginning to despair of finding a good builder in our price range when Stephan McFadden drove up. I knew right away that we'd be able to make an arrangement. He had the large, expensive truck that is apparently a requirement to enter the field, but he had an open, almost angelic face and an effervescence of spirit about him. When I told him what I wanted, he grinned and quoted a price well within our price range, and I knew I'd been smart to hold out for the right person.

Stephan is probably no more than twenty-five, so presumably he is just getting started in his own business. That's why he's still afford-able. I appreciated that he took the time to look around and admire everything we've done to the place.

"That's a heckuva nice mule. It's a mule, right?" he said, when he spotted Lucky. And he also noticed how well the plants in the raised beds were doing for this late in the year.

"It's like a little slice of Eden here, eh?" he said.

I can't tell you how many times I've had that exact thought while looking around Woefield Farm. Stephan was going to be a delight to have around the place.

When Eustace came by the next day, I didn't tell him I'd found the perfect contractor. I'd let him discover my competence as a sub-contractor (if that's what it's called when you hire trades) for him-self when he stopped by and found the construction underway. I gave Stephan an advance to buy all the materials, so it shouldn't be long before things start happening. The sound of saws whirring and boards being hammered together is going to be like music for all of our ears. This place gets more wonderful every day!

With that accomplished, the next order of business was to get serious about training Lucky. After the first day, his personality seemed to get baleful. Eustace speculated that Werner had drugged him the day I picked him up, but Eustace has a tendency to cynicism. I'd been letting the mule's behavioral issues (specifically, his attempts to bite and kick) slide due to my mild case of autumn overwhelm. This afternoon, I offered Lucky a carrot to celebrate the fact that his house would soon be a reality and he nipped me. Thank goodness he only got the fabric of my shirt. Those great yellow teeth could have done serious damage to my bicep. We may have to bring in a mule trainer to get us going. I wonder if we can find someone to work for free or in exchange for gourds?

Sara

I've been reading my mule books and I have a lot of information to share. At Jr. Poultry Club we learned that when you give a demonstration, it's important not to confuse your audience with too much information. First, you have to get their attention. Then you should tell them what you're going to tell them, so they're prepared.

When Prudence and Seth and Earl met me in the driveway in front of the house for their mule lesson, I started by sharing an interesting fact.

"Hundreds of thousands of mules and horses died in World War Two."

"Sara?" said Seth, putting up his hand.

"Yes?"

"You know I'm impressed with your research abilities, right?"

I nodded. He says all the time that he'd like to hire me as an assistant but that his research topics are not child-friendly and his blogging and online magazine writing budget doesn't allow for supplementary staff.

"While I'm saddened by the plight of equines in past military conflicts, I also have a lot on my plate right now. Personally and professionally. I'm not so sure I want to get into another situation in which I and a helpless farm animal could be harmed. Because it sounds to me like that's where this lesson is headed."

He was probably remembering the time we tried to trim and put medicine on Bertie's hooves. Bertie's our sheep. He might also have been talking about the time we tried to shear Bertie and he got kicked in the head and dragged around the yard. I guess he could also have been thinking about the time he got caught cheating at the poultry show by coloring some of my rooster Alec Baldwin's white feathers. My dad misunderstood what Seth was doing and punched him. Seth says he'll never be able to set foot in a show chicken barn again. I don't believe him about that. Chicken shows are really exciting.

"It's okay," I said. "I'm just getting everyone's attention before the main part of the demonstration."

Seth said okay then, that was fine. Prudence yawned, which I've never seen her do before.

I let them know that I would be teaching them about the history and origin of mules and telling them how to handle mules. I told them that mules come from breeding male donkeys to female horses. I explained that male donkeys are called jacks and female donkeys are called jennets. If a male horse mates with a female donkey, the baby is called a hinny, not a mule.

Earl said he knew a hinny once, back in Tennessee, and Seth said he wasn't surprised and did Earl still have her number.

I continued before they could have a swearing argument.

I informed them that male mules are called johns and female mules are called mollies and I told them how mules are sure-footed, which means that they don't fall down, and they have excellent self-protection instincts. I'm pretty sure I had their attention then, because they were all staring at me.

The writer of a book called *Mule Crazy* told a story about riding his mule on a very dangerous trail and how it was best to let it find its own way. One time, he tried to make it go over a bridge and it wouldn't. He finally gave up and found out later that the next horse that went over the bridge fell through. I thought about telling Prudence and Earl and Seth that story, but they were fidgeting too much.

I told them we had to practice leading Lucky. This was especially important because of his previous bad experience on the road.

Prudence stared at me. For once, she didn't have a smile on her face. She's been looking serious lately. And maybe a bit puffy. Normally, she practically runs from place to place on the farm, getting a lot of things done. Seth says she's hyperactive and disturbingly optimistic. I just think she's really nice and so I didn't like to see her looking pale and tired. My mom started to look like that not long after my dad got fired from the bank and everything in our lives went bad.

"Unpleasant experiences can make mules have problems, especially if they have inexperienced handlers," I told them.

Prudence probably felt bad about being inexperienced and giving Lucky a traumatic event, so I tried to make her feel better.

"My books say that it's easier to train a young mule. How old is Lucky?"

"I didn't ask," said Prudence.

"Has anyone tried to catch him since we got him?"

They all shook their heads. I think if I ever become a teacher I won't find it very hard, because I'll have a lot of experience working with people who have a lot to learn.

"I've been reading about it and the books say that we should practice on ourselves first."

Seth looked at his watch, which was bad manners.

I ignored him and got the rope.

"Who wants to go first?" I asked.

When Earl said he would, Seth finally smiled.

I didn't tell them that I'd only read up to the practicing-on-people part of the mule-leading chapter because I've had a lot of schoolwork.

Seth

Little Sara was in the middle of one of her farming lessons, only this time it was mule training, which sounded a hell of a lot more dangerous than building a chicken coop or training a chicken to be a runway model or attempting to shear half a nearly catatonic sheep or any of the other things she's made us do.

She started with a barrage of depressing facts about dead war mules and then started making us take turns being mule and mule trainer. I shit you not. Normally, I'd expect Prudence to get us back on track, but she seemed dazed, and when I gave Earl the old "what the hell?" look, he shot me a look like fifty thunder clouds.

One of us had to close our eyes while our partner put the rope around our wrists and then led us around the pasture. The idea, apparently, was that we'd learn how it felt to have pressure exerted on us and how it was natural to resist that pressure and how the person doing the leading has to immediately let go of the pressure to reward the "mule" for taking a step forward. Only the exercise was flawed because (*a*) our partners weren't mules; (*b*) Lucky is not currently visually impaired, although he might end up like that guy in King Lear if he bolts into my mother's yard again, thanks to all the abandoned twig furniture; and (c) as a group we don't trust each other's competence. At all.

So in that way, it was sort of a genius exercise because our lack of trust immediately became clear.

Sara made me be the blind mule first and she gave my leash to Earl. He yanked on it like he was trying out for the Bulgarian strongman tire pull competition in the over-seventy division. I was like, fuck this. I'm not getting pulled over onto my face by Earl, even if he is world famous on the banjo. I dug in my high tops and he yanked again. "Dude! You're going to dislocate my shoulder. I've got recovery articles to type," I said.

Sara told me I had to keep my eyes closed and that mules don't understand English.

I was forced to admit that if I was a blind mule I wouldn't go one step with Earl. Interestingly, Earl didn't get mad when Sara told him he'd need to be "more sensitive" when leading me or our actual mule.

When Sara let me open my eyes, I saw that Lucky and Bertie, who are now bosom buddies, presumably because they're both trying to survive life on Beat Down Farm, were watching us through the fence with the livestock equivalent of bug eyes.

I wanted to give our beasts of burden confidence, so I shut my eyes again and when Earl jerked my rope, I took a step forward. But he didn't let up. He just kept pulling. It was bullshit, the way he pulled, so I kind of pulled back and we were getting into a bit of tug-of-war, nothing too serious, but Sara broke it up.

She said she'd demonstrate on Prudence. Which wasn't fair because of how Prudence is such a hopeless perfectionist. She'd be the best blind mule in the history of pointless blind mule–leading lessons. At least, that's what I assumed before she crashed over onto her face.

Earl

I don't know what the hell's gotten into Prudence. She might make food that would make a hippie want McDonald's, and be bossy as all get out, but she never used to be snappish. She was always cheerful as the sun is yellow, but as soon as Sara hooked her up to that lead rope, Prudence's jaw set and I had a premeditation that things weren't going to go good.

Sara said for Prudence to close her eyes, and as soon as she did, Prudence started swaying on her feet, like she'd turned herself around in one too many circles.

I told Sara to hang on and asked Prudence if she was okay. But Sara had a hold of the book and the lead rope and was doing too many things at once. She pulled on that rope and Prudence walked a few steps and then stopped. Sara pulled on the rope again and Prudence swayed for a minute and then she came down with a crash, like a tree tied to a tractor.

Seth started jumping around the way he does and cursing up

a storm. Good goddamned thing he's not a paramedical or people would be dying left and right.

Sara just stood there with her eyes wide, looking like she was going to cry.

I went to pick Prudence up but she was already scrambling to her feet and dusting off her skirt and trying to act like nothing happened.

But you fell down! said Sara.

And Prudence said that she tripped because she was so busy. Never heard the like of it. She said it wasn't Sara's fault and that me and Seth should have been paying more attention. That didn't make an iona of sense and I said so. Prudence said that everyone needed to remember that she was in charge and to stop interfering with her ability to do her job. That had a rat's ass all to do with her keeling over, but I let it go. Prudence said that she was very busy and then she told Sara that it had been a very good lesson but that perhaps, in future, mule-leading practice should happen later in the evening, when the day's work had been done.

Then she went stomping into the house. When I went into the main house half an hour later, I could swear Prudence was in bed. I'm talking about a girl who works from five in the goddamned morning until pitch dark every night. It's not right. Not right at all.

Sara

When Prudence fell over I wonder if she might have hit her head. She said she fell because she was so busy but that can't be right, because then she'd probably fall over about twelve times a day. Prudence is a *very* busy person. Also, she said mule lessons should be held in the evening and it WAS the evening. I mean, it was nearly five and that's not afternoon anymore—at least I don't think it is.

I was disappointed that the lesson didn't go better. No one around here can lead anyone and I think that's a problem. I have special leadership training from Jr. Poultry Fancier's Club and even I can't make people follow me.

I hope that Prudence's head injury doesn't stop her from going to my parent-teacher interview next week. Miss Singer asked me again who would be coming to talk to her. She was trying to be nice, but she was asking too many questions. There are other people in my class who have divorces. Target Barton has three dads and not in a gay way. Someone at school said his mom's on the junk and his old man's in the can. I had to look those things up. Being on the junk means that either his mom eats really bad food *or* is on drugs *or* has a big bum. Being in the can means being on the toilet or in jail. I think it might also mean that he works in Alberta. I feel especially bad for Target because of his older brother, Charles, who is in eleventh grade and wears a long black coat. Charles walks Target to and from school and the heels of his black boots are all worn down because he barely picks up his feet when he walks. He just slides them across the pavement. Someone said that Charles and Target have been in and out of foster care since they were born and it's given Charles psychology problems and so he has to take medication.

Poor Target. I barely like having one father, never mind three. I might invite Target to visit the farm. Seth keeps asking if I have any friends my own age. If Target comes to see me, maybe then Seth will stop asking. I guess if Target visits, Charles will probably have to come too. He seems like he might be a good friend for Seth, even though Charles is in eleventh grade and Seth is twenty-one. Seth is very young for his age.

The only problem is that if I start inviting people over, I'll have less time for researching mule training and caring for my birds and helping out around the farm. No one has done anything with Lucky since we got him out of the trampoline. He's tried to kick everyone at least once and he used his nose to shove Earl on the behind when Earl turned his back on him. The books say that mules are very smart and that if they get away with bad behavior, they will repeat that bad behavior forever. We may have a problem mule on our hands if we're not careful.

I can't be responsible for all the animal training around here. I have school. And I have to visit my parents.

Seth

I had a lot of free-floating anxiety after the mule lesson. First, there was my concern that Sara's parents are going to find out the full extent of our incompetence and pull the plug on letting her live here. There was Prudence's bizarre, unmotivated behavior. Then there was the growing concern that I will never meet a woman and never have sex. That's right. I've never had proper sex with another person. Let's not read too much into that. I had all sorts of near-sex when I was in high school, but I had it with a teacher. So that's more like child abuse than sex, I suppose. Though, to be fair, I was into it at the time.

My anxiety, which is probably the major feature of my personality other than loving heavy metal and the Internet, gave me the idea for a new Half Measures column. I think my editor, Tamara, is going to dig it. I'm going to call it "Double Qualifiers" and it will be about being in recovery for your substance abuse issues as well as being highly codependent with other people. That means that you can't be happy because of other people and your worries about them. To be honest, unless you're one of those people who gets wound up about shit you can do nothing about, such as trophy hunting or global warming or whatever, I'm not sure what there is to worry about other than your own problems and other people.

I even talked about codependence at the meeting I went to that afternoon. I rode my bike there, which is some hardcore willingness of the kind that probably deserves its own story in the Big Book. The title of my inspiring story will be "He Wanted Sobriety So Bad He Rode a Bike to a Meeting." I'll describe how the farm's piece-of-crap bike got its hundredth flat tire when I was right across from the high school and how I nearly went face-first into the ditch when the wheel started to wobble and make a screeching noise due to there being no air between the rubber and the rim. Having a transportation meltdown across the street from the site of the worst humiliation ever visited on any eleventh-grade male was just what my self-esteem didn't need. In my Big Book story, which will probably be put into the section about the people who have lost it all rather than the section about people who have only lost half, I might even talk about what happened during the opening night of the school production of *Jesus Christ Superstar* thanks to my sordid affair with the drama teacher, who was the person with whom I was having near-sex/abuse.

I had to get off and push the bike the rest of the way to the meeting. That's why I came in late, which the chairperson, a guy named Sid, noted with a snide little "The meeting starts at six, Seth." Dick. I bet he didn't have to walk a flat-tired bike to a meeting. AA's founders, Bill and Dr. Bob, probably never even went to lengths like that to get to a meeting. I think that my efforts that afternoon made me the soberest guy in Cedar, if not all of the mid-Island, if effort counts for anything. But anyway, I was chosen last to speak as punishment for coming in late. I said that I was glad to be at a meeting, because things were hard on the farm, and that I was becoming more aware of my codependence issues and did anyone else have codependence issues causing them anxiety.

"No cross-talk, Seth," said Snide Sid, the chair-Nazi. "You'd realize that if you'd been here for the readings at the beginning."

So immediately all my willingness was replaced with blazing resentment. How dare Snide Sid scold me in front of everyone else? It was such bullshit. The guy had over three years of sobriety, too. He should be more compassionate.

Eustace is always telling me that I'm hypersensitive and that I am too easily enraged at other people. Yeah, well, no shit. AA is not supposed to be organized, but it should have *some* rules. People who chair meetings should not be allowed to shame people who are just trying to grow, especially people who had to walk a bike with a flat tire to the meeting.

After the meeting, this old dude came over to me and said my talk about codependence belonged in a different kind of meeting. I believe his specific words were "Save it for your women's meeting, kid."

Fucking sexist.

I was standing in the potholed church parking lot and deciding whether or not to leave the bike behind, when this girl who'd also been in the meeting came up to me.

"Hey," she said.

She'd passed when it was her turn to share, and I'd been sorry because she was good-looking and I love hearing good-looking or even average-looking women share.

"Hey," I replied, with undeniable wit and intelligence.

"I liked what you had to say," she said. "I'm codependent too. That chair guy was rude."

I shrugged and even though I sorely wanted to shit talk the guy, the girl had put up her hand when the chair asked if anyone was coming back, meaning she'd just had a relapse. She probably wasn't feeling so great. Like me, she needed to be in meetings, even ones with substandard chairs.

"Ah, he's okay," I said. "How about you? How are you doing?"

She shrugged. She had long, limp brown hair and big brown eyes. Now that she was close to me, I could see that she had the shakes and the distinctive scent of self-destruction was emanating off her like heat off the Florida tarmac. Her relapse might not be quite over.

"Do you have people to talk to?" I asked.

She looked at me, half skeptical, half hopeful. "I'm talking to you, aren't I?"

"Other women, I mean." I realized with a twinge of regret that I was not the kind of guy who was going to go all predatory on her. I was apparently the dude who not only walked his bike to meetings but also referred vulnerable and attractive newcomer/relapsers to other women.

I pointed at a woman who was taking some garbage out to the old dumpster behind the church. "Her name is Heather. She's super nice. You should introduce yourself."

The girl, the kind of twenty-two-year-old who might not make it to twenty-three, made a face and I realized she was probably shy. So like President of the Willing People Who Also Carry the Message of AA, I walked her over to Heather, whom I barely know but who does seem very nice, and introduced the two of them. Heather took it from there, and when I walked my bike out of the church parking lot, they were deep in conversation and I felt good, especially when a couple of other people who'd been at the meeting nodded at me and said, "Nice to see you, Seth," and "See you soon, Seth," and I knew they'd seen me doing my selfless work. Even the Snide Sid nodded reluctantly and I resented him a little bit less.

So yeah, it was a pretty good meeting and a good day overall, especially considering how codependent I am.

Prudence

After mule-leading practice, which nearly caused fisticuffs to break out between Seth and Earl, and which led to me tripping and falling, I felt the need to lie down. The peculiar thing is that I can't even remember going upstairs to my room. All I know is that I woke up at eight o'clock the next morning. Eight o'clock! That's fifteen hours of sleep! I haven't slept for fifteen hours since infancy and maybe not even then.

The only reason I eventually woke up was because Eustace came upstairs to check on me. He was sitting beside the bed when I opened my eyes, which felt like peeled grapes that had been dropped in a bucket of sand.

"How's the mono?" he asked.

"What?" I said, confused and defensive. "Very funny."

"Earl told me that you went to bed at five last night. And here you are. Still in bed."

"It wasn't five," I lied.

The strangest thing was that even after all that sleep I still didn't feel rested. My head felt like a concrete block, which nicely complemented the sand-filled eyes.

"I've never known you to stay in bed past six o'clock."

"My iron may be low. What are you doing here?" I realized as the words left my mouth that they sounded more hostile than I intended.

"Earl asked me to look your gift mule in the mouth."

I pushed myself up and onto my elbows. "Is something wrong with Lucky?"

"He's fine. Earl thought he should have a checkup. Make sure he was up to date on his worming and shots and that his teeth have been floated recently. I have to say, that mule has rotten ground manners. He tried to bite me. Nearly got me in the knee with a savage little kick. He's not safe for you to handle."

"I led him here from Werner's with no trouble. Well, except for a little bit of trouble at the end. Which wasn't his fault."

"Prudence, Werner is a shady dealer. He's perfectly capable of doping an animal before foisting it off on some unwary person."

"I am not unwary!" I said.

"Overly optimistic, then. You expect the best of people. And sometimes that's not the wisest strategy."

"Well, even if he was drugged, he's here now and we need to make the best of it. Of him."

"No, you don't. You need to tell Werner to come and get him. Before someone gets hurt."

If there's anything I dislike, it's being told what to do. Even if it makes sense. To show my displeasure, I didn't respond.

"Do you want me to call Werner? I can borrow a trailer and drop the mule back on his farm myself."

"That won't be necessary. We're fine," I said, trying to make my voice sound chilly even though my throat felt scorched.

The pause stretched out uncomfortably.

"I checked Bertie over, too," said Eustace, finally.

"I don't like to give unnecessary vaccines," I muttered.

The trusty hot-button issue that I could count on to sidetrack Eustace didn't work this time.

"Too late," he said. "Your sheep has been vaccinated against everything from syphilis to gout. You going to let me drive you?"

First he was trying to drive our mule away. Now he was trying to drive me. I struggled to keep up with the conversation. All I wanted to do was go back to sleep, but I didn't want Eustace to know that, so I forced myself to remain upright.

"To the doctor," he explained. "I doubt you've had time to find some alternative quack that meets your approval, so we'll go to a walk-in clinic."

"Absolutely not." I tried to remember my arguments against conventional medicine, which were legion, but my brain wouldn't cooperate. "I'm fine. I've got someone in mind. I just need to make an appointment."

Eustace looked at his watch, which was too large and shiny. "I have an appointment out in Extension at nine. Need to inoculate some piglets. I'll be back to check on you at ten thirty. If you haven't made an appointment, I'll make one for you."

I was gathering my strength to tell him how I felt about giving immune-suppressing shots to pigs and about the swine industry in general and share my distaste for being told what to do, but before I could get the words out, he was gone and I fell back into a dark, rest-free sleep.

Sara

When Eustace brought Prudence home today, she told us she is waiting for results of her blood work but that the doctor at the walk-in clinic thinks she might have a thyroid deficiency. Or adult mono. Prudence said she wasn't concerned, because someone told her there was a fantastic new alternative health practitioner who'd just opened a practice in Cedar.

Eustace kind of smiled at us when Prudence said that, and his smile gave me a funny feeling. Like what if Prudence dies from her thyroid mono and Eustace moves in here and looks after us. He's very tall and I like the way he smells. I don't want Prudence to be sick or to die, but I really like Eustace. I'd be proud to have him represent me at the parent-teacher. Miss Singer would be impressed if a real live vet was my dad or at least the person who went to the meeting to talk about my marks, which are all excellent. If Eustace moved in here to take care of us after Prudence died, I'd be sure to ask him a lot of questions about being a vet so that I'm well prepared if I decide to go to vet school when I'm older.

Prudence didn't want to talk for long, even though me and Seth had a lot of questions. She said she was feeling much better and that after a short nap she'd come downstairs and we'd have a house meeting before dinner. As she talked, Eustace raised his eyebrows at us. He stood behind her, so she couldn't see. I don't know what he meant, but it made me feel like he was on our side and also on Prudence's. If my dad had ever raised his eyebrows like that when my mom said something he didn't agree with instead of yelling and sometimes throwing plates of food, I bet they'd still be married.

Prudence said she was freezing and asked why there was no heat on, and Seth said it was because there was never any heat on because we couldn't afford heat and that's why he had on his thickest Sabbath sweatshirt and his jean jacket and his fingerless gloves. Then Prudence asked me if I did my homework, even though she already asked me that as soon as she came in the door a few minutes before, and I told her I was doing it. My books were open in front of me and everything.

When Eustace and Prudence went up to Prudence's room, Seth didn't even make a remark. Normally, he makes jokes when they have private time. He says it's because he feels like an alien in the face of so much attractiveness. It was good that he didn't start making jokes, because Eustace would have overheard him. He came right back downstairs to get Prudence a cup of tea and to ask if we had any extra blankets.

He made a cup of Sleepytime tea and I got him the orange, yellow and green afghan off the couch. It feels like hay and I've caught my fingers in the holes a few times, but Seth's mom made it and I knew Seth would want Prudence to use it even though normally he stays wrapped in it whenever he's in the house.

"If she has a thyroid problem she should recover quickly," said

Eustace. "One little pill a day and she'll be back to herself in a few days. It's an easy condition to treat in most cases."

Seth said maybe they should give her a lower dose because her speed was often excessive.

Eustace laughed. "But if it's mono, then we all might get it," he said.

Seth held up his hands like he was getting arrested. "Hey man, I haven't touched her."

"No doubt," said Eustace. He's very confident because of being tall and handsome. "Mono can be spread via food and dishes. And it can take quite a while to clear up. If you get it, you'll just have to rest up until you feel better. Good thing it's fall and things are starting to slow down around here."

"Except for the new barn and the out-of-control mule and that six hundred–item to-do list she's asked us to complete in the next day and a half," said Seth. He sounded like he was hoping we all had mono.

"Barn?" said Eustace. "What's going on with the barn?"

Seth looked down at his plate.

I don't think Prudence wanted us to say anything to anyone, especially Eustace. She wanted the barn to be a surprise.

"I think she hired someone," said Seth in a quiet voice, like he was hoping Prudence wouldn't hear him from her bedroom.

"Who?" asked Eustace. He looked sort of upset. Like he had hurt feelings. He must have wanted to build the barn for Prudence. He loves to do things for her.

"Some young dude. Looks like he might belong to one of those churches where they don't let anyone go through puberty until they're thirty."

"I never heard of a church like that," I said. Of all of us, I'm the only one who has attended church regularly. My friend Bethany's parents used to take me to their church. The people there were very nice.

"There is no church like that. At least not around here," said Eustace. I could tell that he wanted to ask more questions about the barn and the guy Prudence hired to build it, but he didn't. He has a lot of self-control.

"While she's sick, can you check on her every so often? She's going to be sleeping a lot. Just make sure she's still eating and don't give her a hard time about her memory or anything else. Don't let her take on more than she can handle. Taking it easy is going to be tough for her."

"I can teach her," said Seth. "Taking it easy is my specialty."

"Just because she's taking it easy doesn't mean you are," said Eustace. "Everyone is going to have to pull together to keep this place going if she's going to be down for a while." Then he took the tea and blanket upstairs to Prudence.

He is so nice!

Seth hooked a finger at me and said never to trust the medical system. "We'll research this terrible situation ourselves using the people's tool."

"The people's tool?" I said.

"Also known as the Internet. That's where the smart money goes to find out what's wrong with them. All you have to do is plug in your symptoms and then you get a diagnosis. Your health is too important to leave to doctors."

So me and Seth went on his computer and it was really fun. We had Ripples chips and No-Name pop for dinner because Prudence was in her room and wouldn't catch us. Getting to research and take charge is part of why I love living on Woefield Farm.

Seth

Holy shit. That's all I have to say. The Interwebs is a terrifying place from a trying-not-to-die perspective. Little Sara and I spent some time researching Prudence's symptoms. Eustace and her doctor were correct that Prudence has many of the signs of hypothyroidism and/or mono, as well as early onset dementia.

What if she's crocked and I get stuck running this place and nursemaiding her? I'm just beginning to flower over here, personal-development-wise. The loss of Prudence could shut me down for real. No time for meetings and recovery. Hardly any time to watch TV or go online to surf music and celebrity gossip. No time to find a girlfriend.

FFS. This could be a nightmare.

Sure, right now Eustace is being Mr. Helpful. Taking Prudence to the doctor and getting her blankets and tea. But how long will that last? He's a busy guy. Got that whole hot vet thing going on. He'll be able to help out with Prudence a few hours a day, max. The rest of it will fall on my shoulders.

They say people stop maturing when they start drinking or getting high in a serious way. That makes me approximately thirteen years old right now. I am on the verge of calling social services on behalf of myself.

Not coping. That's the slogan for the day. Easy does it. One day at a time. Think, think, think, and not coping.

I'm also concerned because Prudence is one of my favorite people. She's got all that energy and she's non-neurotic, which is a rare thing. When things go wrong, she never takes it personally. She just figures out a way to fix the problem. She takes the same approach to people.

When Prudence asks you to do something, you get this sense that she has total faith in you, even if nothing you've ever done or said should give her cause for confidence. Her optimism is so strong it overpowers everything in its path, even advanced incompetence and unwillingness.

So if she's got the early onset dementia or mono or is having a glandular meltdown or any of the other heinous disorders my research points to, I won't let her down. I'll take care of her until the end if I have to. Bury her in the backyard! By hand! That would be some Old Testament shit, because we basically have no dirt here on Woefield. Seriously. There's a half-inch of dust and grass and then it's solid bedrock. If we end up burying Prudence here after a long drawn-out illness during which we (mostly me) tend selflessly to her every need (a feat of kindness and compassion that catches the attention of numerous eligible and attractive women), I may have to put her in one of the raised beds, just on account of my back. We'll call it the Prudence Burns Memorial Raised Bed. We'll plant flowers in it. Not the kind you put on salads, either, which is usually the only kind Prudence lets us grow. Maybe dahlias. I don't think they're edible.

Whatever.

As I was emotionally processing the situation, I found myself getting kind of upset. There may have been a tear, which I tried to hide so Sara wouldn't worry. The kid has had enough trauma in her life, courtesy of her god-awful parents, whose only good quality as far as I can tell is that they let her live here.

What if Prudence doesn't pass away until I am in my mid-to-late-forties and my best days are behind me? Jesus. I'd miss her but I'd miss my youth and sexual peak even more. What if she was in pain? I'd have to score her drugs. What impact would that have on my sobriety? I might end up getting hooked on smack. Just thinking about it got me crying a few more small tears and Sara happened to notice and asked if I had allergies and I said yeah, I did. She said I should take Benadryl. I reminded her that Prudence doesn't believe in pharmaceuticals. That got me thinking how fucking hard it was going to be to take care of Prudence during her hard times. I mean seriously, drugs are so often the answer. She would probably want me to make her mint and grass tea and remedies made out of various ditch weeds, naturally shed tree bark and sun-dried butterfly wings.

There might have been some more tears due to me being so emotionally open these days, but then my email plinked. I opened it and found a message from someone I hadn't seen or heard from in years. I thought things were complicated for me due to our fearless leader being laid up with a potentially terminal wasting disease. The minute I read the message, I knew life was about to get exponentially more complicated. And here I'd been doing so well.

Prudence

I am not a shirker. God, what time is it? It's dark outside. I meant to fix the curtains. Lace would be nice. Or maybe chintz, though I'm not a hundred percent certain what chintz is. Flower patterns? The clock says that it's 5:12, but I don't know if it's five in the morning or the afternoon.

I will take this opportunity to . . . Darn. What was I going to do? There are so many things to do and I can't seem to remember any of them. Worse, I can hardly see due to this darned light. It's hard to see the page when my eyes keep closing.

Where is Eustace? Where is my to-do list? The key to being efficient is

OCTOBER

Earl

This afternoon I headed over for Sara's parent-teacher meeting. I never understood those parents of hers. If you ask me, they don't deserve the title. Sure, they made her and fed her, but kids need more than food to grow up right. I should know. When I was a boy our old man gave us three squares and not much else but hard labor around the farm and hours of music practice every day. By the time I was seven, he had me and my brothers, Merle and Pride, on the road, playing at county fairs in three states. We never saw a damned penny of what we earned, either. He'd have had my sisters up there with us but they all sang like hens with their necks halfway wrung. Just like our ma. No music in any of the women in our family, which was their good luck.

He was never happy, our daddy. When Merle got ideas about how to develop our act and turn us into the High Lonesome Boys, our old man was spitting mad because it wasn't what he visioned for us. He laid a few lickings on Merle until Pride, my middle brother, put a stop to it. Pride once hit Daddy so hard I thought he might have busted his jaw. After that, Daddy let us play how we wanted, or at least how Merle wanted. Our daddy always hated being defied and he stayed mad at us boys forever, even after he saw how much people liked the music. He died before the first record come out, which is just as well.

Me thinking about old family business and not paying attention is how things went wrong at the school. Normally Prudence would have been the one to go to a deal like the teacher meeting, but she's still not on the mend. I didn't want her to get all wound up, so I left her napping. Figured she'd be down for the rest of the day. I told Seth to keep an eye on things while I went to the hardware store. Should have goddamn known better than to leave, and that's the truth.

I parked the truck in the school parking lot to watch for Sara's parents. Figured if they didn't show, I'd go on in and talk to her teacher so her teacher knew there was people looking out for her. It's a fact that we all worry on her, which is probably how there ended up being too many of us at the parent-teacher meeting and not enough of us at home. Just about goddamn kills me that it turned out the way it did.

Seth

I have no idea where to start or who to blame. Well, I guess I should start with blaming myself. That would be the mature thing to do.

The email was from my former drama teacher, alluded to earlier. Her name is Bev, but to me she'll always be the drama teacher. The last time I spoke with her was when she ended our affair right before the big high school theater production of *Jesus Christ Superstar*. I extra-ended the affair and my ability to be seen in public again by staging a public protest over my broken heart. I left school that night and never went back.

As soon as I saw Bev's name, it all came flooding back. The way she'd made me feel like I was this highly fascinating individual, the way being with her was the best high I ever had.

Hi Seth. Bev here. I saw you walking your bike past the school a few days ago. You're looking well. I think about you sometimes.

My response to her email was Pavlovian. I hope I've used that correctly. I felt like I had in eleventh grade: sick with lust, self-hatred, excitement and anxiety. I tried to play it cool. After all, I've had imaginary emotional liaisons with numerous women. But the drama teacher is different. She's real. She's touched me and I've touched her. And that, to be brutally frank, makes her unique in my experience. Agoraphobes do not accumulate much in the way of direct sexual experience, especially when they live with their mothers.

So Bev and I started emailing, then texting, and at first I tried to act like it was all very aboveboard and legit.

Hey, Bev. Long time no . . . restraining order.

That was a joke. She never got a restraining order against me. In fact, the police investigation was all about whether she'd done anything illegal to me.

Funny. How are you, Seth?

Even though it was just five words, I could practically hear them coming out of her mouth. She has a voice like Demi Moore by way of Emma Stone, which is to say she has a fantastic voice.

And she was asking about me.

Yes, our affair had dire consequences for my life, but it was also one of the most intense things that ever happened to me.

I don't need to get into the exchange we had. I will say only that I tried to keep it light. SFW, if you will. But our interaction was a very serious distraction. Which helps explain my role in the parent-teacher meeting. Let me set the stage.

Right before the meeting, Prudence had been diagnosed with some virus named after a Japanese guy. It knocked out her thyroid, just as Eustace had suspected. Prudence went to see some specialist all-natural doctor who just moved to town and was said to be extremely hot shit in the alternative health community. The alternative doctor told her it was going to take some time to get her sorted out and the medications hadn't kicked in yet. Prudence was sleeping about twenty hours a day, she had almost no short-term memory and she'd developed this little potbelly that was sort of cute on her but also strange, like she was wearing a small pillow around her waist. She was also peevish and easily annoyed, which was not like her.

Right after her diagnosis, she put Earl in charge of the farm, but a couple of times a day she'd come flailing out of her room and attack some random problem, such as our superabundance of zucchini or whatever. We'd come home to find her sitting at the kitchen table, pots and pans all over the counter, and strange zucchini-based concoctions in various stages of incompleteness all over the damned place.

Then we'd have to put her to bed and clean up the mess.

It was like having an extremely ambitious toddler in the house, one that could reach everything and did not understand the word *no*.

My editor, Tamara, was getting impatient with me because I was late with two articles about personal growth in recovery, including the one on codependence. I was hiding my correspondence with the drama teacher from Eustace, which wasn't easy because he was over here all the time to look after Prudence. I was also dealing with the raised beds and helping Earl tend the farm, by which I mean I walked past the raised beds on my way to say hello to Bertie and Lucky and feed them carrots and sprinkle some chicken feed into the coop. With all that going on, it's a miracle that I remembered the parent-teacher meeting at all. No, scratch that. I fucked up. We all did. It would have been better if we'd all stayed home.

I only went to the meeting because I knew Earl had gone to the hardware store and Prudence was asleep and I was worried no one from our team would show up. I thought I'd do more good at the meeting than hanging around the house while Prudence slept. And in my defense, when I left, everything was copacetic. Sara was doing something in the chicken coop. Fussing with her birds is a pretty full-time activity for her, so I knew she'd be occupied for a while. When she finished doing mysterious chicken-tending activities, she'd be busy doing some other useful work. I slipped away without saying anything so she wouldn't ask where I was going. Why bring up the fact that I was worried her useless parents wouldn't bother attending her parent-teacher meeting? I didn't want to lie and say I was going somewhere else.

Before heading up to the school, I stopped across the road at my mother's to say hello. She and her boyfriend, Bobby, were playing some kind of trivia game on the TV, so they barely looked up when I came in.

"Season three of *Survivor* was in Africa," said my mom to Bobby. "Don't you know anything?"

Bobby muttered something about Australia but she wasn't listening.

"Got anything to eat?" I asked.

"You know where the gas station is," said my incredibly nurturing and maternal mother.

So I stopped by the convenience store for some refreshing potato chips and a bottle of pop, then headed over to Sara's school. My plan was to hang around casually to make sure at least one of her deadbeat parents showed up. It was never my intention to interfere. Her dad is a volatile guy and her mom is depressing, so I make a point of staying out of their way. I hadn't really formulated a plan for what to do if they didn't show. I guess I thought I'd just make excuses on behalf of the farm.

While I was walking over there, I got a text from the drama teacher. She said she was having some sort of a crisis that only a former pupil could solve. Now that she was split up with her husband, she seemed to think that having proper sex with me was a high-ranking bucket list item. She didn't say so directly, but I could interpret from the tone of our correspondence.

She'd started working me via text, just the way she had the last time. She talked about my "special spirit" and my "limitless potential." At one point, she called me nubile, which I quite liked.

I *am* significantly nubiler since I moved to Woefield. In stark contrast to my childhood diet of Chef Boyardee and Tuna Helper, Prudence keeps us in a constant state of hyper-nutrition. She's a maniac for all things green: heirloom lettuces, Swiss chard, kale, collard greens. She puts mounds of it under, over and inside everything else she makes (everything else being beans and brown rice). Prudence's food causes harsh initial bloat, followed by serious weight loss. Her flavor-free menus, combined with her passion for making strenuous to-do lists for others, result in nubility. If that's a word.

When I first got to Woefield, I had a food gut. Now I'm like Axl Rose in his prime. Or Keith Richards at his lowest point.

The drama teacher had obviously noticed that I was looking good when she saw me walking my bike past the school, and our exchanges had gotten progressively more suggestive.

I'd just about decided that I would allow the drama teacher to ravage me in some out-of-the-way location and assured myself that it didn't count in not having a relationship in the first year of sobriety because (*a*) it would just be sex and (*b*) it would be like taking care of unfinished business.

I'd nearly reached Sara's school when the drama teacher sent me a sext. Only it wasn't a picture of her. It was a picture of a flower. A really explicit flower, like something Georgia O'Keeffe might do for *Hustler* magazine. I was just like, holy shit. This is going to be so hot. I texted her that I'd meet her anywhere. Anytime.

That's when she dropped the bomb.

I cannot wait to finish what we started.

I texted back with shaking hand that I felt exactly the same.

The only thing is that I can't feel completely comfortable and uninhibited until my bed has been treated.

Naturally, I was like, "Treated? What do you mean treated?" I was thinking gonorrhea or crabs, which would not have been a deterrent to me. At all. But no. It was worse than that.

Something's been biting me. At night.

At the risk of sounding like a Marc Maron podcast, I was like WTF? I stopped dead on the side of the road and texted her the all-important question:

Are you saying you have bugs? Like, in your bed?

The second I typed the words, I could feel myself getting itchy.

I'm not sure. I need someone to look for me.

I might not have been worried by the thought that she had STDs, but the news that she might have bedbugs just about derailed me. I develop new phobias with alarming ease.

You should call a pest control company. Just in case.

Now my hands were shaking out of fear.

Bev: You're probably right.
Me: *Definitely* call a pest company.
Bev: That's very expensive.
Me: But worth it.

By this time, I'd reached the school ground. It had become abundantly clear that our physical thing was not going to happen unless I determined whether she had some sort of heinous infestation. It was also clear that if she did, she expected me to deal with it.

She was too embarrassed to call a pest company but she was not too embarrassed to tell me.

Great.

Even though the drama teacher had turned me into an agoraphobic for several years and stopped me graduating high school, this seemed like a new low in our relationship.

By the time I sat on the swing, me and the drama teacher were full-on text fighting, which is a quiet but terrible thing. Those little keyboards seem to amplify messages somehow and make them sound worse than they would if they were shouted from a red face.

I felt the agony of being placed in a terrible *Sophie's Choice* type scenario, if *Sophie's Choice* involved risking getting bedbugs in order to finally get laid or not doing that. On second thought, maybe the bedbug/sex choice was less tough than deciding which of your children you'll hand over to the Nazis. Yes, that was probably an insensitive comparison.

I texted her back to tell her that I was concerned about getting involved too directly with her pest situation because it might activate my phobias, which are legion. She wrote me back that her biggest turn-on is bravery. I wrote her back that it hadn't turned her on when I bared my soul and my underpants for her at the school premiere of *Jesus Christ Superstar* and was pummeled by some jocks and nearly assaulted by her husband. (Extra-Poignant Background Information: I brought a ghetto blaster on stage with me and played Nazareth's "Love Hurts" in a move meant to echo Lloyd Dobler's iconic scene in *Say Anything*. Only I didn't just play the song. I played it and *sang along*. Drunkenly. In front of a high school opening night theater audience. And as I sang, I stripped off my clothes in an effort to demonstrate my emotional condition, which was raw, because the drama teacher had just ended our affair. As I pulled off my jeans, they got caught on my runners and I ended up falling off the stage. It was a pathetic performance, but I think most people would agree it was a brave one, especially considering that I took all the consequences on myself and didn't tell anyone that we'd been involved for months.)

She texted me back that there was a difference between brave and foolish. And I replied that I didn't like splitting hairs or being pressured.

I sat on a bench near the swing set and some sort of wood-and-tires-and-ladder contraption and sent off ill-considered responses to her provocations. Restraint of tongue and pen was completely forgotten for the next half-hour as we texted back and forth.

Fucking technology.

Finally, the drama teacher wrote me back to tell me she'd reconsidered. She didn't want me as a sexual partner or as an exterminator. She no longer needed my help. "Period." She actually typed that out.

I'm not the pushover I was at seventeen. I'm a twenty-one-year-old farmhand, which is similar to being a cowboy, but without a horse, a hat or any cows. So I fired back that I didn't give a shit what she did and I hoped she and her bugs would be very happy together. I texted her that I had a fun life now. God help me. I did.

To drive the point home, I decided to send her a picture to demonstrate just how fun my life was. I wanted to get a shot that showed me behaving in a provocatively carefree manner. So I sat on one of the swings and started swinging like I meant it, pumping my legs back and forth, the whole nine yards. The plan was to take a live action image of my feet way up in the air. But I had some trouble aiming the phone. It was Eustace's old one and a cow crapped on it or a horse gave birth on it or some other medical emergency happened on it, so that it only worked about half the time.

I needed to get some height to adequately convey my extreme level of jaunty, unaffected joyfulness, which meant full-throttle, maxed-out swinging.

Wouldn't you know it, while trying to get my feet into the frame I lost my grip and launched off the front of the swing like I was trying out for the lead role in Cirque du Soleil's Lone Man Cannonball Show. One minute I was looking through the phone at my high tops, the next I was sailing into the fucking void.

Prudence

Running a homestead is a full-time endeavor even in the off-season. That's why I couldn't afford to be ill for any length of time. My wellness practitioner, Dr. Bachmeier, said my energy would come and go as the remedies she prepared for me took effect and helped my entire immune system to come into a state of balance and health. She was clear that her remedies would not be quick fixes, like those prescribed in corporate medicine, but rather complete body and mind treatments that would get at the heart of the problem.

Her words turned out to be true. I was all over the place, energy-wise, and every time I got up, I nearly fainted at the thought of all the work that had piled up while I was resting. I did as much as I could on my good days. Well, they weren't days exactly. They were more like hours. Sometimes half-hours.

The most pressing concern was Lucky. It was a dereliction of duty to ask Sara to train our mule. Sure, we only had him on loan, but I wanted to get the most out of the experience. And my pride was still smarting from Eustace's suggestion that I couldn't handle him.

Lucky was a mule, not a neutron bomb. Any farmer worth her salt should be able to come to terms with her livestock.

On the day in question, I felt well enough in the late afternoon to get out of bed. I made my way outside to make sure that the winter crops were being tended properly. We were growing three kinds of chard—Swiss, rainbow and green—and four kinds of kale. We had cabbages, and three raised beds devoted to various squashes and gourds, one for pumpkins and another for butternut squashes and a third mostly for decorative gourds. We wouldn't be able to compete with the farms with huge you-pick pumpkin patches, but we were growing some fine sugar pumpkins, which aren't easy to find.

I walked the pea-graveled walkways between the raised beds, feeling like I was wading knee-deep through sludge. Still, my spirits were buoyed by the neat rows of wooden boxes holding in all that rich soil, and my soul was soothed by the orderly arrangements of trellises and the efficient network of larger hoses that makes up our automatic drip watering system. My spirit soared even further at the sight of the six deep beds at the end of our enclosure. They're tall enough that Earl doesn't have to crouch over to tend them and they contain layers of newspaper and straw and sticks and regular soil and rich compost. Next spring, we'll use them for potatoes and other crops that like to send their roots deep. I think the future of Woefield may be deep raised beds. Earl is a fan because he hates to bend, physically or mentally, now that I think of it.

After the barn is up, which I hope will be soon—I can't quite remember when Stephan said he would start—the next major project will be a large greenhouse. In the meantime, we are putting frames over top of some of the beds to protect cold-weather crops. The other beds will be left to rest until spring. Rest! Isn't that a lovely way to describe what gardeners and farmers do for their land? It sounded so wise and soothing and made me wish I was resting.

As I made my way through the rows of raised beds, I was hazily pleased to see that all was in order. The soil was moist and any weeds that had come from bird droppings had been pulled before they had a chance to take hold. The weed barriers we'd laid down beneath each bed to prevent invasive plants from poking up were working.

Even those who had scoffed at the idea that anything would ever grow on Woefield Farm were silenced when they saw our raised beds. I spent an enjoyable moment imagining the following spring and the other vendors' faces when they saw our folding table groaning under the weight of our produce. No one would remember the little hot sauce problem or any of our other troubles.

Having thoroughly surveyed the beds, I looked toward the field and saw Sara trying to catch Lucky. She walked after him, holding a halter, and he was making a game of staying just out of reach.

Earl was nowhere to be seen. Neither was Seth, but that wasn't unusual. Earl never went far and if there was work to be done, Seth was often hard to find.

I left the raised bed area, which was protected from deer and birds by a six-and-a-half-foot fence topped with driftwood and a canopy of bird netting, walked past the mobile chicken coop, which we move every day so the birds get fresh grass and fertilize our thin layer of soil, and stood watching Sara play catch the mule.

When Sara quickened her steps, Lucky broke into a lazy trot. At first, I worried that he'd kick out at her, but he didn't. He just kept his rear end between her and his head.

I know there's no room on a functional farm for a mule that can-not be caught, much less worked. If we couldn't do anything with

Lucky, Eustace was probably right. We'd have to send the mule back. But not just yet. Everyone deserves chances, including Lucky.

I've done enough reading to know that mules are highly intelligent and respond well to fairness, consistency, clear boundaries and firmness. Experts agree that in a contest of wills, it's best not to let the mule win if you can help it. Well, I was out of bed and I could help it!

"Sara!" I called, and waved her over.

She walked over to meet me, looking slightly wild-eyed.

"You're not supposed to be up," she said. "Eustace said you should be resting."

I made a mental note to tell Eustace to stop telling everyone to mollycoddle me. Then I promptly forgot the mental note.

"How long have you been trying to catch him?" I asked.

She looked at the orange plastic wristwatch shaped like a rooster's head that she won at a poultry club event in August. "Since I finished cleaning the chicken coop. Five minutes," she said.

"He hasn't tried to bite or kick?"

"No," she said. "He just won't let me get close enough to put his halter on."

"Go get some grain and let's herd him into a corner."

Her face brightened and I could see she was relieved to have me back in action. That gave me a little burst of energy. Enough to sustain me while she ran off to get some grain.

Catching Lucky would be much easier when we had a barn and could confine him. In the meantime, I felt sure that two bright young farmers like Sara and me could outsmart him.

When Sara came back, I armed myself with a halter and lead rope and we began herding Lucky into a corner. Unfortunately, the pasture didn't have many corners because it was designed to take advantage of the infrequent pockets of soil deep enough to sink a fence stake. As a result, the enclosure is shaped like an amoeba, which is not the ideal arrangement for trapping cagey mules. Even a team of highly trained border collies would probably have had difficulties with the task.

Fortunately, Lucky was food motivated, and as he ducked his head into the bucket of grain, we got the rope around his neck and I slipped his halter on. Success!

"You did it!" cried Sara, running over to join us.

"That's right. The key is not giving up," I said. "And rewards for doing the right thing. Behavior that is rewarded is repeated. That's what they say.

"Sara, please get him some carrots. I'm going to lead him around the pasture to make sure he associates being caught with positive things."

Lucky accepted his capture with equanimity. He walked beside me like a perfect gentleman. I stroked his neck. I'm no expert, but I'm sure he's considerably more attractive than your average mule. His red coat, growing thick with the approach of winter, faded to white at his belly and flanks, and the white was flecked with red spots. His marvelously expressive ears were half as long as his head. They swung back and forth in a relaxed yet alert manner as he walked. During our mule-leading lesson, Sara told us that you want a mule to have a "soft eye," meaning that your mule shouldn't glare or squint at you. Your mule should look upon you in a kindly fashion. Well, I could swear Lucky had a soft eye that afternoon.

As we walked around the pasture, even Bertie seemed to look over at us benevolently. She's not a particularly demonstrative sheep, unless you're trying to trim her feet or shear her coat, but she's a stabilizing presence on a farm with so many extreme personalities.

It occurred to me that most of the problems with Lucky's behavior had begun when he'd been spooked by the motorcycle on the road. Perhaps the key to correcting his behavior was to repeat the walk on the road and have it go well and thereby undo the trauma. What was needed was an uneventful road walk followed by lavish treats and plenty of praise.

So as soon as Sara returned with the carrots, which were woodier than I would have liked, I informed her that Lucky and I were going to take a walk up the road.

A flicker of worry crossed her face. Sara is such a fierce little character that I sometimes forget she's so young. I suspect we all do.

"It's okay," I told her. "Eustace told the Morrisey kid to keep his motorbike off the road or he'd call the cops."

"Maybe it was enough just to catch him today," said Sara.

"Don't you worry. I just want to build on today's lesson. I want him to associate being caught with fun and adventure and success." I said this in spite of the fact that my fatigue was closing around me like a lead casket two sizes too small.

"You look kind of tired," she said.

"I'm getting a second wind," I told her. "You wait here. I'll just lead him back and forth on the road out front a few times. If it goes well, we'll walk a little farther to really establish the idea that being out and about is a positive thing. If we run into any problems, we'll get Seth to help. Earl should be home soon from wherever he's gone with the truck. Lucky and I shouldn't be gone long. No more than twenty minutes or so."

So that's how I ended up walking Lucky up and down Woefield Road in front of the farm. We went out the gate, down the driveway and then walked from one end of our property line to the other. No vehicles passed. My confidence rose even though my legs felt like two tree stumps. Lucky also seemed to be enjoying himself. There was a definite spring to his step. It was a pleasure to be out and about with such a handsome animal. Despite the bumps along the way, Woefield was turning into a real farm. Eustace was dead wrong. I could handle our mule.

I felt almost like my old self again.

In order to savor the experience, I decided to take one more trip down the road. We'd nearly reached the turnoff to the road that leads toward the high school and up to the elementary school when an image flashed into my mind. The piece of paper on the fridge announcing Sara's parent-teacher conference. It was happening today. I'd forgotten due to thyroid fatigue.

The distance from where Lucky and I stood to Sara's school was no more than perhaps two city blocks. New York City blocks, but still. To get to the school, we'd have to walk along a road that was quite a bit busier than Woefield Road, but he didn't seem to mind regular traffic. We'd be fine as long as no rogue dirt bike riders blasted past us. There was no way that could happen twice.

Yes, it would be passing strange to show up at a school leading a mule, but I thought it would prove how well I handled our livestock. There would probably be parents there with dogs. And I wasn't going to go inside. I would just be stopping by to let the teacher and the community know that Sara had a lot of support at home in a wholesome environment. People were looking out for her.

I put a hand to Lucky's neck and looked him in his soft, kind eye, which seemed to be brimming with confidence in me, his handler.

"Let's do this, buddy," I said.

He blew softly at my hand with his velvety nostrils and I drew in the deep, calming scent of him.

In that moment, I knew that Lucky and I were a team bound together by trust.

And in that moment, I completely forgot Sara waiting for us in the field. Sure, I assumed Seth was in the house, keeping a low profile in order not to be assigned any work, and that Earl would be home soon from wherever he'd gone. But that doesn't change the fact that my brain misfired and I made a major mistake.

Lucky and I marched resolutely around the corner from Woefield onto Skeena Road and then we hit the Old School Road. The high school and its playing fields sprawled off to the right. My senses were heightened from the thrill of pushing my limits as a mule handler. I also felt quite light-headed in general, thanks to my glandular situation. A nagging sensation that I'd forgotten something nibbled at the edges of my mind, but I pushed it away.

Lucky's head was up and his big ears seemed to swivel at every noise. Ours was an ages-old partnership—farmer and mule, pioneer and mule, homesteader and mule. Our lives were entwined and richer for it.

As we walked, I kept my body between Lucky and the traffic. His hooves made a satisfying crunching noise in the gravel at the edge of the pavement. I would have worried about rocks and the uneven surface of the shoulder of the road bothering him but I remembered all I'd read about mules and their uncanny sure-footedness. All around us, Cedar hummed with the steady sounds of rural life. Birdsong and wind, children laughing. That sort of thing. We passed two boys walking on the other side of the road. I waved. They didn't wave back. The sky was clear and fine. Stands of Douglas fir lined the edges of the farmers' fields, and the deciduous trees were in the final stages of display and undress, splashes of oranges and yellows bursting among the dark evergreens.

We were nearly past the high school when the first car passed, going in our direction. The driver slowed respectfully, probably thrilled to see an actual mule on the road, just like in a bygone era. The next vehicle that passed was a small truck badly in need of engine repair, judging from the white smoke that billowed from the tailpipe.

A teenager with features that seemed to have been dropped onto his face by an unsteady hand grinned at me as he pulled abreast of us. His grin revealed an assortment of teeth going in conflicting directions.

"Nice mule," he said, grinning. At least I think he was grinning. It was impossible to tell with those teeth.

"Thank you," I said. "His name is Lucky. He's in training."

"Lady?" asked the kid.

"Lucky," I corrected.

The boy coughed abruptly. I caught a glimpse of a pipe in his hand. Not an old-fashioned tobacco pipe, but something in the weed-smoking line. Maybe a vaporizer.

"Cool," he said. "What's he in training for?"

Lucky eyeballed the truck and driver. His steps had grown shorter. Mincing, almost. The boy continued to drive alongside and didn't seem to care when another vehicle pulled up behind him.

"What's your name?" asked the boy.

It occurred to me that I wasn't prepared to deal with being sexually harassed during a mule-training lesson. I needed to maintain my focus. Plus, my vision wasn't as clear as I would have liked. I was having trouble feeling my feet.

The car behind the truck honked and Lucky stopped. I could feel him getting tense.

"It's okay," I said, and gave him a reassuring pat on his neck.

Lucky craned his head around to get a better look at the three cars lined up behind the stoned kid in the truck.

"You better get going," I said to the kid as I tried to get our mule moving again. This walk had been a bad idea. My throat felt like a pin-cushion. What had I been thinking? What was I doing bringing an unpredictable mule on a road populated by stoned teenage drivers?

"Need any help training him?" he asked, raising a reddish eyebrow, his jigsaw puzzle of a smile growing even wider.

Another vehicle in the lineup behind the truck honked and Lucky snorted and bobbed his head, which made him sound like a dragon.

I turned to look at the honker and mouthed the words "please don't do that."

The driver was a teenage girl driving a rusted-out sedan. She had what looked like an infected ring in her lip, and it seemed to be nega- tively affecting her outlook and attitude.

"Fuck you," she said, nice and loud through her open window. "Hurry it up. Go fight with your boyfriend somewhere else. Cougar!"

Cougar?

Now there were at least five cars stacked up behind the truck. Lucky was beginning to tremble all over, or perhaps that was me.

I held tight to the lead rope and gave it a tentative tug. It was like trying to move a wharf piling.

"You got a celly number, fine thing?" asked the boy.

The fourth vehicle in the row had had enough. The driver peeled out and roared around the lineup. The others followed. The last rem- nant of self-control snapped in Lucky and he surged forward, dragging me with him. I took giant, hip-dislocating cartoon steps, and thankfully, before he pulled me off my feet he slowed and began to prance.

I ran alongside, trying to keep up. Lucky increased the pace to a brisk trot. The elementary school was fast approaching on our right and I wondered, in a fleeting, out-of-body sort of way, if Lucky and I were about to die in a horrendous mule accident. On some level, the idea was not completely unwelcome.

Gears ground and the little truck's engine backfired and Lucky began to gallop. I hung on, again taking enormous, ludicrous steps, my feet barely touching the ground as Lucky veered into the elementary school parking lot. To my immense relief, once we clattered into the parking lot he slowed to a trot and I was able to get him under control. Sort of. We'd survived.

I was just getting my breath when we walked past the playground. Too late I noticed someone much too large swinging for all he was worth on the swing set. The chain clanked and shrieked against its constraints. With a great rattle and whoosh of wind, the figure hurtled down again.

Lucky spotted him and everything happened at once. The person on the swing shot into the air, arms and legs windmilling. A small, rectangular object flew out of his hand and smacked Lucky in the neck. Lucky reared up to his full height, front hooves pawing the air, Black Stallion (if he was a mule) style. The lead rope was torn from my burning hands.

In his ten rules of writing, Elmore Leonard said one should never, ever write, "And then all hell broke loose." But what about those occasions when all hell actually breaks loose?

Sara

Target and his brother came over to visit about ten minutes after Prudence and Lucky left for their road walk. I was sad that no one was with me to see them coming up the driveway. Seth and Prudence and Earl are always asking me about friends and asking why I don't invite them over. The truck was gone, so I knew Earl was out. He wouldn't be long because he doesn't like to go away from the farm.

I was already tired from trying to catch Lucky and was a bit worried about Prudence because she and Lucky had been out on the road for a long time, but I hoped that I would be a good host until Prudence came back. Prudence is an excellent host and makes even people no one likes feel welcome. Seth was in the house, but he's not as nice as Prudence.

"Hi Sara," said Target, staring at his feet. "This is my brother, Charles."

Charles had on dark sunglasses and his black coat nearly touched the ground. He held out a thin, white hand for me to shake. When I did, his hand was cold and it held mine for too long.

"Did you see a mule on the road?" I asked, when he finally let go.

Charles let his sunglasses fall down his nose and stared at me. I didn't like his eyes. I'm not sure why. He didn't answer my question.

"Charles is only my first name," he said. "My middle name is Manson. My full name is Charles Manson Barton."

"Oh," I said. "That's nice. Was Manson your grandfather's name?" I knew that people didn't like to let names in their family die out.

"Might as well have been," he said. "Have you ever seen *Pump Up the Volume*? With Christian Slater."

"No," I said.

"I saw the mule," said Target. He was picking at a sore on his ear and there was a bit of blood on his finger when he took it away.

"Is your ear okay?"

"Charles pierced it, but it got infected. I had to take out the stud."

"You need to learn to deal with some pain if you want to be a man. Pussy," said Charles Manson.

"Do you want a Band-Aid?" I asked Target, trying to pretend I didn't hear the rude thing his brother said.

"I'm considering starting a podcast," said Charles Manson. He was staring at me really hard. His eyes were mean. Like rocks in his head. "Get the word out. Like Christian Slater does in *Pump Up the Volume*."

"Oh," I said. I was starting to wish Target hadn't brought his brother. I was starting to wish I never invited Target over. It doesn't bother me that I don't have friends that come over. The kids I know mostly live on farms and have a lot of chores. I see them at school and at Poultry Club and that's enough. I don't think Target belongs to any clubs. Charles didn't seem like he'd be a good friend for Seth.

I looked at the house and hoped Seth would notice the visitors and come outside.

"You know what word I mean?" asked Charles Manson.

I looked at Target. His earlobe was bright red and looked hot and swollen.

"We have hydrogen peroxide in the house," I said.

Charles smiled at me and my stomach burned bad for the first time since my medication got changed. "I'd like to see your room."

"Charles," said Target. "You *said.*"

"If you guess what my podcast is going to be about, I won't make you show me your room."

My throat felt like I swallowed vacuum dust.

"There are things in this life, injustices, that need to be brought to the attention of the world."

"*Charles,*" said Target again.

"I'm sorry." My voice was sort of whispery.

Seth says that some people have bad energy, and if they do, I should trust my gut and not be around them. But he never told me how to get away from them without hurting their feelings.

"I'll get my friend Seth," I said. "He's in the house."

Charles's face changed and he frowned.

"Wait here," I said. Then I went up the stairs to the front door.

"Seth!" I said. "There's someone here."

I looked through the kitchen into the living room. Seth's computer sat on the coffee table. His big white basketball shoes weren't in the rack by the front door.

I walked farther into the kitchen and called up the stairs.

"Seth!"

No answer. Seth always comes when I call. So do Earl and Prudence. They were all gone.

When I looked back, Charles was standing in the doorway. The frown was gone from his face. He was smiling and his teeth weren't nice.

"No one home?" said Charles. "No adults here?"

Target was behind his brother. He stared at his shoes, which were not very cool, even to me and I don't have anything cool, really, except my chickens.

"Yes," I said. "Lots of older people are here. Grown-ups."

"Aren't your folks at the parent-teacher meeting?"

"I don't . . . ," I started, then got confused about what to say. I didn't want to tell him my parents didn't live here and that I didn't know if they or anyone else had gone to the meeting. I didn't want to tell Charles Manson Barton that I didn't know where everyone went.

"Not all of them," I said.

"How many folks do you got?" asked Charles.

"My mom and dad. And Prudence and Seth and Earl."

"This some kind of commune?" asked Charles. "Are you nudies? Like the Scandinavians?" He looked past me into the house.

I shook my head. I didn't think I knew any Scandinavians. Then I nodded. I didn't really know what he was talking about or what to do with my head.

"We wear clothes."

He pointed at the stairs. "Is your room up there?"

"Seth's room. Prudence's."

I didn't want to tell him my room was up there. I didn't want him to come into the house.

"Do you want to see our raised beds?" I asked. And then I walked past him and Target very fast, but I still ended up having to touch him. I ran down the front stairs and stared at the driveway. Earl would be home soon. He had to be. Prudence and Lucky would come home any minute. Unless Lucky had run away again.

Seth's mom's house was right across the street. I wondered if I could run over there. Maybe Seth was there? Seth said his mom was quite a drinker and not a gifted parent but basically a decent person. Her boyfriend, Bobby, sold parts for remote control helicopters. He had a mustache and Seth hated that about him. Seth said only Freddie Mercury was allowed to have a mustache like that.

Seth's mom and Bobby have always been very nice to me. His mom paid me ten cents each for fancy feathers from my chickens. I asked her if she wanted any of Bertie's wool when next we sheared her and she said we should probably sell it to pay for sheep depression meds. When you meet his mom, you can see where Seth gets his sense of humor.

I really wanted to run over there, but it would have been rude to leave Target and his brother alone. They followed me outside and I felt relieved. But then Charles Manson Barton noticed my birds. The coop and mobile run were parked to the left of the house, between the raised beds and the pasture. I have two kinds of birds: frizzles and Polish non-bearded. My chickens are extremely nice and have won prizes.

"What the hell is up with those chickens?" he asked. "Why do they look like that?"

"I told you she had fancy chickens," muttered Target.

"Can we catch one?" asked Charles. For the first time since he came, he sounded sort of normal or at least like a young person, which he was.

"We better not," I said. I had a feeling that if Charles went close to my birds, they wouldn't lay again for a long time or maybe ever.

"I won't hurt them." Even though he still had his sunglasses on, I could see Charles's face change. His lips went pale and thin. "I saw this thing on YouTube once. These hillbilly kids chopped the heads off chickens and took bets to see how far they'd run. That was some Mexican drug cartel shit, only on chickens instead of people." Charles giggled at the memory. His teeth were gray. I felt bad for Target. No wonder his posture was so bad.

Still giggling and showing his gray teeth in his white face, Charles started walking toward the coop. He was going to go right past the front door to the house, which wasn't locked. My birds were in their run, pecking around in grass, softly clucking. Bertie, our sheep, grazed just off to the side in her pasture. She was probably missing Lucky. I wished I wasn't alone.

Target just stared at his shoes like he wanted a hole in the toe to open up and swallow him. He wasn't going to be any help.

Then I remembered some of my leadership training from Jr. Poultry Club. Our coach, Mr. Lymer, said we had to learn to master our nerves in moments of stress and think ahead. He said to remember to breathe. Leaders are big breathers. I took a deep lungful of air and yelled at Charles's back.

"It's time for you to go! I'm not allowed to have visitors."

I was surprised at what I said and so was he.

Charles's worn-down boots stopped dragging across the ground. He turned to face me.

"You saying you don't want me to choke your chickens?"

He started to walk back toward me. I gulped more air and tried to think ahead but my brain wouldn't make any good thoughts and the air felt like balloons going down my throat.

Target made a small noise.

"What about you? Can I choke you?" said Charles.

I backed up. I wished someone would come home and I really, really wished Prudence and Seth and Earl hadn't left me alone.

"What are you afraid of?" asked Charles.

I thought about screaming but Seth's mom and Bobby always have their TV on so loud. Sometimes we can hear the game show music all the way across the fields.

Charles reached out a skinny white hand and grabbed me by my jacket, and I remembered that in case of fire, you should stop, drop and roll. I was on fire, at least my stomach was.

I let my knees buckle. Charles was surprised and my coat slipped out of his hand.

One of my knees cracked against the ground. Then I heard the truck. Prudence says it sounds like a gas guzzler, but I love the sound. Charles must not have heard it, because he was standing over me and putting his hands on me. I heard an engine roar, a door slammed and a few seconds later I was jerked off the ground when Eustace pulled Charles off me.

"Sara, honey, are you okay?" asked Eustace. He had Charles by the collar of his long, black jacket. Charles looked like a doll beside Eustace.

I tried not to cry but couldn't help it. I'm not sure what Mr. Lymer's policy is on leaders crying.

Earl

It was the noise finally got my attention away from thinking about old times. Might have dozed off there for a minute, too. There was a thump like a sack of cement hitting the ground and then hooves going hell-bent for election and yelling and some shouting. I looked over by the swing set and saw Seth lying in the middle of the gravel playground. Then our red devil of a mule went by, doing about eighty clicks, Prudence running for all she was worth to catch him.

I'll tell you, at that moment I didn't know whether to shit or get a shoeshine.

Before I could move, a young lady come hustling out of the school. She put her hands on her hips and stared at Lucky, who was trotting back and forth across the parking lot, some parents running beside Prudence to catch him and some running to get out of his way.

Prudence was hollering sorry and excuse me and calling Lucky's name as she ran after him and demanding him to come here right now.

The lady in the doorway of the school noticed Seth lying in the playground and decided to attend to him first. It's not the decision I would have made, but then I'm not a teacher.

She ran over to Seth and I finally got my old body in gear.

That's when I saw the taxicab pull in and the red Buick right behind it. Sara's folks.

I knew we was in trouble. We made a bad enough impersonation on them at the farmer market and now we were putting on a poor goddamned show at the parent-teacher.

Thinking maybe I could get Seth on his feet before Sara's parents saw him, I went over to him first. The young lady was asking Seth if he was okay.

He was on his back in the gravel and he opened and closed his mouth a few times, like a fish. Then he opened his eyes and said something about bugs.

Sir? said the lady. Are you a parent?

That depends, said Seth.

Sir? Have you been drinking? asked the lady.

I told her he'd been off the sauce for a few months. She give me a look like I just showed her a handful of shit. She was a pretty little blond thing. Hardly more than a kid herself, though I think everyone looks like a kid these days. I can't say I blame her for giving me that look.

Sara Spratt, said Seth. We're here for her parent-teacher. We're her guardians. Caretakers.

Like hell you are! yelled Old Man Spratt, storming up on us like we was robbing his general store.

Where's Sara? I said because I finally cottoned on to the notion that if me and Prudence and Seth was all here in the school yard, then either Sara was here too or she was alone. Neither one of them options was any good.

She's our daughter, said Mrs. Spratt, joining us. We're sorry we're late.

This is your fault, said Old Man Spratt to me, his wife and everyone else. And he was right about that, far as I could tell.

I better get home to see to Sara, I said.

Get her things ready, said Mr. Spratt. She's coming home with us.

Which us would that be? asked Mrs. Spratt.

The teacher looked at them.

Just then Lucky trotted by, almost close enough to touch. Nearly knocked Mrs. Spratt over. Would have served her right.

Grab him, yelled Prudence, who didn't seem any too steady on her feet. Worse, she was crying. I never seen her like that and it alarmed me something terrible.

Seth made a lunge for the lead rope, missed and fell down, like an old-fashioned comedy show.

I'm Miss Singer, Sara's teacher, said the young blond lady. I'm not certain what's happening here, but perhaps someone should go home and see about Sara.

She had that shit-smelling look on her face even worse.

That's when the phone lying on the paved courtyard started to ring.

Seth

The whole scene, post-fall, is a blur. Mule hooves galloping by within inches of my head, several types of footwear running by, faces peering down, phones ringing. Chaos. Sadly, it all felt familiar. Everyone probably assumed I was just some random drunk guy who'd passed out in the school yard, which not long ago might have been the case, if I'd been the sort of drunk to leave his house.

First I saw the cute schoolteacher peering down at me and then, like a vision from hell itself, Earl's old turtle head replaced hers.

There were some words exchanged, the specifics of which escaped me, and then I saw Sara's parents looking down at me. We were done for. This conviction was made firm by the realization that our spotted mule was cantering briskly back and forth across the property, with at least eight people in hot pursuit, including Prudence, who was acting completely unhinged.

As it became clear to everyone that Sara was home alone and every single person who was supposed to be looking out for her was at the school, I felt this peculiar panic grip me. I'm not sure why.

I mean, Sara's eleven. Of all of us, except maybe Prudence before she was felled by her Japanese thyroid condition, Sara is the one best able to look after herself. But something in me felt this deep certainty that a terrible mistake had been made. Not just because we'd cemented our reputation for being incompetent fuckwits in the child care department, but because there was something wrong with Sara.

In the midst of all this, the teacher answered the phone I'd dropped. She listened, and reported to the assembled crowd, who'd come out of the school to gawp at the commotion, that an enraged doctor was on the other end, yelling that he'd found someone named Sara being abused by Satanists. The group of listeners included a tattooed guy who turned out to be a social worker.

"Oh my god!" said Mrs. Spratt.

"What have you done?" said Mr. Spratt, staring at her poisonously.

Prudence stood near us, tears streaming down her face. "I'm so sorry. I shouldn't have brought the mule. Is Sara okay?"

"Which of you are her parents?" asked the social worker, his eyebrow piercing rising in judgment.

"Goddamn it to hell," said Earl.

You have to understand, the situation was beyond chaos, what with the mule blasting all over the place and Sara's hateful parents and the mention of Satanists. None of it was helped by my concussion, but I knew we had to get home and find out if Sara was okay. Earl knew it too and started heading for the truck.

I looked at Prudence. She was so fucked up. Crying. Not making sense. I couldn't leave her there. I thought to call Eustace to come and get her, but before I could take the phone, the social worker took the phone from the teacher and talked to whoever was on the other end.

I guess he got the address for the farm, because before we knew what was happening, he was out of there like a shot in his ten-year-old Ford Focus. I made a snap decision and left my boss and landlady to catch the mule. Earl and I got in the truck and tried to follow the social worker, but when the guy accelerated past thirty kilometers an hour, we lost sight of him. On the drive, I called Eustace and told him where Prudence was and what condition she was in.

"You left her there? With that hell mule?" he yelled. "After what I just found on this farm? Sara was very nearly . . . I can't even talk about it. I told you to keep an eye on Prudence. Jesus, Seth. This could have been bad."

"You're at the farm?" I said, stupidly.

"Yes, thank god. I stopped by just in time to prevent . . . never mind."

So Eustace was the doctor who'd found Sara. And screwed as we were, my clenched heart eased a little at the words *could have been* and *prevent*.

When Earl and I arrived, Sara was already being interviewed by the social worker. Eustace was standing guard over some Columbine-looking teenager and a poor little bastard about Sara's age with a badly infected earlobe. We learned later that the social worker had been at the school to sit in on the parent-teacher interview with the sad kid's parents, but they never showed. But Sara's did, too bad for us.

There's almost too much blame to go around.

Sara

When the social worker, who told me his name was Pete, showed up, he wanted me to tell him what happened. So I told him how Charles Manson said he wanted to see my bedroom and about how he said he was going to go Mexican Al Qaeda on my chickens and how he grabbed me but Eustace saved me. Then Pete asked if I'd ever noticed anything wrong with Target, and I said that it seemed like everything was wrong with Target, such as having the name Target and bad shoes and a brother like Charles Manson Barton, who was the worst person I ever met, including my parents. But I didn't actually say that about my parents, partly because they both showed up in my dad's taxi, which was very surprising because they don't like to be in the same vehicle together.

Pete asked if I'd ever seen any bruises on Target and I said about his ear and how it was red and swollen and bleeding because Charles pierced it wrong. Pete nodded. I liked how he took everything I said very seriously. I probably have my training in the Jr. Poultry Club to thank for that. Pete said I was very poised and well-spoken for my age and situation.

That's why I was so surprised at what happened next. Pete said he needed to speak to my parents. He did and I heard them say that if they'd known what kind of place Woefield was they'd never have let me stay. They said they were taking me home, where I could be cared for properly. They said their personal problems wouldn't impact their ability to look after me.

Then the social worker came and talked to me again. He asked if I was ready to go back to live with my parents. And even though I wasn't, I nodded because I didn't want to hurt their feelings.

It felt sort of like one of those nightmares that makes your hands feel like giant erasers when your eyes are glued shut and won't open no matter how hard you try. I wanted to scream and run away, but I tried to think what a leader would do. So I asked the social worker what was going to happen to Target and his brother. Pete said he was going to find their parents and speak to them.

Then Pete went over and asked my parents which one of them I would be staying with. I think he noticed that they don't like each other too much, because he stared at them pretty hard when he said that if they weren't ready to take me back he could recommend that I go into the care of the ministry until they were "in a better place." Neither of them spoke up right away and I realized that they didn't want me to come with them. It was a surprise because I always sort of thought that everyone would want me because of my having so many skills.

That's when my dad said Pete sure as H didn't listen and that they'd already said they wanted me to come home, and my mom said of course they wanted me and what kind of parents did people think they were? But both of them sounded sort of nervous and I felt like a dog that someone was trying to give away to people who would just tie it in the backyard. I don't know why I felt like that, but I did.

My mom said they were just getting their feet on the ground after the separation and that the plan had been for me to come home soon anyway and that I already spent weekends with them, which wasn't really true because we usually skip the visits because no one enjoys them very much.

Then Pete asked me to join them, even though I could hear most of what they said because I was in the living room and they were just in the kitchen. He asked if I understood what was happening and I said I did. Then I asked if I could visit the farm since my chickens lived there.

"I don't think so," said my dad. "This place is a goddamned joke."

And my mom said, "Dean. You know—"

But my dad didn't let her finish. "If you were half a mother—"

And Pete saw that they were going to have a bad fight, so he said he would do an investigation if it would make them feel better when it came time to make a decision about me visiting the farm.

"I don't think that's—" said my mom.

"Just listen to the professionals for once in your life," said my dad.

And my mom said he was the one who dropped the ball, meaning me. They didn't yell though, probably because they didn't want to look bad in front of Pete and Seth and Earl and Target, who were all waiting on the porch.

My dad said a lawyer would be very interested to hear what had happened this afternoon. My mom said it might affect their separation agreement.

Then everyone waited, and nobody spoke to anybody else, while I went upstairs to pack my things. Seth came inside and asked if he could help me, because he likes to give me fashion and decorating advice that he gets off the Internet, but Pete told him it would be best for him to stay put and my dad glared at him.

This wasn't fashion tips. This was moving. I had to try really hard to not cry, because crying only makes things worse. Maybe if I hadn't cried so much when Eustace saved me he wouldn't have called Seth's phone and gotten so mad about me being neglected and I wouldn't have a social worker now or be moving back with my parents.

"Is that everything?" asked Pete, when I had put everything in the plastic bins Seth got for me at the Dollar-a-Day because I didn't have a dresser. We had put a lot of very nice stickers of farm animals on the plastic bins. Seth and Earl were going to make me a dresser, but so far, Seth said, the skills and tools required to make the project had "eluded them." Seth said we should just go buy a used dresser and Earl said hell no, they could make a dresser if they could make a chicken coop. I didn't point out that the chicken coop they made needed to be fixed all the time because of their poor construction techniques. And anyway, I liked my plastic bins with stickers. There were three of them that stacked on top of each other and I think they looked very modern. Almost like Ikea, which I would like to go to one day. Plus, I didn't have very many things because the more things you have, the more things you have to take care of.

Pete took the stack of bins from me and carried them downstairs.

He didn't say anything about how my desk was very neat and how I made my bed every day, which showed that I was cared for just fine.

When we got downstairs, Prudence still wasn't home with Lucky, and Eustace was gone. I guess he went to look for her. Pete and Target sat on opposite sides of the porch, and Earl stood between them. Target didn't look up when I walked past them.

Earl muttered, the way he does when he's pretending to be upset about something, which is almost always, only this time it seemed real.

"There has been a misunderstanding. We didn't mean to . . . ," said Seth.

But no one was listening to anyone else, and my dad was waiting on the porch and my mom sat in the backseat of the cab. When Pete and I went outside, Seth and Earl followed us down the stairs. My dad took my stacked plastic bins and the backpack with my school-books and put them in the backseat with my mom, who was staring straight ahead and not looking at my dad because they hate each other.

Pete gave me his card and said to call if I needed anything. He said he'd be in touch soon and that we'd have an appointment to make sure I was doing okay. I didn't know if I was supposed to get in the back of the car with my mom and all my stuff or get in the front with my dad. I didn't want to get in the car at all. Seth went to hug me but Pete shook his head, so we did our funny handshake that Seth taught me, and Earl patted my shoulder and looked sad and mad. I was worried about Seth and Earl, especially Earl.

"Can you look after my chickens?" I asked him.

He grunted and cleared his throat, which is Earl's way of saying yes.

I handed him my copy of *The Poultry Keeper's Companion*, which is nearly seven hundred pages. He took it from me and then I left the farm.

The cab smelled like air freshener and stink.

We went to Smitty's. Usually I like going there, but it wasn't fun with my parents.

The hostess put us in a booth near the tank with the big goldfish in it. I asked my parents what was going to happen to my chickens and who would look after Bertie and Lucky. My dad said first things first and that we needed to make some decisions. My mom said I needed to decide which of them I wanted to live with and that the other one would understand. But I knew they wouldn't. They don't understand anything, like how important it is for me to live with my chickens and be a junior farmer.

"Sara," said my mother when the waitress came over and asked for our order. "What would you like to eat?"

I go with Seth and Earl to Smitty's at least once a week but we never tell Prudence. Seth says everyone needs a break from steamed kale sometimes and Smitty's is the best place to replenish our fat stores. He and Earl wouldn't have had to ask what I wanted.

"Potato pancakes," I said. "No applesauce."

My dad had coffee and my mom had apple pie. For once, they didn't say anything about each other's orders.

When the waitress went away again, my dad said, "Well?" And my mom said he shouldn't rush me. He said he wasn't rushing me and maybe it was her who didn't want to be rushed. She said she was tired. My mom doesn't swear, but she does sometimes throw things when she gets upset. Mostly she just sits in the car or cleans or scribbles in her diary.

I hoped they wouldn't fight in the restaurant, because then we might have police instead of social workers.

My dad told my mom to keep her voice down.

He said that she needed to recognize that he worked twelve-hour shifts. And she said that so did she, even though that wasn't true. She works three days a week at the Great Little Gas Bar, where she got a job after she got fired from the Price Mart for taking too many sick days. My dad said she was a parasite. She said that wasn't fair. She was getting the house ready to sell and maybe it was time for him to step up as a parent.

That's when I knew that neither of them wanted me to live with them, which would have been okay because I didn't want to live with them either, except I needed to live somewhere! I thought of how Prudence and Earl and Seth used to argue in a joking way over who got to be with me. Prudence wanted me to help with chores and help her decide what to plant, and Seth wanted to show me stuff on the Internet and play me his heavy metal music, which was interesting because he has good stories about the bands. The stories aren't appropriate for kids, but he always gives me what he calls a "trigger warning" before he tells me something that's not G-rated. Earl likes watching television with me and always makes sure I eat enough and get enough sleep, and he gives me candy, which we don't tell Prudence about because of her feelings about sugar.

When Prudence and Earl and Seth argued, no one ever threw anything, although sometimes when Earl and Seth were trying to build something, I could tell Earl wanted to.

Being with my parents at Smitty's made my stomach hurt so much it was hard for me to think.

I told them I didn't care who I lived with but I had to be able to visit Woefield and my birds. And my mom said she was sorry but that Pete said I should stay away from the farm until he did an investigation and that Woefield might become a factor in the divorce.

Then the waitress, who was nice and gave me a special smile like you give to someone you feel bad for, came back and put down my potato pancakes. She asked if she could get me any extra sour cream since I wasn't having applesauce.

I said no. Then I ate all of my pancakes because who knew when I would get to go to Smitty's again.

I pretended I was deaf and didn't listen to anything else my parents said, and when I was done eating they had decided that I would stay with my dad for two weeks and my mom for two weeks. They looked like they wanted to throw their dishes at each other, but I was so full and felt like throwing up so bad that I didn't even care.

Prudence

It is one thing to fail as a novice grower/hot sauce maker at the farmers' market. It's another thing to fail to adequately care for and protect a child. Sara is not biologically ours, but she is the most important part of our family. To say we are devastated and heartbroken about what has happened would be a gross understatement.

I'm the most to blame. I cannot fathom my behavior or my thought process. How could I have gotten it into my head to take a mule to a parent-teacher meeting? There's multitasking and then there's insanity. What happened to my usual calm in a crisis? I went to pieces when Lucky got away from me. I lost my mind the minute I took the mule on the road for a second time. There is no excuse.

As soon as Eustace and I drove into the yard, hauling Lucky in the trailer Eustace borrowed from a friend, I could tell Sara was gone. The farm seemed lifeless and ugly in the evening light.

Eustace unloaded Lucky and put him in his pasture and we fed him and Bertie while Seth and Earl waited anxiously at the fence.

"Her parents took her back," said Seth.

"I know," I told him, because somehow I did.

"They won't even let her visit," he said. "Not until the social worker investigates us. Each seems to think the other is going to bring up the farm in their divorce proceedings."

I felt myself grow heavy as old iron.

"I'll be in soon and we'll talk about what to do. Eustace and I just need a minute."

Seth and Earl went inside and Eustace walked up the wide wooden stairs to stand on the creaky old porch. Cold rain had begun to spit down in bursts. Sara's chickens had gone inside for the night and I knew they'd be sitting cozily under the warmth of the yellow heat lamp. I hoped that someone had remembered to feed them.

Would they be taken away too? Those birds were like an extension of Sara. I couldn't imagine not seeing her out by the run, fussing around with those ridiculous and delightful chickens.

Around us, the farm seemed to sigh with depression as a gust of wind blew leaves across the yard. I tried to catch a glimpse of Bertie and Lucky, but they were huddled under their pathetic tarp lean-to next to Earl's cabin, too deep in the lowering gloom for me to make out their shapes. How much damage had I done to Lucky's psyche this time? Again with the good intentions. Again with the poor results.

"Prudence," said Eustace, reaching for my hand.

I let him take it. "I don't feel well," I said. "My ability to think has been impaired by my Hashimoto's and the less I say right now, the better. I'm glad you got here before she got hurt."

"I'm sorry about the phone call. I should have waited to confirm it was Seth who answered. I never wanted this."

I wanted to collapse onto the porch swing and never, ever get up again.

"This is not your fault. The damage was done as soon as I left her alone and brought a mule to the parent-teacher."

"You're overwhelmed and sick. Can you please just give Lucky back to Werner and go see a proper doctor? Get some medication that actually works?"

I stared into his face, finally feeling calm after the emotional meltdown in the school yard.

"It's not Lucky's fault I put him in a situation unsuitable for mules. It's not Dr. Bachmeier's fault I haven't heeded her directions to take it easy while my medication does its work. I left Sara alone and she was attacked by a young sociopath. It was only by chance that you interrupted him before he did something that could have scarred her for life. The thought of what could have happened sickens me."

"Prudence," he said. "It's not your fault."

"Yes," I said simply. "It absolutely is. And I need to fix it. But first, we need to have a house meeting."

"Do you want me to stay? I might be able to help. I can talk to her parents. The social worker. Explain things."

"No," I said. "We'll handle it."

My mind turned over thoughts like an unmotivated farmworker picking rocks.

"We're going to make a plan to get her back. Or at least make it so she can visit. In the meantime, if you see her let her know her birds will be fine. Let her know we'll be fine. So will Bertie and Lucky. You know how she worries. We'll get all this straightened out. We'll get her back in some capacity. You tell her that."

"Of course."

"What about those boys?" I asked. "The one from Sara's class and the one who tried to hurt Sara?"

"The younger one's name is Target. His older brother's name is Charles. Middle name: Manson."

I winced. "Can you find out what's going to happen to the young one?" I couldn't bring myself to say his name.

"I'll try. Apparently the social worker said he was at the school to talk to their parents. There are some serious concerns about his home situation. If the scene here today is any indication, the boy's probably going to end up in care. The social worker wouldn't give me any details, but I got the impression that the boy has been in foster care before. He and his brother both."

"And what about the other one?"

"The social worker said he will probably be sent to a group home for troubled kids. Up island somewhere."

Another gust of wind heaved past and I shivered. Dr. Bachmeier said once my thyroid levels had stabilized, I wouldn't be so cold all the time. She said I needed to be patient while my body, aided by her remedies, found its balance again. Were patience and exhaustion the same thing? I couldn't tell anymore.

Eustace didn't say anything more about the boys, but I could fill in the blanks. The young one, Target, was not ever going to be fine. Not with who knows what kind of parents and a violent, abusive brother, and multiple foster homes. We'd be reading about the older one in the news one day.

Eustace bent down to kiss me. "I'll call later," he said. "When I know more."

"I can't believe I did this," I said.

"Oh, Prudence," he said. "Life did this." Then he walked down the front steps and got into his big white truck. The noise of the engine starting was a loud comfort that faded too soon.

Back in the kitchen, Earl and Seth sat at the table. I looked from them to Sara's place. She never had to be told to clear her homework away before dinner. For some reason, that made me slightly weepy again. At least it was better than my crying jag in front of a crowd of teachers and alarmed parents.

I leaned against the counter because I was worried that if I sat down I'd have trouble getting back up. Earl and Seth stared at the tablecloth. It was the one that Sara and I had painted. Mostly Sara. Her poultry club had had a fabric arts night and she brought home all the materials to make a tablecloth from a piece of plain cotton. Her painting of a chicken and some eggs looked exactly like the pattern she used. My painting of flowers was half finished, but it was also tidy and attractive. Seth had decided to paint Iron Maiden's name onto his edge of the cloth. His gothic lettering was erratic but perfectly legible. Earl said he would rather watch TV than paint a sheet, so Sara, without the aid of a pattern, painted something vaguely banjo-shaped on his side of the cloth. Earl lit up when he saw it. Said it was a "damned fine piece of work."

I'm aware that this all sounds painfully like *Little House on the Prairie* meets *Martha Stewart Living* and like we were the kind of household that sat around doing crafts of an evening, but I cannot lie. That was part of Sara's gift to us. She made all of us, even me, slow down and pay attention.

"We need to get her back," I said, finally succumbing to my exhaustion and sitting heavily down in Sara's chair. I ran my hand over the cloth. "Or at least figure out what we have to do so she can come back to visit."

I could sense Earl and Seth waiting for me to tell them what to do.

"Can someone get me a piece of paper?"

Seth grabbed a large piece from the pile of scratch paper that I use for making lists and a pen.

With the pen poised over the paper, I considered. Normally, lists are my passion. I relish crossing items off as much as I love adding them. I can think of few things as satisfying as a list with every item crossed off. But on this evening, my list well had run dry.

"I guess we need to stay in touch with social services," said Seth. "That guy. Pete. Get him to hurry up his investigation and write a report. Her parents seem keen on that."

I wrote "Pete" on the paper.

"I think he kind of liked you," said Seth. "He got a look on his face every time you ran past trying to catch Lucky. Would you be willing to sleep with him?"

I glared but also appreciated his ability to give me a little boost of outrage at an opportune time.

"Knew I could make you frown," he said.

"We need to talk to them parents of hers," said Earl. "Even if they's useless as tits on a tree."

"*Are*," said Seth. "*Are* useless as tits on a tree. Actually, I would have a lot more time for trees if they had breasts. If we want Sara back, we're going to have to work on our grammar. Prudence, can you add that to the list? Remembering to use variations of the verb *to be* correctly. Especially in the presence of school officials and child care experts."

Earl and I ignored him. Seth's compulsive glibness is probably connected to his alcoholism in some way that scientists have yet to determine. Eustace, who has been sober for years, suffers from the same malady. Not even active participation in a twelve-step program can fix a bad case of glib.

"You're right," I told Earl. "We need to work directly on Sara's parents. Convince them we're suitable. Sara's mom. What's her first name again? Anyone remember? God, my memory is not working right now."

Earl shook his head.

"Sad Sack?" asked Seth. "The Drip?"

"I'll find out. Who wants to keep in touch with Mr. Spratt?" Then their full names came to me. "Her name is Sally. His is Dean. Sally and Dean Spratt!"

Sara's parents have never liked us much. No, that's not strictly true. Sara's mother, Sally, is too depressive to fully commit to disliking anyone but herself and her husband. Dean Spratt is a man who has marinated for too long in his own unhappiness. They tolerated us because Sara was happy here and we wanted her and they didn't, really.

We needed to win them over. I had no idea how we'd do that, but hoped some brilliant inspiration would come over me.

"I'll be the point person on Sara's parents," I said, and wrote, "Point Person for Parents," after "Pete."

I pondered the piece of paper. "So far, I'm going to work on improving our relationships with Pete and the Ministry of Children and Families and with Sara's parents. What are you two going to do?"

Earl and Seth frowned down at the tablecloth.

"I'll take care of her birds," said Earl. "She asked me special."

"That's great, Earl. And I'm going to ask you to continue handling things on the farm while I work on getting better. So glad to know you're on the job."

The many furrows in Earl's face grew deeper.

"I don't know what I'm going to do," said Seth. "Probably plunge into near-suicidal depression. We need to get Sara back or this place is going to fall apart. *I'm* going to fall apart."

"Seth, you're going to support our efforts. You're very good at that. You keep things interesting and present alternative views. And you're going to continue to look after your sobriety."

"Do you want the rest of my money?" asked Earl, jarringly.

"I'm sorry. What?"

"It seems like we're poorer than a goddamned hairless, tailless, ball-less dog around here most of the time. I still got a little left from what Merle gave me for the old place."

"That's your retirement savings," I said. "You've already invested in this farm. Your half ownership is what allowed us to survive. We're getting by. I've paid the material expenses on the barn. I feel sure we're going to be more profitable come spring."

"We're going to be flat broke by the spring," said Seth. "Unless we start a fracking operation out in the pasture. Or start importing Chinese antiques."

"I was thinking we should open a farm stand," I said. "A thriving little venture that will allow us to sell our wares and help us show the Spratts and the social worker that we're a functional farm as well as a wholesome, well-run place. It will underline the fact that the incidents with the hot sauce and the parent-teacher meeting were aberrations."

"I don't want to be critical, but I think farm stands make places look dead broke. They're basically one step up from a lemonade stand," said Seth.

"Farm stands look welcoming. Homey. One will help us make a good impression on everyone who comes to visit this place. The social worker. Sara's parents, if I can get them to come and evaluate us for themselves."

"Them two hate each other worse than a weasel and a snake," said Earl.

Seth was nodding his head, the Motörhead logo bobbing up and down. "It's true. Those two are so committed to not getting along, it's going to be hard to get them on the same page about anything. They'd probably disagree about whether diamonds are worth money."

Seth and Earl were both staring down at the tablecloth again. I could tell they didn't understand my reasoning. Neither did I, because I wasn't using reason. I was using instinct. And instinct told me that we needed to show that we were part of the community. That we were capable of more than just failure.

Earl

Damned little gaffer. Place ain't the same without her. Marching up and down with her clipboard. Reading her animal books like there was going to be a test. Sara had a way of being interested in things. She wanted to know what TV shows I liked and what I liked about 'em. She wanted to know about my banjo and where I got it and why I wore suspenders instead of belts and what it was like to live in the United States. She even asked what it felt like to be famous. I told her I wasn't famous. My brother Merle was.

She said she thought being famous was probably like having a lot of people think they knew you even if they never met you. She's a helluva smart kid.

She was also bossy as all get out. Like Prudence, but shorter. When she had something she wanted done, you better by god get it done. That kid could make me laugh.

I'll never forget building the chicken house. She made me and Chubnuts do it about four times until we had it buttoned up to her satisfaction. Even after all that, I used to see her out there, taking pieces off and reattaching them with that hammer she likes. The thing's as big as her arm and she uses it to tap here and there. Clipboard in one hand and jeezly great hammer hanging off her waistband, damned near touching the ground. Funny thing to see a little girl packing a great big hammer like that.

Listen to me. Gettin' all sentimentaled again.

There's no time for that now because Prudence has put me in charge of this place while she's getting herself on the mend. She said the first thing I need to do is get an update on the barn. Just keeping my drawers hitched up these days is challenge enough, never mind having to deal with the goddamned trades. But it's got to be done. If that social worker comes around, we'll look like a damned death house for kids and animals if we don't get the mule moved out from under that tarp on the side of my cabin.

I just need to get myself in gear and stop going out to check on the little Sprout's chickens every ten minutes. Alec Baldwin, that rooster of hers with the big white wig of feathers on his head, is off his feed. I think he's missing her. He better get over it. Nothing's going to happen to those birds on my watch.

Seth

Evidence of Prudence's reduced mental capacity: she made me drive her to the nature doctor because Earl was busy looking for the contractor she hired to build the barn.

Dr. Bachmeier, proud owner/operator of Body-Mind Alternative Health and Wellness, came out of the back room of her clinic wearing an orange robe. Unless you actually are a Tibetan monk, I can think of few garments that instill less confidence in me as a medical consumer. And then there was her accent, which is best described as extra-German. She's about two thousand years old and fierce as only a two-thousand-year-old German lady working in a nondescript office in a down-at-the-heels mini-mall can be.

"Pruuuudence," brayed Dr. Bachmeier. "What is to be the problem?"

Prudence, all pale and wan, said she was still feeling tired and sick. She said there had been some problems at home stemming from her condition. She wondered if the medication needed to be adjusted.

"You are following my instructions, yes?"

"Oh yes," said Prudence. "Mostly."

"What is mostly? You are staying in bed except for short walks?"

"Well," said Prudence, evasively.

"Then it's just a matter of some time to take the effect!" said Dr. Bachmeier. "Avoid the goitrogens; go to glutathiones. Protein! Protein!" Then she noticed me.

"This one. He is pale. Looks unwell. Do you wear undershirts, young man?"

I felt pinned to the plain and uncomfortable wooden bench that was the only furnishing in the sitting area besides the heavy wooden reception desk. Outside, Body-Mind Alternative Health and Wellness looked like any unsuccessful enterprise. Inside, it looked like it had been furnished with overstock from one of the nastier Grimm fairy tales.

"Well?" demanded the doctor. "Do you? Is a simple question to answer."

"No," I said, hating the uncertainty in my own voice.

"No one takes care of the liver in this country," said Dr. Bachmeier. "And you like to drink, yes?"

That got my attention. How did the little natural medicine troll know about my drinking?

"Not anymore."

"Too late! Damage is all over you. Your nasolabial folds are like a monkey. Your skin is not good. You wear the undershirts too. Bad liver," she said.

And then she bellowed good-bye at us and swept into a back room.

"Isn't she amazing?" whispered Prudence when the doctor was gone. "Her intuition and diagnostic ability are legendary."

The receptionist had come out from wherever she'd been hiding, a white-blond girl with the spacey look of someone who'd taken one too many acid trips at Burning Man. She nodded. "People come from all over the island and even the mainland to see her. She's only been open for a few months and already she has a huge wait list. She makes all her own remedies. The wait list for an acupuncture appointment is two months long. It's even longer to get in for meditation counseling."

The girl gave us a gap-toothed grin, mouth slightly ajar, and tucked a piece of colored feather back into her confusing arrangement of braided and knotted hair.

Prudence got slowly to her feet.

"So that's it?" I asked her. "You're not going to have a private session or get some new medication or anything?"

"Dr. Bachmeier looked at me. That's all it takes. She's extremely experienced. With patience, my body will heal itself. It's about total wellness, Seth. It's about using your immune system's resilience and nature's wisdom."

"Okay," I said. And I would have thought it was all complete shit except for how the doctor pegged me for a drinker at ten paces in so-so light. That *was* sort of amazing.

Once we got into the truck, I asked if it was okay if we went to Woodgrove Mall so I could get a few undershirts for my liver. While we were there, I picked up a package of kids' undershirts too, just in case spending time with her parents screws up Sara's liver.

Sara

Living with my dad was very depressing. For one thing, there was nothing to do. He lives in an old building with three apartments. There is a tire shop next door and they keep their used tires at the side of the building, which is probably a health hazard. The tires remind me of the documentary Miss Singer showed in class at the beginning of this year. It was about some kids who live in a garbage dump in Brazil. Those kids had to forage in the garbage to find things to sell so they could make money. If I ever had to do that, I would get a wheelbarrow. You need a wheelbarrow or a grocery cart if you're going to scavenge properly.

One thing is that even though those poor kids didn't have material things and were hungry, I bet they were never bored. They got to be outside all the time and do things to stay alive, which is a little bit like farming, if you think about it.

My dad said I couldn't go outside by myself except for the walk to and from school, which only takes about five minutes. He said me being alone and outside was how we got in this mess in the first place. By "mess," I think he meant him having to look after me.

I asked him what I should do and he said I should play or call my mom when she's not at work. That wasn't going to happen because talking to my mother was even worse than being in my dad's apartment. I don't even like playing. I prefer activities that have a point.

All the white paint in the apartment is yellow from smoke. My dad started smoking when he and my mom separated, but since I moved in, he goes outside to smoke near all the old tires. It's too late for the apartment, though, because the whole thing smells.

There is only one bedroom and my dad lets me use it. He sleeps on the reclining chair in front of the TV. I guess I shouldn't complain. Those kids that lived in the dump in Brazil didn't have their own rooms, and if their dads were still around they probably didn't have reclining chairs.

What's interesting to me is how one place can be old and run-down but feel cozy and another place that's old and rundown can feel sad. Prudence's house needs a lot of work. Some cupboards don't have doors because Prudence wants to put on new hinges and handles and most of the furniture has holes and isn't very comfortable due to springs sticking out and saggy cushions. But Prudence made Seth paint the whole house, inside and out, and she's refinishing the hardwood floors, one room at a time. She made new curtains and she recovered the pillows. The house at Woefield smells like old wood and Prudence's vegetarian food and herbal tea.

My dad's apartment smells like used tires and like no one cares.

I couldn't tell him any of that because he's tired after driving a cab for twelve hours and is never in a good mood. He sits in front of the TV as soon as he gets home and barely talks. He just asks if I ate and I tell him I did and that's it.

My homework only takes me about an hour to do and watching TV makes me feel even more lonely for Prudence and Seth and Earl and my birds, so I don't do it. I'm going to have to find something to do after school so I don't have to come home until later.

The other thing I should mention is that I saw Target at school today.

I told him I didn't blame him for anything that happened. He said he was sorry anyway. He said he was living with a new family because when Pete went to his house there were people there who were not good to have around kids. It must be awful to have a brother like Charles Manson Barton as well as a mother on the junk, and three dads, one of whom is in the can. That's worse than living in a garbage dump in Brazil for sure. Social worker Pete and my parents didn't say I couldn't be friends with Target. I don't care if he's different from my other friends who are in Poultry Club. Seth says we all need different kinds of friends or we get insulated.

I know I'm not supposed to visit Woefield until Pete makes his report to my parents, but I'm going to go see my birds anyway. I'm starting to think that a person should not listen to everything adults say.

Prudence

In the old days, people who developed serious thyroid deficiencies ended up with cabbage-sized goiters growing out of their necks and brain damage. Obviously, I wouldn't want that, but nor do I want to end up permanently dependent on synthetic thyroid supplements derived from who knows where. That's why I've chosen to keep my faith in Dr. Bachmeier. In addition to creating several remedies for me, she has me on a strict gluten-free diet that supports thyroid function and general immune health. Under her program, I'll be able to live medication-free and we'll have treated the whole problem rather than a symptom.

On the bad days, I remind myself that health is the most important investment one can make. And I'm pleased to report that the bad days are becoming less frequent. Well, slightly less frequent.

Yesterday was a good day and I made it to the gas bar to see Sara's mother. I found Mrs. Spratt stationed behind the hot dog and nacho counter. Her coworker, a boy of about fourteen who was, according to both his T-shirt and his hat, an enthusiastic member of the marijuana legalization lobby, stood behind the main counter, selling gas and overpriced candy with all the verve of a run-over juice box.

I want more than anything to get Sara back, but I couldn't bring myself to purchase from Mrs. Spratt one of the vile items displayed inside the smeared and fingerprinted glass case. Purplish hot dogs and bile-colored corn dogs rolled lazily on the greasy steel rods. A metal box with a pump on the front burped out a viscous orange substance onto tortilla chips. Mrs. Spratt's face was nearly as shiny as the food she sold. It must have been hot behind that case.

"Oh, hello!" I said when I approached, hoping to give the impression that I was a model of good health and hadn't been bedridden for the past week.

She nodded and allowed her shoulders to slump a bit further. Actually, that's rude. I'm sorry. When I first met Sally Spratt, she'd been pleasant but tentative, like a half-full helium balloon. Since she split up with her husband, all the air has gone out of her. Not for the first time, I marveled at the fact that such an amazing kid had come out of this woman.

"So this is where you work," I said.

Another nod.

"Do you ever get to sell gas or do you just work this, uh, food counter?"

"Sometimes I sell cigarettes. They're locked up."

"I suspect most health care providers would like to see this food locked up too," I said. Then I added a weak "Ha, ha," so I didn't sound so censorious.

She stared at me with dull eyes.

"Do you want something?"

"I was just wondering how Sara is."

"She's with her dad," said Mrs. Spratt.

"That's great. I mean, not for us, obviously. We really miss her."

"We are capable of looking after our own daughter. You don't need to check up on her. Or us," she said, showing a little ice in the water.

"Of course not. We just . . . I wanted to say hello. And to apologize for what happened."

More dull-eyed gazing.

How to reach this unhappy woman?

"Do you actually eat this stuff?" I said before I could stop myself. I gestured at the things spinning in the case.

She nodded. "We get a discount. I'm sorry if it doesn't meet with your approval."

"No, it's not that. I just . . . how does that food make you feel?"

Mrs. Spratt sighed. "Like I'm saving money," she said.

By this time, two teenage boys had come in and were standing behind me, shifting noisily from foot to foot.

"Have you ever had your thyroid tested? I say that because your skin is a bit sallow. Just like mine. I recently discovered I have a thyroid condition. That's part of why . . . well, I'm on the mend now."

Sally Spratt might have been frowning at me but that seemed to be her face's new default position, so it was hard to tell.

The only way I could get her onside was if I convinced her to spend time with me. With us. On the farm. It might be a little unconventional, but it's a good place. She'd see.

"Can I get you something?" she asked.

"No shit," said one of the boys behind me.

"Tell her to go to the health food store if she don't like the food here," said the other one.

136

They were absolutely right. I'd been holding up the line. Criticizing the food. Criticizing Mrs. Spratt's demeanor and appearance.

"Sorry. I just thought I'd come over and say hi. And pass along our regards to Sara. And you, of course."

Another sedated nod.

"Please tell Sara we miss her. And let her know we're taking good care of her birds. They're all doing fine. Earl spends half the day fussing over them."

"Fuuuuuck," said one of the boys. "Hurry up already, lady."

As I turned to leave, Sally Spratt spoke.

"You really think I should get my thyroid tested? Is it like an allergy test? I *am* tired."

I faced her again and both boys groaned. One mimed bashing himself in the forehead with his skateboard.

"All you need is a simple blood test. My low thyroid knocked me on my butt. My skin turned yellow. I couldn't lose weight. Couldn't get warm. My hair started falling out. I slept all the time. Then I heard about Dr. Bachmeier. She's got me on the road to recovery. All natural, too."

I didn't mention that most of those symptoms were still in place. No need to scare the woman.

I tried to think of a way to get her to come to the farm. Then it came to me. I remembered Sara saying that her mom liked to journal.

"Say, are you interested in writing? You should come to the writing group I host at the farm. The Mighty Pens are a fun bunch. We could chat more there about the endocrine system and its effects on general health."

"Ladies! Take it to the free clinic," said the boy who'd left a mark on his own forehead.

Mrs. Spratt didn't answer me or respond to the invitation when I gave her the date and time.

I stepped out of the way and she took the boys' orders for nachos with chili and cheese and a chili corn dog, and I restrained myself from grabbing the poisonous snacks out of their hands and throwing them into the garbage. School had just gotten out and a lineup of teenagers had formed. I was relieved not to see the toothy boy from the truck. Sally was too busy taking orders to keep talking, so I waved and left, relieved that even if we hadn't made much of a connection, at least I hadn't made things worse between us.

I left the store thinking about Dean Spratt. He was going to be tougher. His being is composed of equal thirds pique and rage and offense. Sara said he works long hours driving a cab, so I didn't feel comfortable dropping by his apartment, in case I woke him up or otherwise offended him. I decided that I would consider the matter after a short nap.

I was walking out of the parking lot when Werner Guurten pulled in.

He leaned out of his truck, which was even bigger and louder than Eustace's.

"Prudence," he said. "How's the mule?"

"Oh," I replied, evasively. "We're building a barn. At least we're trying to."

"That's great. Just great," said Werner. "I bet you've got that mule going good. How's everything else at the old farmstead? It's nice when things slow down to a gallop in the fall. We farmers need to take a break now and then. Me and the Missus are going to Paris for a couple a weeks."

"Paris," I said, exhausted at the thought. "Long trip."

"We're leaving the little ones here."

I did not mention that we'd recently had a child apprehended. By her parents, but still.

Werner has been married at least three times and at seventy-something is the father of two eight-year-old twin daughters. He has at least nine kids in total and enjoys telling everyone what disappointments they all are, except for the twins.

"Are you leaving them with your older children?" I asked.

"Hell no. My kids aren't fit to look after potatoes in a root cellar, never mind other kids. Going to get a nanny to come in. It's the responsible thing to do."

Even though I didn't think he knew about us losing Sara, I felt chastised anyway.

"So no new doings on that farm of yours? You got the kind of energy that puts the rest of us to shame."

"Well, in addition to the barn, we *are* thinking about putting up a farm stand. At the end of the driveway. Kind of a community store. Healthy fare."

"You don't say?" He pushed his ball cap back up and scratched his scalp. "I might be able to help you out with that. Got a little building the twins used to play in. Be the perfect thing for you. With a little work, you understand. But if I know anything about you, it's that you aren't afraid of a little elbow grease."

He sat in his truck, happily blocking the entrance.

I loved hearing him talk about my energy and how I wasn't afraid of hard work. I had loved that about myself. So I pretended to be who I used to be before I was felled by my underactive thyroid gland.

"We would love to have it, Werner," I said. "Wonderful. Thank you."

"Atta girl," he said. "You've got what it takes. That can-do attitude."

We agreed that Werner would drop off the building tomorrow and that it would be a simple matter to get it ready to showcase our products. When the social worker came to talk to us to make his report, he'd be impressed. When I enticed Sara's parents onto the property again, they'd also be impressed. They'd remember the fund-raising bluegrass concert we put on in late summer and how well that had gone.

"My son made it after he went to carpenter school up at the college for a semester. He did a nice job on it, considering how he is. I think you're going to be real happy," Werner said.

Earl

I honest to Christ don't know where Prudence gets these ideas. It must be something to do with the seaweed and sawdust and panda bear toenails pills she's been taking. Them pills and potions is a goddamned racket. If they was worth a damn, she'd never have been sick enough to let Old Man Guurten give us his old shack because he don't like to pay dumpage fees. I heard on TV that gland problems like Prudence's can cause permanent damage and I think that may be what we have going on here.

As for the shack, it would take a Harvard architect to turn that thing into a farm stand. When Prudence sent me and Seth down to look at it, Seth said it looked like a cuckoo clock and a wedding cake after a head-on with a Pepto-Bismol tanker. He had a point. Guurten might have been able to fit two little Dutch girls in that shack, but I bet it was a trick to get 'em out again. The shack is about ten feet tall and five feet wide and painted bright pink, except where mold has turned it green. Prudence told us one of Guurten's useless boys made it. Must have been learning to use a chop saw, because the whole thing was covered in scalloped edge trim. There were pointy little turrets on the top. Anyone who happened to fall on it from above would get killed faster than a fish in a field.

Prudence thought that eyesore was the greatest thing since carrots, and she'd been feeling so poorly, 'specially since we lost Sara, that I didn't want to tell her she was wrong.

Me and Seth were inspecting it and she came down the driveway in her slippers and a big housecoat. She walked around it, saying, Oh, Earl! Isn't it perfect? Just imagine it with flower baskets hanging from pretty iron baskets and with our own beautiful produce displayed inside!

And I was thinking: How the hell we gonna get produce in there? And who the hell will be able to see vegetables through them little windows? The smart money who caught sight of that damned thing at the side of the road would hit the gas. I know I would. We might never get Sara back if the authorities and her folks catch sight of that goddamned eyesore.

That was yesterday. Since then, Prudence has come downstairs twice to ask when me and Seth is going to get going on the "renovation." She also asked three times when young Stephan McFadden's going to get cracking on the barn. Lotta pressure on me is what it is. I sure as shit wish she'd get to feeling better. I got a lot on my plate with trying to find that contractor she hired and making sure Sara's chickens is okay. They aren't laying and a few of them is losing feathers. Alec Baldwin's doing especially poorly and I know what a soft spot Sara has for that rooster. I'm going to get Eugene to take a look as soon as I see him.

The only good news I got to report is that I think I seen Sara yesterday afternoon.

Might not of been her, but I saw two kids sneaking across the field on hands and knees, heading in the direction of the chicken coop. I can't imagine any other youngster would want to see chickens so bad they'd go crawling like commandos across rocky scrub. If it was Sara, at least her birds might settle down and get back on their feed.

I didn't let on that I saw her. She ain't supposed to visit until things get sorted out, but what I don't tell no one don't count. Tomorrow morning, I'm going to wheel the coop and run closer to the road so she don't have as far to go to get to her birds. Don't want her to ruin the knees in her pants. The kid don't have many clothes spare. I was real glad me and Seth scrubbed out the coop the day before. It was looking nice in there and hardly stunk at all.

It gives me a little chuckle to wonder what the little Sprout, which is what I like to call her sometimes, will make of that goddamned pink playhouse. She was the only practical one around here. Well, her and Eugene.

Seth

Can you cook anything attractive?" I asked. "Something without green sludge as the base?"

"Why?" Prudence asked. She was out of bed for the first time in two days and cutting and bagging baby greens. How that girl still has a usable back is beyond me. Seriously. I do whatever I can to avoid having to bend over. Earl and I share that particular value.

"If we made a normal-looking meal, it might make a good impression on the social worker when he comes back. Or we could invite Sara and her parents for dinner. We could invite all of them."

"I don't think they'd accept," Prudence said. "Her parents certainly wouldn't come together. All we need to do is show we're responsible and competent."

"Prudence, people deny some pretty obvious things," I said. "Climate change, evolution, the primacy of heavy metal as an art form. They might deny that we're capable of looking after a kid."

She'd tuned out.

"Can you please put these in the fridge? Earl is going to drop them off in town later." She handed me an armload of bagged baby salad greens.

Without so much as looking at me, she muttered, "We need one of those big coolers with the sliding glass doors. Like they have at Sleepy Slope. We'll put it in the farm stand."

I stared at her. She's dragged us all to Sleepy Slope Farms in Chemainus multiple times for what she calls "inspirational tours." Prudence has a major hard-on for the place due to it being organic and sustainable and run by lost backpackers and other forms of exploited free labor. Sleepy Slope has a huge pumpkin patch, you-pick blueberries, and an open-front building with an assortment of glass-fronted coolers, where they keep all their greens. They charge cocaine prices for everything. If Prudence ever got herself a tattoo, it would probably be the Sleepy Slope Farms logo. The contrast between Woefield and Sleepy Slope is, to put it mildly, stark. Although we are improving.

I looked down at the bags of greens. They were filled with young kales in colors from dark green to purple, baby rainbow chard, mustard greens, romaine and cress. Prudence has done a good job with our greens. Considering that I dislike leaves of all kinds, our stuff is pretty tasty. We supply exactly two restaurants in town. They each have about two tables and are open about one and a half days a week for dinner only, so we can keep up with demand. The entire Woefield enterprise is not what you'd call a huge money-maker. I'm basically just waiting for the day when Prudence comes in and announces that we're being evicted.

I may not be very business savvy, but I know that if we're getting a barn and coolers and renovating playhouses, we are going to be bankrupt in no time. Bankrupter? Is that a word?

Someone needs to start being practical so we can get Sara back. The authorities aren't going to let her visit us if we are all living in Earl's broken-down truck. I tried again to talk some sense into Prudence.

"The playhouse is the size of Justin Bieber," I said. "I don't think we can fit a cooler in it."

"The renovation will take care of that," she said, standing up and wiping off her bib overalls, which I have to say were adorable as hell. Christ. I used to be a tube top man. Not a bib overalls appreciator. The second I moved over here, I started to lose all aesthetic sense, especially when it comes to women. First I developed a crush on a sheep shearer I saw on an educational video. Now I find myself with a taste for a nice bib overall. I've begun to admire girls with big biceps and strong backs. If I'm not careful, I'll be getting the hots for Earl's high-waisted work pants and suspenders.

Prudence smiled, all radiant farmer babe who just got off bed rest, and I couldn't argue with her. Thank god she has that effect on people, because otherwise she wouldn't get away with her rat-assed schemes.

"When do you think you and Earl will get started on it?"

"He's still looking for your barn builder," I said. "Maybe once he tracks the guy down, we should get him to give us a quote on building a new farm stand. From scratch. Renovating that pink monstrosity will cost more than building a new one."

She didn't respond, so I kept going. "You know who could make a new farm stand? Eustace. How are things going with you two, anyway?"

She waved a hand. "I'm just getting my head above water here. Eustace already does too much for us. We're not dependent on him."

I could tell that she was locked in some pride mode that did not allow her to admit defeat.

Well, admitting defeat is one of my strengths, along with taking it easy. Eustace is my sponsor, and I am massively dependent on him. He helps me not to get shitfaced and he listens to me complain and talk about my problems for at least an hour a day. But I didn't say that to Prudence. She could keep telling herself whatever she needed to. Far be it from me to get between a delusional and her delusions.

I stood there in the soft afternoon light and realized that the place had started to smell good to me. Which is strange, because to a normal nose it would smell like mule shit, sheep shit, chicken shit, dirt and compost.

"You and Earl are going to do an amazing job on the farm stand," she said. "I want to reuse and repurpose as much as possible. No sense wasting perfectly good building materials." She put a hand on my arm. "Soon things will be back to normal. We'll have Sara back, at least part of the time."

Something caught her attention and she looked behind me.

"We have a visitor. I wonder if she's here for greens?"

I turned around and saw the drama teacher getting out of a mini-van. It was all I could do not to drop my armload of kale and chard leaves.

Sara

Today was very busy. I had an appointment with Pete the social worker after school. He asked how it was going at my dad's. I said it was fine. Then Pete asked if I was looking forward to staying with my mom and I said yes, even though I'm not.

We met in the guidance counselor's office. I'm not sure why we have a guidance office since we don't have a guidance counselor at school, at least not that I've ever seen. The office had pictures from the Big Brothers and Big Sisters club and the Kids Help Phone. I made a note of the number for the help line. Maybe I'd give them a call sometime. It would be more interesting than watching TV.

"Sara?" said Pete. "You in there?"

"Yes," I said, because I was sitting right in front of him.

"Can you tell me about staying at your dad's?"

I thought about telling him that being alone all the time with nothing to do wasn't very fun, especially since I was used to an active life with a lot of outdoor activities and interesting projects. But I didn't.

"Good," I said. "I'm getting a lot of homework done."

Pete had on one of those flat caps. It made him look sort of English, like those people on English TV shows, which is the only kind of TV Prudence watches, even though she's from the United States. I think a lot of farmers like English TV because the actors aren't all good-looking like they are on American and Canadian TV. Farmers appreciate that.

Pete has a lot of tattoos. I bet teenagers who have to meet with him think his tattoos are cool. Because I'm younger, I think he might be sorry about those when he gets old and wrinkly. The holes in his earlobes are big enough to put quarters through. When he takes out those rings, the earlobes will be loose flaps. During our meeting, I kept thinking of all the things his floppy earlobes might catch on. Car doors, fingers, cat paws. His giant earlobe holes were extremely distracting. If his bosses give me an evaluation form, I might point that out. Having smaller earrings might make him a better social worker.

"Sara?" he said again.

"Yes?" I tried to pay attention to what he was saying. I really did. Pete the social worker seemed very nice and concerned and I didn't want to be rude. Plus, I wanted him to write a nice report about the farm so my parents would let me go back.

"Does your dad help with your homework?"

I tried to think of what Pete would want to hear. I tried to think of an answer that would get him to let me go back to the farm.

"Sometimes," I said.

He smiled, like he didn't understand. That always happens when I lie. Nobody understands me.

"My dad is good at math," I said, which was true, because he used to be an accountant. "We might paint my bedroom." That part wasn't true but I wished it was. My bedroom has water stains on the ceiling and all down one wall.

"That's a big job."

I looked at him but tried to ignore his ears. "I designed and helped to build a chicken coop and mobile run at the farm," I said. "I've been showing chickens since I was seven." I said it so he'd know that painting a bedroom isn't a big deal.

His right eyebrow went up, which was extra noticeable because he had two rings in it. Those rings also looked unsafe.

"I like doing things," I said. "That's why I liked being at Woefield. They were very nice. Prudence and Earl and Seth, I mean."

He stopped smiling and the eyebrow rings sank.

"Sara, it's crucial that children are supervised. I can see why your parents were concerned. I'm not trying to be a fascist here. Every kid deserves to have a responsible adult around. In almost all instances, those adults are the parents. I've spoken to your mom and dad. They love you very much and are glad to have you home. They feel terrible about what happened when you were at the farm alone."

"It's not anyone's fault," I said.

"That's nice of you to be so protective. You're very responsible for your age. I can see that about you. I'm going to look into the situation on the farm just as soon as I can, and talk to your parents about what I find. But my caseload is big and it might take me a little while. We just need to make sure that nothing untoward is happening there."

For a person with a lot of tattoos and pierced parts, he used quite a lot of big words that I was going to have to look up, such as *fascist* and *untoward*. I might try to use them in my next essay. Miss Singer has already complimented my vocabulary twice this year. She says it's "extensive," which I looked up. It means my vocabulary covers a wide area, which is good. It's also interesting that the word *extensive* is also used to describe a type of agriculture, which means farms. It means farming big areas without much work. So in that way, it doesn't suit me that well, since I'm used to living on a small farm that is a lot of work.

"I liked living at Woefield. It was fun and I was very busy there."

"Really? Tell me what kinds of things you did."

So I told him about how I looked after the animals and helped tend the raised beds and fix up the house and picked rocks in the field almost every day and he nodded and sometimes made a little note.

"That's a lot of work," he said.

"I know," I said. "Hardly anyone my age works that hard." I could tell he was impressed.

"And who asked you to do all that?" he said.

"Everyone had things they wanted me to do," I said. "I did lots of stuff for Prudence. I got to help Seth and Earl with their work, too."

"Really?" he said, and made another note.

Then my appointment was over and I went out to the parking lot to wait for Target. He was seeing Pete after me and I knew he wouldn't take long because he doesn't talk.

When Target came out of his appointment half an hour later, he just stood in the parking lot and hardly even looked around. He had on new jeans and a new striped shirt and his hair was cut. He had been looking much better than he did at the beginning of the school year and I thought I might invite him to come to Jr. Poultry Club with me sometime. He was looking more like Poultry Club material.

I whistled at him and we walked over to the trail that leads through a little stand of trees and then behind the high school. You have to be careful on that trail because the high school kids hang out in there before school and after lunch and some of them take drugs. It's usually safe after school because they are all in a hurry to get as far away from school as possible. At least that's what Seth said when he used to walk me along that path. He would come to get me after school if he got all his writing and chores done. Earl said Seth just wanted to avoid work, but when Seth couldn't come, Earl would, especially if it was raining or it looked like it might.

Thinking about Seth and Earl made me feel bad, so I tried not to.

"Do you like your new house?" I asked Target as we walked along the path.

"It's okay," he said.

Target is not a good conversationalist. I've spent a lot of time with adults and so I'm quite good at talking. I also have an extensive vocabulary, which I try to use in conversation.

"Are the people nice?"

"They're okay."

I thought about telling him he should say more than a few words when someone asked him a question, but then I remembered his brother and decided not to say anything. It was hard though. Talking to Target was sort of like writing essays for school. Lots of pauses and not knowing what to say.

"I'm staying with my dad," I said. "He lives next to the used tire store."

Target didn't say anything, so I looked over at him. He was staring down at his shoes.

"You should really look up when you walk in the woods," I said. "Sometimes there are branches. You could run into one and get hurt."

Target lifted up his head.

"I like your new clothes. And your hair."

This was the third time we'd gone to visit my chickens. The first couple of times me and Target visited my birds we didn't say much to each other, but today I felt like talking. I was tired of being quiet with my dad. Prudence and Earl and Seth and several people from Poultry Club always liked to talk to me. Each of them talked about different things and that was fun because I was never bored by what they said. Poultry Club is taking a break right now because Mr. Lymer has gone to Minnesota for a big poultry exhibition and conference, so that means I can't look forward to even one fun evening out until we have our Jr. Poultry Fancier's Halloween party. And I'm not allowed to see Prudence, Seth or Earl.

So I talked to Target all the way to Woefield. I told him more about my birds. There's a lot to know about show birds. Most people don't understand how much. When we saw the pink building someone had left at the end of the farm's driveway, I told him how out in the country people sometimes dump their garbage in fields or even in people's driveways and that it's illegal. I said that if he ever sees someone doing that, he should report it to the police or an adult. I talked while we checked out my birds. I showed him what molting looks like and told him that my birds were probably missing me, because more of them than usual were losing feathers. I hoped Earl wasn't worried about it. Alec Baldwin was losing some of his crest feathers, but he seemed okay otherwise. Polish non-bearded chickens can catch colds quite easily and are less strong than some other kinds of chickens. You really need someone you can trust to take care of them if you have to be away.

I showed Target why my frizzles, who are white and fluffy and extremely cute, win prizes and explained why Alec Baldwin, my Polish non-bearded rooster, who is shiny and black and has a big white crest on his head, doesn't win prizes because he has some white feathers where he shouldn't. Seth says that shouldn't matter because Alec Baldwin has tremendous charisma. When Target asked what *charisma* is, I told him how it means that Alec Baldwin breeds a lot of hens. In fact, he bred two hens while we were visiting and I think that upset Target, because he turned red and pretended not to notice.

I was glad to see that Earl was taking such good care of my birds. The coop was very clean and I could tell he'd been giving them treats, such as tomatoes.

A couple of times I wondered if Target was paying attention to what I was saying, but when I looked at his face I saw that he was very interested. He probably felt embarrassed about Alec Baldwin being how he is.

When we closed up the run and left, I started to cry, which surprised me. At the end of Woefield Road, Target spoke.

"I think they're making a mistake," he said.

I was so surprised to hear him talking that I stopped crying, which was good because it was giving me a headache.

"Who?"

"Those people who don't give Alec Baldwin the prizes. He's cool, even if he has some white feathers where he shouldn't. He's definitely charisma."

I think Target was just saying that to make me feel better, but I didn't care, because it worked. So I told him all about the Standards of Perfection, which are the rules about how chickens should look, and I felt much better when he went off to his new foster home and I headed to my dad's. I was nearly there when I saw Eustace driving down the road and he pulled over and asked how I was doing. He looked very handsome and seeing him made the whole day seem better. He said he was glad to see me and he said that Prudence and Seth and Earl sent their love. He asked if the social worker had talked to me and I said yes, but he still needed to talk to Prudence and everyone at the farm.

Between visiting my chickens with Target and seeing Eustace, the day was quite good. It's kind of nice to have a friend my own age, even if we are both disadvantaged and from broken homes. My last friend, Bethany, went off to the Christian school this year even though it's far away from her house. She has special needs mentally and is an extremely nice person. She's also an excellent listener. Since she moved schools, she has new friends who are also mentally challenged, and I don't fit in with them. Prudence always says that when one door closes, another opens. Seth says that when one door shuts, you should take a hint and go home to bed. I guess that applies to friends too.

Prudence

Eustace seems to think I'm too sick to function and it's driving him crazy that he hasn't been able to take over at the farm because another local vet suddenly closed up his practice and referred all his clients to Eustace, who was already run off his feet tending to an outbreak of strangles among local horses. My overweening boyfriend is now doing the work of two and is busy from early morning until late at night. And yet we continue to make progress in various areas without his help.

Allow me to be more specific. In my efforts at building bridges, I've learned that Sara's father, Mr. Spratt, is more than just an unhappy, unpleasant person.

During my awake and lucid moments, I wracked my brain about how to accidentally on purpose run into Mr. Spratt. Then I remembered that I have connections in the local taxi industry. When I first arrived at Woefield, six months ago, I was driven by Hugh, from the Cedar Cab Company. He's a stellar person and he insisted on carrying all my luggage, which was extensive even though I'm not much of a materialist. Since then, he has given me numerous rides because our truck only works intermittently.

He wouldn't think it odd for me to call and ask for a pickup and I knew he'd be able to give me some idea about what hours Mr. Spratt worked, since they were both in the taxi business.

Hugh picked me up and drove me to the Country Grocer and waited while I went in and got our supplies. When I came back, I asked him casually if he knew Dean Spratt.

"He that guy who calls himself Yellow Point Taxi Service?" asked Hugh.

"Yes."

"Why do you want to know about that guy?" asked Hugh as he stood behind the car and organized my shopping bags in the trunk so there would be room for the bags of feed we'd be picking up from Buckerfield's.

"His daughter used to live with us. We miss her. I just wanted to touch base with her dad. Ask him how she's doing."

"He's not a good driver. Gets lost and falls asleep. He makes the customers put their own bags in the car." Hugh shook his head, clearly disgusted with Dean Spratt's lack of professionalism. "Got a speeding ticket the first day on the job! Yellow Point Taxi Service is probably not going to last."

Hugh drove us the fifty-ish yards into the Buckerfield's parking lot.

"Bad driver!" repeated Hugh, looking over his shoulder at me and slamming on the brakes just before we crashed into the side of the farm and garden supplies store. "Don't drive with him!" he warned. "I'll drive you when your truck's not working."

I got out, slowly and carefully because we were wedged in extremely close to the vehicles on either side.

"Okay?" said Hugh.

"Perfect. Thank you, Hugh. I'll be back soon. Is there room in the trunk for a bale of hay?"

"We will make room!" he said. "I'll come in with you. Carry the stuff." But he couldn't get the driver's door open wide enough to get out.

"I'll wait here for you," he announced, sinking back into his seat.

By the time Hugh dropped me back at home, I knew what I had to do. Hugh had told me that Dean Spratt usually worked early mornings until late afternoons. I would call first thing. After I put our groceries away, I had Seth carry the bags of grain and supplements for Lucky and Bertie over to Earl's cabin, where they would be transferred into rodent-proof aluminum bins, and then had him wheel the bale of alfalfa I picked up for a treat for them over to the garden shed for safekeeping. I made Swiss chard and rice, took my thyroid supplements and went to bed at 6:00 p.m. I woke up at 4:30 a.m. and called the Yellow Point Taxi Service dispatch number. A man's voice answered after the second ring.

"Yellow Point Taxi."

"I'd like a pickup at 2210 Woefield Road."

"Name?"

"Prudence Burns."

A hesitation. "What time?"

"As soon as possible," I said.

A grunt and then he agreed.

I was hand-feeding Bertie and Lucky grass through the fence when the cab turned into the driveway. Yellow Point Taxi Service consists of a Prius that has been in a serious motor vehicle accident that causes the front end to make a terrific rattling noise even when the car is in silent mode. The car is painted an otherworldly shade of green and the company name appears to have been lettered using one of those stencil kits. In short, Mr. Spratt's Yellow Point Taxi Service makes Cedar Cabs look like an elite car service catering to Fortune 500 executives.

I expected Mr. Spratt to semi-ignore me or say I was violating some rule by contacting him. But he didn't. He got out of his cab as though pulled by a magnetic force until he stood, entranced, in front of our red mule.

"By god, aren't you a handsome fella?" He held out a hand and Lucky sniffed it.

"I got a glimpse of him at the school but there was so much going on, I couldn't really get a good look. He can sure move, though."

I'd never heard Mr. Spratt so chatty. Maybe he was a morning person.

"This is Lucky. He's our new mule. Well, we're actually borrowing him. To see if we can work with him. It's not going great so far," I said, not sure why I was telling him about our troubles. "We don't know anything about mules."

Dean Spratt was scratching Lucky's big head and the mule seemed to be in heaven.

It was just after five on an October morning and rain threatened from low clouds. We were making small talk about a mule in the dark and there was something fine about that. I felt alert for the first time in days.

"I worked summers as a mule skinner in high school and university. Near Lillooet, Lytton, into the Fraser Canyon country," said Mr. Spratt in the friendliest tone he'd ever used on me.

"Is that right?" My mind was alert to the possibilities. "So you know about mules? About training mules?"

"I should have stuck with mules. Skipped the accounting."

So Mr. Spratt wasn't a morning person. He was a mule person.

I looked more carefully at him while he was busy cuddling Lucky. Sara's father had always had the complexion of a man about to lose his temper and this morning he was ruddy, but he also seemed pale and threadbare. He wore an old man's cardigan and cheap dress pants and no-name running shoes. I wondered how old he was. Mr. and Mrs. Spratt were the kind of unhappy that erases age. Theirs was a timeless discontent, the kind that shifts people into ugly middle age the minute they pass twenty-five.

"Like I said, we're pretty inexperienced and don't really know what to do with him. We may have to give him back."

Lucky was snuffling Dean Spratt's ear. The two of them were practically making out.

"Sara was helping us, but she's new to mules, too."

"Mules take practice," said Mr. Spratt. "A mule can tell when he's in good hands."

He slid his gaze to me, his meaning clear.

"We need to learn to work on catching and leading him. At the very least. He costs a lot to feed."

"Ground manners," said Mr. Spratt. "That's what you need before anything else."

"Right. His ground manners. Ultimately, we want to train him to pull a plow."

"I bet he'd make a fine riding mule," said Mr. Spratt. "And he'd look good in harness."

"Oh?"

"Good conformation. Strong back. Some withers. He'd be a fine all-rounder. In the right hands, mind you. Appaloosa mules are rare."

"I see," I said. "We'd be very interested in getting some help with him. Finding someone to train him *and* us."

Mr. Spratt stepped away from the fence, still staring at Lucky.

"Where you heading this morning? I have other pickups."

He began walking back to the battered Prius.

I walked quickly after him.

"Going to Hemer Park. To see the trumpeter swans."

He had just opened the driver's door and he turned to me as though I'd said something bizarre. Which I guess I had. I doubt many people take cabs to the park at five in the morning to see the swans.

I got in the backseat. After a pause, he got in the front and shut the door and started the engine and the car clattered to life, sounding like a bag of tin cans being thrown into a recycling truck.

"I'm serious about us needing help with Lucky."

"I work twelve-plus hours a day. Got a kid at home. At least two weeks a month I do."

I had to handle this carefully.

"Is she at home alone right now?" I asked.

I saw his eyes in the rearview mirror and I offered up a conciliatory, nonjudgmental smile.

"She can get herself to school in the morning. It's a five-minute walk. Closer than from your place."

"Of course," I said. Then, after a pause, "I'd hate for us to ruin our mule."

"Damned right," muttered Mr. Spratt. "That would be a crime."

"My thoughts exactly. Helping us with Lucky would be like preventing a crime."

"Lucky?" he said. "Who the hell named him that?"

"He came with it."

"Any mule that ends up with a bunch of amateurs is no kind of lucky," grumbled Dean Spratt.

"We could change his name," I said. "We're open to suggestions." I watched the barely visible outlines of trees flash by on the side of the road as he drove. "So are you quite busy in the early mornings?"

He turned onto Woobank Road. We were only a couple of minutes from the entrance to Hemer Park.

"Some airport runs. I drive a few guys who lost their licenses who need to get to work."

"What if you came and worked with Lucky after your shift sometime? Whenever you want, really. We'd watch but we wouldn't get in your way. Then you'd have access to a mule whenever you wanted."

I could tell from the angle of his head that he was listening.

"Do you know how to teach a mule to drive?" I asked.

Slowly, he nodded. "Yeah. Did some selective logging with our mules. Put them in competitions. Took 'em to Mule Days in Bishop, even."

"Mule Days!" I said. "In Bishop!" I had no idea where that was, but I loved the sound of it. "How wonderful!"

But before my enthusiasm could rub off on him, we'd pulled into the dirt parking lot at the entrance to Hemer Park.

"Five bucks," he said. But I saw from the meter that it was actually $8.50.

I handed him a ten and told him to keep the change.

He stared at the bill.

"You must really like swans."

"I feel about swans the way you do about mules," I said, although in fact I had no direct experience with swans.

"Want me to wait?"

"No. That's fine. I can make it home on my own."

"Is this about Sara?" he said.

"We miss her very much. We want you and her mother to know that if we're able to spend time with her again, we will take better care of her."

He nodded. "We shouldn't have left her with you for so long. It was irresponsible of us. I know you didn't mean no harm, but that situation could have been serious."

My heart plunged. He was absolutely right. We'd made a bad mistake and Sara could have paid the price.

"We're so sorry," I said.

"So are we," said Mr. Spratt. "Between the two of us, her mother and I should be able to take care of one kid. It's just that we can't seem to get along. We're worse with our kid than you are with that mule." Dean Spratt expelled a long, early-morning sigh. "I guess we'll just see what the social worker has to say. We agreed on that and we should stick to what we say for once." He turned the car on. "Enjoy the swans."

I stepped away from the cab and it clattered off to greet the day.

It took me over an hour to walk home and I had to go straight to bed, but it was worth it.

Seth

I should renumerate the things I am dealing with at this point. Is *renumerate* the right word? I don't know and I'm too lazy to look it up. Anyway, to paraphrase the great Jay-Z, most metal of rappers, at least in terms of sheer cool:

99 Problems & the Playhouse Is One
- *We miss Sara.*
- *We don't seem any closer to getting her back.*
- *From her sickbed, Prudence continues to devise a variety of impossible tasks for Earl and me to accomplish. There is nothing unusual about her giving us work, in fact that's her main joy in life, but her obsession with renovating the world's ugliest playhouse is so pointless it must surely cross some workers' rights line. A part of me feels like we should be able to handle the job because it is just a playhouse, albeit one that looks like it was designed by a drunk German elf. The part of me that is sane recognizes that we were barely*

able to build a chicken coop to Sara's specifications. If she hadn't pushed us to get it right, it would have been a poultry death house, with weasels coming in the holes in the floor, and rats through the chinks in the roof.

- *I have serious concerns about Earl being the man in charge while Prudence is out of commission. Yesterday, the guy Prudence hired to build the barn dropped off a load of used bricks, half of them busted. The day before, he delivered four unpeeled logs that looked like they'd come out of a slag heap somewhere. That's the total of our building supplies thus far. Earl hasn't confronted the kid about the random loads of salvaged materials and I think it's because Earl doesn't actually know whether the supplies are legit or not. I sense disaster. The only confidence-inspiring thing about the kid is his truck, which has to be worth $75,000.*

- *Eustace is working about twenty-two hours a day due to some horse pestilence that's going around and because another vet came to his senses and fled the profession. Eustace is so busy, he's barely even able to take time to listen to me complain on the phone, which is a real inconvenience for me.*

- *The drama teacher. The drama teacher. As noted in a cliff-hanging way in my last entry, she showed up. Here. At my place of residence. And things got weird. Weirder. Let me explain.*

When the drama teacher showed up at the farm, she pretended not to know me.

She greeted Prudence in her slightly dumpy yet highly sexualized way. The contrast between the two of them was stark. Prudence was all efficient practicality in denim overalls and tidy kerchief around her hair. The drama teacher wore a pilled, bagged-out black pantsuit ensemble. Prudence, even struggling with her Japanese glandular disorder, was lean and toned thanks to a steady diet of ancient grains and other things that are not delicious. The drama teacher seemed to be composed mostly of hips and thighs and breasts squished into a too-small bra. How do I know about the bra? In the old days, her bras were always a couple of sizes too small and a bit tattered. Damn, she was a sexy beast. Like an old she-cat who has been prowling around for years, initiating all the neighborhood tomcats into the ways of the world. That's probably reductive and sexist. So sue me. I'm a product of my time and the Internet. I will just say that she looked mad, bad and dangerous to know. Not to mention hot.

What the fuck is wrong with me? I'm pretty sure I'm a bad person.

The drama teacher spoke only to Prudence.

"I see you've been bagging your greens," she observed in that voice that sounds like Darth Vader after a Fisherman's Friend lozenge.

Prudence lit up. Nothing makes my boss and landlady happier than selling the things we've grown. There are probably people who've organized mergers between major corporations who feel less satisfied than Prudence after she unloads a few wormy radishes or an acorn squash on an unsuspecting consumer. The average smallholder is every bit as fiercely capitalist as the worst developer in the local Chamber of Commerce. If you doubt me, just look at the way those farmers eye each other at the markets.

"Yes!" said Prudence, beaming, proud. "We're just picking and sorting them now. I'm so pleased you've heard of us."

The drama teacher gave Prudence her best Mona Lisa, not quite a smile, not quite a frown. It was a look that said she'd memorized the Kama Sutra and made some additions.

"How much for a bag?"

"Five dollars," said Prudence. "Same price as Sleepy Slope."

The drama teacher's face changed almost imperceptibly the way it always did when she thought a comment was dumb. I remembered talking to her about my hopes and dreams, which I will not share here because I am now in possession of a modicum of self-esteem, and feeling proud when I didn't get the look. It meant she thought I was a creative, worthwhile and non-frivolous person. It meant she thought I was worth taking seriously.

I hated to see her use the face on Prudence.

The drama teacher looked strange standing near the raised beds. The farm is not exactly an idyllic tourist destination but it looks immeasurably better than when we first started. The fence posts are upright. The house and porch are painted. Everything is trimmed and watered and weeded and things are growing, even this late in the fall. It's not a total embarrassment to be associated with the place. There is a neatly stacked rock pile the size of an African elephant in the far corner of the field. Prudence thinks we're going to make stone walls with the endless supply of rocks that burp spontaneously out of the ground. Prudence is out of her mind. But back to the drama teacher.

There was something a little unhealthy, even malignant, about the drama teacher in that setting, but she emanated sex appeal like a fresh Glade PlugIn. I was reminded, as I so often am, of "Free Fallin'," that Tom Petty song about nice girls. A little unhealthy can be a very compelling thing.

"Do you have change?" the drama teacher asked Prudence, pulling a wrinkled twenty from the gaping maw of her purse, which was a leather patchwork job in shades of dead-body blues and bad-bruise purples.

"How many bags would you like?"

"One should be plenty," said the drama teacher. She still hadn't looked at me. We hadn't spoken since the text fight the day of the parent-teacher interview. But she hadn't been far out of my mind. Black hole suns don't need to look at people to get their attention.

"Let me just pop inside and get you some change," said Prudence. She plucked a bag of greens from my arms and handed it to the drama teacher. "Soon our farm stand will be open. It'll be in that building at the end of the driveway."

The drama teacher stared at the dilapidated pink shack at the edge of the road and another look flitted across her face. "Huh," she said. "Drive-through lettuce."

"I know!" said Prudence. Then she dashed into the house to get change, leaving me alone with the drama teacher.

"I've been waiting to hear from you," she rasped.

"Yeah," I said. "About that. I'm uh . . ."

"You're afraid," she said. "Of me. Of us."

If by *us* she meant her pest situation, she was absolutely right. And I was also a little afraid of her.

She absently scratched her inner wrist against her own right breast. Something about the gesture felt like a sexual challenge.

And then, because Prudence is nothing if not speedy, even when she's sick, she was back with fifteen dollars AND a receipt book.

The drama teacher waved a hand at the receipt book. "That's okay," she said. "We don't need to tell Revenue Canada about this little transaction."

Prudence snatched another bag of greens from me and handed it over.

"Two for one on your first visit," she said, smiling broadly.

The drama teacher finally smiled. "Like a crack dealer looking for new customers," she said. Then she walked back to the dented blue Aerostar.

Those greens would probably get tossed on the floor of the backseat and stay there until they turned into a puddle of dragon snot.

I went in the house and used all the room I had left on my credit card to order bedbug supplies: an industrial-strength steamer, how-to video and booklet, talcum powder–lined trays for under the legs of furniture.

Then I used the errand as an excuse to ask Eustace to drive me to a hardware store in town. I'm well aware that he only took time out of his insanely busy schedule because he wanted to pump me for information about how Prudence is holding up without him and because he wanted to issue more detailed instructions about all the things I should do to help her out. None of that was very enjoyable, but sometimes a person needs his sponsor around when he's doing terrifying things, such as buying diatomaceous earth, which is supposed to be deadly to crawling insects. I bought double-sided tape and two cans of spray-on carcinogens aimed at household pests. I asked the sales guy if he had any over-the-counter DDT on offer and he gave me a lecture about birth defects. When I said I didn't plan to serve it in cookies for pregnant ladies, he shook his head.

Eustace watched all this with concern.

"Don't tell me the farm is infested with something," he said. "Because that's not going to help you guys get Sara back. I leave you all alone for a few days and everything goes to hell. Are you sure you're keeping a close eye on Prudence? Her condition is serious and I can't be there."

"Everything went down the crapper as soon as we lost Sara, but we don't have an infestation. At least not yet. Prudence is fine. Asleep ninety percent of the time, but basically fine.

"We're here because I've decided that pest control is going to be my new sideline. For the winter. When there's not much farming to do. Sara's parents will respect me having a job."

"I'd have pegged you as a little squeamish for a gig like that."

My sponsor must be given some credit for understanding me.

"Pest control professionals can make excellent money. By the way, do you have a pair of tall rubber boots I can borrow?"

"I can give you an old pair, but I warn you that they're a size thirteen and have been through the wars."

We were in the lineup and, at his words, the checkout clerk's head came up and she frowned at us. Then she saw Eustace and her frown turned upside down.

"As long as the boots aren't covered in bedbugs," I said.

The cashier's mouth reverted to a frown and the man behind me backed away quickly.

"It's bedbugs, not meningitis," Eustace told everyone in earshot. "Don't worry."

We walked out of the store, and once we were in his truck he asked if I was sure we didn't have an infestation in the house. "Because I can send over an exterminator. One who is qualified to deal with the problem. This strangles outbreak is a nightmare. If you all have bedbugs it would push me right over the edge."

I couldn't tell him that I was trying to have sex with my former abuser/dramatics instructor. Something told me he wouldn't approve. I was in favor of rigorous honesty except when it came to my romantic relationships, which did not bear close scrutiny.

Eustace would say that my plan was propelled by low self-esteem and that the drama teacher was taking advantage of me. He wouldn't like it when I told him that of course she was and that people like me had to go that extra mile to get laid. Fine for him. He would never have to exterminate one of the most odious pests in the world in order to gain a woman's favor.

"Are you sure, one hundred percent certain, you're cut out to be a soldier in the bedbug wars?" he asked, starting the truck. "Given everything else that's going on?"

I hoped my racing heart and shortness of breath wasn't a prelude to a full-scale jammer.

"It's fine. Face your fears and do it anyway," I said, badly paraphrasing Prudence, who is as unfamiliar with fear as Eustace is with ugliness.

Earl

I came in from checking the chickens to find Seth messing around in my cabin. There's never a good time for that.

I asked him what the hell he thought he was doing and he tried to distract me by asking how I made out with hanging the decorative kale baskets on the farm stand.

How the hell do you think? I said, trying to figure out what he was up to. Looked like cleaning of some kind. But what the hell kind of house cleaner squirts white dust all over everything? I live in a wood cabin and anyone who knows anything knows they're already dusty as a retired preacher's throat.

Did the baskets add the touch of polish and charm that Prudence thought they would? he asked.

You know goddamned well they didn't, I told him.

It'd been raining steady for a few days, so we hadn't painted the shack or settled on how to renovate it so we could sell vegetables out of the damned thing. I was going to ask Stephan McFadden, the young feller who was getting ready to build the barn, but he'd been scarcer than a fart in a tornado since he dropped off that batch of bricks. Every time Prudence gets out of bed, she asks me when he's going to get cracking, so I better find out.

It's too damned bad we turned that ticket booth we built for the concert last fall into a toolshed. Then we wouldn't have had to try and turn Werner Guurten's eyesore into a road grocery.

Did the screws hold the brackets? Seth asked.

The third one did, I said.

The first two had pulled right out of the punky wood siding, leaving holes so big it looked like somebody shot up the place with a Desert Eagle. When I finally found some solid wood, I put up the braces and hung the two baskets of kale. Sure as shit they'd be dead from neglect in a week. One basket was about four feet off the ground, the other maybe two feet. The baskets were planted with them fancy rabbit leaves Prudence likes so much.

Seth quit squirting the white dust all over everything and he started waving around this contraption with a nozzle end that leaked steam and made a noise like an old lady who'd eaten too many beans. He held his hand in front of it and when it burned him, he screamed and swore and called it a stupid piece of shit. He's always had filthy language. Must be the way he was brung up. That mother of his ain't exactly Mrs. Manners.

I got tired of waiting for him to tell me what the hell he was doing in my cabin, so I just come out and asked him direct. If he was learning to clean houses, I thought I'd let him stay. I could use the help.

Bedbugs, he says. I'm doing a treatment.

What the hell are you talking about? I don't have no goddamned bugs unless you brung 'em in here just now.

I know, he said. This is a test treatment. A trial run. You can even think of it as a preventative measure.

I told him to get the hell out and take his bugs with him.

Can't, he said. Prudence will get suspicious if I practice in the main house.

If she's bit to hell every morning she's probably suspicious already, I told him. 'Specially considering how much time she spends in bed these days.

No one here has bedbugs. I'm just learning how to get rid of them for a friend. I bought the supplies and equipment on the Internet. Now I need to practice so I look professional and competent when I do it for real. I've got to do it right the first time because my nerves will not allow me to go through this more than once. Please notice that I'm not using the pesticides in here. Just the steam treatment and the diatomaceous earth. I haven't used the passive traps either. This is just a test.

I asked who the hell his friend is and why didn't he just tell the guy to get a terminator. Back when I was touring with Merle and the High Lonesome Boys, in the old days, we stayed in a few places that had them damned things. Nothing worse than waking up covered in bites and itchy as hell.

He said his friend had special circumstances, whatever the hell that was supposed to mean. Right then I knew it was probably a woman. She must have special circumstances alright, if she was hanging around with Seth.

What if you bring the little bastards back here? I asked him. On accident.

I'm going to wear protection, he said. Boots and overalls. A hat.

That ain't enough, I told him. Them things can spread like scabies. I told him he should stick to his business, although I couldn't have said what his business was other than wasting time on the computer and listening to that racket he calls music.

I tried to think how Prudence would handle the situation, back when she was in her right mind. She always wants us to be more supporting of each other and so I held my tongue. Mostly.

You sure you're not putting any bugs in here? I said.

He said my place would be clean as a porn star's privates and I didn't even have to thank him. And I said, good thing because I wasn't planning to thank him.

Then he went back to steaming the ever-living-shit out of my kitchen chairs.

He don't drink no more but he still don't make much sense.

Sara

Today was exciting and also disturbing. Target and I snuck over to Woefield again. We went in an opposite direction from how we normally go, by taking a shortcut through two fields. One field was fenced with barbed wire, and Target's shirt got caught. I pulled him free and showed him how to pin the wire with one hand or your foot and use your other arm to keep the top strand from poking you. Barbed wire is extremely dangerous. I read a whole book about it just before school started and it gave me nightmares. Prudence said the book was too old for me and she said I should bring my books to her first so we could read them together.

Then she read the barbed wire book and got even more upset than I did. She said she couldn't believe man's inhumanity to man and that she really hated war, which is where barbed wire started from, or at least where it got really popular. I won't write the details about the barbed wire because it would make you sick. Prudence made us sit and meditate for almost fifteen minutes so we could try and get our emotional balance back. We were supposed to send positive thoughts to all the people who have been hurt by barbed wire and also all the animals. She said she thought she might want to spearhead an anti-barbed wire campaign after she got the farm under control.

Anyway, when we finally got to Woefield Road, I thought it would be okay if we walked by the driveway, because we were already sneaking onto the property to see my chickens. I was hoping that Prudence and Earl and Seth might be out there chopping up that old pink building for firewood. Me and Target could say hello and have a visit as long as we stayed on the road.

But no one was outside. I wondered why they hung those nice kale baskets on the old shed and I wondered why no one measured so they hung at the same height. Earl and Seth are my friends but they don't take as much time with their work as they should. They do not have perfectionist personalities.

Me and Target were standing on the road in front of the little pink house and I was just telling him about how much water kale needs, when Target made a little noise and I looked in the direction he was looking, which was the front porch of the house.

What we saw there was a big shock to us both. Seth was standing on the porch and he didn't have any clothes on! Well, he had his underpants on but it was still a bad thing to see, especially because we are young and have good vision. The rest of his clothes were all in a pile at his feet and we saw him bend over, which was especially terrible because we weren't expecting it. Target made another noise. He's had a hard life and seeing Seth naked wasn't making things any better. Seth was shaking all his clothes over the side of the porch like there was sand in them or something.

We were so embarrassed that we ran and ducked near the shed so we couldn't see any more. What if he took off his underpants?

That would be terrible! I explained to Target that Seth and Earl and Prudence are very nice people and that they aren't usually in their underpants that I know of. I said it would be best if he didn't tell anyone what he saw, especially not Pete the social worker. He said okay, and then I was going to suggest that we go see my birds, because they are very good for taking your mind off things and their run was parked near the edge of the property, but when I looked down the road I saw my dad's taxi coming. His signal light was on and that meant he was turning up the driveway to the farm! We weren't supposed to be there! What if he saw Seth in his underpants on the porch? He'd for sure never let me come back no matter what Pete's report said.

Then I thought maybe he was looking for me! I told him I was going to a library club meeting after school, and there is no library club!

I grabbed Target's arm and pulled him into the little building. As I was closing the door, I heard my dad's car turn off the paved road and up the gravel driveway. My heart was really pounding but probably not as hard as Target's. He was breathing loud, which is a sign that your heart is going fast.

I said he should try to be quieter, and at first he didn't answer. He just kept breathing loud and then he started making a wheezing sound.

I wished I had a bag for him to breathe in. I know from first aid classes that bags are very effective for hyperventilating.

His breathing was so fast and loud that I wished I got to take the adult first aid and not just the youth one.

"It's okay," I told him. "When I get scared sometimes my stomach hurts."

He kept puffing.

"It's very safe in here," I said. Even though it didn't seem safe at all.

The shed was tall and skinny and I thought I could hear something moving over our heads. I hoped it wasn't a weasel or a badger. Badgers can be extremely dangerous. Fortunately, they're rare.

"Don't worry about all the mold that's probably in here," I said. Then I sniffed again, trying to be evidence-based, which is what my *Home Science Guide* says you should be when you try to understand the world. "There is probably some animal feces in here, but as long as it's not from mice we won't get hantavirus."

Then I told him about how hantavirus comes from mouse droppings and how if you ever feel bad because your family doesn't have a cabin in the woods, at least you have less chance of getting hantavirus when you clean your cabin up. I'm not in foster care, but I *do* know what it's like to wish you had a nicer life.

His breathing got even louder.

I said maybe we should sit down so we wouldn't get too tired. I said it for him. I wasn't tired at all. I kind of liked being in the little playhouse. Now that we were inside, I could see that's what it was. My eyes were getting used to the dark and I pulled back the curtains on the little windows to let in more light. There was a stool near a ladder that went up to the second floor.

"The kids who had this house before must have been really small," I said. Then I told him that I never heard of any kids around here getting hantavirus and so he shouldn't worry.

"Do you want to sit on the stool? You can put your head between your legs if you feel like you're going to faint."

Target sat on the stool and put his head down on his knees.

I was going to ask him if he was okay, but then I didn't because that question never helps. It just makes you remember that you might not be alright.

Instead I commented how the house was pretty cool inside, even though it looked sort of dumb from the outside because it was pink and had all those pieces of wood glued all over it. I started hoping that Prudence wouldn't chop the house up for firewood. Maybe we could paint it brown and use it for when someone needed alone time. I wondered if Prudence got the playhouse for me, for when I get to move back to the farm. She probably did. Prudence is very fond of me. She probably thought I'd like the kale baskets on my playhouse since I'm interested in crops. I'm kind of old for playhouses, but gifts are nice and I definitely like kale more than most people my age.

Next time I see Pete the social worker I decided I would tell him about the playhouse, but I'd call it a fort because you can use forts even when you're a teen, which I will be in a few years. I wouldn't say how I knew about it, though, so he wouldn't know I'd been back at the farm against my parents' rules.

Target said something but I couldn't hear it because he was talking into his knees. I had to get him to say it again.

He said it again.

"Closetphobia," he said.

I said I didn't know about that but that he should be fine if he stayed out of closets. I doubt kids who are in foster care have a lot of closet space. Living with my dad is like living in foster care. My closet at my dad's is extremely small, with a folding door that's broken and stacked inside, so I couldn't go inside and get closetphobia even if I wanted to.

"I don't like small spaces," he said.

"This isn't that small," I told him. Then I put out my arms and turned in a circle to show him how big it was. When I did that, I accidentally hit him in the ear.

"Oww," he said, and then we both laughed.

It was pretty funny, even though we were both afraid of quite a few things inside our fort, such as badgers, viruses and small spaces.

"Wait down here," I said. "I want to look upstairs."

I thought there might be boxes full of interesting things up there. If there was a badger or some other wild animal, I'd come right back down. There might be bats, but that would be okay. I like bats because I like Kenneth Oppel's bat books. He's a very famous Canadian author who came to our school once. He was funny and he taught us a lot about bats. Without bats, we would all have malaria from too many mosquitoes. I don't know if Kenneth Oppel said that or if I read that in a book.

It felt very risky to climb the ladder. I don't usually like to be risky, because if you get injured it's hard to help others and take on a leadership role. But no one could see me inside the fort except Target, and I would always be more of a leader than him, thanks to his bad family life.

The ladder had six rungs and when I poked my head through the hole in the floor of the upper part, I was at least four feet off the ground, maybe even five.

Whoever built the fort was very careless about the safety of kids! Seth says that about the equipment every time he takes me to the school playground, which isn't that often because I'm too old for playgrounds, but he seems to enjoy it, so I go with him sometimes.

There were no boxes full of cool stuff upstairs. In fact, there was nothing up there at all except for some straw on the floor. It wasn't completely dark, because of a small window that faced the house and Bertie and Lucky's pasture and Earl's cabin. I really wanted to see what my dad was doing. Maybe he was returning my things so I could move back.

Target asked if I was okay and I said I was.

Then I climbed all the way onto the second floor.

Target asked what I was doing and I said I was just looking around some more. He said he thought he'd stay downstairs. That was okay. There was even less room upstairs than there was downstairs.

I crawled on my stomach over to the window and tried not to breathe in any viruses. When I pulled the curtain across the rod, the fabric ripped because it was rotten. Me and Target would need to make new curtains, although forts didn't usually have curtains. Maybe we could hang wool blankets.

The window on the top floor actually pushed open, which was a nice feature. I looked outside. I'd never seen Woefield from so high up. It looked like a storybook farm. The raised beds were very neat and the house, which had been painted after the concert, also looked nice, except for the roof, which still had a couple of blue tarps on it. Seth had gone inside, hopefully to put some clothes on over his underpants.

Then I noticed someone in the field. It was my dad and he was walking after Lucky and Lucky wasn't running away like he did when other people walked after him. Instead, Lucky just waited and my dad put a halter on him and led him over to the hitching post that Eustace put up near Earl's cabin. My dad tied Lucky to the post and started brushing him and then he picked out his hooves. It was incredible to see my dad doing that!

Maybe it was from all the dust on the second floor of the fort, but I started to feel funny in my face.

Target asked if I was okay and I had to be careful so my voice didn't show anything when I answered him.

Prudence

I was stunned when Seth ran upstairs to report that Mr. Spratt had just driven up. Seth was shirtless and carrying some sort of vacuum cleaner wrapped in a plastic bag. I'd been fast asleep, so it took me a moment to decide what to react to first.

"Sara's dad!" cried Seth from the doorway. "He's here! What do I do?"

He saw me looking at the compact vacuum cleaner and hid it behind him.

"What's he doing?" I asked, trying to clear my head. "What are you doing?"

"I don't know what he's doing, but I'm under a lot of stress right now," said Seth. "I think I better leave the Angriest Man in Cedar for you to deal with. I've got to shower. A few times."

Then he disappeared.

I pushed myself out of bed and tried to get some saliva into my mouth, which felt and tasted a bit like the bottom of a rabbit's cage. That was another side effect of the Hashimoto's, or perhaps of Dr. Bachmeier's remedies.

Fortunately, I'd been too tired to get undressed after my long, slow walk home from Hemer Park, and so all I had to do was pull on a big sweater and find my slippers. I opened the door and found Mr. Spratt standing at the foot of the stairs.

He wore the same outfit he'd had on early that morning when he drove me to Hemer Park to pretend to look at the swans.

"Where's the halter and lead rope?" he asked, dispensing with greetings, when I stepped outside onto the porch. It occurred to me that it would be an interesting experiment to seat Earl and Mr. Spratt beside each other at a dinner party to record what, if any, conversation occurred.

I pointed at the gatepost where the halter hung from a large nail.

"Should keep that out of the rain. Going to rust," he said.

It was more likely to rust from disuse because, post-incident at the school, we were no longer able to catch our mule, but I didn't mention that. Each of us had tried and given up after nearly getting kicked. I hadn't mentioned this fact to Eustace, either.

Before I could let Dean Spratt know about Lucky's reluctance to be caught, his kicking, his biting or his tendency to bolt at loud noises, Mr. Spratt had let himself into the pasture. I stood on the porch, hugging myself in the chill of the afternoon and watched Sara's father walk right up to our mule.

Lucky watched him come with interest, big red ears swiveling like scanners. The afternoon sky was a light blue wash and I was glad to be out of bed. I was reminded how handsome our mule was when he craned his head around to get a better look as Mr. Spratt walked right up to him, slipped the rope around his neck, slid the halter over his nose and buckled it up.

The scene was tremendously affecting and Hashimoto's can cause emotional volatility, which is probably why I found myself verklempt. When Mr. Spratt led Lucky to the hitching post, Bertie following them like a lumpy gray pilot fish, my hand went to my heart. Not only had I succeeded in making a connection with Mr. Spratt, I may have found us a mule trainer!

I couldn't savor the moment because Seth swept outside in his Volbeat bathrobe, feet clad in dollar-store plastic slip-ons. He'd purchased the dressing gown on Etsy. It was gunmetal gray and the arms were printed with what looked like full-sleeve tattoos. Random Volbeat lyrics ran down the back, and the band's name ran down the front in bold letters. The garment was clearly the work of a disturbed fan and has upset my stomach many a morning, and not just because of all the copyright violations it represents. If Seth hadn't spent so much of his money on a heavy metal dressing gown, he might have had the funds for new underpants. The ones he leaves lying around our only bathroom are in desperate need of replacing.

Seth held the phone receiver out to me.

"For you," he said.

"Is it one of the Sandhus?" Anoop and his mom keep in touch quite regularly. She checked on my relationship status and told me about her family farm back in India. She understood the heartache of the agricultural life. Anoop checked on my relationship status and talked about how hard it was to be an elite gamer in a family that didn't understand gaming. I'd begun to think of them as good friends of the farm and, in my more coherent moments, I considered what I could do to help Anoop find a path that would make his mother happy. The answer hadn't yet come to me, but I knew one would.

"I don't think so." Seth pressed the receiver into his bare chest and I made a note to clean it before I put it near my face again.

"She's called about six times. I'm really busy. The hot water keeps running out for my shower. Either you need to take it or I will have to unplug the phone."

"What if someone calls in an order?" I said. "For greens. Or gourds?"

"What if James Hetfield calls to get my advice on how to invest his money?" said Seth.

"Who's James Hetfield?"

Seth sighed. "Metallica. Anyway, I think it's Sara's mom," he added. "Sounds depressed enough to be her."

I took the receiver.

"Hello?"

"Is this Prudence?"

"Yes. Is this Mrs. Spratt?"

"Call me Sally. I'm sorry to keep calling like this, but I've been thinking about what you said."

What had I said? People don't realize how devastating a thyroid condition can be. Those of us with underactive thyroid glands don't get enough nutrients to our brains. For some people, Hashimoto's is just the first skirmish in a terrifying onslaught of autoimmune problems. Rheumatoid arthritis. Lupus. Diabetes. That's the reason I've chosen to get serious about underlying causes.

I tried to remember my conversation with Mrs. Spratt. I could recall the revolting hot dogs, the rude skateboarders and absolutely nothing else.

"I think I'd like to do what you suggested," she said.

What had I suggested? I didn't want her to think I hadn't been paying attention. That was how we'd lost Sara in the first place.

"Great," I replied, still having no clue what we were talking about.

Then I was seized by the sight of her husband, the man with the least charming personality in all of Cedar and perhaps the world, achieving some sort of spiritual communion with our recalcitrant mule. Mr. Spratt had tied Lucky up and groomed him and was cleaning his feet. Lucky was not only tolerating it but seemed to be basking in the attention. His long ears had relaxed out to the sides of his head and the expression on his face was one of bliss. I thought back to the spring when Earl and Seth had attempted to tend Bertie's hooves. There'd been bits of hoof, hunks of sheep's wool and splatters of blood as far as the eye could see. None of us had even considered touching Lucky's feet.

I shook my head and stared around the porch. No, I had not been transported to an alternate dimension in which everything was upside down. I returned my attention to the phone and Mrs. Spratt.

"So would that be okay?" she said.

"Of course," I replied.

"Thank you."

A pause.

"Thank *you*," I said, because it seemed the only thing I could safely say.

"And I'll pass along your greetings to Sara. Thank you for looking after her birds. See you then," said Mrs. Spratt.

"Right," I agreed. "See you then."

She hung up and I wondered when I'd see her and for what. I sank onto the porch swing to rest before heading back to bed.

Seth

When she came dragging back into the house, phone in hand, to ask me if there was anything on the agenda this week, I realized she'd officially lost it. For one thing, thanks to her list-making obsession there are always at least twenty things "on the agenda" at all times. For another thing, only a seriously ill person wouldn't realize that I had the air of a guy with too much on his mind already. For a third thing, she looked almost as out of it as she had the day we lost Sara. My heart sank.

Prudence was so groggy, she didn't say anything about the fact that I was applying antibacterial gel over my arms. She did, however, notice the odor.

She stopped on her slow shuffle to the staircase, sniffed, and a whiff of her old alertness came into her face. "Seth. Are you drinking again? It stinks like a distillery in here."

"No."

"Well, you *smell* like you're drinking."

"It's this," I said, squirting alcohol and antibacterial solution onto my hand and smearing it onto my bare chest.

"You are killing all of your good bacteria when you do that," she said, with very little conviction.

"No such thing as good bacteria," I told her. "And I don't know about any agenda other than the to-do list you gave us."

"I need to lie down again," she said. Then she trudged slowly upstairs.

It was hard to see her like that. So unlike herself. So unable to right our sinking ship.

At risk of sounding like a Stark, winter is coming and there's a good chance I have seasonal affective disorder as well as resentments, irritability, sexual obsession, bedbug phobia, codependence and barely restrained alcoholism. Maybe I *should* go see Prudence's naturopath. I may need more than just undershirts to survive this season, especially if we remain Sara-less.

Fuck, I am sad. I need to take a break.

* * *

Okay. I'm back.

Here's what I did. I went to a meeting. Of course, Eustace, King of All Women, All Animals and All AA, was there. He said he was glad to see me getting myself to a meeting on my own steam for once. Which was bullshit and majorly unfair because I got myself to a meeting not that long ago.

"I had to walk," I said. "Truck's broken and the bike tires are flat and it looks like it might rain."

"That's very upsetting," he said, in an uncaring, busy professional voice.

His tone made me mad, so I didn't talk to him during the meeting. Which is probably just as well, because he hates it when I talk to him during meetings. He thinks it's rude. He also hates it when I check my phone. He's like Prudence that way. They are a pair of courtesy fascists.

Anyway, the topic of the meeting was fear. Most people shared about how they discovered that they had a lot of fear and anxiety when they first sobered up. One woman said she developed a job-related anxiety disorder and had to take a medical leave, which was sort of funny, because she worked alone doing data entry. A young guy who didn't even look old enough to drink, never mind sober up, said he was scared to talk to everyone except for Jehovah's Witnesses and he was worried he was leading them on.

When the chairperson, a heavily tattooed biker in her forties, asked me to share, I found myself talking about how I was trying to become a pest control specialist but was going out of my head due to a fear of catching bedbugs. I told the group that my employer thought I was drinking, because I covered myself in antibacterial goo after I tried doing a practice treatment in a room. Instead of everyone in the meeting edging away from me, they started cracking up. I was killing. For real. I was telling them the truth about what was going on inside my brain and they thought it was the funniest thing they ever heard. One guy laughed so hard he cried.

I said that we'd lost a member of our family recently and were sad about that, and the room went silent.

The girl with the brown hair was at the meeting and when she was asked to share, she said she had a sponsor for the first time ever and she felt like she was really getting somewhere. She was sitting next to Heather and she looked way better than she had the last time I saw her. Steadier hands. Better color. Even her hair had more volume. She said people had been really nice at her most vulnerable time and she looked at me when she said that and I felt fucking great. When the meeting was over, a few of the crustiest old bastards came over and clapped me on the shoulder and told me to keep coming back. Another guy came over and said he thought there was a rat in hiding in his house and he might call me to help get it out when I was done my pest training. All the encouragement made me feel excellent and I wasn't even mad at Eustace anymore.

When he asked if I wanted to go for coffee, I said yes and ended up telling him about the drama teacher and her pest situation and about feeling like I was ready to get laid, even though I don't have the requisite amount of sobriety.

"Seth," said Eustace. "I'm not going to tell you what to do."

A bullshit statement of the very highest order. Eustace does nothing BUT tell me what to do and cast doubt on my decision making and pretty much everything else about me. Taking my inventory, which is what it's called in AA, is his main community service, right up there with having the hots for Prudence and doing a lot of stuff for Prudence. In fact, it was a minor miracle that he wasn't with Prudence, since he hadn't been able to visit her for a while. I mentioned it and he said that he'd needed a meeting.

"Plus, I called twice today already and she told me to focus on taking care of myself," he said.

"Ah," I said.

"The point is, Seth, that if you think that getting into a sexual relationship with the woman who has already triggered a years-long bout of agoraphobia in you is worth developing a new phobia, I won't judge."

I stared into my coffee. Which was lousy, by the way. Prudence, being a New Yorker, has changed the way I think about coffee. Tim Hortons just doesn't cut it anymore. Which is too bad, because I can barely afford Timmy's, never mind some organic, hand-picked, free-trade, shade-grown, rare-bird-turd blend.

"Well, when you put it that way," I said.

"She's doing okay?"

"The drama teacher? No, not really."

"I can guess how your drama teacher is doing from the bits you've told me. I mean Prudence. Between losing Sara and her illness, I'm getting really worried about her. You know how she is. She just won't ask for help and I can't be there right now. It's driving me crazy."

"As you know, Prudence is in bed most of the time, but when she gets out of bed it's like a very tired cyclone hitting the place. You should feel grateful that you've been working nonstop while you deal with strangling horses."

"Horses with strangles," he corrected.

"Whatever. You're busy, so you don't have to see her in action. It's so disturbing. Like watching a hummingbird tied to a rock. She's determined but she's not getting anywhere."

Eustace stared into his own cup, which was nearly hidden by his hands. A quick glance around the harshly lit interior of the restaurant told me that he was, as usual, the focus of intense interest. The ladies behind the counter, many of whom were old enough to be his mother, and in some cases his grandmother, cast sly glances his way from under polyester visors. Other customers stared openly.

It occurred to me that under all the handsome, he was just a guy hurting for his woman. Although he was quite a bit further along the so-called road to happy destiny, he was still a boozehound with issues, just like me. The road to happy destiny, which is what the program promises, sounds kind of lame. I'd be more motivated by the spa of happy destiny or maybe the massage parlor of happy endings. That sounds creepy, so I won't say any more about it and will instead attempt to focus on someone else's needs for a change.

Since Eustace started sponsoring me, last June, he has probably spent forty solid hours listening to me. He listens to me when I call him on the phone, which I do once or twice a day. He listens to me when he drives me to and from meetings. He listens to me when I join him and Prudence on the swing he made for her.

A woman I've seen at meetings always says that when we put down the substances, we have to "talk ourselves into being." At first I didn't understand what she meant. But the longer I'm sober, the more it makes sense. I've been talking nonstop for the past four months and Eustace has listened. And listened. And listened. Maybe it was time for me to return the favor.

"What's going on with you two? You doing okay? All things considered?" I asked.

Eustace smoothed back his curly hair and considered. The girl wiping the table next to ours sighed.

"She doesn't want me to help so much. I'm not supposed to 'overwhelm her with kindness.' Even now, when things are so fraught. If I wasn't so busy, I'd just . . ."

"Ignore her request to respect her boundaries?" I said.

He sighed.

I refrained from saying how fucking stupid he was being. Prudence too. Seriously. The only way to have time in life is to do the bare minimum. Do the maximum in one area of your life and it will eat all the other areas. For instance, if I were to get too hard-core about looking after our raised beds, I'd end up working on them eight or ten hours a day. I wouldn't have time to blog or watch YouTube or research my recovery articles or eat or take naps or develop fascinating new phobias and obsessions with women. But I didn't say any of that. I just nodded. Thoughtful, active listener. That was me.

"I'm not trying to take over her life," he said. "Or the farm. But things seem sort of dire at the moment. And my hands are tied with my schedule."

"Of course," I said.

"If I see things I can do for her, why wouldn't I do them? It doesn't mean I don't think she's competent," he said, double negatively.

"Exactly."

"I respect her independence. Even when she's sick and making terrible decisions."

"Hmmmm," I said, being provocative and open ended, just like the article about active listening in *Psychology Today* had suggested.

"I don't know if she's ever going to let me in."

And right then my sponsor looked like a six-and-a-half-foot-tall seven-year-old.

I nodded sympathetically. Here's what I wanted to say: Prudence is a maniac and so are you. If you two crazy kids insist on killing your-selves with work from dawn until dusk, go for it. You can start with figuring out how we can get Sara back. Then help me to get rid of the bugs in the drama teacher's bed so that I can have sex without fear of catching something. Then you and Prudence can drag Earl out of his cabin, and the five of us can kick back in the living room, eat oven snacks and live the good life. But I didn't say any of that because I'm respectful and a good listener.

"She said she feels 'emasculated' by her illness. She actually used that word."

Prudence is possibly the least masculine woman I've ever seen. Yes, she's fiercely productive and likes dirt and hard work more than is normal or healthy, but she's also a wisp of a thing with no real muscles, at least not the kind I associate with women who get concerned about being emasculated.

"I hate talking about this stuff," he said. "In fact, I hate talking about any stuff."

At that, I put a forefinger to my lips, as though deep in thoughtful agreement. What I actually thought was: No wonder Prudence hasn't let you in. You need to talk to her. And you need to get an inner life, for fuck sake.

"I don't talk about anything very personal and neither does she."

"Lotta silence," I said, starting to relish my role as therapist/sponsor.

Eustace sighed and ran his hands down his chiseled face.

"I'd like to build her a farm stand. And the barn. But she wants to do it herself."

"No, she doesn't," I exclaimed, forgetting that I was being a terrific listener. "She's got Earl trying to track down the contractor who's supposed to be building the barn, and she's making me and Earl fix up that playhouse at the end of the driveway. *Me and Earl*, if you can believe it."

"That thing? Jesus. *That's* why I want to help out. So she can avoid pointless, time-wasting projects like that."

"She has this idea it's going to be cute."

"It looks like a low-rent whorehouse for tiny Bavarians. Who would want to buy produce out of some kid's half-rotten playhouse?"

Even though I agreed with him, I also hoped he'd hear himself into being less of a dick about Prudence's ideas, which were admittedly terrible.

But before all my silence could allow him to experience emotional growth, his cell phone buzzed. He listened, then clicked off.

"The Townsends' mare is in labor. At least she doesn't have strangles. Drop you off on my way?"

I agreed and we walked out of the restaurant into the parking lot. I don't know what it is about listening to other people's troubles, but I felt calmer about my own life and strangely hopeful.

Earl

There's guys you expect to see riding mules and guys you don't. That's why I was so surprised when I come out of my cabin this afternoon and seen Dean Spratt riding Lucky around the pasture, Bertie trucking along behind.

Prudence must have put Spratt up to it. She's still tuckered out from her Japanese disease, but that don't mean she's not still getting into everybody's business and putting everybody to work.

First time I seen Spratt out there with Lucky, I thought for sure he'd get his headlights kicked out, but he turned out to have a way with mules. Still, it's a helluva step from brushing a mule and picking up his feet to having him in full Western riggin' a week later—saddle and bridle, crupper, the whole shitaree—and riding him around.

That mule looked straight out of *Lonesome Dove*, which is the only book I ever read twice. The show was good too. Lot of mules in *Lonesome Dove*.

I'm not saying Old Man Spratt looked like Augustus McCrae or Woodrow Call or any kind of Texas Ranger. He had on his regular cab-driving clothes and some rubber boots with a little heel, almost like a lady's rubber boots. I don't know where that guy's money goes, but it's sure as hell not on boots.

Anyhow, I come outside to feed the animals and there's Spratt trotting around on Lucky, and Prudence and Seth are leaning against the gate like it's the top entertainment they ever seen. Bertie did her damnedest to keep up. It was good to see our old sheep showing something other than blackest despair.

The light was nearly gone when Spratt dismounted. Lucky stood stock still, which was a good thing because Spratt looked sore as hell. He grunted when his feet hit the ground. Must have been a helluva big woman who had them boots before him.

Prudence started clapping and so did Seth.

I believe Spratt may have smiled, which was damned near a miracle in itself.

He stood in the pasture, holding Lucky's reins and giving that mule pats on his neck. The rest of us come into the field, keeping a close eye on Lucky's ass-end, since he does like to kick. But that spotted red mule seemed almost as happy as Old Man Spratt. Maybe being good with animals runs in the family. I wonder if little Sara knows that her old man is good with mules. She never had much to say about her pa, which I can understand since he's a miserable sonofabitch, but it's good for kids to respect their parents. That's not something me and Merle and Pride got too much of because of how we was raised and our old man being mean as a bag of rattlesnakes.

It would be good for the little Sprout to be able to see her dad riding on that mule that no one else can handle.

That's what give me the idea to leave her a note in the chicken coop. Sara always did like to be kept informed.

Sara

I was so excited to get Earl's note, even though I already knew what he told me, which was that my dad is good with mules and is riding Lucky and that things are fine on the farm. I have read his note over twenty times so far and I enjoy it every time.

I hope he likes mine as much. I told him that things are fine at school and that I am staying with my mom and that I am happy he is taking such good care of my chickens and that he should be careful with Alec Baldwin and the Polish non-bearded hens when the weather gets bad, because they get colds easily.

For some reason I didn't tell Earl that me and Target have been sneaking into the pink fort almost every day so we can watch my dad train Lucky from the upper window. I want Earl to feel good about telling me news even if he's telling me stuff I already know.

My dad visits Lucky even if it's raining, which it often is now because it's fall. Sometimes my dad just catches Lucky and brushes him, and sometimes he holds a long rope and makes Lucky go around him in a wide circle. That's called lunging and it's cool that my dad knows about it.

My dad has even started riding the mule! Once he rode him down the driveway before he turned around and went back. Prudence walked partway down the driveway with them and I heard her ask my dad if it was safe, and my dad said it wasn't time to take Lucky on the road yet due to him having had some negative experiences, but he didn't mention that they were Prudence's fault, which was nice of him.

My dad has a lot of patience for mules. He doesn't have as much patience for people, such as me or my mom.

I wonder if Lucky will turn out to be an incredibly fast mule. Then we could race him. My books said that mule racing is quite popular in some parts of the United States and Alberta. If Mat Morrisey rides his motorcycle by when my dad's riding, everyone will find out how fast Lucky can go.

Like I told Earl in my note, I've been staying with my mom. We're not living in our old house because it's for sale and she told the real estate people it's empty. She said empty houses are easier to sell. The first few days we stayed with my aunt, but then my mom said that my aunt's house is a "toxic environment." At first I thought it was because my aunt only cleans her house once a week on her day off. My aunt is an RCMP officer and a single parent, so she's very tough and also practical. She told my mom she needed to "get off her butt" and get herself together. It was right after that that my mom said the thing about my aunt being toxic.

Now I meet my mom at her work when her shift ends at the gas bar and then we go to Smitty's or A&W for dinner. Then we visit the big library downtown until it closes. When she's sure it's too late for any realtors to show the house, we go there. She keeps our sleeping bags and stuff in her car. Last night when we went to the house, there was a fancy car in the driveway. My dad said all real estate agents have expensive cars due to highway robbery. I'm not sure what he meant, because they'd all be in jail if they really did robberies on the highway. Anyway, we couldn't stay in the house because a realtor was showing it. Instead of waiting for them to leave, my mom said we were going to have an adventure, and she drove us to a campground. When she thought I was asleep, she got out of the car and went away until four in the morning!

A lot of people might be scared to sleep alone in a car in a dark campground, but it was okay, I guess. I hoped the campground got locked at night so no one could come in. Still, I wondered what the social worker would say if he found out I was staying overnight by myself in a car and that it was partly his fault.

I also told myself that no matter how not fun it is with my mom, I probably have it better than Target because he's in foster care. I'm going to visit his foster house for dinner tomorrow, and I have a feeling that will make me feel better about staying in our car, even though we have a perfectly good house.

I decided not to ask my mom where she went last night. Sometimes, kids don't need to know everything. I also thought about telling Earl about how I was staying in the car in my next note, but decided not to because then he would worry.

* * *

I would be much better off in foster care.

Target has two older foster sisters and two foster mothers who are married to each other. All four of them are extremely nice to Target. I don't usually feel jealous of other people because I've got a lot of leadership qualities and I own several of the top show birds in the mid-Island, but I think I feel a little bit jealous of Target.

One of his foster moms is a yoga teacher and the other one is a personal trainer. They look very healthy, which is quite different from what I'm used to with my parents. There are wedding pictures everywhere, and Esme and Fran look like they should be on TV in all of them! Esme has on a white dress and Fran is wearing a white suit, but they both look like they're about to go for a run or do an exercise class. If I ever get married to someone, I hope I look as energetic as them in my pictures.

Target's foster sisters are both in eleventh grade. Stephanie is biological and Ariel is spiritual. When I asked what that meant, Esme told me that Fran gave birth to Stephanie and they adopted Ariel.

Our dinner was just like dinners used to be at Woefield, only much more delicious. We had green smoothies that Fran made in a fancy blender. The smoothies contained Herbal Matay, which is a kind of tea, kale, romaine and Swiss chard as well as mint and pineapple plus pine pollen, which is this yellow powder. Prudence doesn't like things that have to be shipped from far away, so she probably wouldn't have approved of the pineapple, but I know she'd like to have a blender like that. It's called a Blendtec and when I asked Fran about it, she said it was the Lexus of blenders, which I think means it is a really good one.

We also ate wild rice and a coho salmon that Esme caught. Esme is an avid fisherwoman. There are almost as many pictures of her fly fishing as there are of her and Fran's wedding.

Dinner was so amazing!

I also really liked Target's foster sisters. Ironically, because she's biological and her moms are into fitness, Stephanie doesn't like to exercise. She would rather play video games, such as World of Warcraft. Ariel skateboards. They are probably the coolest people I ever met.

Esme and Fran don't get mad at Stephanie about her video games, even though they worry that her lifestyle has too much sediment. They made her sign a contract about how long she is allowed to play. I think it's neat that they did that. It shows clear communication.

Fran told me that sitting causes inflammation. So do sugar and wheat. I pointed out that means sitting at school must be dangerous for kids, and Fran and Esme agreed. Fran said that when I'm studying, I should try to get up every twenty minutes to half an hour to walk around, and that if I couldn't do that, I should at least stretch out my legs.

I think that was great advice.

Their house is full of opportunities to not sit around. Esme and Fran's office has a treadmill with a tray on it instead of a desk and a chair, like most people. Esme says she walks while she pays their bills and does other household activities.

Fran, who teaches yoga, put mats and balls all over the house so everyone can do yoga or stretching whenever they feel like it. Bouncing on exercise balls is fun. I would like to have a big exercise ball, but I don't think it would fit in my mom's car. I guess I'd have to leave it at my dad's, but then it might get the smoke and tire smell on it.

Ariel sat on an exercise ball at the dinner table because she says she needs to work on her core strength. Ariel has straight blond hair and arched eyebrows. Even her smile looks athletic!

Stephanie has curly brown hair, just like Fran's. The front of her hair is dyed bright green, which she said is a hard color to get.

Target's foster family is sort of like Prudence and Earl and Seth, except without the swearing and arguments and men. They are so nice to Target, only they call him "T." I shouldn't be jealous because he has a terrible brother and a sad family life, but I sort of couldn't help it.

They kept asking him if he wanted any more green smoothie and they asked us how our day was and they asked if I wanted to sit on an exercise ball or a yoga mat to watch a movie. It was a movie suitable for kids that had a good message about not littering. Even when I was at the farm, I didn't get to watch many youth movies. Seth likes documentaries about dead musicians and Earl likes TV shows about home improvements and cars as well as people who run pawn shops. Prudence doesn't sit still long enough to watch movies. She probably has zero inflammation in her.

If I was Target, I'd want to stay with Fran and Esme forever. I told him that when we went to see his room, which has a blue checked bedspread and books and a desk and a lamp and everything.

He shrugged his shoulders and said that placements never last. I asked why not and he said the system was why.

It must be terrible to live with the nicest people ever and know that the system is going to make you leave at any moment. I felt less jealous after I heard that, but then I remembered that my mom was coming to get me at eight. What would Fran and Esme think of my mom, who is probably one of the most inflamed people ever? I wished Prudence would come to get me and that made me feel guilty as well as jealous.

For some reason, feeling bad like that made me ask Target about his brother, because I know he never wants to talk about his brother.

"He's going to a special school," said Target. "To get the help he needs."

"Oh," I said. Then I even felt a little bit envious of Target's brother because nothing in my life felt very special lately. Which is terrible. But I forgot about all of that when we went to play in Fran and Esme's gym.

That's where Esme trains people and Fran gives yoga lessons. We all went in together and Fran showed us yoga moves, such as crow, where you kneel on your elbows. And Esme spotted Ariel on the climbing wall, which means she held the rope so Ariel wouldn't be injured if she fell. Stephanie used the time to play one of her video games. If I was her, I wouldn't want to miss any physical activities with such a fun family, but Esme said that at least her body was there even if her mind was not.

Fran and Esme and Ariel asked Target if he wanted to bust a few moves and he said no. He just sat on one of the exercise benches and watched. I did want to bust moves, so they showed me how to do Zumba. It was incredible. I think I even felt some inflammation leaving my body.

Before I knew it, it was eight and the doorbell rang.

Fran and Esme answered the door together and they were very polite to my mom, who looked more tired than usual, as well as inflamed, probably because she stayed out all night when she should have been in the car with me.

Fran said how much they enjoyed having me and said she hoped I could come over again soon. Esme said she was glad I was T's friend. Stephanie said I was hilarious! I don't know why she said that, but I liked it.

My mom thanked them for giving me dinner and said that we had to go. I was hoping the realtor wouldn't be at the house, so we could stay there. Like I said, I wasn't too scared in the campground because I think they have good security measures, such as a gate, but I do feel better in our old house, even if we have to sleep on blow-up mattresses on the floor. I felt a lot of relief when we pulled into our driveway, but then I started to feel jealous again when I thought of Target and his two fit moms and two cool sisters. Just a little bit.

Prudence

Seth would tell you that optimism like mine is hubris. Only Seth would not use the word *hubris* because he did not complete high school and I doubt it's a word used often in the heavy metal blogosphere.

I am beginning to think the word *farm* actually means "land upon which things go wrong in surprising and unexpected ways" or perhaps "place where it's impossible to get good help."

Oh dear, thanks to my illness, my defenses are down and Seth's negativity is rubbing off on me. I really must get back to Dr. Bachmeier for another assessment.

I was so thrilled at Mr. Spratt's progress with Lucky that I decided to try to catch the mule myself. Specifically, I wanted to show the members of the Mighty Pens, my writing group, that Woefield is a safe place for livestock. Some of them are inveterate gossips, and I thought word of our prowess with mules might get back to the social work office. An absurd notion, I realize, and one based in bruised pride and our desperation to at least get visiting rights with Sara.

Her father has not yet broached the subject of her coming for visits and I'm slightly afraid to ask. He seems to think if he reverses his
decision to keep Sara off the farm for her own good, he'll be letting
his ex-wife win the argument. And it's clear that he'd remove one of
his own molars with a penknife rather than do that. I remain hopeful
that exposure to us and the farm will convince him to do the right
thing and let Sara see us. I also wonder if Sara knows he's spending
his afternoons here, but haven't had the courage to ask that, either,
even though it seems grossly unfair.

Back to the writing group. Seth calls them the Untalented Pens.
I have some sympathy for a lack of talent in the writing department,
thanks to my experience of publishing one of the least successful
young adult novels ever. The less said about it, the better. But somehow, my lone novel convinced the local writers that I'm qualified to
help them. I'm too broke to disabuse them of their mistake.

As noted, some of the Pens are under the mistaken impression
that the animals of Woefield Farm are lucky to be alive from moment
to moment thanks to the shocking incompetence of me and my staff.
More than once in free-writing exercises, they've written about the
things they've seen here. I've stopped giving them nature-based writing prompts because one of them inevitably writes about the time
they saw Bertie's feet covered with maxi pads and duct tape (from
when we tried to trim her hooves ourselves) or that time one of the
hens turned blue when Seth added too much bluing to her pre-show
bath. It seems there's nothing quite like a Smurf-colored frizzle hen
to capture the novice writer's imagination. They never write about
the leaves turning color or the heady scent of turned earth. Not that
we do much earth-turning on Woefield, except in the raised beds, as
there is almost no topsoil on the farm. But that's another story.

I headed into the pasture to catch Lucky a few minutes before the Mighty Pens were due to arrive. I thought they'd be impressed and even creatively inspired to see me working with our spotted mule.

As I approached Lucky in his field, I tried to copy Dean Spratt's posture and attitude. Mr. Spratt exuded a calm confidence, so I put a half-smile on my face that I hoped conveyed that same feeling. Lucky and Bertie were grazing at the far end of the pasture near Earl's cabin, and at first both ignored me.

I waded through the damp, ankle-high scrub grass until I was about ten feet away. Lucky lifted his head and stared right at me. Bertie also raised her head to watch. I waved at the two of them, feeling like an uninvited kid showing up at a sleepover. I'm not sure why. Perhaps because I'm not a farm animal and Bertie and Lucky are.

Lucky's head rose higher, making him appear impossibly tall and imposing, and a stiff breeze of doubt swept through me. I'd read that horses, dogs and, presumably, mules have an uncanny ability to sense fear and uncertainty.

The key was to fight the negative feelings.

I smiled wider and kept moving. My gaze slid over to Bertie. Her normally vacant face seemed to register concern and I felt a wave of missing Sara. She'd had a way with our depressive sheep.

I raised the halter in a friendly gesture at Lucky, hoping that he'd interpret it as a signal to lower his head so I could slide it on. In the driveway, a vehicle pulled up to the house. One of the writers was in time to see me in action.

"Hello!" I said brightly to Lucky, who pinned his ears back and, more swiftly than I would have thought possible, pirouetted his body around so his hind end faced me. He was in the perfect position to deliver a coup de grâce.

When Mr. Spratt visited, Lucky had begun to walk or even trot over to greet him at the gate. But here he was, giving me the old ass-end routine again.

"Very funny," I said. "I'm just going to put this halter on you."

I tried to walk around his substantial spotted hindquarters to reach his head. As I moved toward his front end, he pivoted away.

"Lucky," I said sternly. "Stop that!"

Lucky did not "stop that." Instead, he bunny-hopped forward a few steps, like a . . . well, like a mule. I leaped backward. Lucky hunched his back and gave a small buck. This was followed by another, more exuberant buck. When he was out of range, he lashed out with both hind legs and took off at a gallop across the pasture. He raced up and down the fence line a few times, slowing only to buck and release explosive farts, loud as a backfiring car. By this time, two of my writers had arrived and were watching, spellbound and delighted. There were oohs and aahs when Lucky went into another spasm of fart-bucking in the middle of the pasture, like a bronco that'd just been given a can of beans and a jolt with a high-powered cattle prod.

I let the halter and lead rope, which I'd been holding in front of me as though to ward off attack, drop to my side.

Ego has no place on a farm and especially not in one's work with farm animals, but that doesn't stop it from coming to the party. I tried not to feel like a failure when I walked over to my writers. Brady and Portia clapped and looked pleased beyond all measure. Brady is a plumber, given to wearing garish Hawaiian shirts, even in winter. He is writing what he refers to as "a novel of the erotic." He says it's "like *Fifty Shades of Grey*, only it's about a plumber and a female electrician and there's no bondage." Fortunately for me and his fellow Pens, he's a three-sentences-a-week man, so there's only so much dampness and plunging and heaving and thrusting between the trades that we have to listen to at each workshop.

Portia's memoir is 750 pages long, and she adds to it every time she has a fight with her ex-husband. We've talked about the need to trim the account of her failed marriage to a more manageable size, but then she and the man referred to in the text as "Little Shit Face" have another encounter in the parking lot of the Country Grocer or similar and the book grows by another two thousand words.

We used to have a mother-daughter team, Laureen and Verna, but they dropped out when Laureen, who is sixteen, stopped smoking a duffle bag of weed every day. Verna, the mother, was under the mistaken impression that Woefield was a treatment center, which is how they came to join the writing group in the first place. Long story and I'm too tired to get into it. Suffice it to say that Laureen and Verna have been replaced by a father-son team. Winston Phelps, fourteen, is the only son of Orson Phelps. Orson is laboring under the delusion that Winston is a genius. Maybe even a super genius. Among helicopter parents, Orson Phelps is the Apache model, loaded with warheads and ready to raze the village of anyone who dares to impede the progress of his son, who truly is awful. Orson works "in government" as he puts it, which means that he issues parking tickets at the Departure Bay ferry terminal.

All anyone is likely to take away from a meeting with Orson Phelps is that he's a blurry white man in his fifties. That impression lasts until he opens his mouth and begins to talk about Winston's accomplishments. Winston is an OUTSTANDING (the capitals are Orson's) student, achieving "almost all As." Winston is in eighth grade and he plays badminton AND fences AND is on the chess team AND has a flute and a drum set. Winston has his own blog.

Winston once foiled a crime in progress (he tattled on a more popular and attractive kid who was trying to shoplift a package of condoms from the gas bar). Winston started a charity for "the orphans" and got himself written up in the *Cedar Town Crier*.

Winston himself is round, dour and makes Augustus from *A Confederacy of Dunces* look socially skilled. He has a face like a cottage cheese–filled pierogi and writes derivative fantasy stories that are, I suspect, torn straight from online games.

"*We're* applying to U of T," says Orson, if you let him. "Or *we* might go the American route. Yale, maybe."

Orson and Winston are often late for writing group because of Winston's many extracurricular commitments, or because Orson is at Winston's school, threatening to sue various teachers or administrators for interfering with Winston's "path to success."

"We should have put him in Upper Canada College," said Orson, after one of these meetings made them late for the Mighty Pens workshop. "That Mickey Mouse school doesn't know what to do with him."

At the last group meeting, Orson handed me a towering stack of pages. "Winston's novel," he said. "We want you to read it and pass along your comments. Then we'd like you to put us in touch with an agent." Orson's voice became stern. "But please, only give us comments if they're *actually* helpful. Not like what we got from that asinine English teacher up at his school. She seems fixated on interfering with Winston's path to success. Well, I 'fixated' her. Lodged a complaint with the principal and the school board when she tried to give him a C+. She said his work wasn't original just because there are orcs and wizards in it. Well, you find me the fantasy story that doesn't have those things. I dare you."

I took the pages away and read the first few. The novel was a cross between *Lord of the Rings*, World of Warcraft and something downloaded off PornHub. It was a miracle Winston hadn't been kicked out of school for handing that in to his English teacher. She was probably off on stress leave due to having to deal with Winston and Orson.

For this evening's workshop, I'd already prepared my comments on Winston's manuscript, which was entitled *Game of Fire and Heat*. My praise was effusive in the extreme and included a referral to an agent in NYC. I went to prep school with her and she was kind of a bitch to one of my friends, so I felt justified. If teaching the Mighty Pens wasn't such a moneymaker, I think I would quit. It was hard to take any of it seriously after losing Sara.

Winston and Orson were late, as usual, so they hadn't joined the others at the fence. Just as well. It was bad enough dealing with Portia and her ironic applause.

"Very nice," she rasped.

"We're working on it," I said.

As Brady and Portia and I walked inside, an early model Buick pulled up and Sara's mother got out. She had on one of her depression-inducing outfits of I-quit-caring polyester pants and nothing-can-make-me-shake-these-blues blouse.

That was what I'd forgotten! I'd invited her to join the Mighty Pens. Had she said something about a memoir? A novel? I couldn't recall. Well, whatever she was writing couldn't be any worse than the other things being produced by the Pens. Or could it?

"Hello!" I said, as she walked toward us, managing to look both ruddy-cheeked and pale, like a diseased English rose.

Mrs. Spratt offered a wan smile.

"So you're going to join the Mighty Pens?" asked Brady. "Or, as those of us with a historical bent like to call ourselves, the ink-stained wretches."

Portia rolled her eyes.

"Hi," said Mrs. Spratt in a voice so low and glum it could only be heard by suicidal worms.

"Hi, Sally. Funny to see you out from behind the counter. You're looking well," said Brady.

Portia and I shot him a glance, wondering what part of Mrs. Spratt looked well. Certainly not her defeated hair, her hunched posture or her haunted expression.

"Come on in," I told Mrs. Spratt and the rest of the Pens. "Seth is waiting for us inside."

I've developed a routine for workshop nights. I make a zucchini bread to serve with tea and coffee. Once the writers are set up around the living room, they take refreshments and we get to work. This week, due to my energy deficit, I'd had Seth make the bread.

I give a brief lecture on the topic for the evening and then I assign a writing exercise. When we finish that, we workshop the writing they've done since our last session.

I have sometimes dreaded the workshops because they take time away from farming. But as the weather has grown colder and the rain has set in, I've almost begun to look forward to our time together. The work produced by the Mighty Pens is sometimes offensive and often boring, but I've grown fond of my writers and their unpublishable projects. Also, with my health troubles, any work that doesn't demand much from me physically or mentally is welcome.

When we entered the living room, Seth was already ensconced in the best chair, taking enormous bites from a buttered slice of warm zucchini bread.

"I did great with the baking," he said. "If I do say so myself."

I looked at the table and saw that he'd made two loaves. The butter was out and so were the small plates and knives. I gave him a grateful look. He had come so far from when he first moved in.

"How'd the mule catching go?" he asked.

I pretended I didn't hear and instead showed Mrs. Spratt where to sit.

"That mule of yours can sure move," said Brady. "Gassy, too."

"He's obviously real fond of Prudence," said Portia. "I could sense the affection when he tried to kick her head off her shoulders."

"Well, not everyone's on the same psychic wavelength as Mr.—" Seth cast a glance at Mrs. Spratt and caught himself. "Uh, people who are good with mules."

I shot Seth another grateful glance. The point was to build our relationship with each of Sara's parents so that they'd agree to allow Sara to come back or at least visit. If neither of them knew the other was coming around, that was probably for the best right now.

"Okay," I said, when they all had tea or coffee and a slice of zucchini bread. "Today, our writing prompt is fear. We all feel it from time to time—"

"My husband sure as shit felt it when I caught him with that guttersnipe out back of the Black Bear Pub," muttered Portia.

"—and we all respond to it. They say two of the main sources of creativity are fear and love."

"Plus hate," said Portia. "Hate's big, too. I got nearly nine hundred pages of hate right here."

She'd brought along the complete manuscript for her divorce

memoir, which she pulls around in a rolling case to save her back.

"I'm more of a love writer, myself," said Brady.

Orson and Winston had come in and sat down without saying hello to anyone.

"Dad," said Winston. "Did you bring anything for me to eat? I think I'm experiencing a drop in my blood sugar."

Orson started rustling around in a Winston-oriented duffle bag he carries everywhere. He pulled out an organic juice box and an egg salad sandwich, which announced itself in a sulfurous cloud of stench as soon as he pulled off the plastic film.

I steeled myself. Winston is a messy and noisy eater. He chews his way through every workshop like a pig snuffling for truffles. His father says it's because Winston is so intellectual that he burns more calories than the average person. My guess is that the boy is simply a glutton. Not that I'd risk a lawsuit by saying that.

I tried to ignore the wet smacking sounds Winston made with his sandwich, but Seth, who has nothing to lose in the event of a lawsuit, stared and made wincing faces at each new slurp.

"Before we talk about our works-in-progress, I'd like you to write about something that scares you," I said.

"You going to write about that spotted devil in your pasture?" asked Portia.

"I won't be joining you in this exercise," I said.

I turned over the ten-minute hourglass timer I found at the Salvation Army Thrift Store and watched the assembled writers go through their usual routines.

There's something soothing about watching writers settle into their work. Each has his or her own distinct tics and methods.

Portia leans her head way back and unhinges her jaw, like a young walrus checking the sky for rain. When she starts writing, she does so as though her primary aim is to punish the paper.

Brady stares into the middle distance, his pen poised over his paper. He can sustain this position indefinitely. He usually begins writing a minute or two before time is called, and then when time is up he acts exhausted, as though he's been hammering out the words for hours.

Winston writes on his iPad in between taking bites of whatever food he happens to be eating. He brushes crumbs and bits of egg or whatever else briskly off the device and onto our couch or the floor. The food that gets caught on his shirtfront is eaten later, when he finally notices it. His father pretends to write on his own iPad, though he's really just checking sports scores and reading the paper. The two iPads are networked and Orson occasionally checks what his son has written, nodding with grim satisfaction.

Seth writes like what he is: a person who writes a lot. He bows his head, giving me a good view of the Iron Maiden logo on his hat. Then his fingers fly until time is called.

I'd never seen Sally Spratt write, but she seemed to take to it.

When the sand had run through the glass, I asked the writers to stop.

"Okay," I said. "Remember that you only need to share your writing if you feel comfortable. We're just warming up."

I looked at the faces around the living room. Writing for even a short time can change someone's whole expression. People who were tense when they sat down appear calmer and more relaxed. People who'd been angry seem lighter. Everyone always looks as though they've *done* something, and that is a fine thing.

Brady started.

"Slick and throbbing, he drove his," he said. "That's as far as I got. Man, I'm pretty happy with that."

"Where in god's name is the fear in that?" asked Portia.

Before he could tell us, I asked her to read her exercise.

She read out a piece about how a woman feels just before slamming her husband's head into the side of a Ford F-150.

"Her heart's racing," she said. "Then she drives the shitsmear's head into the quarter panel. It makes a noise like a head hitting a truck."

"That's good," I said. "Lots of specific detail. Winston? What did you write?"

"I wrote about a really annoying prince who gets liquid gold poured on his head by his sister's boyfriend."

"Scary," I said.

"Isn't that what happens to Daenerys's brother in—" started Seth.

"Great!" I said. "That's SO terrific, Winston."

Winston smirked. His father fished out another egg sandwich for him.

"Orson?" I asked, knowing the answer.

"I'll pass," he said.

"Sally?" I said, to Mrs. Spratt.

She cleared her throat. I felt sure she'd pass too, but she blinked her large eyes once and began to read. As she spoke, I felt my jaw drop open. Her writing was lyrical and full of startling imagery. Her sentences were works of art. The sensibility behind it all was sensitive and wildly inventive.

By the time she finished reading her piece, my hand was clutched over my heart. I pulled my lower jaw closed.

"Oh," I said. "That was so good!" I couldn't keep the surprise out of my voice.

Sally's smile was vulnerable.

"Thanks. I just . . . thanks."

"What else have you written?"

"I've been working on a story. I guess it's sort of a novel . . ." Her voice trailed off.

It had been so long since I'd heard writing that good that I was disoriented. True talent has that effect, I find. It's so unexpected and undeniable. Like a poltergeist in the room.

Most of the other Pens hadn't noticed Sally Spratt's eloquence. Portia was texting furiously. All of Portia's communications were furious. Orson and Winston stared at their iPads. Brady stared at his page.

Only Seth had twigged to the fact that something extraordinary had occurred.

"Holy shit, that was seriously excellent," he said, half admiring, half accusing. "You Spratts are full of surprising talents."

I glared at him and he again remembered himself.

"You know how Sara's good at so many things. Not just chickens but all kinds of stuff."

The quizzical look left Mrs. Spratt's face.

I could understand Seth's feelings. Extremely fine writing was a new thing in our group. I wanted to talk about what made what she'd read so good but didn't want to break the spell. Instead, I let the moment linger.

"Thank you, Sally. Seth?"

"I don't think I want to go after that. Between the two of us, there's apples and oranges, or turds and candies type contrast."

"I'd like to hear it, Seth," said Brady. "Your stuff's always lively."

I wasn't so sure I wanted to hear what Seth had written, but it was true he had a distinctive voice and was capable of lively turns of phrase, even if he was a little too dependent on curse words to get his point across. I nodded at him to go ahead. You have to treat people as though you have confidence in them, even if you don't. That's how you build self-esteem and competence.

Seth exhaled noisily at his computer screen. The brim of his Iron Maiden hat hid his face.

The room around us was cozy in the lamplight. Outside, day had slid into dark and through the window I could see a single light on in Earl's cabin, a firefly resting on the window. Lucky and Bertie would be having their evening feed of hay under the tarp. Soon the barn would be up and they'd be tucked as neatly away as Earl. Woefield Farm was getting organized. For some people, beauty is all. For me, it's organization. Order and efficiency. Self-reliance. We'd convince the Spratts to change their minds. We'd be complete again.

A strange peace rose in me and floated up to include the assembled writers.

Then Seth began to read. "Of the many, many things that currently scare me, the number one item would have to be bugs. Specifically, bedbugs." As he spoke, he scratched himself. First his forearm. Then his neck.

He suddenly had the sharp attention of everyone in the room. My feeling of well-being evaporated.

"People may not realize it, but bedbugs are tremendously difficult to eradicate. An infestation is wildly expensive to treat. A bedbug can live for two years without taking a blood meal. Two *fucking* years!"

He gave a twitchy shrug inside his jean jacket as though there were at least twenty bedbugs on his body at that exact moment.

The Mighty Pens began to shift in their seats.

"The funny thing is that bedbugs aren't dangerous to your health. But they are revolting nonetheless, as well as psychologically devastating. And itchy. Some people even develop a form of post-traumatic stress and chronic insomnia. Scary fact: at least fifty percent of people don't react to the bites. So you could have them and you might not even know."

He scratched at one of his ankles. So, seemingly without being aware, did Portia, who was gazing at him like he'd just thrown up his dinner on the floor and begun to eat it again. The others had begun to inspect themselves and their seats and the space around them.

"I think of my life as PBB and PoBB. Pre-bedbug and post-bedbug."

"Seth," I interrupted. "You can stop saying *bedbugs*. It's getting repetitive." I tried to laugh, even though once the words were out of my mouth, I knew I'd just made the situation worse.

"Dad!" wailed Winston. "This place has bedbugs!"

"We'll sue," said his father. "If I find one bite on Winston, we'll sue this place to the ground."

Seth was too gripped by his subject to sense the unease rippling through his audience.

Only Sally didn't fidget. I could see that she was missing no detail. The woman, for all her low energy, was a writer. She had that ability to be in a situation and outside it, taking notes. We'd probably end up in some ineffably beautiful Alice Munro–type story about hapless, bankrupt rubes with bedbugs.

I had to put a stop to this.

"Seth." I tried again. "Why are bugs on your mind? Since *we don't have them here*."

In full-on obsessive mode, he ignored me.

"If you call a pest control company for help, you could end up on the bedbug hot list. In other words, everyone will know you have them. If you try to get rid of them yourself, you could end up in a downward spiral of do-nothing pesticides and diatomaceous earth, spending all your online time poring over steamer models and passive traps."

"Oh, I see," I said, casting wildly about for some excuse for his behavior. "You're doing a reprise of the opening of Philip K. Dick's *A Scanner Darkly*, only with bedbugs rather than aphids. Interesting approach."

"Huh?" said Seth.

I'd hoped the literary reference would calm the group, but it was too late. The Pens were gathering their belongings, brushing off the seats of their pants with extra violence, shaking out their books and their pant legs and their purses, rubbing at their sleeves. Some were shaking their heads as though trying to dislodge crawlies from their hair.

Finally, Seth realized what he'd done.

"Oh," he said. "Not us. I mean, we don't have them. I was writing, uh, fiction. Fuck, I'm sorry. Ever since I started reading about them and spending time on Bedbugger.com, I've got this horrible crawling feeling all the time. Once you cross the bedbug barrier and understand the true nature of the menace, there's no going back, psychologically speaking."

"Seth!" I said, my voice a near-shout. "Stop talking. You're scaring people."

"You'll be hearing from our lawyer," said Orson, who I know for a fact acts as his own counsel.

"At least there's one kind of animal they can keep alive around here," muttered Portia. "Come on, Brady."

Brady seemed torn between being creeped out by the thought of an infestation and sorry to cut the lesson short.

"I stayed in a few places in Manila with bedbugs," he said to Portia as they walked out together. "Have you been to the 'Pines?" He pronounced it "peens."

I didn't get to hear her answer. I was too busy trying to process what had just happened.

Sally rose reluctantly. "Thanks," she said. "That was very interesting."

I wanted to rush after everyone and assure them that Seth was just having a relapse into alcoholism. We did not have bedbugs. How could we? We didn't travel and rarely had visitors. I always cleaned and inspected my thrift store finds before bringing them in the house. The only way we could get infested would be if one of the Mighty Pens brought them in. But everything I said was going to sound like an excuse. Plus, there was Sally and her strangely luminous work to consider.

I have numerous mottos, most of which I can't remember lately. But one I have not forgotten is "Always follow the productive thread."

I put my hand on her shoulder before she stepped off the porch.

"Sally, I'd be happy to read your novel, when it's done. I know some people in publishing in New York."

"Really?" she said. "You'd do that?"

"I'm very interested. And if what you read is any indication, you're really, really talented. Marvelous voice."

She wrinkled up her nose, which made me laugh.

"Will you get bedbugs on my manuscript?"

"Oh, dude," said Seth, who'd followed us out. "No. We don't have them. I just know someone who does. Who might. And I have to treat . . . Never mind. Sorry if I gave everyone the wrong impression."

"I would infest everything I own with bedbugs if I thought it would get me published," said Sally Spratt with an unexpected but welcome spirit.

"That shouldn't be necessary. We don't have them." A thought occurred to me. "Sara was never exposed to anything like that."

"Good to hear. I'm getting close to finishing my novel," she said. "With this encouragement, I'm even more energized." She grinned at me and the smile turned her face young. "This was really fun. I'm glad you invited me. It's such a relief to be around people who understand what it's like to be completely consumed by writing."

I didn't understand, actually. Back when I was working on my novel, I wrote enough each day to make sure the book was done on time. I added all the elements books are supposed to have. And that was it. For me, writing was like baking cookies, but without the deliciousness at the end.

Seth stood behind me and watched as Sally walked to her old car.

"Bye!" he called.

She waved, got in and drove off.

After everyone was gone, I found myself back in the kitchen and trying to see through the now-familiar cloud of exhaustion. There were things left to do: I needed to give Seth hell for scaring off my writers. I needed to find out where his phobia was coming from. I needed to take extra thyroid remedy because stress had obviously reduced the effectiveness of the dose I'd taken that morning. But first, I needed to take a short nap. Who was I kidding? I had no idea how long my nap would be.

Earl

Prudence went at dinner tonight like a squirrel who just found a hundred-pound bag of peanuts. She come downstairs and right away she was going in so many directions at once it was enough to make your head spin. Even though there was just me and her and Seth for dinner, she made enough food for the Russian army after Stalingrad, which I just saw a TV program about. Helluva thing, that. Helluva thing.

I heard her on the phone, inviting Eugene, but he must have had some veterinary emergencies, because he couldn't join us. We had fresh corn and squash and kale and scalloped potatoes and kale and something else with kale. She even let us have some cheese on the taters and kale, which was a nice change from not ever having cheese. I figure dairy is the only thing standing between me and a half-dozen broken bones. I'm not a young man anymore, so I keep a big block of Superstore orange cheddar in the cabin, just to make sure my bones is taken care of.

She said she felt bad that she forgot about Canadian Thanksgiving and so she was making up for it with a special "late gratitude" meal. Getting moving like that seemed to light a fire under her, because now she's on me and Seth about Halloween, which is coming up soon, and even Christmas, if you can believe it. Who the hell wants anything to do with Halloween? I'd like to know. Well, the answer is Prudence.

I told Prudence I couldn't do much Halloweening and I was going to tell her it was because I had my hands full with tracking down that little bastard she hired to build our barn, but Seth interrupted me and shook his head like I should say nothing about that. So I said I had some shows I liked to watch.

She said she was sorry I preferred TV to life but that she has to dedicate due to compromising health. Well, shit, I said, because I didn't understand what she was getting at.

She said we had to pull out the stops, whatever the hell that means, and turn that rotten old shack at the end of the driveway into a Halloween attraction that would make everyone sit up and take notice.

So I said, Jesus Christ, you must be jokin'. Parents won't let their kids anywhere near that thing unless they're trying to get rid of them. Prudence said nonsense, that we'd decorate it to the ninth degree and hand out candy to kids and give their parents cards for the farm. She said it was branding and it would make a good impression on Mr. and Mrs. Spratt and on the whole neighborhood.

Then she said if I didn't want to help decorate the shack, maybe we could turn my cabin into a haunted house. I said no goddamned way I was having no strange kids in my cabin. I already had Seth in there with his bug steamers and dust bottles and dope.

She said, Dope? Is Seth using drugs?

No, I told her. I mean bug dope.

Earl, do you have bedbugs? she asked me.

Honest to god, talking to Prudence and Seth is enough to give a headless man one of them migrainers.

No, I told her. I don't got bugs. Seth said he was practicing for his new business.

And she said it was high time he got a job, especially now that he scared off her writers.

She said we'd all have to pull together and make the holidays count. So I went down to the end of the driveway to see what we could do with it. I was halfway there when I saw something that give me a start. There was Old Man Spratt long-lining that mule of ours up and down the pasture. The two of them looked straight out of one of them animal training videos Sara used to make us watch. Lucky was harnessed and Old Man Spratt walked behind him, calm as you please. He pulled on one rein and that mule turned one way, and he pulled the other and by god that mule turned the other way. When Spratt clucked at him, Lucky picked up to a trot, the whole thing slicker'n snot from a fifth grader's nose.

Beside me, Prudence nearly had a catastrophe, she was so excited. She hopped up and down at the sight of that renegade mule being driven by a bad-tempered cab driver in lady's rubber boots.

You know what this means? she says to me.

I said, Yeah. Means that mule was already broke for driving.

This means Lucky can pull a cart at Christmas, she says.

Not unless you got a whole shitload of insurance, I told her. My name is on this place now.

We'll start with the Halloween party at the farm stand. That will be mostly for branding and community relations. Then we'll blow everyone out of the water at Christmas with mule rides around Cedar. That will be the real revenue-generator. This farm is going to become an integral part of the holiday experience on Vancouver Island!

I didn't understand half of what she said. I'm not even sure it made sense.

She went to stand against the white tape fence until Spratt finished his teaching lesson, though the mule didn't seem to need much instruction. I knew she'd have a hundred questions for Old Man Spratt, which I was happy not to hear. I know how Prudence can be when she starts in with the questions.

I went down to the end of the driveway and took a real close look at that shack.

The shack still looked like a disgrace in three languages, but not as bad as I remembered. And them baskets of little kales was still alive, which was a surprise.

I'd tell Sara about the farm stand and the Halloween party in my next note. Me and her had a communication system going. Every few days, she'd leave a note for me in the chicken coop and the next day I'd leave her one back.

Hers were the goddamnedest things. She told me she was getting As in her classes, which didn't surprise me. She said her little friend Target liked her birds too, and that she was going to her Poultry Club Halloween party in a Leghorn costume. I get the biggest kick out of that kid. Sounds like she's doing fine, so I don't let on about things here that might worry her, such as that Prudence is still sleeping all the time and Seth is acting even stranger than usual. And I sure didn't tell her that someone stole the barn money. She asks about that barn every time she writes. She's real thoughtful that way.

I'm just glad she's okay living with her parents. It's ironical, in a way. Them two is around here all the time, but they won't let us see her. Sure as hell wish it was the other way around.

Sara

I know leaders don't complain, but Esme and Fran said it's not good to keep things inside because secrets and bad feelings can cause just as much inflammation as sitting, so here are some of the things that I'm not enjoying right now:

Staying in the car, alone, when my mom goes out at night, which she has for the past two nights. She doesn't even try to take us to the house to see if the realtor is there.

Getting yelled at by one of my teachers for getting up every twenty minutes because I'm trying to prevent inflammation.

Not spending enough time with my birds.

Too much rain.

Not having enough baths because of staying in the car.

My mom tries to make it nice—the car, I mean. But it's not. I can't sleep when she goes out with her headlamp on. I don't know where she goes. When she comes back, usually around three or so, I finally fall asleep. But we have to get up early to go to our old house to have showers and get dressed and then my mom needs enough time to clean the bathroom again.

Today, we both slept in. It was after seven when the campground attendant knocked on the driver's window.

"Everything okay?" he asked.

My mom, who is getting skinnier every day, woke up and rolled down the window.

"Yes?" she said.

"You sure this is the best place for a kid?" He wasn't being mean. I think he felt sorry for us. Personally, I think most people would feel sorry for us.

"We were just too pooped last night to put up the tent," she said. "But we had a nice fire and s'mores and everything. Just a little mother-daughter getaway."

It was strange to hear my mom lie like that. Maybe she thought Oreos were s'mores. They are sort of similar, when you think about it.

My mom's probably very tired from hardly sleeping at night, even though lately she's in a way better mood and doesn't cry as much. Yesterday, when I went to meet her after her work, she was already outside and asleep in the car with her journal in her lap, even though she doesn't officially get off until five and I got there at quarter to.

Because of waking up late today, Mom said we didn't have time to go by the old house before school, because the real estate agent might be showing it to people. I doubted that. The house has been for sale for two months and no one's bought it yet. My dad said he doesn't care when it sells because there's no equity in it. He wanted to rent it out to cover the mortgage, but the strata board said no. They also said I couldn't keep my chickens at home. I wouldn't rec-ommend stratas to anyone.

By the time me and my mom brushed our teeth using water in a coffee cup from a tap a few sites down, it was almost seven-thirty. My mom told me I was going to have to get ready at school. I didn't want to do that. It was extremely foggy outside and we were the only people in that part of the campground. My hands and feet felt cold and my nose was running. My mom went through my things and put a hairbrush and some clothes in my backpack. When I told her that left no room for my books, she put my homework in plastic grocery bags.

I wanted to tell her that I couldn't go to school with my books in plastic grocery bags. Nobody carries their books in grocery bags. The plastic isn't strong enough and there are other problems with it, too, such as it looks bad.

I was starting to realize that things were really not good in my home life and I tried to think of who I could tell. I drew on all my Jr. Poultry Club leadership training but it didn't help. I couldn't tell Pete the social worker, because he didn't listen and made things worse. I couldn't tell my dad, because he'd be mad at my mom for moving us to a campground. I wondered about saying something to Esme and Fran, but I didn't know them very well, and if I got taken from my parents they probably only had room for one foster kid. I just wanted to go back to Woefield and Prudence and Seth and Earl so I could have a normal bedroom and get up early to feed my birds and do some chores and go to school with just books in my backpack and have people to do fun farm things with.

The other thing is that it was extremely embarrassing to have a mother who went out at night and left me in a car in a campground, even though we have a house to go to. That was not something I wanted to tell anyone. When we still lived with my dad, my mom sometimes spent hours in the car, parked in the driveway. She said her car time gave her stress relief from their fighting. But now I had to be in the car with her and sometimes *instead* of her and that was worse. Seth once told me that my mom tries hard but her and my dad's bad relationship is probably the reason I have so much stomach trouble. He said I had to watch out for internalizing their problems. He said I'm a complete champion. Thinking about Seth made me feel like crying.

"I think we'll switch campgrounds tonight," said my mom, when we pulled away from the campground, which was almost empty because it's only camping season for a few old people who live in their RVs and some fishermen.

I wanted to ask if we could go stay with my aunt again. My aunt would not like my mom making us stay in campgrounds, but once my mom decides to leave someone, she does it. She left my aunt just like she left my dad. I wouldn't mind if she left me if that meant I could go back to Woefield. I felt bad for thinking that, so I ended up not asking if we could go back to my aunt's.

I also didn't point out that she forgot to give me breakfast again, because then she'd feel guilty.

When I got to school, I tucked the plastic bags tight around my books like I was trying to keep them dry. Other kids got out of their parents' cars and trucks and I felt jealous knowing they didn't have to sleep in their vehicles the night before. I'm feeling jealous a lot lately. I never used to be that way because my self-esteem was excellent from Jr. Poultry Club. It's surprising how fast self-esteem can get ruined!

"Bye, Sara," said my mom, and I waved.

One interesting thing about my mom is that she looks sort of the same whether she sleeps in the car or not.

It was even foggier at school than it was at our campsite, sort of like the ground was being smothered by the sky. I kept my head down and went straight inside to the first washroom. My mom hasn't been in school for a very long time. She probably thinks that the school bathrooms are like the ones at the aquatic center, but they aren't. The toilet takes up most of the space in the cubicles and the toilets don't have covers, so it's extremely risky to get changed in there. Also, there are girls who hang out in the bathroom who aren't very nice.

I just couldn't do it. I couldn't get changed in the bathroom with the open toilet. I hoped my pajama bottoms looked like track pants, but I knew they didn't because they had snowmen on them and were fleecy.

When I walked in, two of the bathroom girls were in there doing stuff to their hair in front of the mirror. The first one looked over at me and wrinkled her nose.

"Something stinks," she said. "And it's wearing pajamas to school on a non-sleepwear day."

"Personal grooming much?" said her friend.

Girls like them usually never notice me, but they could probably sense my weakness. The same thing happens when people keep wolves or wolf crosses as pets. I read about it in an animal behavior book. A wolf will act like a dog and be nice to its owner until the owner gets a limp or the flu or something. Then the wolf will turn on its owner and attack her or him. This is one reason that wolves are not good pets.

My new self-esteem problems were my weakness. I don't know what wolf owners do when their wolves attack them, but when a chicken gets sick, I isolate it for its own safety. I turned and left and tried to think of a good place to isolate myself.

There is a special bathroom for guests and special needs students in the nurse's office, so I went there. It only fits one person and has a lock and everything. It would be a good place to get some isolation.

Miss Singer was in the nurse's office with Donald Fisker. He's a volunteer firefighter and paramedic who is in teacher school and is volunteering as a nurse and school helper to get experience. I guess he can't decide what he wants to be.

"Can I use the special bathroom?" I asked.

Mr. Fisker makes jokes about everything. His jokes are not that funny, but they make him happy. I could see that he was going to make a joke, but Miss Singer looked at me and then put her hand on his shoulder to stop him.

"Of course, Sara. I'll let you in," she said. Her voice was nice.

For the second time that morning, I wanted to cry. When everything is hard and you are tired, if someone is nice it makes you feel like crying.

I spent a long time in the special bathroom. I washed my face and brushed my hair, which was getting long because no one was cutting it, and put it in a ponytail. I changed my clothes and put the old ones in the plastic bag. I put my schoolbooks in my backpack.

Part of me wanted to lie on the bathroom floor and go to sleep. But it was still a bathroom floor and that wouldn't have been hygienic.

The first bell went and Miss Singer called my name from the other side of the door.

"Sara?" she said. "Everything okay in there?"

I said it was.

She asked if I was ready to come out and I said I was.

"Are you sure you're okay?" she asked again. Then I really started crying, even though I actually was okay right then, and she brought me into the nurse's room and asked Mr. Fisker to go and start her class.

Miss Singer asked what was wrong and I told her nothing.

"Is your stomach okay?" she asked. All the teachers have to know about my stomach condition because of my medication.

"I'm just tired," I told her.

"Why?"

I was also hungry, but I didn't say that because it was embarrassing. Part of me wanted to tell her about staying in the car, but something stopped me. A kid with extremely excellent leadership would tell, but I just couldn't. I had to leave the farm even though what Charles did wasn't my fault. What if I got taken from my parents, who are not very good at child care but are better than no one? It would be okay, I guess, if I went somewhere very nice like Fran and Esme's, but what if I went somewhere that had mean people and no place for my birds and maybe not even a yard for gardening?

"I don't know," I said.

"Maybe you should see a doctor," said Miss Singer. "I'll mention it to your mom."

"She's at work," I said, even though I wasn't sure she was. She didn't have her work clothes on when she dropped me off. If my mom lost her job, that would be another thing I couldn't tell anyone.

"How about you lie down for a short sleep? I'll come and check on you after one hour. If you feel up to it before then, join us in class. Mr. Fisker will be in the next room with Ms. Ouillette. They are putting together the health library."

I didn't want to lie down, but I thought it would probably be good for me to get some sleep in case we stayed in the car again tonight. I needed to get extra energy for car nights because they were quite stressful.

So I lay down under the little red blanket on the little bed. Some kid must have gotten sick on it, because it smelled like old barf, but I didn't mind. I liked hearing Mr. Fisker and Ms. Ouillette whisper as they sorted books. I was very surprised when Miss Singer woke me up and told me I'd been asleep for two hours.

The rest of the school day was fine. We had Art and Science, which are two of my favorite subjects. Miss Singer gave me my homework for Geometry and Math, which are also my favorites.

I knew I could do my homework in the big library downtown that night. The library is relaxing and warm and has an excellent selection of books. It's good that we go there every night, because there's no desk in our old house anymore and it's too dark to read in the car, even though my mom got me some little LED lights at the Dollarama. She got herself a nice LED headlamp from the camping store and we went to a bookstore and she got herself three fancy new journals to write in. Now when we go to the library, she types stuff from her journal into their computers and saves it on a thumb drive. It's nice that she has a hobby, but I think it would be better if she found one that gave her more exercise.

When me and Target left school that afternoon, I was feeling much better. A few more nights and I could go back to stay with my dad. My schedule is unusual, even for someone whose parents are divorced, but I know from leadership training that people can get used to anything if they try to be adaptable, which is similar to being flexible.

I worry that Target isn't adaptable. He's very quiet, even though he has such nice foster moms. I asked him why he didn't go home right away after school to play with the exercise balls and the climbing wall and have healthy green drinks with Fran and Esme. He said he liked to watch my dad train the mule. That's probably not true. I think Target just finds it relaxing to be around me because I'm his friend. He doesn't know that my mom makes us sleep in the car, but I think he can sense that I have problems in the same way the fancy-hair girls at school can sense it, only my problems make him feel nicer toward me. Target is the opposite of a pet wolf. He's more like a pet deer.

I was telling him that my dad was teaching Lucky to drive and he didn't know what that meant. So I explained that when horses and oxen and mules and donkeys are tied to a cart or a wagon and they pull it, that's called driving.

"Should be called towing," he said.

"Target!" I said. "You made a joke! That's so great." I didn't point out that his joke wasn't all that great, because people have to start somewhere.

Target smiled and looked at the ground.

Man, that was such a good moment. The day got even better when we got to the farm stand and I found Earl's note. He never says very much but I always know exactly what he means.

Prudence

I'm pleased to report that my head is clearing nicely, if not quickly. I slept for most of the past two days and that seems to have done me wonders. I'll have to tell Dr. Bachmeier that the medication is finally working. Now that I'm on the mend, I absolutely have to get some traction on the Sara problem. I thought I was being so brilliant involving her parents in farm life, but now I feel like I'm juggling two incendiary devices. We have to make sure their paths don't cross and that they don't feel pressured or manipulated. Plus, I underestimated their mutual dislike.

I began by broaching the subject with Sally Spratt when she stopped by to say she hoped the manuscript was going to be finished soon. She said that to be "on the safe side," she wanted to wait for the social worker's report. She didn't want to leave her husband "any openings."

So I called the social work office and left a message asking when Pete would be available to interview us. I told him that we were having a family-friendly community Halloween event and that he should drop by. I hoped that if Mr. or Mrs. Spratt showed up, they wouldn't do so at the same time. And although I'm not religious, I also prayed that one of them might bring Sara by so we could see her.

In addition to the Halloween event, I've made an excellent plan for Christmas. We will have Lucky pull a wagonload of people around Cedar to various attractions. We'll call it the Cedar Christmas Mule Tour. Can you imagine anything more delightful? People will buy a ticket and get a ride to a place selling bottled cider, then to one selling candy apples. We will drop wagon customers at the afternoon showing of the Yellow Point Christmas Music Revue, the local musical production, which I'm told is terrific entertainment. When the customers have visited all the holiday hot spots, we'll drop them off and pick up another batch for evening shopping.

I think most people would be willing to pay top dollar to be driven around town in a cart pulled by a spotted mule. We'll probably make him a festive outfit. I am so excited about the concept that I can barely contain myself. A shower is in order so I can feel even more refreshed.

* * *

Post-shower, I got dressed and went downstairs, just like in the old days. At the kitchen table, I made a long list of people to contact about the Cedar Christmas Mule Tour. The McHales, who have the beautiful corn maze, and the McGuires, who have an apple orchard. We could get Jimmy Samuels, who runs the fish hatchery for the band, involved. People on the mule ride would probably love to see the smolts or whatever they have down there at the hatchery.

I'd invite all the local artisans to take part: the potters and the painters and the woodworkers. Cedar is full of artistic talent. Then there are all the merchants in downtown Cedar. The possibilities are endless.

I called Eustace to share the great news. He'd been so busy since the other vet closed up shop and keeping on top of the strangles outbreak, I'd hardly seen him at all. He was talking about bringing in another vet to help him, but in the meantime, he was working nonstop. That meant that he was mostly too busy to come by. He still called a few times a day, but it was mostly to offer suggestions for what I should do, and so I was forced to tell him to mind his own business, in a nice way. Still, I missed him terribly. Sure that he'd be busy on a call, I was surprised when he answered his phone and immediately asked if he could come over.

Ten minutes later, his truck pulled up outside.

He stomped up the front stairs and, when I opened the front door, his wide-shouldered body filled the doorway.

"Sorry," he said. "I promise I wasn't driving up and down the road out front waiting for you to call. The Genovas' goat had an accident."

"Is it okay?"

"It'll live, but the car it fell onto won't. Or rather, the car it fell *into*."

I waited for him to explain.

"You know that old Ford Ranger Mr. Genova drives? Well, their goat likes to stand on the roof. Their daughter came home from Vancouver, driving her new soft top convertible, and the goat decided to try it out. Took three of us to get him out of the front seat. The seats will never be the same and the roof is now ventilated. But the goat's fine."

I love Eustace's stories about his work and not just because they remind me that most people who have farm animals seem to operate from a base level of incompetence.

"You look good," I told him. It was true. All six-plus feet of him seemed to radiate strength and good health.

"I got most of the half-chewed car seat out of my hair," he said, noticing me staring at his curls. "The goat kept hacking up bits of upholstery onto my head when I was doing my Jaws of Life routine."

There is almost no way to talk about someone like Eustace without lapsing into romantic clichés. Tall, handsome, competent. Vet. It was too much. He was ridiculous. The way I felt about him was ridiculous, even if I did feel smothered from time to time.

We walked into the kitchen and I could sense him watching me as I made us tea.

"You too," he said. "I mean, you look good too. A little bedridden, but good."

Insert dead metaphor about a prickle of heat sliding up my body. All I wanted to do was lead him to the bedroom. My hips felt loose, my legs unsteady. Eustace always had that effect on me. Between his sexiness and his helpfulness, Eustace sometimes felt like a bearskin wrapping around my body and sometimes like a bear trap shutting around my torso. But that feeling, I reminded myself as I carried the tea to the table, was my problem. Not his.

"How are you feeling?" he asked.

"Good. Almost better."

"You been to see a proper doctor yet?"

The only thing that keeps my beautiful boyfriend from being perfect is his tendency to be bossy, conservative, reactionary and unsustainable. Even so, I wanted him. Always.

"It's really good to see you," I said.

He didn't smile back and I felt robbed. Eustace has gorgeous teeth.

Usually, when we sit together at the table he has trouble keeping his hands off me. He's always reaching over to rub my forearm, which drives me crazy. Or he stretches a long leg over and nudges my foot or my leg. Which drives me equally crazy.

Our kitchen table visits always end up in the bedroom.

My thyroid condition has had a dampening effect on my libido, but Eustace was bringing it back to life.

Earl was in his cabin. Seth was out somewhere. The timing was perfect.

I was just about to go to him and sit in his lap, the way he liked, when he began to speak. His words sounded like they'd been practiced a few times.

"Prudence," he said. "I've been thinking. In order for us to have a real chance to develop an equal partnership based on respect, I need to let you find your way, just like you keep asking me to do."

I waited, not liking the direction of the conversation.

"You've told me a hundred times that you are in charge of this farm. That you can handle things here by yourself. That I need to stop interfering. Stop criticizing. Things are hard right now with everyone missing Sara, and with your illness. It's hard for me to sit back and not help. But it's disrespectful of me not to trust you to handle these problems."

"Well," I said. "I wouldn't say that, exactly."

"I've been talking to a few people and it's been pointed out to me that I'm too attached. A *lot* too attached. I need to get my needs met on my own."

I leaned forward to stare into his beautiful, troubled face.

"What needs?"

"Emotional ones," he said. "You aren't responsible for me."

My mouth was hanging open. I closed it and tried to think of something to say.

"You are right to set boundaries with me," he said.

"I don't want boundaries," I said. "I mean, I do. But not big ones. How about porous boundaries? Can we try some of those? You've been working too much. Is that what this is about? I'm sorry I've told you to mind your own business. The Hashimoto's has made me testy."

He ignored my words. "Right now, for instance, I want you so bad I'm half-sick with it. I need to learn to interact with you as a friend and as an equal."

Finally I croaked that we could have sex as equals.

"No," he said. "Sex is just going to confuse things. We need to learn to talk. The more I do for you, the more we have sex, the more I want to do for you, the more I want to lose myself in sex with you."

His grin finally appeared and I nearly fell over from the perfection of it.

"This is going to be hard. Because I really, really want to be with you. To help you. Build you a new barn and fix your truck and weed your raised beds. Top up your RRSPs. You get the picture."

I swallowed. Oh, I got the picture, alright. It was a picture I missed already.

"I'm going to respect your boundaries," he said. "And we'll be stronger because of it. I'll do my helping from a respectful distance."

My face felt like old wax as I tried to smile.

He got to his feet and came around the table, leaned down and kissed me.

"I love you," he said. "And I think we're going to be stronger for this."

I watched him leave, all long legs in jeans and broad back in green canvas work coat, felt lining showing at the collar and where it had ripped at the shoulder seam.

I sat at the table for a long time.

Seth

I was too shattered at the prospect of dealing with the drama teacher to respond intelligently when Prudence came into my room and asked if I'd been talking to Eustace about boundaries. She must have seen my boundaries worksheets and the books I got from the used store, which I planned to semi-plagiarize for my article for Half Measures.

I was sitting at my desk chair, which I'd rolled over so I could stare out the window at the field in a pensive way.

"Seth," she said, when I shrugged in response to her question. "What's going on with you? Are there bugs in here? Do we need to call a pest control company? It is going to be very difficult for me to make a case to get Sara back here in any sort of regular way if people think we're infested."

She was dressed, which was an unusual thing for her these days. Her sleek brown hair was styled neatly, and her skirt, worn over wool tights, and old pink sweater with an owl knit into the front managed to look practical, warm and cute as hell. But she had on so many socks her runners wouldn't tie up, and dissatisfaction came off her in waves. I could understand. If anyone is familiar with dissatisfaction, disappointment and most every other kind of dis, it's me.

"Are you okay?" she repeated. "Because to get this farm straightened out, we need you to be okay."

"Are *you* okay?" I said, sounding like a whiny preteen.

She sighed. "I'm getting there. We have had a difficult fall. Some serious reversals of fortune. Mistakes have been made but we need to keep our attitudes positive."

Prudence sat in my Director of Rock chair and leaned forward. She used to have skin like fresh ivory paint. But now her face had a yellow-gray tint.

"Seriously, Prudence," I said. "You should go see a regular doctor."

"Dr. Bachmeier *is* a medical doctor. And a doctor of traditional Chinese medicine. A certified naturopath and acupuncturist as well as an ordained monk, though I can't remember from what order. That's why I know that she's going to get me sorted."

"You sure you're not just defying Eustace?" I asked. Prudence, like a lot of people, is not in love with being told what to do.

"Of course not. I'm doing what's best for my health. Was it you who told him to boundary me?"

"No."

"Then why is he doing this? Is AA telling him to boundary me?"

"*Boundary* is not a verb. And AA is not a coherent organization. It's mostly just a bunch of suggestions that hardly anyone follows, except for the one about not getting loaded. None of the suggestions are about boundaries. The only reason people in AA talk about boundaries all the time is because hardly anybody has any. We're all trying to work it out. Including Eustace."

"Why don't you have boundaries?"

"To be honest, I don't even know. I'm supposed to be writing an article about boundaries and the concept is a complete mystery. That's probably all Eustace is trying to do: develop an understanding of the concept. After all, you have told him to let you figure it out on your own about a thousand times."

"He's a good man," she muttered. "A really good man."

I stared at her.

"Several of my friends in New York had bedbugs in their apartments. They're a pain, for sure, but they aren't dangerous. We'll find the money to treat the problem. But if you have them in your room, they might spread. That means they'll be more expensive to treat. The key is to get on top of the problem before it escalates."

Now this was the Prudence I knew. Direct. Practical.

But as soon as she stopped speaking, her eyes started to close.

"Halloween stand," she said, drowsily.

"Pru? Are you on something? Seriously. You don't seem right. It's gotten worse since Sara left."

"That girl took a big part of this farm's soul with her," she said. "I better get back to my room." She held out an arm and I got up and helped her to her feet.

"Don't worry about anything Eustace says. He's as codependent as ever. Completely ass over teakettle in love with you. Even when you're a mess, like you are now."

I deposited her on her bed. Her room was like her: neat and thoughtful. Rows of hardback books about growing things and building things. Clothes in clean colors put neatly away. Shoes lined up on a rag rug. Cool little details, like the row of small mismatched vintage vases with a single leaf or flower in each. But the flowers and leaves were wilted and the inch of remaining water thick with sludge. The quilt that covered her bed was bunched up in the middle of the wrinkled sheets. I'd never seen Prudence's bed unmade during the day.

She slid under the covers with all her clothes and her shoes on.

"Do you want to take those off?" I asked, and pointed to her feet.

She moved them out from under the covers and I pulled her shoes off.

"Can I borrow one of your boundary books?" she asked.

I went down the narrow stairs to the living room, where I paused to look around. It had changed so much since I moved in. Prudence had hung framed paintings and prints that she'd begun collecting from local artists, and a few pieces of art she'd brought with her from New York. Colorful blankets covered the armrests and backs of old couches and chairs. There were antique lamps and old area rugs. The room smelled like beeswax candles and wood soap. The windows were covered in simple curtains in some kind of soft green embroidered material.

When I first moved over here from my mom's place across the street, the house, and the living room in particular, had the unmistakable air of a house in which an old man had slowly checked out of life. Its signature scent was stale pizza, cheap coffee and cheaper gin. All the sheets in the place smelled like they'd been moldering in a garbage bag for years. The pillows were few, flat, and greasy from age and use. Prudence had had us paint and clean and refinish, and she'd found lamps and rugs and furniture from second-hand stores and Craigslist. She'd splashed out on new sheets and towels, and now the whole house was comfortable and attractive but not fussy. The transformation was amazing. It was maybe not so surprising that Prudence had exhausted herself and her thyroid gland.

I picked up two boundary books from the stack on the coffee table in front of the couch. I chose the smallest ones because I figured the simpler, the better, given Prudence's condition.

When I got back upstairs, she was sitting up with her feet hanging over the side of the bed. She was staring at her running shoes like they were a sudoku puzzle she wasn't sure she wanted to tackle.

"I don't want to go back to bed again," she said. "I'm missing everything. I still haven't figured out the Sara situation."

"I'm not sure it's figure-out-able right this minute," I said. I put the books on her nightstand. "It'll all work out. We'll get Sara back. Eustace will stop having boundaries. You'll grow a shitload of vegetables. Be the bionic farmer again."

"You promise?"

I promised and she lay back down and closed her eyes.

I went to my room and got dressed in my work outfit of white jeans, leather jacket and fingerless gloves.

When I got down to the playhouse for the great Halloween Decorate-a-thon, Earl's old truck was parked alongside the pink shack. Maybe Eustace had taken a moment after setting boundaries with Prudence to repair it.

In the bed of the truck lay our sad collection of construction tools and equipment: a hammer, a handsaw, some kind of electric saw that works one time out of five, a level, a package of sandpaper from the 1970s. Like that.

Earl stared at the playhouse, which had not been improved at all by the addition of two unevenly hung pots of infant kale.

Piled at Earl's feet were several shapeless plastic bags from Pattie's Party Palace.

The farmers in that American Gothic painting looked less

250

defeated than Earl in that moment. At least that old farm couple had pitchforks and appeared to know how to use them. Earl held a heavy-duty stapler in one hand and a hammer in the other.

"What's happening?" I asked.

Earl grunted. "Don't know where to start," he said.

"May I suggest a gallon of gas and a match?"

Earl lifted the stapler at me. Must have weighed four pounds.

The craptastic pink playhouse with its ornate scalloping, pointless turrets and general sense of airborne pathogens and unwholesome elves sat at the edge of the property like it had fallen off the set of an unsuccessful Tim Burton movie.

"It's pretty scary the way it is. Maybe we should just leave it," I suggested.

Earl let the big stapler fall to his side.

"Goddamned death trap," said Earl.

Even though the day was bright, I could see the giant TV flickering in my mom's living room across the street. She's a heavy consumer of daytime entertainment. She does her crafts and drinks Superstore pop until about three, at which point she switches to afternoon television and Old Style beer. She moves to rye and Coke after dinner.

"The idea is to get people to come here?" I asked. "To look at this thing?"

"Prudence says we want to build a brand, whatever the hell that is, for the farm and get people coming to us for their fresh vegetables. She even invited the social worker feller so he'll put in a good word with Sara's parents."

Sara's parents should know by now that we are a safe place for her to visit, at least. But neither seemed ready to budge without a report. They were both idiots, as far as I was concerned.

I thought about Prudence's plan. She's a maniac. But she's such an enthusiastic maniac that it takes a person's mind off his own difficulties. Which are numerous, at least in my case.

"Here's an idea: instead of fixing it up, we'll make it even more shitty. What does it remind you of?"

Earl cocked his head, looking even more turkey-esque than usual.

In my pocket, my phone chimed to let me know I had a text. I felt for the button, turned it off and immediately felt better.

"Come on," I said.

"A waste of wood and paint?" said Earl.

"Besides that."

"A fairy house," he said.

"A fairy house! Exactly. But is it a nice fairy house?" I pressed, feeling like a teacher of non-gifted second-graders. "Earl?" I prompted. "Is it a nice fairy house?"

"Hell no," he said.

"That's right. It's a bad fairy house. What we need to do is play up that aspect. In any kind of decor or design, you need to tell a story. This story is going to be scary fairy."

"I never know what the hell you're talking about."

"We'll use it to recreate fairy tales with a twist. Wolves will win. Princesses will stay single. Kids will never get out of their cages. Little pigs will be killed in tragic construction accidents. Prudence wants a Halloween party centered around this eyesore. So we'll make it high-concept. Worth looking at."

Earl had his head cocked even harder. Maybe everyone who lives on a farm, successful or not, eventually starts to look like poultry.

"It's going to be cool," I said. "People love fractured fairy tales."

"I don't know how to do all that," said Earl.

"I'll tell you who knows everything there is to know about making pointless stuff," I said, jerking a thumb in the direction of my mom's house. "People will be lined up to see the Scary Fairy House on Woefield. We'll need major, major candy supplies to deal with the crowds."

Earl looked about half convinced. And for the first time since we lost Sara, I felt useful and nearly happy.

"We need a special guest to give out the candy," I said. "Someone who can fit inside that little shack."

"The little Sprout?" said Earl.

"That's right. Sara's the person for the job."

"She can't. She's got her poultry club party."

I wondered how he knew that. Before I could ask, Eustace pulled up alongside the pink shack. He leaned out the driver's side window of his massive vehicle.

"How's it going?" he asked. "Need any help?"

"Weren't you just here? Setting boundaries with Prudence?"

Eustace turned off the truck and silence returned to the countryside. Several crows cawed noisily from a barren tree at the edge of the property.

"I can't hack it. I've tried. Just now I stayed away for—" he looked at his gleaming hubcap-sized watch—"nearly forty minutes. You people need my help. If I'm not out on a call, I'm here, helping. As much as she'll let me."

"What the hell is he talking about?" Earl asked me.

I shrugged. It would be too hard to explain to someone of Earl's emotional range.

"I feel pointless without Prudence," said Eustace, baldly.

"Hmmm," I said. Because really, what is there to say when a man feels pointless without a woman? Eustace and Prudence would work it out like the ridiculously good-looking, overly hardworking people they were.

"We got to decorate this bastard," said Earl, getting to the point.

"He doesn't mean me," I said. "He's referring to the shack."

I could see Eustace wanting to make a snide comment but holding his tongue. Maybe he'd learned more than he thought during his few hours of setting boundaries.

"Okay. I'm in," he said. And the three of us headed up to the house to plan the Scary Fairy Halloween Farm Stand.

Earl

You never seen anything like the goddamned production around here getting ready for Halloween. First it was me and Eugene and Seth drawing up plans. Eugene had to keep taking breaks to see if Prudence needed anything and tend to sick animals. He must have done a good job looking after Prudence, because the next afternoon she got out of bed and got in on the action.

Seth had covered about ten sheets of paper with sketches that all looked like a jumble of sticks laying this way and that and some blobby circles that was supposed to be blood. I don't have a clue what goes on in Seth's head, and from looking at those drawings that's probably best.

Anyhow, after a half-hour he said he had to go "confarb" with his mom, and that was fine as frog's hair with me because Old Man Spratt come driving up the road, only he wasn't in his taxicab, he was riding passenger in a tow truck with a flatbed on it, and on that flatbed was the sorriest wagon you ever saw.

Prudence came high-tailing it outside, Eugene right behind like a mother duck. By the time I got out there, Prudence had the gate open and that tow truck drove right into the pasture. Anyone else's farm, and that truck would have sunk, tires spinning like ball bearings on fresh ice, but we don't got hardly any dirt on this place.

There was a whole lot of beeping and blinking while the driver unloaded the wagon. When he was done, he got out, stood back, looked at it and said, Good luck with that. Then he drove out again, leaving us staring at the thing. The wagon looked like it was built by the same outfit that made the shack at the end of the driveway. Not up to code is what I'm trying to say.

Seth had come back from his mother's place across the road. He caught my eye and I saw that he was thinking along the same lines, but we didn't say nothing because Prudence was acting like she'd been wanting a dog for ten years and someone finally brung her a Labrador retriever puppy.

A wagon, she kept saying. A chariot! It's just what I'd hoped for. Perfect for my plan.

If her plan was to get some people killed by a mule pulling a cart made of cracked, splintered wood with wheels so worn-out they were practically squares, then she was in luck.

Needs some work, said Old Man Spratt. But I figure it'll do what you're after.

How much do we owe you? asked Prudence.

Spratt said he got a deal on it from a guy who just wanted it out of his barn.

Seth said that was probably because the guy's whole family died in a tragic wagon accident.

Prudence and Eugene told Seth to hush up and call his mother to ask when she planned to deliver the bodies.

I'll say this for Old Man Spratt. He minds his own business. Least-wise, he didn't say nothing about the bodies comment.

By this time, Lucky and Bertie, who'd both run off to the edge of the field when the tow truck come in, had decided it was safe to come close again. They stood right behind Spratt. The big red mule flared his nostrils at the wagon.

Old Man Spratt said, Now Luck, and I swear that mule looked embarrassed. Spratt said he was going to work on the wagon out in the field so that Lucky could get used to it. Once he had the wheels replaced and some other things fixed up, he was going to hook Lucky up to it and start driving him.

Where the hell you going to drive him? I asked. That mule's a runner. Things could get dicey if he had a cartload of people behind him.

We'll start by going around the field, said Spratt.

While Spratt caught Lucky, me and Prudence wandered back down to meet Seth's mother at the shack. She drove her goddamned Tempo across the road and sat in it with the driver's door partway open while Seth unloaded the car. She kept her eyes squinted shut against the smoke leaking out of the cigarette she kept tucked in the corner of her mouth. Seth pulled the most ungodly shit you ever seen out of that vehicle, but I had to admit it looked right for the job. There was dolls made of plastic and dolls made of socks and stuffed animals of every description. There was fake blood and cobwebs and little outfits and you name it.

You have as much stuff as Pattie's Party Palace, said Prudence, who is always full of compliments.

Used to work at Harvey's Halloween Emporium, said Seth's mom.

Must have been when she was a teenager. I've never known her to work and I been living across from her for twenty years.

Oh, this is going to be great, said Prudence. She held up a cardboard box marked "Zomby." I might not be an eleventh-grade English teacher, but even I know that's not how you spell it. *Zombie* ain't one of your harder words.

When Seth had everything out of the car, his mother started the car. Aren't you going to stay? he asked her, and she said she'd come over later. It was a Halloween marathon on TV, and her boyfriend, Bobby, was bringing back chicken wings from Costco.

Prudence made a face.

Seth made a face too, but it was the opposite kind of face.

Can he bring enough for us? said Seth.

You got money? asked his mother, who is not exactly a mollycoddler.

I could see he was about to complain or get into it with his mother and I was thinking I might just pay the woman. Me and Prudence's late uncle Harold used to eat them Costco wings all the time.

Before I could say anything, Prudence piped up and said we don't need any wings. She's got dinner all planned out. She told me and Seth she'd make us soy fingers with her special hot sauce instead.

Me and him exchanged a look because of all the things Prudence feeds us, probably the worst is them pretend chicken fingers. It's like eating rotten erasers. Not only that, she keeps trying to sneak that liquid heartburn she calls hot sauce on everything, even after what happened. She says she cut it with vinegar and some other ingredients so it's not as hot, but you might as well put your ass directly into a tub of ice if you take so much as a bite.

It was obvious from Seth's mother's face, all scrunched up under the stream of cigarette smoke, that she didn't care what the hell we ate.

If you want wings, tell me in the next minute, she said.

We have all we need right here, said Prudence. If these guys don't feel like having soy fingers, maybe I'll have enough energy to make zombie brain for dinner. Get us in the mood for Halloween.

We all looked at her, even Seth's mother, who couldn't wait to get back to her TV.

Baked celery root on a bed of mushrooms and barley, said Prudence.

Yeah? says Seth's mother. I saw that in Jamie Oliver. Looks like shit on a plate. Does it taste good?

I don't know. I only just looked at the recipe in Thrifty's. I've got the book on hold at the library.

Prudence don't buy new books. Just gets 'em out of the library. She's pretty economical for a city woman.

I can loan you mine. Bobby got it for me even though I don't like him bossing me about eating healthy food, said Seth's ma.

Thank you, said Prudence. I'd love to borrow it. This one mentioned that he'd like to learn more about vegetarian cooking. She gave Eugene a playful poke with her finger. He give the rest of us a fake smile.

Then he left and Seth's ma left and the three of us stood there, staring at dolls and crafts and glue guns and Zomby boxes.

Prudence took a long gander at the pink shack.

I've asked a girl from the International High School to hand out the candy. She's the only one I can think of who will fit easily in the playhouse. Her name is Anulka and she's from Cameroon. She's very excited to experience a real North American Halloween.

Also, we need a big sign to advertise our farm stand and the Halloween party. Maybe put a spotlight on it so people can see it in the dark, she said.

You mean for the two people who drive past every night? said Seth.

And let's put the candy in little bags that advertise the farm, for Anulka to hand out. People will find that charming, Prudence said. She put her hands on her hips. And we should put seeds in the bags! To encourage people to do what they can at home.

Absolutely. Seeds. That should be a big hit with the children seeking candy, said Seth.

Prudence was nodding, happy as a clam in love. We'll do the major renovation in the spring. Right now, we'll focus on getting Sara back and the barn built. Those are our top priorities!

She went back up to the house to bed and Seth got to unpacking decorations. I went to write my note for little Sara.

Sara

I had an extremely memorable Halloween.

I was staying with my mom and I wasn't feeling good. Also, a lot of things were going wrong in my life, even things in my life that are normally really fun, like Poultry Club. There's so much to tell that it's probably best just to tell it and not try to explain it too much.

Jr. Poultry Fancier's Club was having a dress-up party after our meeting and then we were going to go trick-or-treating to local farms.

My mom forgot that it was Halloween and about the party. I had to wake her up that morning. We had stayed in our old house on the floor because I told her I might be getting a cold. She said it would be okay for one night. She didn't even blow up her air mattress, but instead she wrote in her journal for most of the night.

After I got up, brushed my teeth and got dressed, I put my foamy and sleeping bag in the car. Then I woke her up.

She looked at me like she didn't know who I was.

"Don't you have to go to work?" I asked.

She shook her head. "Not today," which means she got fired.

"What are you going to do?" I asked.

She sat up. She was wearing her jean-look slacks. They are way too big on her now. She also had on a green dress shirt. It made me sad to think of her going to bed in her clothes.

I didn't say anything, because I didn't want her to think I was being critical. Other kids' mothers didn't wear their clothes to bed and sleep on the floor of their empty houses or in cars in empty campgrounds.

"I've got a lot to do around here," she said, which was true now. The realtor said we might have to repaint inside the house because my mom had washed so much paint off the walls.

"Are you okay to get to school by yourself?" she asked. "I thought I'd do a little more writing this morning."

"I just need my Halloween costume," I said.

I wear the same thing every year. A few years ago, Mr. Lymer's wife, Bonnie, made four Leghorn costumes for kids whose moms don't sew. I'm the only one still wearing mine three years later. Good thing it's one size fits all. I really love it. It's got a lot of very realistic details, such as a red comb and yellow legs.

My mom sighed and put her hands over her face and dragged them down. She probably shouldn't do that, because her wrinkles are getting worse every day from lack of sleep and staying in the car and losing so much weight.

"Do you really have to have it?" she said. "Maybe this year you could go as something else. How about a ghost?" That meant she wanted me to wear a sheet because she was too depressed to find my Leghorn costume in storage. It wasn't fair. Plus, our sheets all had flowers on them, so I'd just look like a sheet!

I started yelling at her even though I didn't mean to. I've never done that before in my whole life. I have an extremely even temperament. Everyone comments on it. But I was screaming that I had to have my Leghorn costume and that she was being mean and that she didn't care about anyone except herself and her stupid journal and she was supposed to be my mother. There was this part of me that felt like I was watching the fight from far away, maybe from the little fort at Woefield. My mother just sat on the floor, still tangled in her sleeping bag, and stared like she had never seen me before.

I was crying and I told her not to bother finding my costume. I told her I'd go to the party without one. Then I grabbed my backpack and left without having a granola bar or anything. Mrs. Mooreland from next door was in her driveway. She is always watching when we come and go, and she's seen us bring our sleeping bags and bedding into the house. She's very nosy. She asked me what was wrong, but I pretended I didn't hear her. I stopped crying at the end of our subdivision cul-de-sac, and by the time I got to school I didn't feel anything at all except for a runny nose, headache and a sore stomach from not eating breakfast.

To be honest, I think my mom might be having a breakdown and that she might be giving me one, too.

Anyway, the school day went okay except for me falling asleep in Math and getting sent to the nurse's office. Mr. Fisker let me nap for a half-hour and Miss Singer came to the nurse's station and left an apple and a Fruit Roll-Up and a box of chocolate milk for me. She's an excellent teacher. I bet she's going to be principal one day.

At lunch, I asked Target if he wanted to come to the Poultry Club Halloween party with me and he said he couldn't because he was going out with his foster moms and his sisters. I asked what he was going as and he said Esme made him a professional wrestler outfit with big muscles and everything. He told me the name of the wrestler, but I didn't know him because I don't know much about wrestling except what I know from reading one of my favorite books of all time, *The Reluctant Journal of Henry K. Larsen*, which is about a kid who has a sad tragedy in his family and who likes wrestling. I usually feel sorry that I don't have any siblings, but if I did, I didn't want them to be extremely tragic ones.

I told Target his costume sounded amazing.

He asked if I wanted to go with them. He said Esme and Fran had lots of de-gendered costumes from when Stephanie and Ariel were younger.

I said I couldn't because I'm really active in Poultry Club and they would be expecting me. I said that even though part of me didn't feel like I was very important to the club anymore. It was hard for me to visit my birds and I didn't live on a farm. I barely even lived in a house anymore. In fact, since I moved away from Woefield, I didn't have very many leadership qualities at all. Also, I didn't know what *de-gendered* meant.

Target seemed kind of excited about Halloween, so I didn't tell him that I didn't have a costume. After meeting his brother, I bet he's had some Halloweens that were not that fun. I wanted him to enjoy this one.

Thinking that actually made me feel better. I used to have caring thoughts like that all the time before the parent-teacher meeting when everything went wrong. In fact, I used to be very interested in problem-solving and helping others. I remembered Seth telling me about the Principle of As If. He said it was one of his main techniques that he used to stop drinking. He said he acted as if it wasn't hard to stay sober. Then he acted as if he didn't hate going out in public. He used As If to make himself do work, which is another of his least favorite things. He said faking bravery was an excellent technique for overcoming fear.

Back when he told me that, I felt bad for him being a grown-up and having to pretend about so many things, but now that I am getting a lot of fears too, I think it's an excellent suggestion. I guess I always had fears, though the doctor said it was anxiety, which I think is different. My anxiety is why I need stomach medication, but I used to be mainly afraid of my parents fighting. I had no idea there were so many ways life could go wrong. There are A LOT of opportunities to act as if!

I decided to act as if I didn't need any help getting ready for Halloween. Instead, after I ate my snack at the nurse's station, I asked Mr. Fisker if he had an extra plain white sheet I could borrow. He said he didn't think so and why did I want one. I said I forgot my Halloween costume and needed to make another one for the party at the Fancier's Club.

He asked what the Fancier's Club was and I told him it was for people who like poultry.

He had a lot of questions about what we did and really seemed impressed with my answers. I acted as if I didn't mind answering all his questions, even though anyone who lives in a rural neighborhood and eats eggs should already know at least the basics about chickens.

Miss Singer came along when we were talking and said she could help me get a costume together after school. She asked how I felt about robots and I said they were okay.

When the bell rang, I met her in the art room and she started pulling things out of the supply cupboard.

She made a robot body out of a big box with holes cut out for my arms and legs. She covered the whole thing with tinfoil and then she glued plastic pieces on it to make buttons and knobs. Miss Singer found another box for my head and made a slit for my eyes. The art teacher, Ms. Ouillette, came in and helped glue tinfoil on the head box, and they asked if I wanted antennae and I said I didn't think robots had antennae. They looked sort of disappointed, so I said antennae would be cool, even though I was supposed to be a robot and not a radio.

I looked at the costume in the mirror and said I wondered if it would be neater if we made the robot into an iPod. I really want an iPod so I can listen to educational podcasts, but my parents say Apple products are too expensive.

Ms. Ouillette looked at her watch and said she had to take her kids out trick-or-treating, but Miss Singer said an iPod was a good idea. Ms. Ouillette told us to have fun and then she left. Miss Singer pulled all the buttons off the body box and then we drew a touch screen and glued it to the front of the box and cut a slot for my eyes and covered it with a screen so it was sort of invisible.

"What are you playing, iPod?" asked Miss Singer.

I answered her in a funny robot voice and said I was playing Volbeat. I know about them from Seth because they're his favorite temporary group.

"Volbeat," said Miss Singer. "Let's print out an album cover."

So she got on the computer and printed it out. She even played one of their songs on YouTube and I was embarrassed because they are so noisy. I don't even like them that much. I just like how much Seth likes them. Anyway, Miss Singer put the cover on the photocopier and blew it up and put it on the touch screen. Then we drew on the controls. We used her iPod as a model. I saw that she was listening to *This American Life*, which she said is an entertaining program.

Being an iPod was even more excellent than being an old-fashioned box robot like I was before!

The only thing that was missing was the headphones, but Miss Singer fixed that too! She grabbed an old electric cord and punched a hole through the head box and threaded it through. Then she spray-painted two foam balls black, like huge earbuds!

"What time is it?" asked Miss Singer. She was sweating quite a bit.

"Five," I said.

"What time's your party?"

"Five-thirty."

"Are your parents picking you up?"

"I'm going to walk to the high school."

"But your parents are going to pick you up from the party?" said Miss Singer.

"Yes," I said, even though I didn't know if my mom would remember.

"I'm going that way. Can I give you a ride?"

I said no because I didn't think I could sit down in her car in my box and I didn't want to have to put it on in the parking lot, because then everyone would know it was me and I wanted it to be a surprise.

She said she understood.

It was raining a little bit, so Miss Singer gave me her umbrella. She said she was glad I was reflective, which I was from all the tinfoil on my box. Then she hurried and got her coat. She said she would walk me over. That was nice, because I was scared to walk along the path by myself on Halloween when it was getting a little bit dark. I could already hear people setting off firecrackers.

When we walked out of the school, I looked around the parking lot to see if my mom was waiting for me in the car, but she wasn't.

Walking through the trees to the school would have been scary if Miss Singer wasn't with me. There were no high school kids smoking in the clearing, which was a relief. Miss Singer took me into the main doors of the high school.

"Everything's bigger over here, isn't it?" she said.

That was a good observation because it was true. The hallways were very empty and bright.

"Where's the party?" she asked, but I didn't know. If we were going to a Pony Club meeting, we probably would have known from the music, because the Pony Club kids are pretty wild, but Poultry Club is quieter.

"That's fine," said Miss Singer. "We'll find them."

We walked down a couple of hallways until we saw someone dressed as a big blue egg go into a room.

"There they are!" I said.

"A giant robin's egg," said Miss Singer. "How pretty."

"That's Dmitri. He raises Ameraucanas."

"Oh," said Miss Singer in a way that told me she didn't understand what I meant.

So I told her that Dmitri was dressed as an Ameraucana egg and that only three types of chickens lay blue eggs: the Ameraucana, the Araucana and the Cream Legbar.

"If I was him, I'd raise Araucanas or Legbars. Araucanas have cool ear tufts and Cream Legbars have really nice feathers."

Miss Singer looked at me. "Is that right?"

"If you want to learn more about chickens, you can come to the party," I told her. "Everyone likes to talk birds."

268

Miss Singer smiled. She has a very nice smile, even when she looks tired, which she sort of did, probably from working so hard to make me into an iPod for the party.

Is it wrong that I wished for a minute that Miss Singer was my mom instead of my actual mom? Sometimes I also wish Prudence was my mother. I feel bad when I do that but I can't seem to stop.

Miss Singer said she'd love to know more about chickens, even though I've written quite a few essays and stories about them and so she should know some stuff already, but she had to go home in case she got some trick-or-treaters. I bet she has a pretty house and a carved pumpkin and hands out those little chocolate bars and everything.

I asked where she lived, in case the club went trick-or-treating near there, but unfortunately she lives near one of the malls in the north end of town. There was no way we were going to get to go all the way to the far end of town, even though I bet they have the best candy over there.

She told me to have a great time and I went into the room. There was some Christian rock music playing, because some of our members won't listen to other kinds of music, which is okay because the music they play is cool. I could tell who almost everyone was from their costumes. That's because most of the outfits were bird-themed, but not all, luckily, or I would have felt bad, even though my iPod costume was pretty good.

Jennifer Wong, who just turned twelve, was dressed as a bantam rooster, which was good because she's the size of an eight-year-old. If Miss Singer had stayed, I would have explained the joke to her. (The joke is that bantams are small. They are also kind of feisty, which Jennifer also is. She's been known to argue with judges when they disagree with something she says at shows. I would never dare to do that!)

Tommy Bristol was dressed as an ugly chicken coop, which was really funny because the costume was so big he could hardly move and pieces of wood kept falling off it. There were even fake chickens on the top. I like that Tommy can laugh at himself. I also like that I have now seen a coop worse than the first one Earl and Seth built for my birds.

Rylan Smith, who only goes to Poultry Club because his dad owns the biggest organic egg farm in the mid-Island, was dressed as a feed sack. He never makes much of an effort. I bet he's going to quit the club soon, and that's fine with me because poultry fancying is not for people who don't take it seriously.

Mary-Ellen Scottolini, who just turned sixteen, was dressed kind of like a sexy chicken. It was weird. Her outfit had feathers but you could see half her boobs and she had on those tights that are made of nets, a big feather headdress and a lot of makeup. The boys in the club kept asking her if she wanted to dunk for apples and she said yes! Even Tommy stayed as close to her as his chicken coop let him.

During our meeting, which was really just a party except for Poultry Club announcements, we played poultry-themed games for prizes and dunked for apples, and then Mr. Lymer, our leader, took us all out in the special needs bus, which was loaned to us by Bethany Blaine's parents, who bought a bus to take Bethany and all her friends around to do activities. When I first started at Poultry Club, Bethany didn't have any friends except me, but then her parents put her in Christian school and a special after-school social group and now she's way more popular than me. I guess that's nice for her, even if I do feel sort of left out sometimes. In fact, Bethany is probably one of the most popular people I know.

Her and her friends were all dressed like princesses, which wasn't very original but they did look pretty with their shiny blond wigs and pink gowns and wings. They said I looked neat, even though I had to tell them what I was and even then I don't think they quite got it.

Mr. Lymer drove us to some farms that have chickens and we got some good candy, but all the places were very far apart, so we didn't get as much stuff as kids who live in the suburbs where the houses are squished together. Also, quite a few of our members are older kids and they seemed sort of embarrassed about trick-or-treating and so they hung around the bus and stared down Mary-Ellen's top.

Then I told Mr. Lymer about the Halloween party at Woefield and he said we could go!

"I bet you had a hand in this," he said when we pulled up and saw the fort all lit up and a lot of people standing around it and a fire and everything! Seth and Prudence and Earl were there, and Eustace too. Seth's mom and her boyfriend, Bobby, who sells parts for remote control helicopters, were there, along with lots of other people I didn't know and their kids. Everyone was gathered around the fort. Some people were drinking apple cider and some people were making s'mores on a fire. I bet Eustace built it, because Earl and Seth are very bad at making fires.

The best part was that the fort was decorated like a haunted house. It was cool and I wished I got to help with it, but I was glad that Earl wrote me a note and told me about the party.

Then I noticed that there was a kid in the fort and the kid was handing out candy, which should have been my job.

I went to Bethany's church a few times last summer. The minister gave this one talk about how envy is one of the worst sins. He said it's extremely deadly and that people go to hell for less.

That made me worry, because I felt really envious seeing that other kid in the fort. There were other kids around too and they spoke all kinds of different languages.

At first, I was so upset that I stayed near the bus. All the other Poultry Club people were looking at all the decorations. Even the older kids thought they were excellent.

Mary-Ellen said that if you looked through a window, you could see three mean dolls in fancy dresses stealing a red shoe off another doll in an ugly dress who was tied up with duct tape. Jennifer, who always has to correct everyone, said it was a scene from Cinderella, only it wasn't accurate. She said all the stuff in the house was from fairy tales but that whoever decorated didn't know much about how the stories actually went. Rylan said to Mary-Ellen that if he told her she had a beautiful body would she hold it against his grain sack, and Tommy punched him, but not very hard. Rylan said, "I'm sacked! I'm sacked."

I think they had too much candy, even though they are teenagers and should be able to handle candy. Them being so immature helped me forget to be envious of the kid who got to be in the fort to hand out the candy. There were three stuffed pigs outside lying under a pile of bricks and sticks and straw, which was from the story of the three little pigs.

A blond princess doll hung by a braided noose made out of her own hair from the window and there was a wolf with a big water gun.

"That doll is supposed to be Rapunzel," said Jennifer. "But that's not what really happened in the story."

Behind the fort, there was a tiny bed with a doll lying on it. Her eyes were covered with a tiny leather mask and there was a weird leather strap with a ball on it in her mouth. No one understood who she was supposed to be and I heard two parents saying that it was "too much."

Seth and Prudence and Earl and Eustace didn't recognize me at first because I was dressed as a box.

"And what are you supposed to be?" Seth asked Tommy when a couple of pieces of wood fell off his costume. "Let me guess? You're a building here on Woefield Farm?" Seth was dressed all in green, like an elf, but there was a fake pitchfork sticking out of his back. The tines showed in the front of his chest and there was a lot of fake blood. It was awesome and I felt proud that I know him, even though I didn't know what he was supposed to be and he didn't recognize me.

"Lotta chickens in this group," said Earl, who is more observant than most old people. I don't know why. He was just dressed like himself.

"That's right, sir," said Tommy, who has excellent manners.

"This the chicken club?" asked Earl, who was the only one really paying attention, because Eustace and Prudence were leaning against each other in a boyfriend-girlfriend way and Seth kept checking his phone. "Sara with you?" asked Earl.

"Sir?" said Tommy.

"I'm here," I said, and waved my hand. "In the box. I'm an iPod."

Then before I knew it, Prudence and Seth and Earl and Eustace were all around me and Prudence hugged me, as much as she could with me in the box. Earl kept patting my box so it made a funny, hollow sound.

"Looking awesome!" said Seth. "Sweet Nano Sara!"

Eustace was smiling and looking handsome.

I don't know when I have ever been so happy.

"Off with your head!" said Seth.

"Let's get a look at you," said Earl.

"Let me help," said Prudence, when I couldn't quite get it off by myself.

Her and Seth helped me get my head off and they all crowded in front of me, staring at me, and I felt really good, even though another kid was giving out Halloween candy from the fort.

Prudence put her hands on either side of my face and stared at me really hard, like she was trying to see if I had something in my eye.

"What?" I said.

"Are you okay?" she asked. "Getting enough sleep?"

I nodded. It was a lie, but at least I didn't say the lie out loud, which would have been worse.

Mr. Lymer was standing there watching us and he said he thought I lived at Woefield. And I said I had gone back to stay with my parents for a while.

Prudence and Seth and Earl all got funny looks on their faces then.

"We invited Pete," Seth whispered to me. "But he hasn't shown up yet. We hope he'll come, see what a good party we throw, and make his report."

"Who's Pete?" asked Mr. Lymer, who can be a bit nosy because he's in charge of Poultry Club. "What report?"

Then Bethany, who doesn't really know about not saying things, said I wasn't allowed to visit the farm because they didn't take care of me properly. She said Pete was my social worker.

When I first had to leave the farm, I told Bethany that my parents and Pete the social worker thought Seth and Prudence and Earl didn't look after me right after Target's brother tried to hurt me. I didn't think Bethany was even paying attention, because her and her new friends were playing some game on their iTouches at the time. I was wrong. At the Haunted Fort party, she started saying almost everything I said but getting it all wrong.

"Yes," said Bethany. "A boy hurt her here."

She looked at Seth, who opened his mouth, which was already sort of scary because there was fake blood dribbling down his chin.

"Jesus! Not me!" he said.

"You said the Lord's name!" said Bethany. Her friends looked shocked.

"Not him," said Prudence in that voice she uses when she's trying to get people to calm down. "He didn't hurt Sara. It was another boy. A stranger. It's all a big misunderstanding. Sara is part of the family. And she wasn't really hurt. I mean, Eustace got there before anything happened."

Even I knew that didn't sound very good.

"My mom said they have bugs here," said Bethany.

"Categorically untrue," said Seth.

"We only have the ones we should have. The ones indicative of a healthy ecosystem," said Prudence.

"Bugs that live in beds," said Bethany.

Then Earl said a swear, which I will not repeat in case younger people read this.

"It was a misunderstanding. I'm in training to become a pest control specialist," said Seth. "I'm going to treat other people's problems."

"I told you to go to Courtenay to buy your supplies," said Eustace.

"Sara," said Mr. Lymer. "Are you allowed to visit the farm right now?"

I didn't answer because I didn't want to say.

He sighed. "We ought to be going. I don't want to upset anyone."

By "anyone" he meant my parents.

"It's really fine," said Prudence and her pleasant voice didn't sound very calm anymore.

Mr. Lymer told all the Poultry Clubbers to head for the bus.

I said I needed to go check the coop. If there's one thing a Poultry Club leader knows, it's that you can never check your chickens too many times, so he said okay. While everyone else was getting on the bus and eating candy and shoving each other, I tore off a piece of my box and got a pen out of my pocket.

I wrote as fast as I could and left the note on the front door of the coop, tucked into the latch.

When I got back on the bus, no one would sit near me. I heard Mary-Ellen say I had bugs and she didn't think I should be allowed on the bus. Tommy said she should shut her mouth and then he came and stood near me, but because we both had on boxes, we needed our own seats and couldn't even really sit down properly. Tommy has excellent leadership.

Anyway, I don't care if even people at Poultry Club except for Tommy don't like me now because of what Bethany said. I have other things that are worse to deal with, such as sleeping in a car by myself.

I was so upset that I barely remember getting to the high school. All I know is that my mom was waiting for me in the parking lot, and after everyone got out of the bus, her and Mr. Lymer talked and she shook her head and said she hadn't seen any bites. I got out of my iPod costume, which I sort of wished was an iTouch outfit, and got in the car and my mom asked me if I had a good time and I said yes and she said that was good. Then she drove us to the campground again.

Earl

I couldn't tell you what made me check the chicken coop after the party. I checked them birds at least twice that night already. But I stopped by to take one last gander before going in for the night and there was the little Sprout's note.

Took me a minute or so to make sense of it.

Hi Earl,
   Sorry I couldn't stay longer. It was a fun party.
   Sincerely,
   Sara
   P.S. I think we'll be staying at the campground again tonight. It's scary being alone there at night, especially on Halloween.

Jesus, Jesus, I said, and I ran for my truck.

I was thanking the good lord that the damned thing was running for once as I pulled out of the driveway, going as fast as I dared, considering I can't barely see a goddamned thing at night.

What the hell was she doing alone at night? In a campground? I knew her old man lived in one of the units near the used tire store, so she must be staying with that mother of hers. Useless damned woman.

I had no idea what time they'd get to the campground or whether her mother would go out and leave her alone right away. My old head felt like it might blow right off my shoulders if I didn't calm the hell down and figure out what to do. I'd end up in a ditch if I wasn't careful.

As soon as I saw the gas bar, I pulled in, parked and collected my wits. What would Prudence do if she wasn't down with the thyroid troubles? I had no goddamned idea. All I knew was that she'd do something.

First I had to find Sara and then I'd figure out the next step.

They weren't in the first campground I checked. The place was nearly deserted except for the attendant's RV and a few permanent residents parked close to the entrance. I drove up and down all them little gravel roads. It was damned near impossible to see in there.

When I got to the Little Lake Campground, the entryway was closed for the night, I guess due to it being winter. Hell and damn, that was no good. Lucky for me I brung my headlamp with me. So I left the truck on the side of the road and started walking. Same as the other campground, there were a few sites occupied around the entrance and then it was empty.

I passed one truck and camper, shut up tight for the night, but I knew Sara's mom drove an old Buick.

Them campgrounds is bigger than you would think. My feet was hurting something fierce when I finally saw the car. There was a little light on inside and I stood on the road, wondering what the hell I was going to say if Sara's mother saw me. I didn't know if people was allowed to make their kids sleep in cars or not. Prudence was trying to get on the good side of both Sara's parents, so I needed to keep myself calm and not tell her what I thought about her mothering.

I walked into the campsite and saw someone move inside the car. Then Sara's pale little face, eyes wide, scared as hell, staring out the window at me.

Ah, Jesus, I said, and stopped.

I couldn't see anyone else in there with her.

She rolled down the window an inch or two.

Hello? she said. Brave goddamned kid, I'll tell you. Rolling down the window like that.

It's Earl, I said.

Her little face changed and I could see some of the scared leave it, and by god I didn't know what the hell to do with myself.

She was having a little cry and I walked over and told her it was okay.

Her mother hadn't made a fire or anything and they didn't have no camping chairs to sit in, so I just stood beside the Sprout. She was in her pajamas and wrapped in a couple of blankets.

So you and your mother are staying here? I said.

She nodded and wiped her nose.

We've been coming here at night and then she goes out. She comes back in the morning, really early.

I didn't ask Sara where her ma was going. I didn't tell her that I couldn't think of a thing to say to her mom that wouldn't make things worse. That woman could make sure Sara never came back to the farm again.

I don't like it here, said Sara.

It's damned dark, I agreed. But it's peaceful though.

Even though we was in the trees in a campground, we could hear firecrackers going off somewhere.

Yes, she said, being real brave. I like the woods.

I'll tell you what, I said. You got school in the morning, so you better turn out that light and get some sleep. And I'll scamper out of here when I hear your ma coming back. Then we'll figure out what to do. You get some rest. I'll be right here.

Then I thought about them dark circles under her eyes. You getting enough to eat? I asked her.

Sara held up a bag of candy.

I mean proper food, I said.

She shrugged. My mom's really distracted lately.

I could have kicked that woman right then. But I didn't say nothing and I wouldn't until I talked it over with Prudence and Seth.

We'll make sure there's a good lunch and snacks at your school tomorrow. Now you go to sleep and I'll be right here at the picnic table until your mom comes back.

Do you want to sit in the car? she asked.

No, darlin', I said. I might fall asleep and then your mother would wonder what was going on.

I took myself over to the picnic table, uncomfortable goddamned thing, especially in that cold, and sat down. Sara turned out the little light. After about five minutes, I heard the car window roll down.

Earl? she said.

I'm right here.

Okay, she said. And she rolled that window back up.

I sat there all night like that until I heard the sound of gravel crunching under somebody's feet. I'd already looked around and knew I could duck onto a little trail that led off to another campsite without going on the road. The path was mossy and my eyes were used to the dark and so I didn't make too much noise or have to switch on my light.

I turned around and saw the headlight bob into the campsite. It stopped and moved around, like Mrs. Spratt had heard me moving. I held my breath.

Then the car door opened and the interior light came on. Quick as a wink the door shut and the light went out.

And I made my way back to the truck, wondering what in god's green earth to do next.

Seth

The night of the Halloween party, I dreamed about the drama teacher. We'd had words the night before. Hot words, if you'll forgive my directness.

She'd come to the party but hadn't gotten out of her car. Instead, she'd texted me a series of funny, sexy little messages.

Example:

Bev: What are you wearing?
Me: Zombie elf farmer.
Bev: Is that a pitchfork through your heart or are you just happy
to see me?

Okay, so maybe our texts weren't that funny or sexy, but I liked it.

Me: Come have a s'more with us.
Bev: I'll stay here thanks. I just like watching you. You're
beautiful, you know.

Obviously, that was weird as hell considering I had a pitchfork through my chest and pointy ears and green overalls, but I never really doubted that she found the sight of me pleasing. It is such a rush when someone finds you appealing. This is doubly true when you don't find too many things about yourself appealing.

She didn't ask when I would be ready to handle her pest situation and I liked that, too. The lack of pressure made the task feel more manageable.

I decided I would do it soon. Treat her pests, I mean. And she would find me even more beautiful. How many guys get a sophisticated woman saying something like that to them?

So I was sitting at the kitchen table, drinking coffee and thinking about how she would react when I heroically debugged her house, when Earl interrupted my reverie.

He knocked once, quietly, like he didn't want to wake Prudence, then came on in.

"We got to have a staff meeting," he said.

I was still tangled in the drama teacher's well-used but bedbug-free sheet in my mind, so I had trouble following what he was saying.

"Now?" I said. "What about Prudence?"

"We're going to let her rest. Come on down to the cabin," he said. Then he marched on out of the house.

When I got to his cabin, he had coffee made and was sitting at his oilcloth-covered kitchen table.

"Speaking as the only staff member at this meeting, since you and Prudence are management, I'd like to say that my shift doesn't start until eight thirty. I'm lobbying for ten, but so far no dice. Let's add that to the agenda."

He didn't grumble or react to my amusing comments.

"We got to talk about Sara," he said.

I noticed then that he looked wiped out. His stubble was gray against his pale cheeks. Normally, Earl's natural grumpiness keeps his cheeks rosy. Not this morning.

"Why? What's wrong?"

I remembered him leaving in his truck the night before. "Did something happen?"

Earl sighed. Rubbed his hands roughly over his face, like he was trying to clean cobwebs from it.

"It's her mother. She's got them staying in a campground. At least, she's parking Sara in the car in a campsite while she buggers off doing who knows what till the morning."

"I don't understand. They have a house. That place in the subdivision. It's for sale, but I don't think it's been sold."

"I got no idea why. That woman makes ferns look smart, at least when it comes to looking after her kid. I mean, Jesus. They took Sara away because we left her alone for an hour. And now her mom's got her spending all night alone in a dark car."

My head spun. Heart raced. The whole deal.

"We'll tell the social worker. Or her dad."

"So the social worker gives full custody to her old man? He's not going to change his mind on us even if we get him a whole herd of mules. 'Specially not if his Mrs. could tell on him. Or maybe the social worker decides none of us is any good and they put her in care."

"They can't!" I said.

"Course they can. And they will. It's a goddamned mess."

"What's her mother thinking?" I said. "Is she using drugs? Turning tricks? What the fuck?"

Earl just shook his head.

287

"All I know is Sara's scared. I stayed with her last night and high-tailed it out of there when I heard her mother coming."

No wonder he looked like a three-day-old dinner. Earl is no youngster. He couldn't be staying out all night.

"Okay. So we'll take turns. Her dad has her half the time. We'll figure out when her mom's taking her to the campground and make sure she's not alone."

"The damned woman is forgetting to feed her, too," said Earl. "We need to go to the school this morning. Drop something off."

My heart was racing so bad. Who the hell leaves her kid alone all night and forgets to feed her?

"I'm on it," I said. "You go to sleep. I'll give Sara my cell phone and take lunch to the school this morning. They won't be open for a couple of hours. She's not staying alone in that campground again."

"What are you going to put in her lunch?" asked Earl.

"She likes apples. And boiled eggs. I suspect that's rare in kids her age."

"She hasn't been getting healthy stuff. You better put some carrot sticks in there," said Earl. "And crackers and peanut butter."

"They don't let peanut butter in her class. There's that kid with the allergy. He could die if she breathes on him."

"Goddamn it. You're right. I forgot that," said Earl.

In the end, we decided we both better go to Country Grocer to stock up on lunch and breakfast supplies for Sara. We gave her two boiled eggs, three granola bars, two fruit bars, a cheese sandwich, a jam sandwich, a thermos of hot noodle soup, a bottle of apple juice, a container of milk, some of those weird cheese and cracker packages, a bag of chips, two apples and a banana. We put it all in a large paper bag and left it with the school secretary, who looked at us quizzically.

I hoped no one in the office recognized us from our performance outside on parent-teacher day. I thought I saw a blond head poking out of the principal's office. It could have belonged to Miss Singer, Sara's teacher. But Earl and I hustled out of there before she could get a good look.

In the bottom of the bag, we'd left Sara a pay-and-talk cell phone and a set of instructions for when to get in touch.

Earl

Sara was back with her father for the next two weeks, so I wasn't staying with her every other night anymore, and I figured it was time to find the guy who stole Prudence's barn money.

When Eugene come out of the house, just about a week after the party, stretching his arms over his head like he wanted to hug the sky, which was gray as a barfly's teeth, I told him that the little bastard ripped us off and that Prudence asked me to find the guy and I couldn't, goddamn it.

I should have cleared my throat to warn him I was there, because he nearly jumped out of his big rubber boots.

Holy Christ, Earl, he said. I didn't see you.

I was standing against the side of the house, taking a gander at the place, trying to figure out where I should park the chicken coop for the day. It needed to be someplace Sara could get to it easy, and Prudence has rules about not leaving the birds on one patch of ground too long because of leaving the exact right amount of chicken shit and destruction behind so the grass'll grow extra fast.

Me and Eugene stood there for another minute or two until he spoke up again.

So how are things? he asked.

How do you think they are? I said. I guess the not sleeping was catching up with my attitude, even though I was glad to do it. Me and Seth had started packing chairs to sit in and rain gear and big umbrellas and blankets, but we were still sitting outside in the goddamned weather for between four and five hours. That wears on a person. But old Eugene knows how to mind his business. All he said was that was a very good question.

What's going on with that pile there? he said, pointing to the bricks and logs we didn't use for the pig death scene at Halloween. You going to make a brick outhouse with some log detailing?

Supposed to be for the barn, I said.

Going to be small.

Like I said, that goddamned constructor kid ripped Prudence off. Got money for the materials and all he done was drop off some old bricks and them old logs there. He's buggered off and took the barn money with him. She told me to find him and I can't.

Ah, said Eugene. He stared out over the fields. Looked at Lucky and Bertie, grazing together near my cabin. This place has come a long way, he said.

It's Prudence, I told him. She's a hard worker. Least she was till she took sick.

That's true, he said. She's something.

But that don't help us with the social worker or Sara's damned fool parents, I said.

Yes, he said, and I don't think losing Sara is helping Prudence feel any better.

He checked his phone and then put it back in his pocket.

My new locum has started. I'm supposed to be off today, unless an emergency comes in and she can't handle it. What do you say we go find the builder and Prudence's money?

I said, Jesus Christ, that would be good.

We got into that big white rig of his—probably burns two gallons of gas every time he turns the key—and went to Tim's to fortify, as Eugene called it, with donuts and coffees.

We was in the lineup and he says to me, Earl, if we're going to spend time together, I think I should let you know that my name is Eustace, not Eugene.

That right? I said.

Then we had a helluva good laugh.

We sat in the parking lot at Timmy's and he looked up things on that phone of his. I remember when people had phone books. I never liked them, either.

Well, he said. Stephan McFadden's not listed, but I think I know his uncle. We'll start there.

So we drove way the hell into the back of beyond and into the Nanaimo Lakes area. Lots of logging up in there. The second- and third-growth trees are all spindly as fourth-graders' legs and too close together. When I first come to this island, there was trees so big it'd take three men holding hands to circle 'em. Not many of them left these days.

We drove through the skinny little forests and Eustace pulled over on the side of the road near an unmarked driveway and checked his phone again.

This is it, he said. I should know it by heart because I mailed about twenty-four invoices to him before I sent him to collections. In exchange, I've been paid exactly zero dollars.

He turned up the dirt track and stopped in front of a trailer tucked into a scrubby old clearing. There was toys and bags of garbage and pieces of cars all over the yard.

I asked Eustace what kind of work he did over here, because I didn't see no farm animals and he said, Just wait and you'll see.

So we got out of the truck and went to the front door. It was even more full of junk than Seth's mother's place. There was a path cut through piles of newspapers and magazines and boxes. Some of the crap was wrapped in tarps and some wasn't. Six foot high if it was an inch. I'll tell you, I didn't like being in among all that garbage. Smelled like old diapers in there. I seen a show on TV once about the people who can't get rid of nothing, and young Stephan's uncle should have been on the season premiere.

Eustace knocked on the door. Nobody answered. He knocked again.

Then the door opened and a little feller looked out. He was dressed better than I would have thought. Glasses and brown sweater. Like a college teacher. Condition his yard was in, I wouldn't have been surprised to see him wearing a goddamned tarp with mouse traps hanging off it for decoration.

Yes? he said.

Hello, Brian, said Eustace, polite considering his bill was never paid.

Brian didn't answer. He whipped his head around and bellowed, I hear you, Willa! You need to stop that RIGHT NOW.

I was thinking Eustace needed to get on that phone of his and call the police if this was how the feller talked to his wife.

So no repercussions from Willa's illness, I take it? asked Eustace.

Oh, she's a going concern, said the little feller. Willa, come here and see your doctor! he said.

You could have knocked me over with a piece of dandelion fluff when a big pig come around the corner. She was pink and whiskery and her eyes was nearly buried in fat. She snuffled at us.

Hello, Willa, said Eustace. You're looking well.

The pig snuffled again.

You going to come and say hello to your personal physician? asked Brian. After all, he's been kind enough to make a house call.

That old pig squeezed through the hallway, which was every bit as crowded as the yard outside, her belly nearly dragging on the ground, and that face of hers, well, it was so damned ugly you couldn't help but like her. The fat under her throat hung almost as low as her stomach and swung from side to side when she walked.

She come right up beside the little feller, squishing him into a pile of what looked like old clothes. Eustace bent down and give her a friendly scratch behind the ear and she grunted. I swear to god that pig sounded like she was talking. You'd think a hog living in them hoarder conditions would be dirty, but she seemed clean enough.

You did a superb job, doctor, said Brian, who talks kind of fancy for a feller who lives in a trailer filled with garbage and a huge pig. Willa has been breathing just fine since her treatment. No recurrence of her walking pneumonia. As you suggested, I'm keeping her as stress-free as possible.

That's good, says Eustace. I also look forward to being paid for my services at some point in the future.

The knock on his bill-paying habits didn't faze the little man one bit. Of course, doctor, he says. You are my first priority.

I started to get worried about how that pig was going to get herself turned around. Brian was smashed against the clothing pile and me and Eustace was packed together like tinned oysters. What if that pig panicked and run right over us? Ever since we got the mule, I'm more aware of stampeding.

The pig didn't seem in a hurry to go anywhere. She had her head tilted so she could see us out from under the ridges of fat over her eyes.

The little feller didn't seem to be in any hurry either. The two of them looked like they'd be happy to stand in that little hallway all day.

We're looking for your nephew, said Eustace. Wondering if you know where we can find him?

I've got a lot of nephews, doctor, said Brian. We're Irish Catholics of the old type. The relations back in Ireland stopped breeding like laboratory mice some time ago, but my seven sisters haven't gotten the message. They don't understand that the world has limited resources and so they keep having babies. Not like Willa here—right, girl? You're not going to be bringing bucketloads of piglets into the world, are you? Not while I'm in supervisory capacity.

Willa grunted.

The little feller didn't seem to have no shortage of resources, at least if you count garbage as a resource. I was thinking his sisters probably didn't invite him to too many family functions. Him or his pig.

We're looking for Stephan. He agreed to do some work on Earl's farm, but he disappeared after he got paid.

Ah, the wee shite is famous for it.

Brian looked as unworried about his nephew as he had about his unpaid bill.

Never give a McFadden money before the job is done, he said. Except me, of course. I'm reliable.

Of course, said Eustace. In your case, get the money before *starting* the job.

Oh, you're a card, doctor. Anyway, I want to help you out since you were so good to Willa and here you are checking up on her again. I suggest that you look for young Stephan down at the casino. He's a complete stereotype, he is. If he's not on a toot, he'll be in there.

Then the little feller grinned like he couldn't be more pleased with life.

And if he's drinking? asks Eustace. Where do we find him then?

In that case, you'll have to wait for him to sober up and get paid for someone else's job, then take the money from him before he gets to the casino and pisses it away on the slots. The little feller lowered his voice and leaned as close as he could, considering a two-hundred-pound pig had him pinned.

He's got addictions, he said, like he was telling us a Pentagon secret. I'm just glad the family curse skipped me. Then he give us that big smile again and Eustace thanked him and backed away.

I didn't leave right away because I was too taken at the sight of that big sow moving down the hallway in reverse, like a fat pink semitrailer backing into a loading dock. Her big bum brushed against the piles on either side, but she kept herself more or less in the middle. When she hit the turn in the path, she turned, neat as you please. I half expected to hear them beeps trucks make when they're backing up.

The little feller noticed me staring. Oh bless her hide, he said. Isn't she a beauty?

Me and Eustace didn't say nothing until we got into the truck and he turned us onto the Lakes Road.

Have you ever? he said.

And I said, Holy Christ on the cross, I sure as hell have not.

Then we had another big laugh.

I'll tell you one thing, them vet doctors probably have one of the most interesting careers a person could have.

Seth

Feelings of uselessness and helplessness are at war in me. I'm not sure which one is winning.

Yes, I feel good that I've been able to help Sara in some small way, but long-term, I have no idea what to do about that situation. Her mother has the worst decision-making skills of anyone I've ever met, including me. But she's the mother and she has all the rights. Her dad is basically a prick who would rather hang around with a mule than spend time with his excellent kid. So in relation to them, I feel needed and useful if basically ineffectual.

The same sort of calculation is at work in my dealings with the drama teacher. She needs my help and I need hers to relieve me of the bondage of my virginity, if you'll forgive me for paraphrasing AA's Big Book.

I may be the only person in the rooms (twelve-step slang for "person who attends meetings") who is a technical virgin. Could anything be less heavy metal than being a full-blown alkie who couldn't even break the virginity barrier? Any normal alcoholic would have at least two entrenched STDs to go with a severely checkered sexual history by the time he gave up the drink. There is no area of life in which I am not ass-backward.

The night before my date with the drama teacher—though *date* doesn't seem quite the right word for the afternoon of pest control and devirginization we had planned—I didn't sleep at all. I'd pushed the day back three times already, partly because I was on call if Sara was going to be alone and partly because I was scared.

I compulsively watched the DVD that came with the bedbug supplies, the one that showed in careful detail how to start at the outside of a room and work your way toward the bed. It showed a hugely unconcerned guy hosing harsh pesticides into corners and crevices.

Then I reread the online tutorials and message boards again, and stared at the images of bedbugs in their different life cycles until my eyes quit focusing.

By the time dawn lightened the sky on the big day, I was in pieces. I thought about trying to go to an early meeting, but the only one I knew of was in downtown Nanaimo and the truck was on the fritz again.

It occurred to me that without wheels, I had no way to get to the drama teacher's place with my stand-up steamer, handheld steamer, talc-lined passive traps, bottles of diatomaceous earth and assortment of pesticides, not to mention huge rubber boots, face mask, full protective mechanic-style jumpsuit, boxes of heavy-duty contractor bags, packages of gloves, and hat (in case one of the little bedbug bastards threw himself off the ceiling into my unsuspecting hair, perish the fucking thought).

If I was a normal guy trying to get laid by a normal woman, I could walk over there, weighed down only by a few premium condoms and modest expectations. But no. Nothing is ever simple for me.

I considered calling Eustace and asking him for a ride. He'd been keeping his thoughts about the whole thing to himself and I appreciated that. I'm well aware that the drama teacher is sixteen years older than me and that's the least inappropriate thing about our liaison. It's never a good sign when your potential lover has already been questioned by the police about your relationship, as happened after we broke up the first time.

No. If I was going to make shitty choices, I wanted to make them without assistance from my support network.

I couldn't ask the drama teacher to pick me up, because (a) it would make me feel twelve and (b) it could land her in jail, or at least get her fired, given the accusations that flew after the school concert.

My breath was labored, like I was about to give birth to a goddamned fear baby, when my computer chimed that I had a new email.

Tamara: HM! Where's my column on codependence and boundaries?

My editor at *The Cure* always calls me HM, short for Half Measures, after my column. It's kind of endearing but also kind of dismissive of me as a man.

Me: It's coming. If I don't die of stress first.
Tamara: It was due weeks ago. I've been patient, but I have to ask what's going on. Why the delays, HM?
Me: Women.

I hoped that response would make me sound like I'd had extensive experience.

Tamara: Didn't your spons say no relationships in the first year?
Me: It's complicated.
Tamara: Complicated is a Facebook status. Talk to me HM. I'm
trying to avoid work here. Help an editor out.
Me: I'm in trouble.
Tamara: New cell phone, right? Send me your digits.

I sent her the number for my new cell, bought because Eustace's old one had quit not long after the incident at the parent-teacher meeting, and the phone rang ten seconds later.

Before I knew what was happening, I was telling my editor everything.

I told her about us losing Sara. About how her parents wouldn't let us see her, even though they were perfectly happy hanging around here themselves. I told her how me and Earl had been sitting with her at night for several nights while her mother fucked off who knows where. I told her about the affair with the drama teacher and about the incident at the premiere of the school production of *Jesus Christ Superstar*. About the years-long bout of agoraphobia that had followed. I didn't have to tell her about sobering up and getting a life again, because she'd read all my columns. Then I told her about what I had planned for the afternoon.

"Well," she said. "I have to say I wasn't expecting that."

"I know," I said. "It's too much."

"Look, I don't believe in telling people what to do, even though I run an online recovery-advice and how-to-live-your-life magazine. But maybe you should just focus on getting the kid back. The other thing, with that teacher, it doesn't sound great."

"I don't know what else to do about Sara. Until the social worker comes around, her parents won't budge. It's this point of pride with the two of them. And I told the drama teacher I'd help her out."

"You sure it's worth it? Being around the teacher and her bugs? What if you go full phobic?"

"Already there," I said. "At least this way I might get laid in the bargain."

Tamara made a sympathetic noise.

I could hear the roar of traffic in the background.

"Where are you?" I asked.

"Montreal."

"You don't sound French."

"Because I'm Anglo. I only sound French when I speak French."

"Oh."

"If I was there, I'd help you out," she said.

"You know how to get rid of bedbugs?"

"No, dumbass. I know about sex with virgins. Deflowering boys used to be a hobby of mine. Back in my using days."

"Really?"

"Nah. I just said that to be shocking. You sure you don't want to wait for a woman who loves you? One who isn't a borderline pedophile?"

"The drama teacher likes me. And I'm not . . . I mean, I wasn't a *child* . . . at least not in terms of years. She finds me very attractive, which makes her unusual."

"The drama teacher sounds like a deeply troubled person, if you don't mind me saying. But I understand where you're coming from. The pathologically selfish and perverted heart wants whatever the fuck it wants, as Woody Allen might say. Just don't go getting a busted heart to go with your new phobia."

"I won't."

"At risk of sounding crude, HM, wouldn't a hooker be cheaper and simpler? I'm not talking about some desperate addict. I'm talking about a mature call girl. Someone with experience and discretion who is just planning to work until she's maxed out her RRSPs."

"I don't know anyone like that, and even if I did, I spent all my money on bedbug supplies. Plus, Prudence would freak if she knew."

"Didn't you say Prudence is bedridden? How would she find out?"

"She's only in bed half the time. Plus, she has a finding-out way about her."

"Well, if you insist on going over to the predator's house, take a cab and send me the bill. This would make a killer feature story."

"No," I said. "There's no way I'm writing about this. It's private."

"I know. Your sponsor knows. Why not tell the world? We'll call it 'Half Measures Takes the Plunge.'"

"No, we won't."

"'Bedbug and Beyond'?" she said.

"I have to go," I said.

"Call me! I want to hear every detail," said Tamara as I hung up.

At 3:30, I called a cab. At 3:45, Sara's dad, the Mule Man, showed up.

I considered canceling due to possible complications from him knowing me, but my nerves were too shattered to think things through any further. Also, he never seems to notice anything or anyone around here except for our mule.

"Where to?" he asked, after I had wrestled all of my equipment into the backseat with me.

I gave him the drama teacher's address.

He didn't respond. He just drove his rattlecrap Prius down the driveway. I hoped Prudence hadn't seen me go. She'd been on the couch in the living room for most of the afternoon, reading what I think may have been Mrs. Spratt's manuscript. When I left, she was on the phone, talking to one of her friends in New York.

Lucky and Bertie had come to the fence when Dean Spratt pulled in, and Lucky trotted along the fence line after us when we left again, like Old Yeller, only red and a mule and without rabies. At least not yet.

"That mule is sure attached to you," I said, trying to sound calm, even though I felt like my heart was racing so hard it might go off in my chest like a badly assembled IED.

"He's a . . . ," said Mr. Spratt.

"Sorry? I didn't quite catch that."

Mr. Spratt muttered something else.

He obviously struggled with giving compliments or saying anything else that was positive.

"What's the plan now that we have the wagon and everything?" I asked, making small talk, even though what I really wanted to do was burst into tears. Arriving with a tear-stained face probably wouldn't be a sexual deal-sealer for any woman. Suddenly, I wanted a drink. A coffee mug full of vodka would go down nicely, followed by two or three beer. Then I'd start drinking for real. Why did I have to do terrible things just so I could have a normal life experience that other people seemed to get in a matter of course?

I could not handle people's opinions, my own expectations and desires. I couldn't handle disappointment or worrying about people I cared about.

I could not handle life.

Mr. Spratt said something about the wagon, but I wasn't listening because I was deciding which liquor store he should take me to.

I would get a bottle and *then* go see the drama teacher. The trick was to avoid AA people on my way into and out of the store. I thought of Eustace and my stomach curled up like it'd been hit by a car and left to die by the side of the road.

Fuck it. The decision was made. I would tell Mr. Spratt to drive me to the Wheatsheaf. I'd give him five bucks to go in and get me a case of beer and a bottle of vodka. That would leave me with enough money for cab fare, and it would keep me out of the public eye. Then I reconsidered. Skip the vodka. The family drink was rye. I'd get cola to go with it. I could mix up a wet-your-pants-size drink and put it in one of those no-spill coffee cups while I was treating the drama teacher's house. She wouldn't care. I hadn't told her I was sober. It'd been long enough between drinks that I'd be painless in about ten minutes. Painless, fearless. Less. That was always the goal.

Finally I tuned back into what Dean Spratt was saying.

"Got a feeling he was already trained as a driving mule. Going to give him a three bells if that's the case."

"Huh?" I said.

Dean Spratt was talking about putting bells on Lucky's tail, and the part of my brain that wasn't engaged in plans for self-immolation wondered at the wisdom of that idea. On the other hand, at least if he had multiple bells tied to his tail, innocent passersby would have time to get out of his way when he went charging all over Cedar at 160 kilometers an hour after something spooked him.

My phone vibrated in my sweaty hand. It scared me so bad, I nearly flung it into the front of the cab but settled for dropping it onto the dirty leather of the backseat.

The screen lit up and I saw a text flicker across the top.

Tamara: Whatever you do, HM, DO NOT DRINK. That's a direct order from your editor. Repeat. DO NOT DRINK.

Then we were pulling up to the drama teacher's little house. It was a small, wood-shingled cottage. The drama teacher used to live in a larger house when she was married.

I would have to ask Dean Spratt to back out of the driveway and take me to the liquor store. He couldn't do it quietly, due to the jalopy nature of the car, but too bad. He wouldn't care about the booze run. Like the drama teacher, he didn't give any sort of crap about me or my sobriety. He didn't even know I had any sobriety to protect.

Dean Spratt seemed to be in a hurry. He was rambling on about all the things he had planned for Lucky when he got back to the farm. He's obsessed with that mule. If I didn't have so much on my mind, it would be very concerning to me. I wanted to shout at him that maybe he should be a little more obsessed with his daughter and what his wife was doing when she was supposedly looking after her. But no. That wouldn't help Sara or us. We'd kept the campground thing a secret. We were committed now.

He leapt out of the front seat, pulled open a back door and started removing my steamers and bags and boxes from the seat. I sat with my cell phone in my hand.

"Okay," said Dean Spratt, standing in the open door, hands on the roof. "That'll be $8.50."

"I was wondering if we could make one more stop," I said.

He was shaking his head before I finished speaking.

"I've got to get back to the farm before it starts raining. I'm off shift now."

I wanted to say, *Look, I'm attempting to relapse here,* but thought better of it. We were trying to get Sara back, and doing my Charles Bukowski impression in front of her dad wouldn't help that cause.

And then there was that word: *relapse*. It had a serious ring to it, suggesting severe complications and harsh difficulties to follow.

"Okay?" said Mr. Spratt, barely trying to hide his impatience.

I dug into my pants and pulled out a tenner.

"Can you pick me up?" I asked. "In about . . . well, later."

And as I spoke, I realized with stunned relief that I *would* be leaving this place, eventually. I'd lost sight of that fact. I might be covered in bedbugs and no longer a virgin, but eventually I would leave this cottage of tainted dreams, and life would go on.

Dean Spratt shook his head. "I'm off," he said. "Call Cedar Cabs if you need a ride." Ten seconds later, I stood in the round gravel clearing in front of the house, surrounded by equipment, watching him back out of the narrow driveway, pressed in on both sides by the overgrown laurel hedges that surrounded the front of the property.

Please come back, I thought but didn't say.

My phone buzzed again.

Tamara: I'm serious, HM. Don't make me have to come over there and deal with your little issue myself.

Hard on the heels of that text came another one.

Eustace: Pick you up for the meeting tonight?

How was I supposed to get lost and get less with people after me all the time?

For the sake of my self-respect, I could halt the story right here, but I feel like some explanation is required. It's the difference between reading the back cover of a Stephen King novel and reading the whole thing.

I stood in the driveway and waves of revulsion and fear at what lay ahead, pest-eradication-wise, crashed into the waves of wanting to get laid. I'm sorry not to be more poetic, but that was really the situation, wave-wise.

It's impossible to say how long I stood there, surrounded by my steamers and two grocery bags full of sprays and powders and safety goggles and face mask and plastic booties so I wouldn't get bedbugs and bedbug babies on any part of me.

I gave serious thought to knocking on the door, handing the drama teacher the supplies and educational DVD and telling her to take the Mike Holmes approach. She was strong enough to handle the work. I'd wrestled with her enough times to know that. She wasn't toned, it's true, but she was sturdy.

Or I could sneak up and leave the supplies on her doorstep and run away.

Before I could decide on the right cowardly path to take, the front door swung open.

The drama teacher was dressed in a robe, heart-attack red to match the color of the front door. She cast a glance around to make sure we were alone, then opened the robe to reveal what can only be described as a sex garment. I have spent a lot of time on the Internet. A lot of things scare me but few things surprise me. So when I say I was shocked to my core by the drama teacher's outfit, you can be sure it was quite the sight.

"It's steampunk," she said. "Do you like it?"

I couldn't speak for a second.

"I'm writing a steampunk play. I plan to make the costumes myself."

I hoped the play wasn't for a younger audience. The drama teacher's steampunk negligee was hugely not safe for work or for children.

There was a green velvet corset that squished her stomach and chest and armpit flesh in a way that reminded me of Yorkshire puddings spilling out of a tin.

Then there was her bra. It was like something you'd use to hang volleyballs in a gym. Each individual boob was wrapped in some sort of green netting. The effect was beyond screwed up, but it was also extremely sexy, which is the inexplicable part. *One* of the inexplicable parts.

There was a garter belt and some ornate, steampunky decorative necklaces hung between her net bra and old-fashioned granny heels, and everything about the outfit had a severe falling-apart quality. I have a lot of sympathy for anyone with a less-than-perfect physique. It's not the drama teacher's body I'm talking about. What I mean is that thing was coming apart already. Some of the metal grommets that kept the lacing in place had been torn out. Stray threads poked out everywhere and the boob netting was, well, it was just incredibly strange and looked super harsh on her nipples. In summary, I was pretty much open-mouthed, which I would have been even if she'd been dressed in regular clothes.

So what did I say to her? I said what every virgin of twenty-one years says to the woman who will only sleep with him if he takes care of her extermination needs. "You look nice." I followed up that erotically charged gem with "I brought the stuff."

The drama teacher smiled a lascivious smile. I bent down and looped the reusable grocery bag handles over my arms in order to leave my hands free to pick up my power tools. That's what I'd been telling myself they were, so I wouldn't be so scared. I kept reminding myself that I was a handyman with *legitimate* power tools.

As I walked past her, the drama teacher swayed a bit and I caught a whiff of eau de old vino and realized that not only was she dressed like a steampunk porn star who was just learning to sew her own clothes, she was very drunk.

Fuck. Fuck. Fuck.

She staggered in behind me.

"They're in there," she said, gesturing expansively toward the back of the little house. I saw that her sewing machine was still set up and bits of fabric and netting lay around the table. My heart felt knotted up at the idea of her putting all that effort into an outfit that was frankly terrifying.

"They?" I said.

"The bugs."

"Right," I said. "Are you one hundred percent sure you have an infestation?"

The drama teacher wandered unsteadily over to the table with all the sewing paraphernalia on it and grabbed for a Big Gulp–sized glass of what I assumed was white wine.

"Huh," she said, licking her lips.

"Is that a yes?"

"What do you think?" she asked and let her open robe fall down her shoulder as though to demonstrate something. It was a white shoulder. Not exactly muscular. But solid.

"I don't see—"

"Look at it!" she said, waggling her shoulder at me.

I took a few steps toward her, feeling confused now as well as scared and horny. A trifecta of out-of-control emotions.

Her shoulder looked fine to me. Quite nice, really. After all, it was a woman's shoulder.

"Closer!" she urged. So I drew nearer. I hadn't been that close to the drama teacher since we used to make out in her car. When I was her student. Her eleventh-grade pupil.

The whole thing was so bad. But my head swam from the heady bouquet of herb-scented candles, hormones and disrepute in her house.

"Do you see?" she asked, sounding like the killer from *The Silence of the Lambs*.

I did not see. I'd spent hours staring at bedbug bites on the Internet. When people react, they get everything from tiny red dots to huge red welts. Three welts in a row is a common reaction. The pros call that arrangement "breakfast, lunch and dinner." It's revolting, but I saw nothing like that on the drama teacher's shoulder or on any of the other parts of her squeezing out from under her ill-fitting sex outfit.

"Oh, yeah," I said, hoping to defuse the situation and tell her what she wanted to hear. "Now I do." Part of me felt a flutter of hope. Maybe the drama teacher was just being dramatic.

Then she turned around and let the robe fall in a heap on the floor. Her lower back was covered in red welts.

The breakfast I'd eaten hours before nearly came up.

I was really going to have to treat the place. The poor woman was being eaten alive.

"Are you sure you don't want to call a professional?" I asked, realizing that I was putting my chances of having sex at risk.

The drama teacher swayed a little, then propped herself against her sewing table.

"I don't have the money for a pest company. And I can't let my ex-husband find out. He hardly lets me see Daisy as it is."

"Daisy?" I repeated, stupidly. "You have a kid?"

"Our dachshund. After our divorce, we split custody of the puppy. He took her and left me, not long after that thing happened with you. She was only ten weeks old. We'd had her for less than two weeks. I missed so much of her childhood. If he thinks she's going to catch bedbugs over here, he won't let her come at all. He uses her like a pawn."

I couldn't think of anything else to say, so I got to work. I followed the directions I'd found on the Internet and on the how-to DVD. I did the same thing I'd done in Earl's cabin, but this time I unleashed the full arsenal: pesticides, diatomaceous earth. I placed talc-lined plastic cups under all the bed and table legs. I went over her carpets as carefully as a cokehead who just sneezed on the mirror. I vacuumed and steamed every object in the bedroom, starting on the outside edges of the room and working inward. I bagged every piece of fabric that could be laundered. I put all the books in plastic bags and knotted them shut. She could vacuum each individual novel, if she wanted to. There were limits to how much vacuuming I was prepared to do, even if there was sex to look forward to at the end of it.

As I worked, I saw all these little indicators about the drama teacher's life that were even more disturbing than her homemade sex outfit and her bug bites. For instance, it was obvious she'd cleaned up before I came, but she'd missed a few things. There was a dish of dried-out macaroni and cheese *under* the bed. It wasn't homemade either. It was Kraft Dinner. Don't get me wrong. KD was a regular feature in my house. My mom loves it and is probably eating it right now. But after living with Prudence for a few months and watching movies and reading health magazines, I know KD is a food product eaten mainly by children, teenagers and people who have given up all hope for a better life.

Part of me thinks that my mother's extreme reliance on KD and associated meals, such as Chef Boyardee ravioli and Spaghettios, has a self-conscious aspect to it. She's living the white-trash dream. She watches daytime TV, smokes like a grass fire and eats KD in order to have a consistent self-presentation. And to be fair, my mom's kind of funny about the boxes of KD in our house. She calls it "Killer D," for no real reason, and is always talking about how she likes to "spice it up" with black pepper.

I could tell the drama teacher didn't eat KD to be consistent or funny or anything else. She's a drama teacher, for chrissake. She is conversant in the works of Tennessee Williams and, you know, other playwrights. When she hangs out with drama nerds, or as I used to think of them, drama turds, she sure never lets on that she spends her evenings sewing sad sex costumes to wear while former students try to do pest control applications to her cottage. She doesn't mention that she eats Kraft Dinner in bed.

She had some serious books, too. I checked them out before I bagged them. She had a copy of the play *Waiting for Godot* on her bedside table, and another one called *Present Shock*, which looked sort of interesting but also looked like it had never been opened. Equally unread was the copy of *Underworld* by some guy called Don DeLillo. She might have cracked the paperback copy of *Oryx and Crake* sitting on top of *Underworld*, but it was a library book, so who knows. A small, cold part of me wondered if she'd put those books out so I'd see them and be impressed.

Her furniture was fairly tasteful, so far as I could tell with my limited experience of taste. It was in line with what you'd expect from a professional woman. Made of wood and upholstered. Nothing in light blue fake velvet.

When I approached the bed, things took a turn for the serious. Bedbugs can live at a considerable distance from their target. They might be nestled in behind a picture or a bedside table or any number of nooks and crannies. You have to remain alert for signs, such as blood smears and larval castings, but so far I hadn't seen anything like that. Chances were that the drama teacher's bugs were being predictable by living *in* the bed. Maybe under the box spring or in the bed frame. Close to the food source, anyway. Fuck me. Food source. I wanted to sleep with a food source. What did that make me?

I stripped off the sheets with the care of someone defusing a bomb and put everything into the extra-large garbage bags I'd brought. I hoped bedbug eggs and particulates weren't cascading onto the floor and onto my protective gear. I saw no evidence of blood meals on the sheets or the mattress cover, but the drama teacher hadn't taken my earlier advice to get white sheets, so it was hard to tell.

"See anything?" she asked, leaning in the doorway like Mrs. Robinson in *The Graduate*, only significantly less together.

"Well, the sheets are dark pink, so it's hard to see if there's any sign on them."

"I like passionate colors," said the drama teacher.

Had she always been such a cheese ball in the conversation department? I never really noticed before because she was so hot, in her semi-terrifying way, and I had usually been a little or a lot drunk.

After that, I couldn't really maintain the chitchat, because I was steaming the edges of the mattress and turning it and steaming the other side and then unzipping it and looking for evidence of bedbuggery. Nothing. Unblemished surgical-unit whiteness.

The drama teacher watched, motionless but for the steady movement of glass to mouth. Maybe she was fixated on how manly I looked. Probably not.

"I'm going to be spraying the whole thing down before I put it in a bedbug-proof mattress encasement. You might not want to stand there without a mask. The spray's pretty poisonous."

The drama teacher heaved a deep sigh.

"You know something else that's poisonous?" she said.

She didn't wait for me to respond.

"Other people."

"Yeah," I said. I remembered finding other people incredibly poisonous, too, especially when I drank.

I was marginally better at liking humanity since sobering up. Mostly because quite a few people have been nice to me.

"Passion basically overflows from me," said the drama teacher.

"Tell me about it," I said. I didn't mean for that to sound dismissive or ironic, but I *was* familiar with her passion. She had seduced me when I was in high school, with the result that I didn't graduate and I mentally and socially imploded. The only reason she didn't get fired then was because I told the principal and the cops who interviewed me that I had an unrequited love crush on her. I swore that she hadn't led me on or been inappropriate. Except those fifteen times in her car, parked out by the industrial grounds near Jack Point and a variety of other out-of-the-way locales. She'd been a *little* inappropriate on those occasions.

"You really should go in the other room while I spray," I told her, and then gave a silent prayer that I wouldn't have to do the whole house. It would take hours and I wasn't sure my nerves could stand it.

She didn't reply, and I looked up and found myself eye level with the crotch of the drama teacher's homemade steampunk panties. There were laces up the sides and some little metal doohickeys hanging off the edges, which swayed hypnotically from side to side. I stared and it occurred to me that I don't really get steampunk. I know it's supposed to be like early industrial machinery and Victorian style and time travel. What I don't understand is why anyone thinks those things are appealing or sexy. The fucking Victorians never time-traveled. Their machines were a menace, always tearing up peasants who moved to the cities to work in factories. Victorian fashion looked heavy and uncomfortable, and as a society, they spent way too much time worrying about whether table legs were provocative or not.

I was self-aware enough to know I was mentally trashing steampunk because I was scared of the drama teacher and all her uncontrolled passion. During our affair, we never went beyond, well, certain things. It is hard to write about this without sounding disrespectful of what was not a respectful or healthy thing. Our affair was the most intense thing that ever happened to me up until the time I sobered up. The thought that a mature woman, a creative person, could want to be with me was the fulfillment of every dream I ever had. Van Halen was hot for teacher and so was I.

Having our thing be unacceptable on every possible front just turned me on more. But there was a high price to pay when it fell apart, as I've noted several hundred times now. Judging by our current situation, it seemed like the drama teacher's life hadn't been on a rocket-like trajectory to fame and fortune, culminating in a hit Broadway show and a national teacher of the year award.

In spite of all that, on some level I always felt lucky that she'd chosen me.

But as she thrust her steampunked business in my face, something shifted. There was something so vulnerable about her in that moment, I knew there was no way I was going to try for sex. She was blind drunk and just . . . unwell. As the recovery types like to say, she was making poor decisions and she was trying to make them with me. I didn't pity her, exactly. I guess I felt empathy, having made a few catastrophically unexcellent decisions in my time.

She didn't pick up on the change in my attitude. Instead, she was trying to do some sort of burlesque-style shimmy and it wasn't happening.

"Maybe before you bag that mattress, you should bag me," she said.

I took a deep breath.

"Oh, I think I should just, you know, get your room sorted out. So you can go to sleep," I said.

A hurt look passed over her face. Just because a person is in full-scale alcoholic meltdown mode doesn't mean they can't be hurt.

"I got dressed up for you," she said, tears creeping along the edges of her voice.

Suddenly, I found myself talking to her like I was the grown-up, which I patently am not. This was a situation for which I was singularly unqualified.

She'd sunk onto her knees on the mattress on the floor. Her dark hair was a complete mess. It was arranged into what I assume was some sort of special steampunk hairdo, reminiscent of a top hat, that had begun to slide down the side of her head like a haystack after a hungry horse had gotten into it.

Her face, which when she wasn't hammered was so wry and smart, was puffy and a little yellow. I wondered how often she got loaded like this. I had a feeling this was not an isolated incident.

She didn't speak. Instead, she made a noise somewhere between a retch and a sob and collapsed onto the mattress.

"You're okay," I said, as gently as I could. "You're okay."

"No," she moaned, "I'm not."

In that, she was correct. I'd never seen a woman less okay than the drama teacher right then.

I worked my arms under her and propped her up. Then, with tremendous will and greater effort, I got her to her feet. She was soft and that gave me a feeling or two, which I shut down right away.

Once she was up, I wedged myself under her arm and carry-dragged her into the living room. She mumbled unintelligible nonsense and I muttered back what I hoped were comforting words, along the lines of "Almost there," "Doing good!" and "Oh, shit, my back."

When we reached the couch, she crashed headlong onto it.

"You want to?" she asked, lifting her face off the seat cushion. I guessed she was talking about sex, but I could tell from the way she rolled over and closed her eyes she didn't mean it.

All I wanted to do was leave, but I'd promised the drama teacher to deal with her problem and I would. I am an immature asshole in a lot of ways but I'm not mean.

I pulled a blanket off one of her chairs and put it over her. I felt sort of bad leaving her in the outfit, which was probably going to leave permanent marks due to a poor fit, but I wasn't about to take it off her.

While I was taking a minute to collect myself and make sure she wasn't going to come at me again, she groaned and flung one arm over her eyes. She used the other arm to reach down to the floor and pull up a flat cushion shaped like a bone. It was covered in brown dog hair. She slid it under her lower back.

I thought for a minute about the placement of her bedbug bites. They were concentrated in the same place she'd just shoved the bone pillow.

"Oh, Jesus," I muttered. I thought of the hundreds of dollars I'd spent buying steamers and traps and bug dope. All because the drama teacher had a habit of getting hammered and using a dog pillow to support her lower back when she passed out on the sofa.

But still I finished steaming and spraying her bed. I found no bedbugs on the frame, none in or near the nightstand. I vacuumed, sprayed and dusted everything, even though I was ninety-eight percent sure it was pointless. When I was just about done, I texted Eustace and asked if he'd come get me.

Eustace: You okay?
Me: Yeah. Can you bring me a Twenty Questions pamphlet?
Eustace: Got a candidate?
Me: You have no idea.

I waited for him in the driveway. As I stood in the afternoon light, I felt something strange come over me. It was a fullness that had a quality of lightness to it, for lack of a better description. What the fuck was happening to me? Pesticide poisoning? My spine was straighter and my head was clear. I actually felt like I might be taller. Jesus. I wasn't poisoned. I was feeling self-esteem. Unbelievable. Prudence is always yammering on about how every good decision makes it easier to make the next good decision, and how self-esteem is built one good decision at a time. I mostly tune her out, but I think she might be right.

I had tackled bedbugs, resisted sex with a woman dressed in a fishing net and put some serious sober time together. Result: tallness!

Possibly even not-terrible-lookingness. And a sense of being at ease in my own skin. It felt nothing short of revolutionary.

The air in my lungs was sweet, even with the faint top note of pulp mill.

It occurred to me that the next excellent deed I could do would be to help Prudence find her way to making a good decision for herself and for all of us. Earl and I had been doing our best for the farm and for Sara. We'd done everything Prudence asked, and sat with Sara at night and smuggled her proper food. But we needed Prudence's bionic powers of getting things done and we needed them right now. We'd been keeping things from her and that wasn't helping. It was time for her to learn what was going on with Sara and to see a regular doctor.

Prudence

A few days—I'm not sure how many—after the Halloween party, I was woken by the ringing phone. I looked at my alarm clock and saw that it was nearly eleven in the morning.

Once again, I'd missed half the day. As much as I would not give anyone the satisfaction of saying so, I had to admit that I wasn't completely pleased with the results of Dr. Bachmeier's remedies for my thyroid condition. The phone continued to ring.

"Why doesn't someone pick that up?" I muttered. Probably because no one else was slothful enough to stay in bed until nearly noon. It was disgusting.

With my head aching as though I'd been doing Jell-O shots off a bouncer's bicep the night before, and my body stiff with worrisome aches and obscure pains, I got myself downstairs. When I reached the kitchen, the phone had gone quiet.

I was about to sit down at the table when it started up again. I lunged for the receiver.

"Yes," I said, feeling nails being driven into my skull by an unskilled handyman.

"Prudence. It's Jeanine!"

"Oh, hello," I said, trying to force a bit of verve into my voice.

Jeanine is a friend from college and the author of several wildly successful young adult novels, one of which is being turned into a television series. Her first novel for adults just came out. It's a romantic crime caper about a teacup Chihuahua who helps solve crimes with the help of his nail technician owner. Jeanine is the person who encouraged me to write a young adult novel. I don't know that she completely understood how unsuccessful it is possible for an author to be, since she's experienced nothing but devoted readers and large royalty checks, hard on the heels of massive advances and enormous film and TV options.

"That book you sent me is amazing. God. What a voice! Pyrotechnical use of language. The author must be so interesting. I can't think of another novel half so profound about a woman overcoming a stiflingly provincial life. And I don't know when I've read such a developed voice in a first novel."

I thought of Mrs. Spratt. *Interesting* was not the word that came to mind. *Oblivious*, yes. But not *interesting*. Still, Jeanine's opinion could be trusted. We received excellent educations at our small private college. And she followed up her undergraduate degree in creative writing with a master's degree in literature from Stanford. Her cotton candy writing is perfectly formed and she knows what serious work looks like.

"She's a bit older," I said.

"Sixties? Seventies? That will affect the size of the advance if they think she's only got one book in her. But who the hell cares? This book is going to make her reputation."

"I don't know how old she is exactly," I said. "Much younger than that."

"Wonderful. The advance just went up by a hundred grand easy."

Besides knowing how to make money and how to sell books, Jeanine knows everyone who is anyone in the New York publishing scene. A source of serious revenue for publishing types, she lunches with the most influential writers and editors. The highbrows admire her intellect and taste, and the businesspeople admire her bottom line.

"I'm going to send it to Rich Dalton at Apex. He'll have every prestige-hungry editor in town slavering over it. I don't even think the book needs much editing. She must have been working on it for years."

From our discussions, I'd gotten the sense that Sally Spratt had been working on her novel for something closer to weeks. Sally said the story had been in her mind for some time. All she had to do was write it down. She said she'd been in a creative fugue for the past few weeks. Working all night and all day.

I didn't tell Jeanine any of that. Let Rich Dalton decide how to package the story of how a depressed, divorced mother from Cedar turned out a genius novel.

"Must have," I said.

"Well, thanks, Pru. It's going to do nothing but good things for me to pass this on to the right people. Writers like this come along once a generation. She makes Alice Munro look ham-fisted! She makes Junot Díaz look unvivid! You can't see, but I'm rubbing my hands together in glee right now."

"That's good. I'm glad."

"And the farm? It's thriving? How about those characters you're living with? They sound so fabulous! When are you coming to visit us?"

The way I felt at that moment, I would never leave the kitchen, never mind the farm, again. New York City might as well have been an outer ring of Saturn. I didn't tell her that we'd lost one of our "characters" and that I had no real idea how the others were doing.

"Not sure," I said.

"Don't make us come to you. Ruth and Kimi have been talking about it. We miss you, Pru. We're unsustainable without you!" She lowered her voice. "Are you okay? You sound odd. Flat. Are you being held against your will by overall-clad hillbillies?"

"No. I'm fine. Just getting over a . . . health thing."

"Please tell me you aren't trying to treat it using one of your extra-alternative health approaches. It's bad enough that you insist on cooking your own cosmetics and gathering wild yeast for your sourdough by leaving rotten potatoes around in bowls of water. Remember when you got strep throat and you tried to cure it using that Australian honey?"

"It was from New Zealand and it's a miracle product," I told her. "Some of the best doctors in the world recommend manuka honey."

"Yes, but it won't cure strep. You ended up in hospital."

"One time. For two days. It was not a big deal."

"Promise me you'll go to a proper doctor if you need to."

I ignored the request but I did promise to tell Mrs. Spratt to call Jeanine so they could discuss her book.

I was too tired to head down to the gas bar to tell Mrs. Spratt about the call, and I didn't have her phone number. The thought of looking into that glass case full of crimes against nutrition was too much. Instead, I went back to bed. Telling Mrs. Spratt she might be headed for literary stardom would have to wait until the next day.

My eyes had just closed when Seth came barreling into my room, by which I mean he slouched in faster than usual.

"You need to get out of bed," he said.

"I'm sorry?"

"Don't be sorry. Go to another doctor and get some new medication. We need your help around here."

Then he told me what he and Earl had been doing at night. He told me where Sara had been spending her evenings. I thought her mother was probably writing and hadn't gone far when she left Sara. But I was equally sure she was so involved in her writing she hadn't told her daughter what she was doing.

"I don't know what I can do," I said.

"Get yourself right, even if it's some big point of pride that you don't like conventional medicine or whatever the fuck you call it. I know that you'll know what we should do when your brain is working again."

He was absolutely right. I wasn't thinking clearly to begin with and being stubborn only made my decision-making abilities worse. I'd dug in because I didn't want Eustace to be right. In that way, I was no better than Sara's parents.

I got up and slipped on my runners over my three pairs of socks.

"Fine. Let's go to a walk-in clinic. See what some conventional doctor has to say."

"Truck's not working," he said.

"Fine. We'll call Hugh."

And so we did.

Sara

I'm staying with my dad right now. It's better than staying in the car with my mom, but it's also more boring, especially since Earl and Seth started visiting me at night. We never talked much because they wanted me to sleep, but it was fun having them there. While I'm at my dad's, we can still leave each other notes.

The fort has been nailed shut. I don't know why. I didn't tell Earl and Seth that Target and I had been going in there to watch the farm, because then they'd feel bad about nailing it shut and feel even sorrier for me. Lots of things about me were embarrassing, such as that I couldn't stay alone at night even though I'm eleven and should be mature enough, and I keep hanging around a place where I'm not allowed to be. I didn't want to add to it.

Target said we could use a hammer to pry the door open, but I told him they probably closed it for a reason, such as safety. I told him that pretty soon the social worker would do his report and then my parents will let me go back to the farm, but Target said I shouldn't "hold my breath."

It was interesting to hear him say that, because Target doesn't talk in a mature way like that very often. I told him he sounded sophisticated, which is a word that means smart and old. We learned it in school a while ago.

He just shrugged and said social workers don't always do what they say they will, because they get new jobs and move away.

That made me worried, so I called social worker Pete's office and they said he was out. I asked when he'd be back and they said they'd take my number, but instead I just hung up.

Then I sat around in my dad's apartment. I knew he was over at Woefield working with Lucky. I should be over there, too. It's too bad my parents are not leaders enough to decide what should happen with me. They're just waiting for the social worker to tell them so they can't blame each other. I asked my mom about it and she said things would work out and that I should be patient.

Some people at school have started calling me Bedbug Spratt, but then Target told them to stop and they were so surprised that Target talked that they stopped. That was really neat. I'm lucky to have Target for a friend. Maybe I'll call him up and see if one of his foster moms will invite me over.

Earl

Me and Eustace went to the casino three times before we found him. A young feller working the front door said hello. He was the only one in there who didn't look like a three-day-old TV dinner left on the back porch.

Tell me if you see him, said Eustace.

So we start walking around, and that morning the casino looked like the saddest geezer convention you ever seen. There was a few younger people glued in front of them machines but not many. None of 'em looked like they had money to lose, not even dimes or quarters or whatever you have to feed into them blink boxes.

If I ever end up sitting in front of some blinking, squeaking, farting machine on a Thursday morning when there's things to do outside, you can go ahead and shoot me.

With the loud music and the machines making a hellacious racket and who knows what all going on in there, I started to lose my damn bearings. Got to feeling like I might have some kind of fit if I wasn't careful. But then we come around a corner, just around from some kind of gambling tables with nobody sitting at 'em, and there was young Stephan McFadden. Never would have thought his uncle Brian living with a pig in a hoarder trailer would look like he had himself a nice situation, but he looked a damn sight happier than his nephew.

Young Stephan had a red baseball hat pushed halfway off his head. The place wasn't none too warm, but he was sweating and muttering to himself while he shoved coins into the machine and jammed down the lever.

That's him, I told Eustace.

Eustace stood right next to him and said hello.

Young Stephan didn't look over. Not now, he said. I'm due. I had this one till closing last night. I was first in line this morning so none of these old fuckers could try to scoop me. This bitch has eaten like four grand. I'm fucking due.

Would that four grand happen to belong to a young lady with a farm on Woefield Road? asked Eustace, cool as you please.

The little bastard looked up, red face and little mustache and a scruffy beard.

No, he said. I spent her money in here weeks ago. This is money I got from another lady to buy stuff for her new bathroom.

Get up, says Eustace, but before the kid could do anything, I got in there and knocked his damned hat off his head. It was the way he talked. Like it didn't matter worth a shit that he took Prudence's money. I would have liked to smash every machine in the place and make the little bastard sweep it up.

Hey man, said the kid. I'm not saying I *won't* build her barn. Or whatever it was. I'm just down a little. But I got this other advance for materials for the other lady's bathroom. She wants a lot of high-end shit in there. Soaker tub. Double sink. The works. So I brought her money in here to win back *the other lady's* money. Fuck, you can't just hit me like that. I came in here like first thing to get the job done!

Let's all settle down, said Eustace.

What's going on here? asked a feller in a red coat who come walking up. A manager or a security guard.

Everything's fine, said Eustace. We're just talking to Stephan about some business matters.

Keep it civil or go outside, said the security guy, who looks like he lost everything he ever had on one of those goddamned fancy pinball machines. What do they call them guys who can't quit gambling? Degenerators. Stephan and the guard were both degenerators as far as I was concerned.

Absolutely, says Eustace. You could tell he was used to dealing with scared farm animals. Even I simmered down some.

Look, Stephan. We need to talk this over. I'm sure the casino would be interested to hear that you're spending stolen money in here.

I'm sure they wouldn't give a shit, said Stephan.

The security guy made a confused face like he wasn't sure if he was supposed to give a shit or not.

Let me put it this way: I bet the newspaper would be interested to hear that this casino let you spend money you stole from pensioners.

They weren't pensioners! said Stephan. The girl in Cedar is young. Hot, too. And the bathroom lady is still working. Volunteering and doing charity stuff and teaching gardening classes. It's fucking depressing, actually. She must be terrible with her money.

Unlike you, genius, said Eustace. Come on. Let's go outside.

Dude, the kid says to the security guy. You need to get them to leave. They're ruining my entertainment experience. And this thing is just about to deliver.

By this time, a guy in a black suit had come up and he seemed to have a little more thread on his spool than the guy in the red jacket.

Come back when you've got yourself sorted out, he said to Stephan.

My machine, man! said the kid. He sounded like he was going to cry.

The manager and the security guy walked us outside.

Shit, said Stephan when we were standing on the sidewalk. Now my whole investment is going to someone else. You guys have quite the timing. He sighed, like he was already done being upset.

Can you give me a ride home? he asked.

What about that fancy truck? I asked.

Sold my truck. Well, sort of lost it in a wager. Fucking Canucks. Should have stuck with Montreal.

You're a full-blown addict, said Eustace.

Oh, for sure, said the kid. That is not in doubt.

We walked through the parking lot to Eustace's big truck.

Nice ride, said the kid. You need any work done around your place?

Eustace give him a look and the kid said, Just kidding.

Here's the good news, said Eustace. You're going to be too busy building Prudence's barn to let that casino take any more money from you. But before you do that, we're going to take the lady's bathroom money back to her.

He stopped. Looked at the kid. You *do* know how to build, don't you? he asked.

Are you kidding? Got my ticket and everything. Born to build, said the kid.

I'll say this for him, he's a cheerful little bastard, considering there are probably quite a few people around who want to break both his legs.

That Eustace feller has a way of making you feel he has things all under control. If we can just get Prudence on her feet, I do believe the two of them can get our troubles sorted.

Prudence

Twenty-four hours after I saw the new doctor and started the new medication, I began to feel like myself again. It was like a miracle. I got out of bed to find the farm thrumming with activity. Normally, Earl and Seth operate at what is best described as a leisurely pace. When Sara was here, she was steady but not swift. I'm the only truly speedy person on the farm. When I emerged from my room feeling like a vampire that's finally had a drink of blood after a years-long fast, I shuddered to think of what I'd allowed to happen due to my stubbornness. I thought of Sara left alone all night in a cold, dark car. I thought of the things half done and the things done so badly I'd have to redo them myself.

I couldn't afford to get overwhelmed or wallow in guilt. All that was left was to redouble my efforts. It was time to move forward. The thing I know about me, Sara's parents, and everyone else is that people are almost always doing the best they can. It sounds trite, but it's true. Thinking people are setting out to do their worst never helped anything or anyone.

I was reminded of that when, instead of finding the farm in disarray, I went outside to discover Earl and Seth and Stephan McFadden preparing a foundation for our new barn. My god! If you've never seen a building go up on your very own land, you have no idea what true satisfaction is. I could see why people became developers!

As if that wasn't exciting enough, Eustace was helping Sara's father wheel the wagon over into the middle of the field. The wagon seemed to be moving smoothly on its wheels. Then I saw that Lucky was harnessed up and standing like a docile little lamb at the hitching post.

Well, I couldn't contain myself. I just had to go out and peek at the building supplies that lay neatly stacked under a blue tarp.

"Oh, it looks fantastic!" I told Stephan McFadden, Earl and Seth. "It's all so tidy. You are all marvels of responsibility."

Seth coughed into his arm.

"Seth? Are you sick?"

"No," he said. "Just glad to see you up and around."

"Thank you, Seth," I said. "I needed that talking to."

He grinned and ducked his head under his Judas Priest ball cap. He's too old to still be growing, but Seth actually seems taller lately. It's the oddest thing.

I gazed around. The farm seemed to sparkle in the early winter light.

"I was worried things wouldn't move forward without me, but look at this! You guys don't even need me."

"Nice to see you again," said Stephan McFadden, coming over to look at me in a caring manner. Seeing him again reminded me why I'd hired him. In addition to his low quote, there was a lovely, clear-eyed farm boy innocence about him. Total confidence. That's what his rosy cheeks inspired in me.

"Get to work, Stephan," said Earl to the boy.

Seemed like a strange way to talk to our contractor, especially one with the face of an angel, but Earl has his own communication style.

"How long until the barn will be ready? Bertie and Lucky will be so thrilled to move in!"

"We'll have it framed up by the end of tomorrow. Another day for the roof. Then we'll finish up the walls. Put in the windows and whatnot. Pretty simple. Should be ready for the weekend."

"That is just incredible," I told Stephan. "I could kiss you."

He beamed at me. "I'd allow that," he said.

"I wouldn't," said Eustace, who'd come up behind me. "Get to work, Stephan."

A thought popped into my head and I called Stephan over again.

"You're doing wonderful things here, and I know a young man who would love to help. His name is Anoop and his mother will be so thrilled to see him working. Are you interested in an assistant?"

Stephan didn't say anything at first, but Eustace beamed at me. "Stephan here was just saying he'd love a helper. Maybe someone to handle the money for him. Right, Stephan?"

Stephan nodded and I made a mental note to call Anoop and his mother as soon as I went back inside. I knew I'd remember, too. What a wonderful feeling to have my memory back as well as my energy!

After that, I practically floated over to watch Lucky being harnessed up to the wagon. After I watched Dean Spratt drive him around the field twice without incident, I knew we were in a new era at Woefield Farm. The era of competence. Finally, we were on the right road.

Seth

Now that Prudence is back on her feet, she's doing her very best mongoose impression. I don't mean that she giggles when she mates, which the Internet informs me is what actual female mongooses do, but that she's tackling the problems big and small, hers and others', with an indomitable will.

Like me and Earl, she was horrified by Sara's situation but stymied about how to handle it. No parent wants to be told they're doing a bad job. So Prudence went to each of them and, without making accusations, asked directly if they'd reconsider their decision not to let Sara visit.

If you want any further evidence that they're idiots, here it is: they both said no. They said they couldn't afford to give the other one "ammunition" in the divorce and that they thought it was best to wait for the social worker's report.

This is unbelievable on several fronts. Prudence got Mrs. Spratt some massive book deal and has given Mr. Spratt a new lease on life by letting him work with our mule. But no, that wasn't enough.

Bloodied but not beaten, Prudence has decided to renew her efforts to impress the social worker. This is exhausting for everyone.

She's trying to get the Great Christmas Mule Pull off the ground, and it doesn't seem to be going well but I don't like to ask, because then she might feel compelled to tell me.

She says she's having trouble getting what she calls "community buy-in." In other words, no one wants our mule wagon bringing customers to their places of business. I guess they must have talked to their lawyers about liability or something and decided to take the opt-out position. This is a small community. You can only afford to have so many of your customers maimed and killed in preventable mule-wagon accidents before it takes a toll on the bottom line.

So far, Sara's dad has driven Lucky around the pasture and up and down Woefield Road a few times. He hasn't taken our unpredictable mule onto any of the busier roads, and I sure as shit wasn't planning to be sitting on that wagon when he tried.

She's got that guy who faints when he eats spice and who wears nothing but jogging suits over here helping the young fraudster Stephan McFadden. Anoop's mother has come to take video of him cleaning up the construction materials. I think she's going to send it to some woman to prove that Anoop has a job. This interference is very much to Prudence's taste, and she gets this look on her face like she's just seen a sensational ballet performance whenever she catches sight of anyone doing anything even slightly productive. Indomitable. That's what she is.

Prudence is also cooking up some other scheme for the holidays, but she hasn't shared the details and I haven't asked, because again, I don't want to risk her telling me. All I know is that I have been put in charge of Christmas decorations. Which is fine, because my mom is dying to get her leathery hands on the new barn and she loves to festoon every available surface with holiday garlands and other shit.

What else?

Earl and Prudence and I are all leaving notes for Sara. And in true thoughtful Sara fashion, she's leaving notes for each of us. Her notes are matter-of-fact recitations of current events in her life, and she makes sure to give each of us a useful fact that we can use in our lives. They're sort of like fortune cookie notes, only factual and not mass-produced.

The note I received today informed me that she's in her school Christmas play and will be playing the role of the partridge. This means she'll be on the stage "the longest out of anyone." Then she told me some partridge facts, which I will treasure forever.

I think she's been writing to Earl about Alec Baldwin, who still seems to be ailing. That rooster has tremendous star quality, so it's a bit of a worry. Sara's told Earl everything he should be doing, but I don't see a lot of change in the white-crested Casanova. He's hardly humping any of the hens in his harem and his crest is looking threadbare. Sara's last note said she's not sure how old he is, and so his problems might be age-related. On the plus side, the lull in Alec Baldwin's sex life makes my nonexistent one look better by comparison.

What else? I finally wrote my overdue articles, and my editor, Tamara, loved them. She and I have been talking quite a bit. She is coming to BC for some online magazine awards gala deal in Vancouver, and then she's going to Victoria to see some relatives, and while she's on the island she's going to visit the farm. And me. Will I sound like less of a man if I say I'm scared to meet her in person? She's so cool, it's kind of paralyzing.

Finally, every few days, I get an incomprehensible message from the drama teacher, who has apparently taken a leave from her job. She says she's using the time to finish her steampunk play, but I think she got suspended for showing up for class drunk. I've tried twelve-stepping her a few times, and every time she's told me to get lost. Or to come over to finish what I started.

My guess is she only remembers a little bit about what happened between us. That's probably a blessing.

Anyhow, life is not a total drag now. But we definitely need our Sara back, even if her mother isn't leaving her in the campground anymore.

Sara

Miss Singer was the one who gave me the role of the partridge in the Christmas play because she's very fond of me. I really appreciated that, because of how having activities can make everything better. Well, maybe not everything.

My mom has also learned that it's nice to have useful things to do. That's good because cleaning things that are already clean and sitting in the car while squeezing stress balls used to be her main hobbies. Back when we were sleeping in the car, I used to dream that Prudence or Seth or Earl would find out that my mom was leaving me alone in the car at night and they'd come and rescue me. Then Earl did! But first I had to tell him. And even when he found out, he couldn't really do much about it except stay with me. That was an eye-opener.

Adults can do lots of things with kids and no one will find out if the kids don't say anything. Target says I'm lucky it wasn't worse. He says he would have been better off by himself in a car than he was with his family. Anyway, the interesting part is that it turns out that my mom wasn't being a neglectful parent when she left me in the car in the campground. She was writing on her book!

She told me that she left me and went over to the campground activity hut and worked on her book with a headlamp strapped to her head. In the cold! And the rain! My mom is very serious about writing and it paid off, because now her book is getting published for a lot of money. Since she finished her book and some people in New York like it and want to publish it, she's a different person. She moved us back into our old house, but I'm mostly staying with my dad because my mom keeps having to go to Toronto and New York and other foreign cities to have meetings with agents and editors and other publishing people. My mom is way skinnier than she used to be and she smiles sometimes and only cries about twice as much as other mothers instead of ten times as much.

I'm staying with her this week, and this morning before I went to school she said she needed to talk to me. There still isn't much furniture in our house, but at least she's moved our beds back in and we have a kitchen table and two chairs. My mom says prospecting buyers will just have to imagine our furniture doesn't exist.

Because she's going to be a published writer, my mom has started hanging up pictures of naked ladies and rotten fruit. The realtor told my mom she might want to rethink the decor if she wanted to leave the house on the market, but my mom said her life was just starting and she intended it to include art. She put a bottle of wine with the bottom part wrapped in string on the kitchen table and a candle in it. She didn't drink the wine, I don't think. She just bought the bottle like that, with the half-burned candle in it and everything. The real estate lady rolled her eyes when she saw it. I bet she hides it in a cupboard when she shows the house, which doesn't happen too often.

Maybe my mom will get very famous from her book and then people will want to buy our old house, including her wine bottle and candle.

My mom showed me an email from an editor in London who said she was the "natural heir to Sylvia Plath and Erica Jong by way of Gillian Flynn and Edward St. Aubyn." I don't know who any of those people are. At first I thought it said "natural hair" and my mom had to explain *heir* to me. I tried to use the word when I talked to people but almost everyone confuses it with *hair*. It's not a very useful word for that reason. Still, it's great that my mom's book is like so many other people's books.

When we sat down at the kitchen table, she kept using her finger to turn the wine bottle with the candle in it around and around.

"Sara," she said. "Now that I've produced something I'm really proud of, I feel like I need to see where it will take me."

I could have been offended when my mom said that, since my mom also produced me, but my mom doesn't really think about other people that much. That's something I've realized about her.

"You know how passionately you care about your chickens? Well, that's how I feel about my work." She paused. "And you, of course."

That last part wasn't true.

My mom can be slow to get to the point. I hope her book's not like that. I shifted my backpack, which just had my books in it, which was nice, on my lap. I wanted to get going because there was a cast meeting before school and I wanted to sneak over to the farm and get my notes. I get notes from Earl, Seth, Prudence and Eustace now. It's a lot of work to write them all back, but I don't mind because it makes them feel good.

"I've decided that to truly explore this side of myself and the opportunities that my writing has brought into my life, I need a change of setting. I considered Paris. Mavis Gallant and all that. But it's so French there. I've spoken to my agent and my editor and they've found me a six-month sublet in New York."

"What's a sublet?" I asked. Since my mom became a writer, she's really a good source of new vocabulary words. I wouldn't have expected that from her.

"It's an apartment that you rent from someone else for a period of time."

"Oh," I said. "When are you going?"

"Next week," she said. "Of course, you're welcome to join me. I really do feel badly that I haven't . . . I mean, we haven't been connecting."

"I have school. And the play. I'm a partridge," I said.

"I know the timing's not ideal. I'm going to speak with your father. I'm sure you can stay with him. Six months isn't that long. Maybe you can come visit me in the spring. There's probably a farm museum in New York," she said.

So that's how I found out my mom is going to sublet New York City.

Earl

Christmas music gives me a headache. That's what I told my brother Merle when he called today and asked for the fourth time if I wanted to do a holiday bluegrass record. He asked if I'd do one if we could record it at the farm, and I pretended not to hear what he said. He ain't going to come all the way to Nanaimo again.

I told Prudence I can't stand that music when she asked me and Seth to put up speakers in the barn, loud enough so people'd be able to hear the racket all over the farm. But we done it anyway. Borrowed speakers from some friend of Seth's and hung 'em up. Sara's chickens isn't laying much right now, and if we play too much goddamned Christmas music, they might never lay another egg and I wouldn't blame them. That's my opinion. I'm real worried about Alec Baldwin. I been doing everything Sara says in her notes but he still ain't right. He's off his feed almost completely now. I hate to see it.

After we got done with the speakers, Prudence came down to the farm stand to watch me and Seth try to put up a string of Christmas lights. So many of 'em were burned out or missing, it looked like a bum's smile when we plugged it in. Prudence asked me if I would mind driving down to the store to get her more spices for her Christmas cookies. Well, Jesus. The only time I liked going to the grocery was when Sara came with me. She's quite the shopper. Comparing prices and explaining labels. And them grocery stores is the worst for playing the Christmas music. Always got it on extra loud.

I asked Prudence if I could get the stuff at the gas bar and she said it would cost too much. She's full of piss and vinegar again and there was no arguing with her, so I got in the truck and went down to the Country Grocer.

Might as well have been the grand opening at a Walmart. People drove around that parking lot, wearing goddamned Santa hats, fake antlers sticking out of their windows, every one of them looking like jackasses.

I was in no mood to be civil by the time I got past the people from the Salvation Army wanting money and the junior hockey team wanting money and the radio station and the firemen wanting money out front. Jesus Christ. Half the town was standing outside that place looking for handouts.

I pushed through all the Christmas begging and into the store and it was worse than a rodeo circus convention in there. Every person in Cedar must have been in that store, carts piled up with food and drink like they figured the holidays was a major earthquake and they had to lay in a month worth of supplies, even though the store is only closed for two days. I'll tell you, I was in a helluva foul mood by the time I got one of them little fellers in an apron to show me the spices and then I couldn't read the little writing on the bottles because I forgot my specs. I was holding one of them bottles about an inch from my eyes, trying to see if it was that cardamom Prudence wanted, when somebody said, Mr. Clemente?

I turned and seen a young lady with blond hair.

I'm Miss Singer. Sara's teacher, she said.

Even though I was in a bad mood from all the Christmas, I knew I had to make a good impersonation. So I said hello.

Mr. Clemente, I wonder if we could have coffee?

Well, lord help me Jesus. I never had coffee with no young ladies before. Except Prudence, but she's so goddamned speedy she's more like a jackrabbit than a young lady.

Before I knew it, that young Miss Singer helped me find the cinnamon and cardamom and allspice and jar of molasses that Prudence had on her list, and she came with me through the checkout.

Doing some Christmas baking? asked the checkout feller, a friendly young guy I seen before. Always has a nice word for everyone, which makes his lineups too damned slow.

Yup, I said.

Then Miss Singer and the young feller started talking about the kinds of cookies they like to eat and I told them I liked all of it except for Christmas cake because it tastes like gum picked off the sidewalk. They laughed and so did some people in the lineup. Turns out a lot of people don't care for Christmas cake.

I got to feeling better then. Even the Christmas music headache eased some.

When we walked back through all the beggars out front, I gave each of 'em a couple of dollars. What the hell. I followed Miss Singer over to the coffee shop near the A&W. I never been in that one before. It's even fancier than Tim Hortons, but I paid for both of us, because she's a young lady. It was an expensive trip to the grocery, let me tell you, but Miss Singer said that was very kind of me, so I didn't mind.

The only place to sit was at one of them tall round tables with high stools. I was glad I had my suspenders on, or my backside would have been hanging out. I don't know who invented them goddamned tall tables.

I wanted to speak to you about Sara, said Miss Singer. The thing is, she's an amazing girl. But she's been struggling since she left the farm.

Misses her birds, I said.

Not just her birds, said Miss Singer. She loved living on the farm with all of you. She's told me this several times.

Yup, I said. Because I know she did. We all liked it better when Sara lived on the farm.

I've seen you and your coworker bringing her food in the morning.

Just treats, I said. When we see something we think she might like, we get it for her.

And you drop it off at the school? said Miss Singer.

She's not supposed to visit the farm. Her parents don't get along and they can't make an agreement on where she should go. They want to get a report from the social worker before she comes back to visit.

I'm sorry to hear that, said Miss Singer. If anyone asks me, I'll tell them the farm seems like an entirely appropriate place for her to visit. And stay, if it comes to that. I think that what happened at the conference was an unfortunate accident.

Damned right it was, I said. That little bastard who tried to tom-fool with her. If I ever see him dragging his ass around—

Mr. Clemente, she said. It's not my place to tell you what to do, but when the social worker finally gets in touch, it would be best not to threaten any kids. Even if they are . . . difficult.

Creepy little bastard, I said.

She smiled and said, If you think Charles Manson Barton is bad, you should meet his parents. But T is a nice boy and he's really flourishing with his new foster family. They're hoping to adopt him.

Miss Singer took a drink of her fancy coffee and it left some foam on her top lip and she reminded me of a kid herself. That's what it's come to. Kids teaching kids. I guess that's who has the energy.

Do you think Sara's parents are taking good care of her? she asked.

Hell no, I told her. Don't misunderstand me. They aren't doing nothing wrong to her. But they sure as shit aren't doing nothing right, either. Too focused on their own business. It's like they never got to do what they wanted when they were young and now that they got a taste of it, nothing's going to stop them.

She nodded. That's what I thought, she said. Sara's so intense. She needs people who support her growth. Well, I better go. I'm helping with the Christmas play. It's a multicultural retelling of the Twelve Days of Christmas. Sara has a major role.

The teacher stood up. You are all invited as my special guests. It will thrill Sara to have you there. Just please don't bring the mule.

Then our visit was over and I was already looking forward to telling Sara about it in my note. I would tell her about meeting her teacher and how everyone thinks she's the cat's pajamas.

Prudence

Not one business owner has signed up to be a stop on the Cedar Christmas Mule Tour. I've called every farm in the area, every local gift shop, every artist's studio. I even called the local strip malls. I asked the manager at the gas bar if he'd like to take part. Turns out he's the same boy I saw when I went in to speak to Sara's mother—the kid with the pot leaf T-shirt who looks to be about fourteen.

He said he wouldn't be taking part and that he and the other members of the Downtown Cedar Business Association had discussed my proposal and had serious concerns about liability. He actually used those words, which suggests that he isn't actually fourteen.

I called Werner to see if he could put in a good word for us, but he was on a two-month holiday in Spain and Italy and couldn't be reached.

So I've been forced to call it off. We aren't going to drive Lucky around Cedar this Christmas, and perhaps it's just as well.

I'm optimistic that we'll have a wonderful holiday anyway. We'll decorate just as we'd planned, and if the weather holds we'll offer wagon rides around the acreage.

I went to discuss the matter with Dean Spratt, who had Lucky tied up outside the new barn. It's so much more impressive than I dared to dream. It has three stalls and a loafing shed attached to the side, plus a room for hay and grain and another room to store tack. There are few things more satisfying than seeing your live-stock snugly housed.

It was cold and the sky was a smudged white, hinting at the possi-bility of snow. Dean Spratt didn't hear me walk up, because he was using an electric shaver on Lucky's tail.

I watched him cut a horizontal ridge into the outer tail hairs near the top, then another and another, so the top of the tail looked like a tassel with three layers. The rest of the long hair fell down toward Lucky's hocks.

When he finally shut the device off and ran a hand over the neat three ridges of hair, I cleared my throat so as not to startle him.

"Lucky's Christmas look?"

Spratt almost smiled.

"He deserves it," he said. "He's what they call a three-bell mule."

He ran a hand appreciatively over Lucky's spotted hind end. "The military used to cut bells into mules' tails so you could tell what they were broke for. One bell for a mule broke to pack, two for a mule that can pack and drive, and three for a mule that can pack, drive and be ridden."

"I'm a committed pacifist, but I still find that fascinating," I said, patting Lucky's neck. The big red mule inclined his head toward me. Lately, Lucky has been more warmly inclined toward all of us. He visits us when we're working in the pasture and lets all of us catch him. He hasn't run away or tried to bite or kick anyone in weeks, not even me. Dean Spratt says Lucky just needed more handling, clear boundaries and to feel useful. Those are things every living creature can benefit from.

"The plan for Christmas has changed. I've had to cancel the Cedar Christmas Mule Tour of local attractions."

"Maybe because there aren't any attractions around here," said Mr. Spratt.

"I just think it's going to take time for people to understand the concept and to trust us to pull it off. In the meantime, I've decided that we'll host a party here. We're going to decorate every inch of this place. Have a marvelous meal. We'd like to ask you to drive the wagon if weather permits."

Now it was his turn to clear his throat.

"Yeah," he said. "I can do that, at least until Christmas. After that, I'm going to be making a change."

"A change?"

"I took a new job. Just a temporary thing for a couple of months. Maybe three. Going to work at an outfit that runs mules in Arkansas. On a visitor work visa. They need me to start before New Year's."

I stared at him. His rawboned face was alight with something that looked like happiness.

"I think it's great that you're following your dream. I followed mine and it led me here."

He made a little face but I ignored him.

"And, uh, what about Sara?" I asked.

"Her mother and I will be working that out."

My mind raced. Which one would be taking Sara with them? I

had a sick feeling neither one of them wanted to. Sad as that was, it could be our big chance.

"I'm going to invite the social worker to our Christmas party. Try to get him to write that report."

Dean Spratt kept stroking Lucky. "We've got to have it," he said. "Sally might not seem like it, but she's got a vindictive streak."

"I'm hoping you can help get him here. I think he's more likely to show up if you encourage him."

"I can do that," he said. And my heart set sail.

Seth

lec Baldwin wasn't looking so hot. Eustace and Stephan McFadden and Anoop, who is actually pretty handy, built him a little rooster convalescence hospital with heated shed and small run for when he felt well enough to take a walk outside. The hospital was parked on Earl's porch. I'd opened the back of the rest box and saw that the no-longer shiny black bird with the droopy Liberace head crest was crouched inside.

Prudence came bustling over. She still gets cold easily, so she was bundled up, three times her usual size, in sweaters and coats and hats and gloves under mittens.

"Seth!" she yelled, which was unusual for her. Even when she's in full speed mode she usually has one of those calming, nicely modulated voices.

"I've had an idea!"

Oh shit, I thought.

"Sara's parents are leaving. And they're taking Sara with them. Only for a few months, but who knows what might happen? This is our last chance to get her back. We've got to get that social worker here and convince him to write a report that they can bring to their divorce lawyers."

"I don't think that social worker is going to write a report. Sara's not part of his caseload. That's why he's not showing up. He just said that to get Mr. and Mrs. Bitterspratt to stop fighting."

"They won't change their minds unless they have something in writing from an authority."

"The whole thing is just so unfathomably stupid. They know she'd be better off here. They know we aren't unsafe. Well, we are, but mostly to ourselves."

"We need to give them space to change their minds. To retreat with dignity from their entrenched positions."

"How about they think about what's good for Sara?"

"Someday they'll think in those terms, but they can't seem to do it now. The social worker and the party is what we have. We've got to make it count."

"Are you sure inviting the social worker to one of our events is a good idea?" I asked, trying to sound like I didn't think she'd lost her mind. "Not everything we do around here is an unqualified success."

"Those situations were different," she said. "The Cedar Christmas Mule Tour idea is dead. This is the only option we have. We'll put on a Christmas party so amazing that no one could possibly object to Sara coming back to stay. The social worker will be dying to write a glowing report."

"Okay," I said, wishing we had a viable Plan B. What would happen if we didn't get the report? Would Mr. or Mrs. Spratt take Sara with them? Leave her with her aunt in Duncan? How would we ever get to see her then?

I glanced into the box. The rooster hadn't moved. Damn it.

"My friend Hugh, from Cedar Cab, called. He said that the botanical garden in Nanoose has decided not to put on their annual Christmas display. They have thousands of dollars' worth of lights they're not using and they've agreed to rent them to us!"

"For what? A few bags of greens? I thought we were nearly broke."

Prudence laughed merrily. "I made a special arrangement. We're going to let the woman who runs the botanical garden ride Lucky! Her name is Tai and she loves mules. I told her she can come over anytime."

"I hope Tai has a lot of insurance."

Prudence wasn't put off by my negativity. "Now we just need a little help putting up all those lights in time for the party. We need to gather cedar boughs. We need a menorah, just in case we get Jewish visitors. We'll need ribbons. Call everyone you know. We've got to make this thing happen."

Then she zipped away, inasmuch as anyone shaped like an over-dressed egg can zip.

By the end of the next day, the farm looked like one of those traveling carnivals setting up in the Walmart parking lot.

Earl

She got all of us, the volunteer fire brigade, the local tree-chopping service, two loggers and three roofers involved. There was guys hanging out of every tree on the place and two of them cherry-picker platforms, one parked by the house so the guys could string lights along the roofline and another one parked near the tallest stand of fir trees at the far edge of the property.

Problem was, there was more lights than there was things to hang 'em on, so Prudence got them doubled up. We ended up with so many lights crisscrossing the new barn, it looked like a Vegas casino.

My cabin was the worst. Practically falling down under the weight of them sparklers. The commotion probably didn't help the sick rooster living on my porch. I kept his hospital covered in an old sheet so he could get a little shut-eye and not be bothered by all the goings-on.

Most of the young guys who come out to help did it because Eustace promised them free vet services for their dogs. Seth got that mother of his and her boyfriend to pitch in with decorating, along with his aunt and some of their barfly friends. There was about six of them gals, and I'd guess that they all watch a helluva lot of decorating TV. Every one of them smoked and swilled wine from plastic cups. The more wine they drank, the more directions they had for Bobby, Seth's mother's boyfriend.

Bobby, said Seth's mom, I think we need another cedar bough on the porch. Then she got to hacking and said she needed another drink.

Bobby, said Seth's aunt, a great big lady in a checked work shirt and long skirt. Can you straighten the plaid ribbon on the compost bin?

Goddamn it if old Bob didn't do everything they said, running all over the place, mustache twitching. I guess working with model helicopters has made him good with his hands, because he made at least eight damned nice wreaths, and the boughs he tied with pinecones and ornaments was even nicer.

Looks good, Bobby, said Seth's mom. She was in a blue snowsuit with fur around the hood and didn't look half bad. Having Seth out of the house was agreeing with her.

There was an argument when one of the ladies said we needed a blow-up Santa on the roof of the house and some of them ladies agreed that was what was missing, but Seth's mom and his aunt said the idea was to make the place look classy, and those blow-ups was about as classy as hot dog night at the homeless shelter, and the lady who suggested the blow-up got offended and said she always put up Santa and Frosty and Rudolph, and someone else said that was exactly the point.

I guess Seth seen this kind of argument go wrong before, because he got in there right away and said how inflatables were real festive but you had to blow them up every day, pretty much, and because of having to farm, we wouldn't have time to do that. He said everyone should just pour themselves a fresh drink from the wine box and enjoy the afternoon.

When it was all done, the place looked like hell, all covered in wires and branches, but then it was daytime, so maybe it would look better at night and with the power turned on.

Prudence come over to where I was standing with Eustace and Seth and we were watching the ladies and Bob share what was left of their box wine with some of the young guys, and Prudence put a hand on my shoulder.

Tonight we test, she said. I've invited the social worker to attend tomorrow. Both Sally and Dean have also asked him to stop by and so did Sara's teacher, Miss Singer. He can't ignore all of us.

Her cheeks was all red and she was smiley as hell and I hoped this was all going to work out.

Seth

Imagine that moment when a metal supergroup stands on the stage to rehearse the show for their world tour. They look around, prepared to be amazed at the array of seizure-inducing lights, the huge staircase rising out of the stage, the massive video screens, enormous smoking volcano, the works. If they're control freaks, like David Lee Roth, they have also poked around in the dressing room to make sure there are no brown M&M's in the candy bowl.

Well, if the band was me, Prudence, Earl and Eustace waiting for the big Woefield Light-Up, they would have been seriously fucking disappointed. The volcano would eject a single puff of electrical smoke, the stage would stall halfway out of the floor, and the video screens would be cracked and dark. The candy bowl in the dressing room would contain exclusively brown M&M's.

It turns out that thousands of Christmas lights require a shitload of electrical capacity. When we plugged the extension cords into the power bars, there was a brief pop and all the power went out. Not just on the farm, but over half of Cedar.

We stood in the dark.

"Guess it's too much draw on our system," said my sponsor, the genius. "I'd have thought someone would have caught that."

The porch was black as an outhouse hole, so we couldn't see each other at all.

"This is why David Lee Roth put the brown M&M's in the concert rider," I told everyone. "Putting on a major show means paying attention to the details. He didn't want promoters who would cut corners setting up Van Halen's stage show."

"Goddamned candy wouldn't have helped this outfit," said Earl.

A light flared on when Prudence clicked on her LED headlamp.

"Thank goodness we tested it before the actual evening!" she said, completely unconcerned. "So how do we get more power?"

"Once BC Hydro gets the power back on, you mean? Let's go to Home Depot or one of those equipment rental places and get a generator. Maybe two," said Eustace.

"Great," said Prudence. "Let's do it now! I think Home Depot is open until nine."

She hurried off to Eustace's truck and he hurried after her.

Earl fumbled his own LED headlamp, which he keeps in his pocket, onto his head and his beam appeared.

We stood in silence for a minute.

"Think this is going to work?" I asked.

"I don't even know what's going on around here," he said.

We were quiet for a long moment.

* * *

The day of the party, I was pretty much going to pieces. Not only were we in a make or break situation with regard to getting Sara back, but my editor, Tamara, was on her way.

Prudence was in the kitchen, preparing what she called "holiday party fare," and like the supremely confident, non-shaming person she is, she kept trying to encourage me.

"You look amazing," she said, when I came downstairs in my light wash blue jeans.

"Even better," she said, when I changed into a dark wash pair.

"Those are the best yet," she said, when I switched into my black skinnies.

Tamara texted to say she'd left Victoria and would be about an hour and a half getting to the farm.

"This is exciting," said Prudence the fifteenth time I came back inside after going outside to stare at the road.

Eustace was less gentle with me, partly because Prudence had given him all the annoying jobs, like rolling the shortbread dough into tiny balls, pressing thumbprints into them and then spooning in a teaspoon of Prudence's raspberry jam. When he got done that, she put him to work making the molasses cookies and cheese tarts.

"Don't you think three hundred might be too many?" he said. Followed by, "Maybe Earl should help."

"He's sitting with Alec Baldwin."

Eustace, who'd been checking the bird three times a day, made a face I chose to ignore.

I reached for one of the thumbprint cookies from a wire rack where dozens of them cooled and Eustace jabbed a jam-covered spoon at me.

"Leave them. We need all three hundred cookies because I think Prudence invited about four hundred people."

"Nearly," said Prudence, laughing merrily and dumping more cinnamon and nutmeg and cloves into a bowl. "Tonight is going to be talked about for years."

Eustace's voice softened. "Please don't get upset if this doesn't go the way you want," he said.

Prudence was preparing apple cider spice mix for people to take away with them in little brown envelopes printed with the name of the farm. "I just want tonight to be nice," she said. "I want to show people who we are and I want Sara back here when her parents leave."

The telephone rang for about the twentieth time in the past couple of hours.

"Seth, would you mind getting that?"

"I'm sorry," I said. "I'm going to have to decline. My nerves are shot. Can't answer any more questions about the party."

I heard the engine and darted outside to see a brown car coming down the driveway. Even the car, which she'd borrowed from her sister, was cool and French. Not *literally* French. It wasn't a Peugeot or a Renault or anything. But it was the kind of car a certain kind of cultural person in Montreal should drive. Staffers at *Vice* magazine. Quebecois filmmakers and musicians who haven't hit it big yet.

I panicked and ran back inside.

"Get back out there," said Prudence, cheerfully. "It's going to be so great! She's your editor. She's Team You!"

"Oh god," I said. "I think I'm going to be sick. I might have IBS."

"Enough with the fear," said Eustace. "Grow a pair. You're a new man."

I forced myself back outside. By then, Tamara had gotten out of the car.

I had sent her my photo to run next to my column, so she had some idea what I look like, but her editorials are accompanied by a drawing that makes her look like a smart cartoon character. In person, she looked like Prudence if Prudence used to be a junkie punk rocker and was able to see and appreciate the bad side of everything.

That is a wholly inadequate description. Tamara, my editor, had brown hair that was unkempt and she wore a scarf around her neck in a way that was careless and perfect and tight jeans and motorcycle-ish boots and a light brown motorcycle-ish jacket, and I swear to god my heart nearly stopped when I caught sight of her.

I realize I'm gushing. I can't help it.

She spotted me and grinned. "HM," she said.

I felt my face crack into an uncontrolled, ear-to-ear smile.

We stood like that for a minute. Me on the stairs of the house, Tamara in front of her car. We grinned at each other like a couple of idiots. Or kids.

I could feel my chest cavity expand to fit my swelling heart.

She walked over to me, her boots crunching on the gravel.

"You're cute," she said. "Just like in your writing."

Like the recent winner of a seventh-degree black belt in social ineptitude, I couldn't seem to make any words.

"You going to show me around?" she asked.

I nodded.

"First the mule. Then I want to meet Earl."

I puffed out a big breath that I'd been holding and took a few steps toward her. Then I stopped. "I can't believe you're here," I said.

Tamara's hair fluttered across her intelligent face. Her dark eyes were free of makeup and her lips were pale.

"Life is full of startling things," she said. "Haven't you noticed yet?"

Then we went to see Lucky, and as we were leaving the pasture, the gleaming new Lincoln Town Car swept up the driveway, looking about as out of place on Woefield Farm as it was possible for a vehicle to look.

Sara

The play was about the Twelve Days of Christmas, but some songs were in Cree and some were in French and there was singing in Dutch and English and Spanish and Chinese.

It was a big honor to play the partridge, because the partridge, which is also known as a grey partridge or English partridge, was on the stage the whole time, along with the pear tree, which I carried around. Good thing the tree was made of cardboard and wasn't very heavy. A lot of people don't know this, but a partridge is actually a type of pheasant. They do not migrate and like to nest at the edge of cereal fields. I find that really interesting.

My costume didn't really look like an actual partridge but more like a dove. It was made of white fleece with wings on the arms and I had an orange beak and gray legs. Miss Singer gave me these big, stuffed yellow slippers shaped like chicken feet to wear. I hoped no one in the audience knew anything about birds, because they might have noticed that the partridge wasn't realistic and they would have had a hard time enjoying the play. I didn't complain, though, because Miss Singer was very busy.

The three French hens were played by Target and two of the meanest girls in school. I was worried that they would bully him, and at our first rehearsal, one of them called him "Bull's-eye" when the music teacher wasn't listening, but they never said it again after his foster sisters, Ariel and Stephanie, showed up to watch. Target's foster sisters are very cool and everyone wanted to impress them. The mean girls complimented Stephanie on her hair, which has purple in it, and told Ariel her skateboard was awesome, which it was because she decorated it herself.

The French hen costumes are okay, but I don't think there's any such thing as a French hen, so accuracy isn't as hard to get as it is with a partridge.

The play was pretty long due to medleys and I had to stand on the stage the whole time, but that was okay. Standing there gave me lots of time to watch the audience, which was very big. Every seat was taken.

My mom and dad came. My dad wore his best cardigan and sat in the back row. My mom sat in the middle. What was really exciting was that Prudence and Earl and Eustace and Seth were there too! And Earl's brother was there in his hat! Earl's brother is very famous but he's too old for anyone my age to know about him, which was too bad because it's hard to brag about famous people no one is aware of. I met him at the bluegrass concert in the summer. I was surprised no one told me in a note that he was coming to visit again.

Practically every kid in school was in the play but only some of them sang, because not everyone has a good voice. The stage was already crowded when the seven swans came on, and by the time the twelve drummers hit the stage, no one could move. But it probably looked impressive. I couldn't see the audience anymore, but there was a lot of clapping.

At the end, everyone stood up, which is called an *ovation* and it's a really good thing to get when you're in a play.

My parents came backstage and told me I was an excellent partridge and I explained about how a partridge is similar to a pheasant. They didn't seem very interested. Instead, they acted like they were nervous.

"Are you ready to go?" asked my mom. She handed me a bouquet of flowers. At least, I think it was a bouquet. There was a stick with some red berries on it and a big waxy red thing that looked like a fan and had a yellow sticker coming out of the middle. When my dad said the flower looked obscene, my mom said it was a very artistic arrangement and he wouldn't understand that because he didn't have an artistic bone in his body.

Prudence and Seth and Earl and Eustace didn't come backstage. But I wished they had. All the other kids were telling their families about what happened during the play, even though their families had just watched it, but me and my parents just stood there and didn't know what to say to each other. Prudence and Seth and Earl would have had a lot to say.

I wanted to go over and tell Target he'd been an excellent French hen, but his foster moms and sisters were all around him and they seemed really excited and he didn't notice me. I forgot to mention that Target has a good voice. I would not have expected that.

I went to the girl's changeroom and took off my costume and gave it to Miss Singer.

"You were terrific," she said. "Even better as a partridge than you were as an iPod."

"Thank you," I said.

"Okay, bye, Sara," she said, and it kind of hurt my feelings that she didn't say more about how good I was because she was busy helping another kid get out of her golden ring, which was a big cardboard ring stuck to her head. It looked pretty and sparkly from far away, but up close it just looked like spray-painted tinfoil.

In the parking lot, my mom and dad and I stood between my mom's car and my dad's and they looked at each other.

"So what now?" my mom asked.

"I need to talk to you both," he said.

"Out here?" asked my mom. She was wearing a blue jean pantsuit with a yellow silk scarf. It made her look like she was a pilot. It also didn't look very warm.

"We can talk in my cab."

My mom rolled her eyes. She hates his taxi. I guess she really just hates him.

But she got in the front seat and I got in the back.

My dad turned the taxi on and the heater started to blow cold air all around.

"I have an opportunity," he said.

"What opportunity?" she asked.

"Sara," he said, ignoring my mom. "As you know, I'm not totally happy driving a cab."

I could feel my mom being tense in the passenger seat. She was waiting for him to say something mean and so was I. I wished I was alone.

"Well, the thing is, I'm planning a trip," said my dad. He sounded like a different person. Like a person who didn't hate everyone he talked to. "It's the fulfillment of a lifetime dream."

"Where are you going?" I asked.

"Arkansas," he said. "To a mule ranch. I'm going to work as a mule skinner for a couple of months. Maybe three."

"What do you know about mules?" asked my mom, who doesn't know that my dad goes to Woefield to train Lucky almost every day.

"Where's Arkansas?" I asked, because I thought it would be best to change the subject.

"Bill Clinton's from there," said my mom.

"Who's that?" I asked, even though I know and am not dumb.

"He used to be the president of the United States," said my dad. "Who the hell is teaching you history at that school?"

"Dean," said my mom. "Enough with the hostility."

"Does she know who our prime minister is? The taxes I pay to the government, she should know every world leader."

Before they could fight more about what I know, I said, "Am I going too? To Arkansas?"

"Yes, Dean. Is she going with you? Because I'm also leaving. I'm going to New York for six months. It's the fulfillment of *my* lifetime dream."

"And when were you planning to tell me this?" my dad asked.

"Just as soon as I had the details worked out," said my mom. That was not true. All the details had been worked out for a long time.

"Sara, I'd love for you to visit me in Arkansas," said my dad. "But I don't think the ranch is set up for kids."

"So you think I'm going to pull her out of school and take her to New York with me? You are unbelievable. What kind of a father are you?"

"And what kind of a selfish bitch are you, Sally? Have you asked yourself that?"

"Stop it, Dean." My mom's voice was all crackly, like she was going to cry. "You've never understood me."

"Well someone is going to have to reconsider their plans," said my father. "And it's not going to be me."

"Can we just go home?" I said.

My mom got out of the car and slammed the door. I waited and for a second couldn't remember which one of them I lived with.

"You better go with your mother," said my dad.

So I did. We went home to our cold, quiet, mostly empty house, and I listened to her cry in her room because her dreams might get ruined from having to look after me.

Seth

When we got home from the Christmas concert, we were all nervous as hell. I couldn't say why, really. I guess it was all the drama swirling around the place. There was the drama of Earl's famous bluegrass brother showing up unexpectedly. The tension stretched between them like a high wire with a fat guy balanced on it. The question of what, if anything, was going to happen between me and my editor, Tamara, was another factor. There were a bunch more issues besides, such as whether Prudence would end up poisoning half of Cedar with her food. The big question was about Sara, of course. Would the social worker show? Would he feel moved to write a report that would be so persuasive Sara's parents would stop acting like stubborn fuckwits? I knew her dad was going to be here to give wagon rides. Surely the social worker would be impressed by that.

Me, Earl, Prudence and Eustace stood on the porch, greeting people. It was a strange scene. First of all, it was cold, so we all sort of wanted to go inside, but that wouldn't have been very impressive and welcoming, and Prudence insisted that the party had to be both. It was like she was trying to overcome our sparse vegetable output with masses of decorations and bizarre outpourings of hospitality.

The play ended at three and we were home by 3:10. People were supposed to arrive at three thirty but started arriving at a quarter after. They came in cars and trucks and the closest ones came on foot. They had presents and they brought things to eat.

The Sandhus were first. Anoop was dressed in his usual outfit: dark blue tracksuit with stripes on the arms and legs.

He was followed by his mother, who wore a glittery purple dress with red harem pants.

"Hello," she said, in a disapproving tone.

Anoop was playing it cool. "I just wanted to say that I can eat anything at the party, man. Hot sauce is not a problem for me."

"Anoop!" said his mother. "Leave it alone or you'll have a real heart attack. Not just a pretend one."

"I've been jogging. Lost some weight," said Anoop, casting a glance from Prudence to Tamara.

"He never jogs," said a boy who came in with them. He was probably another cousin, but not the lawyer cousin, because he was too young. "Literally never."

"Dinesh! You mind your business," said Mrs. Sandhu, ushering them both into the house.

My mother, Bobby, my aunt and their bar friends showed up next. Between them, they carried two large boxes of red wine, a dried flower arrangement that has been on our bathroom entertainment center—which consists of a rickety, two-piece, white plastic shelf unit containing a tiny analog TV and some bathroom-themed knick-knacks—since I was twelve, a ham and a turkey Prudence had asked my mother to cook in her oven.

"Bobby," said my aunt Elsie, who was only carrying her slippers. "Watch that you don't drop that bird."

The enormous bird in its tray must have been heavy and awkward to hang on to and it started to tilt in his hands.

"Bobby!" said my aunt. "Watch it!"

Eustace hurried down the porch stairs and took the foil-covered pan from Bobby's overtaxed arms and carried it into the house.

"I hope there's enough food," grunted Elsie as she climbed after it.

Then came Portia and Brady from the Mighty Pens. They'd carpooled in Portia's new Jeep Cherokee.

"Got two kinds of taters here!" said Brady. "A pan full of scalloped potatoes and a pan of mashed."

"Thank you," said Prudence, leaning over to kiss him on the cheek.

"Glad it was a false alarm on the bugs," said Portia. "That would have been disgusting, even for this place."

The good-looking kid from Sara's chicken club arrived by himself carrying a tupperware container of cookies. I was impressed again by the maturity of the young farmer set.

Hugh the cab driver arrived on foot, announcing that he'd got a flat about a half-mile away.

"Carrots are cold," he said.

"Oh Hugh," said Prudence. "You're such a doll."

Hugh nearly floated into the house.

Anulka, who'd given out candy from the haunted farm stand at Halloween, and two of her friends from the International High School arrived in a giggling mass.

"Snow!" she said. "Snow!"

One of the girls was from Ireland and she teetered along in

strange blue platform boots that made her tower over tiny Anulka. For some reason, the Irish girl was wearing a furry blue tail.

Earl and Merle looked at me.

"Does she know this is Christmas, not Halloween?" asked Earl.

"I have no idea," I said.

"Cosplay!" whispered Tamara. "That would be my guess."

"If you say so," said Earl. "I think she might just be real confused."

Then Mr. Spratt pulled up in his taxi. And my heart fell when I saw that Sara wasn't with him.

Prudence

Not every social event needs to have a goal other than showing people that they matter and offering them an opportunity to enjoy one another. Our Christmas gathering was wonderful. Such a delightful and unusual assortment of people enjoying food and drink and each other. But we had another, even more important agenda.

I looked around as people loaded up their plates with local, organic turkey or took helpings of the delicious cauliflower dish I made for the vegetarians, mashed or scalloped potatoes, Brussels sprouts with local bacon (cooked as a special favor for Merle, who said he loved bacon with his sprouts), carrots, mashed turnips, roasted onions and gravy.

Seth's mother, displaying a charmingly retro taste in home economics, brought a baked ham encased in rounds of pineapple and some sort of sweet potato dish covered in marshmallows. Earl, Seth and the youngest guests really enjoyed that, though they probably all have diabetes now.

Tamara, Seth's editor, made a baked brie dish with basil and sundried tomatoes and pine nuts. I really like her and so did every-one else, especially after they tasted the dish. T's foster mothers, who came with their daughters and T, brought a fabulous baked salmon and some sort of wild rice pilaf.

Stephan McFadden, our builder, brought a bag of Doritos, which made me laugh and give him a hug. He let go as soon as Eustace cleared his throat.

There was spiced apple cider on the woodstove, and all the decor-ations looked lovely and traditional, like the small fir trees we'd hung with popcorn and homemade ornaments, and the centerpiece of cedar boughs and branches with crab apples still on them and bees-wax candles.

I wished Sara could see it. Mr. Spratt was outside hitching Lucky to the wagon and I didn't know where Mrs. Spratt was. I'd hoped all three Spratts would show up, but of course that would have meant Mr. and Mrs. Spratt agreeing to a cease-fire for the evening.

It killed me that Sara wasn't with us and it killed me even more that the social worker hadn't shown up.

And that's why my heart nearly split in two when there was a knock on the door just as we were finishing dinner and Seth opened it to find Pete the social worker.

I leapt to his side and began to babble.

"Pete!" I said. "Mr. Pete?" I gave a weak giggle. "Welcome! We're just having a little community gathering. Good local food. Friends. Families."

Pete looked over my shoulder at all the people eating and laugh-ing and relaxing.

"Looks like a great party. I'm sorry it's taken so long for me to get over here. I've had some, uh, tough cases."

"Of course," I said. "Please come in and help yourself to some food. We've got so much. Always a lot of food. Healthy, too."

I led him over to the kitchen table, where most of the dishes sat and waited while he took a polite amount of food.

Then I led him to where T and his foster family and Sara's teacher sat and saw his pierced eyebrows go up. He knew all of these people. That would work in our favor.

"You remember T and Fran and Esme and Stephanie and Ariel and Miss Singer?" I said.

"Call me Jamie," said the teacher.

"Yes, of course," he said. "How do you all do?"

They smiled and said hello.

Pete stepped out of earshot of the group and gestured for me to follow.

"Sara's not here?" he asked, quietly.

"Her parents are really counting on a report from you," I said. "Before they're comfortable letting her visit."

He didn't seem to follow.

"They're worried the farm will become a factor in their divorce. That the one who lets her come back here will be vulnerable to charges of . . . something."

"Ah," he said. "That kind of divorce."

I nodded.

"We've got a light display," I told him. "When dinner is over, we're going to turn it on." I hoped we wouldn't overload the entire electrical system in Cedar again. "There will be mule wagon rides in the field and caroling."

"Sounds nice," he said.

Then Pete the social worker smiled at me before going to sit with Fran and Esme, Miss Singer and T.

I breathed a deep sigh of relief. We would get through this without making anything worse.

Then the doorbell rang. Anoop, who has been a delight around the farm since he started helping Stephan, was up and getting more gravy for his third helping of mashed potatoes and answered it. A woman I vaguely recognized staggered through the front door, paused in the kitchen and then lurched into the doorway of the living room. She had on a red one-piece snowsuit with white fur trim around the hood. The top was unzipped far enough to reveal that she had on nothing underneath.

The assembled crowd gasped as she swayed in the doorway.

She held a hand to the snowsuit's zipper as though about to embark on a striptease involving cold weather gear.

"Seth!" she cried and started to move the zipper down.

Fran and Esme put hands over as many kids' eyes as they could reach. The International High School students screamed with joy, perhaps thinking the woman was also into cosplay. Seth froze in place and his editor, Tamara, sat with her mouth open. Then she hid a grin behind a hand. Eustace was up and heading for the woman, but Merle and Anoop got there first.

"Damn it," I muttered and forced myself not to look at Pete the social worker.

Earl

I was real pleased when the feller with all the tattoos from the government showed up. We just had to make sure that we kept things civilized while he was there. Of course, not ten minutes later, the lady in the puffy red long johns or snowmobile suit or whatever that outfit was supposed to be showed up. I saw that social worker's eyes get big. He watched while my brother Merle and that little fainty fellow from the farmers' market went over to deal with her. She looked at Merle and the little feller like they were Jesus and the Holy Spirit come down from on high.

You're fine, sweetheart, said Merle. Seventy-four years old and half the ladies in the place were looking at him like he was dessert. I think even them ladies who is married to each other was giving old Merle the hot eye.

Your outfit is very nice, said the little feller to the lady in the red snowsuit. Spicy, even.

His mother got up and sat across from the lady. She stared at her hard. Are you single? she asked. My son Anoop here is single.

The lady was so pie-eyed, she didn't answer.

She's not right for you, said the little feller's mother to him. Not a conversationalist.

I play video games, said Anoop. I'm very good. I'm also adventurous about food.

He is not, said a teenage boy who got up and stood beside Anoop's mother. The kid had at least eight cookies balanced in his hand. Anoop even passes out sometimes when he eats, like, pepper. Anoop's got issues, said the boy.

Anoop ignored him and continued staring at the lady in the red snowsuit. Her eyes had begun to close.

I decided to go and take a look at Alec Baldwin and finally get some fresh air.

Sara

My mom was still crying in her room and I was sitting in the living room and thinking about what might happen and where I might go, when Seth's phone vibrated in my hand.

I'm not supposed to have the phone, so I usually keep it turned off and only use it for emergencies, such as telling Seth things to tell Earl about my chickens and letting Seth and Earl know when I was alone in the campground.

But after the school play, I turned the phone on and muted it. Having it on made me feel less lonely. I might end up being one of those people who spends all their time on their phone if I'm not careful.

I answered the call, keeping my voice low so my mom wouldn't hear.

"Hello?"

"Sara?"

"Yes?"

"It's Seth. Alec Baldwin's not doing so good. Earl and Eustace are with him. Eustace said you better get your mom to drive you over."

I knew that meant it was a serious emergency, so I hung up the phone and told my mom we needed to go to the farm. She said she didn't think she was up to it. I put on my coat and boots and started walking over there by myself. My mom picked me up about five minutes later.

"Come on, Sara," she said. "Let's go."

Seth

Me, Earl, Eustace, Prudence, Tamara and Merle all stood on the porch of Earl's cabin. Mr. Spratt had unhitched Lucky and he stood at the foot of the cabin stairs. We'd asked the rest of the guests to please stay in the house while we dealt with a personal emergency.

"How long?" Prudence asked Eustace, who had moved the rooster into a shoe box lined with a towel, under which he'd placed one of those hand warmers.

Alec Baldwin was half collapsed in the box, one wing spread as though to steady himself. He stared up at us, his strange eye visible for once with his crest brushed out of the way.

"Not long. Do you want to go get her?" he asked Prudence.

"We can take the Lincoln," said Merle.

But before anyone could decide, Mrs. Spratt's Buick pulled up and Sara jumped out and came running through the gate and across the pasture.

She charged up the stairs and stopped in front of Eustace. He handed her the box and she sat down with it on her lap.

I could swear that old rooster looked up at her and something in his body changed, unclenched. Sara had that effect on animals.

She used her finger to stroke his feathers and he pulled in his wing and settled further onto his side.

"You should have won the prizes," she whispered.

Alec Baldwin's eyes were closed now, the lower lid sliding up to meet the top.

A stillness fell over all of us when the rooster died. Some electrical charge gone out of the world. The feeling lasted until Mr. Spratt spoke up.

"Nice job, Sally," he said. "Now you've really done it."

Prudence

Sara held the box containing her dead rooster and didn't look up when her parents started in on each other.

"Excuse me?" said Mrs. Spratt.

"Did she really need to see this? Who gave permission for her to be here?"

"What are *you* doing here? Looks like a party. Nice to know Sara and I couldn't come because we were abiding by the rules you and I established."

"I've got a job to do here. It's none of your business," said Mr. Spratt.

"You have never been supportive of Sara's poultry," snarled Mrs. Spratt. "You small-minded, nasty little—"

"Stop it!" yelled Sara so loudly that we all jumped. "Do you want my stomach to start bleeding again?"

"Oh my god, honey. No," said Mrs. Spratt. "We're sorry."

Mr. Spratt nodded.

"I want to come back to the farm. I don't like living with either of you."

Her parents stared at her with open mouths.

"You aren't good parents. It's okay. I don't mind. But you need to let me come back here."

"We . . . ," Sara's dad started but couldn't seem to think of what else to say.

They didn't approach her. The two of them just stood on the cold ground, in the near dark, and stared up at their dry-eyed daughter, who held the box with her dead pet clutched to her chest.

"I want to bury him now," said Sara, looking at me.

"Okay," I said. "We'll have a ceremony."

Sara, ever considerate, looked toward the house and all the people, some of whom had come out on the porch to stare, concerned, toward Earl's cabin. "What about the party?"

"It can wait. We need to take care of Alec Baldwin."

Merle took in the situation. "This seems like an event for immediate family. I'll go see if the folks want a tune or two to keep 'em occupied."

Tamara, Seth's lovely editor, followed.

Merle made his way back to the house. He gestured to his driver, who stood with several of the other guests on the porch of the house, and the driver went over to the car and retrieved Merle's guitar.

Sara walked down the cabin stairs, carrying her box. The rest of us fell in behind as she led us around behind the new barn.

"Here," she said. "The ground is soft here. And he liked this patch of grass."

"Are you sure you want to do this now?" I asked, as gently as I could. "We could do it tomorrow."

"Now is best," she said. "I don't know when I'll be able to come back." Then she asked us all to put something in the box with Alec Baldwin so he wouldn't feel lonely.

We each went off to get a farewell object. Seth offered up a tattered Guns N' Roses T-shirt, Earl an old work glove. I got a photo from my room of Sara holding Alec Baldwin. She was grinning widely and Alec Baldwin looked resigned. Eustace added a chicken-shaped key chain Sara had given him. Sara's parents stood like statues. Adding nothing. Saying nothing.

Earl and I dug the hole, and when Sara had organized all the items alongside the bird's body, everything covered with Seth's T-shirt, she put the lid on and placed the box in the cold ground.

"Good thing it's not frozen yet," she said.

"Do you want to say anything?" I asked as we stared down at the little shoe box, sad but also strangely life-affirming.

"He was a very good chicken," she said. "Probably my favorite."

That made me cry.

"A great chicken," said Seth. "A rock and roller."

"The best goddamned chicken," said Earl.

And with that, we took turns shoveling dirt onto Alec Baldwin's body.

Seth

The guests went quiet when we walked back inside. Then Merle started playing bluegrassy Christmas carols again and people started singing along, quietly, I guess out of respect.

I looked around and saw Prudence usher Sara's parents and the social worker upstairs.

The drama teacher had, thank Christ, passed out on the couch in her red snowsuit, which someone had zipped up to a decent height. Eustace and I carried her up to Prudence's room and put her to bed.

Not long after, Prudence came down by herself. When Merle stopped playing, she announced that it was time to have dessert and then we would turn on the lights. Soon Sara was helping serve pumpkin and strawberry pie, stopping now and then so people could tell her they were sorry to hear about Alec Baldwin. The boy from the chicken club put a hand on her shoulder and I saw her wipe her eyes. That was a throat-tightener, for sure, and I caught Tamara looking at me.

Jesus. I wondered what she thought about all of this. About me.

When most people had finished their desserts, we all started trooping outside for the light show.

"This is going to be great. We need something great right now," said Prudence, who is the definition of whatever word it is that means a person doesn't easily get fatigued or discouraged.

It was cold outside and pretty soon we were stamping our feet and trying not to develop that condition you get from damp cold— chilblains?

"All together now!" shouted Prudence. She sounded like some over-amped track and field coach, trying to cast off the pall left by the death of our poor rooster.

I sprinted for the stereo and Eustace started the generator. Music blasted out over the farm, probably spooking livestock for a two-mile radius. Thousands of lights came on. Everybody oohed and aahed in spite of the fact that the display was a bit wonky. I have a theory: in order for Christmas lights to look really good, what they're illuminating should be halfway attractive. But when we flipped the switch and Woefield Farm became the Vegas of the Pacific Northwest, it was clear that inexperienced light hangers and a less than gorgeous setting combined to make the whole farm look like there'd been an explosion in the lights section at Canadian Tire. Bright though. It was definitely bright.

Sara's parents came outside and they whispered something to Sara's teacher, Miss Singer, who nodded and went in the house.

Prudence gestured to Mr. Spratt, who seemed embarrassed.

"Ready?" she said.

"You sure you want me to drive him?" he asked. "I haven't done a lot of good around here tonight."

"You've changed the fortunes of that mule and this farm," said Prudence. "And Lucky's been waiting patiently for his chance to shine."

She turned to the group. "Who wants a mule ride? Dean is just going to get Lucky hooked up again and you can take a tour around the pastures. Enjoy our light show up close. Listen to the music."

"Do you have a death wish?" Portia asked Brady, her fellow bad writer.

"I once took a donkey ride through Tijuana," said Brady. "Mules don't scare me."

"Don't even think about it," said Anoop's mother to him when he started toward the pasture. "Mules are not like video games."

Pretty soon, Dean Spratt had Lucky hitched to the wagon, and Sara and the boy from her poultry club and Brady and Anoop's young cousin climbed aboard and pulled blankets over their laps.

Mr. Spratt said something to Lucky, who moved off smoothly.

I waited for the mule to startle and run off, crashing and maiming everyone on the wagon and perhaps several people in the crowd of watchers, but he was as docile as Bertie and only slightly faster.

"I had no idea he could do anything useful," said Mrs. Spratt. I wasn't sure whether she was referring to Lucky or to Mr. Spratt.

I nodded noncommittally. I'd thought the same thing about her until I read her work. In fact, before learning about their hidden talents, I assumed the only useful thing the Spratts had ever done or ever would do was create Sara. Maybe they thought that themselves and were troubled by the notion.

"If you're open to it, we'd like her to come back here to stay, at least while we're away. The social worker agrees this is a good place for her," she said, with no preliminaries.

In spite of myself, I let out a strangled cry and hugged her.

She smiled wryly. "This fall and winter have not been my finest seasons as a mother. Not by a long shot."

I wasn't going to argue. But all my animosity toward Mrs. Spratt and Mr. Spratt disappeared as I watched the wagon, which was also lit up like a gas station at two in the morning, move around the field.

Earl

You know, I never had much time for Sara's parents because of how they weren't worth a turd in a septic system from a looking-after-kids perspective. But I guess Old Man Sprout showed he had some worthwhileness when he got the mule going. And Mrs. Sprout might be the saddest excuse for a woman I ever seen, but Prudence says it's because she was writing a book.

That argument don't work for me. There's things you should do with your time and things you shouldn't. Writing about yourself, or worse, writing about people you made up, is no activity for a grown-up. But I respected that they told that social worker Sara should come back to us, even though it hurt their pride, since it was up to them all along.

We've all talked to that social worker two or three times now, and I'm starting to get the feeling he just likes coming around. Not just him, either. Old Mrs. Sandhu is over here for tea all the time, and them international kids who wear fuzzy tails and ears and whatnot stop by a lot, and my brother Merle shows no sign of leaving.

He's got himself set up at the Coast Bastion Hotel. Has himself the nicest room in the place. But he's here every day when he's not keeping company with that lady in the red snowsuit. The one who showed up at the party and tried to take off her clothes.

Him and his driver took her home after the party, and him and her have been hot and heavy ever since.

Even that little Anoop feller has a romance. His mother sent the video of him picking up construction garbage to a lady in India. I guess she liked the look of him, because he's talking to her on the computer all the time when he's not working or playing video games.

Me and Seth were talking and he said he figured my brother Merle's hanging around because he's lonely. And you know, Seth might be right. I feel bad for Merle. So I told him I'd do a holiday album with him, even though I hate Christmas music. Might be the only way to get rid of him. And we could use the money. I even asked Merle if he remembered Ella Grace, the gal from when we was young. The one who rode a mule. He said he sure did. I said I might look her up and see how she was doing. He give me a funny look then, but he didn't say nothing. Just give me a pat on the back and said I should do that.

Prudence

Sara moved back to the farm a few days before Christmas Eve, and we decided to celebrate the occasion by renaming Lucky, even though I'm starting to think his name is actually perfect. We were also having an open house to celebrate Sara's return and our first Christmas all together.

Seth said that whoever came up with the winning name wouldn't have to taste the beans and kale dish I was preparing.

Earl said he didn't give a goddamn what the mule was named, so long as it didn't try to bite him anymore.

Sara organized the naming session, handing out small slips of paper for people to write their suggestions on. She tried to get T to read out the suggestions, but he shook his head shyly. I liked the way he let Esme, his foster mom, put her arm around him.

"Okay," said Sara, happily. "I can read them."

How I have missed that girl.

"According to the papers Werner gave me," I said from where I stood at the kitchen sink, trying to chip burned beans off the bottom of the pot, "his full name is Lucky Ginger Sprite SSH."

"What does SSH stand for?" asked Sara.

"Stubborn Shit Head?" asked Portia, who brings her cynicism to open houses as well as writing groups.

"I don't know," I admitted.

Sara began to read the suggestions.

"Kicker," she said. "That's Earl's."

Everyone clapped.

"Guacamule," she read. "That's Brady's."

More clapping and I felt a strong relief that Brady was able to write at least one thing that wasn't erotica-related.

The names kept coming.

Elrod, Zebediah, Pox.

Sara's father, displaying a surprising bit of whimsy, suggested Pepperpot. Everyone agreed it was a strong contender.

The names kept coming.

Chuck, Jimmie Rodgers.

Eustace suggested Haywire.

I grinned at him. The night before, we had had another good talk about boundaries. That is turning into one of our favorite topics. We have agreed that if one of us is sick or otherwise indisposed, we will accept more help from the other, and that we cannot allow things to fall apart due to pride. Other than that, we will respect each other's decisions. That usually lasts about two days and then Eustace tries to tell me how to do things. Then he apologizes and I enjoy his apologies. We really are a good match. But back to the mule renaming session.

Sara's mother suggested Tecumseh Sherman and we all stared.

"He was the general who gave each freed slave forty acres and a mule," she said. The award for continuing to be the most surprising person in Cedar goes to Sara's mother.

Jeb and Stirpot, Blind Crake and Catbrain were all put forth.

Spot and Splat, suggested Pete the social worker, who had stopped by to check in.

Neddy and Nod. The last was via text from Tamara, Seth's editor, who apparently has a drug history and who is back in Montreal but hopes to visit again soon. I think she must have slept with Seth, because he is glowing brighter than any of our holiday displays.

My suggestion was Buckley.

Seth's was Secretariass. Everyone loved that.

Then Sara read her own: Stan of Green Stables.

We had a winner.

"We can call him Lucky Stan at first," said Sara, beaming at her success. "So he doesn't get confused."

Her father patted her on the back, awkwardly but with obvious pride, and her mom squeezed her hand. The fact that the two of them were able to sit so close together, with only Sara between them, was a testament to the powerful healing powers of Woefield Farm.

We put the Christmas lights on at six-thirty, after first making sure the generator was full, and people started to arrive as they had in increasing numbers each night since the dinner party. We really had become a local attraction. Earl went out to meet some music students and his brother, and soon the sounds of bluegrass music floated across the field. The sound engineer from Merle's label was there with his recording equipment. Every part of the farm sparkled and twinkled erratically.

"We still don't really know how to operate him," I said to Dean Spratt as he pulled on his boots. "Stan, I mean."

"I'll be back in April. Just keep catching him and brushing him. Stay away from the road and I'll teach you how to work with him when I get back. You got yourself a real nice mule there."

I nodded. We did.

Mrs. Spratt was on her way home to finish packing.

"Do you think she's going to be okay?" she asked, looking toward the field where Sara was pointing out things about her chicken coop to T and his foster family.

"Absolutely," I said.

"I have been a terrible parent the last while. It's the writing. It just took over everything. My behavior is a little hard to look at."

I didn't respond. What was there to say? She *had* been a lousy parent. Mr. Spratt had been a terrible father. There was nothing to do about it now except move forward. I wasn't very proud of my actions while I was sick, either.

"She knows you love her," I said.

Mrs. Spratt gestured over to the living room where the Mighty Pens were sitting and laughing over something. "Do you know why my book is so good?" she asked.

I shook my head. It was a complete mystery to me.

"Me neither. It started as a journal. I've always kept a diary. But then one night, the real estate agent was showing the house late, so I took us to a campsite. I couldn't sleep and I didn't want to wake Sara. I went into the picnic shelter and started writing. Something about writing in that dark hut cracked me wide open. The story just came pouring out. I felt like I had a fever. I made us stay in that campground for nights on end. Sara caught a cold because we were sleeping in the car. Well, she was. I was in the hut. Writing in my journal. And every evening, I'd make her spend hours in the library while I typed up the manuscript."

"I know," I said.

She blinked. "You do?"

"Sara told Earl. She was scared when you left her. So Earl and Seth took turns sitting with her. While you were away."

Mrs. Spratt's eyes filled. "Oh my god," she said. "That makes me feel awful."

I didn't reply. I'd thought about not telling her, but maybe Mrs. Spratt needed to feel awful, at least for a while.

At least she didn't get defensive or try to justify her behavior. Instead, we agreed that she'd be in touch when she was settled in New York and I'd make sure Sara had her passport ready when it was time for her to visit. I thought the visit probably wouldn't happen, but we'd cross that bridge later. I'd given Mrs. Spratt the names and numbers of my friends in the city. I wondered what they'd make of her.

I was left standing on the porch, watching people walk around the property in little groups. Laughing. Listening to music. Behind me, in the house, the writers wrote, badly. Mr. Spratt drove the mule, competently. Eustace came up behind me and I leaned against him. Around us, people made their own entertainment as we waited for the growing season to start.

Acknowledgments

Thank you to Bill Juby and Andrew Gray and Susin Nielsen and Stephanie Dubinsky for being terrific test readers and advisors; my marvelous editor, Iris Tupholme, Noelle Zitzer, Stacey Cameron, Helen Reeves, Alan Jones, Sarah Wight, Kelly Hope, Jason Pratt, Julia Barrett and everyone at HarperCollins for making it much better; and Hilary McMahon for being a stalwart and elegant advocate (such a great combination!).

Thank you to all those who have embraced the residents of Woefield Farm, particularly all the readers who pitched in with suggestions ranging from brilliant to deranged for mule names and book titles: Emily Olesen, Elena Bonar, Tai Deacon, Linda Boyd, Tony Lapadat, Jen Klassen, Elizabeth Jones, Kelly Oswald, Stu MacDonald, Jade Seabrook, Barbara Zatyko, Jackie Hamilton-Irving (the winner, with Stan of Green Stables!), Leah Isherwood, Mat Snowie, Camille Cavanagh, Heather Clouston, J. Penney Burton, Roz Kromhoff, Jean Anderson, Libby Murphy, Heather Davis, Tim Mcdiarmid, Kevin Storrie, Anne Klein, Michael

Campbell, Lynn A KJ, Kim Martin, Cyndi Freistadt Cunanan, Joe Racanelli, Sunny Taylor, Leslie Milligan, Vicki Grant, Paul Forster, Diane McIntosh, Susie Sovereign, Trevor Boytinck, Lisa Karuna, Karen Rivers, Suzanne Crawford, Ros Davies, Mj Mcgee, Megan Bailey, Theresa Moleski, Ross Murray, Karlin Creed, Andy Sibbald, Sheree Fitch, Colleen Purcell, Lee Anne Smith, Dian Borek, Valerie Sherrard, Maggie L. Wood, Jody Kihara, Jocelyn Reekie, Jodey Wilson, Susin Nielsen, Sherry Conly, Lisa McGregor, Judy Millar, Myranda Jayne Bolstad, Pattie Turcotte, Stephanie Dubinsky, Charlotte Gray and Jenny Gibb.

Finally, thank you to my boys, Jimmy and Rodeo.